Shaping Up

Isabella opened her account books and allowed herself a dignified smile, a cigarette and a sparse nightcap of brandy and soda. The fact that all over Alba people were paying well into three figures to enjoy nightcaps consisting of hot water made the brandy tingle on the back of her tongue in an even more delightful way. The figures were looking good, very good indeed . . .

Not everything, of course, ran as smoothly as it appeared to Alba's cosseted clients. She had too much to think about, too much to organise, too many worries. She was, after all, rising seventy-five, and however good she looked, even she couldn't go on for ever. She needed someone to pick up the reins, someone to ease the burden from her shoulders. She needed an heir, and to her intense irritation there was only one available. Her granddaughter Cordelia. That Woman's daughter.

**Also by the same authors,
and available from Coronet:**

SWAPPING
TAKING OVER

About the authors

Shirley Lowe and Angela Ince met on the
Daily Express early in their working lives.
They have been friends ever since, in spite of
collaborating on four novels, television scripts
and countless newspaper and magazine
articles. They recently created *Bluebirds*, a
major children's television series, for the BBC.

They are both married, with children, and live
in London; near enough to get in touch when
the plot thickens, but far enough apart to stay
on speaking terms.

SHIRLEY LOWE
A N D
ANGELA INCE
Shaping Up

CORONET BOOKS
Hodder and Stoughton

Copyright © 1991 by Shirley Lowe and Angela Ince

First published in Great Britain in 1991 by Hodder and Stoughton Limited

Coronet edition 1992

Printed and bound in Great Britain for Hodder and Stoughton Paperbacks, a division of Hodder and Stoughton Limited, Mill Road, Dunton Green, Sevenoaks, Kent TN13 2YA (Editorial Office: 47 Bedford Square, London WC1 3DP) by BPCC Hazells Ltd Member of BPCC Ltd Photoset by E.P.L. BookSet, Norwood, London.

British Library C.I.P.

Lowe, Shirley
  Shaping up.
  I. Title   II. Ince, Angela
  823[F]

ISBN 0-340-56456-3

Shaping Up

PROLOGUE

'What we seek for at Alba, what we achieve, is nothing short of perfection. I will not suffer incompetence or slackness.' The autocratic old lady raised an imperious hand to thwart any possible interruption. A quite unnecessary gesture, since it wouldn't have occurred to three of her audience to have the temerity, and the fourth was bored. 'You might think that the temperature of the underwater massage bath is a trivial issue. You would be wrong.'

Isabella Cordoba de Zarate, owner and Directrice of the Alba Health Manor, sat at the head of a long oak refectory table; hewn, as her family tradition had it, from the same trees that supplied the Armada timbers. Her head and shoulders were framed by a noble chair that had supported the bishops of Toledo, until an earlier Cordoba took a fancy to it while attending a policy meeting regarding Henry Tudor's divorce plans. When in the mood, Isabella recounted the story most amusingly.

Table, chair, and Isabella; three finely-carved patricians who suited each other to perfection. Isabella was very aware of the effect of her bone structure and her white hair against the polish of centuries. Under the chair was curled another elderly patrician; Flora Macdonald, the impeccably-lineaged, evil-tempered Scottish terrier who followed Isabella about like a dusty, dangerous lady-in-waiting.

There was not much of the patrician about her four heads of department, who, seated at contrived and unnerving distances round the table, were gazing at Isabella with just the shade of apprehensive attention she liked to see. At least, three of them were; the fourth had a look that could be described as 'quizzical' by a generous-minded observer, which Isabella certainly was not.

Sister Monica, chunky, with eyes that looked best over a blood pressure monitor. Her face had gained its freshness on the hockey fields, and she had ankles to match. Monica was in charge of the four nurses, trained at vast expense by the National Health Service and employed by Alba at roughly five times the salary the state was prepared to offer them. As Alba's brochure put it, 'A fully-trained nurse is on duty twenty-four hours a day; guests should not hesitate to call on their help at any time, no matter how trivial their problem might appear to be.'

Nobody at Alba appeared to find it eccentric that intelligent young women, taught to staunch the blood of children and soothe the burns of the elderly, spent their working days calming the fears of perfectly healthy people who thought they might have pulled a tummy muscle in the gym; they were, after all, operating in a commercial world. Monica was a good deal more commercial than she looked. She was thinking, No wonder the old lizard's looking so pleased with herself, the amount she's raking in. High time she upped my pay. Extras were *my* idea, after all.

Matt Lawson, the chief masseur, headed the team of two girls and another man. Or, as Matt never missed the opportunity to point out, almost another man. Isabella considered him to be vulgar. He was, as he was the first to admit, in it for the money; he had a deplorable sense of humour, and he regarded the guests as a bunch of self-indulgent foodies. Irritatingly, he possessed hands of high calibre. Depending on the client (and Matt was very quick at sussing out clients) his fingers could say, 'Nasty knot in those shoulder muscles; we'll have to see what we can do to put it right' . . . 'You have a very beautiful body and my interest in it is purely professional' . . . 'You have a very beautiful body and why don't we do something about it?'

All the longstanding clients preferred Matt, saying pityingly to newer clients, 'Oh, do you have Lucy? Nice little thing. Of course, Matt insists on doing me himself.' Matt couldn't tell one of them from the other, and right then he was thinking, Oh, do stop sitting there looking smug, Princess, and get on with it. Half past five already, Mary will never get my supper on time at this rate.

Matt's wife Mary was, as she liked to put it with a cheerful laugh, i/c Steam Cabinets, Underwater Massage and Aromatherapy. Cosy, jolly and chatty, she was just the sort of person the ladies liked to gossip with when locked in steam cabinets or having underwater jets directed at upper-arm flab. Mary was uncomplicated but worried a lot. She was careful not to moan to the clients, of course, that would never do, but she did sometimes hint that juggling work, Matt, and two young children left her a bit ragged at the edges. Though she was careful to add, while tactfully whisking a concealing towel between wizened bodies and interested eyes in other Steam Cabinets, 'All part of life's rich pattern, that's what I always say.'

While Mary's face kept an attentive and conscientious gaze on Isabella, Mary's mind was scampering fretfully through lists of chores and worries. If Matt doesn't stop fidgeting, Madame will give him one of her looks . . . did I remember to get the potatoes? . . . we'll have to collect the kids from Sue on the way home, Matt won't like that . . . I still haven't tidied away those old photographs of dad's . . . if the ironing's dried out again, I'll have to damp it, never quite the same . . . Sam has football tomorrow, did I do his boots? . . . I do wish Matt hadn't insisted on a roast, it'll take ages . . .

Rosemary Meadows, MA Edin. Dietetics, Degree diploma, ran the kitchens at Alba; not in itself a testing task, you might have thought, what with lunch being soup and salad in the Dining Room and fruit and yogurt in the Light Diet Room. And dinner being not all that dissimilar. True, it did say in the brochure that 'Clients' Individual

Requirements Will be Catered For'; but Rosemary briskly interpreted that as giving them what everybody else was having, and explaining in long words why their Individual Requirements would be quite fatal to their current regime. Rosemary had a lot of time to spare to think about money, a particular fondness of hers. Now, pretending to take notes in a capable way, she was thinking, Two more years and I'll have paid off the mortgage. I might get that new little Renault, could run to a GTS this time. That dreary cow Monica is in cahoots with Madame about something. Might be worth finding out.

Isabella smiled in a manner which made Matt keep his feet still, if only temporarily, and handed Rosemary some papers. 'Distribute these, will you, dear? The guests arriving next Sunday. Any comments, anyone?'

Matt said 'No,' without looking at the list (Mary would have to warn him about that, when he was in a good temper after the roast).

Monica said, 'That dipsomaniac back again already. I'll have to remind the maids to search her wardrobe every day.'

'And that poor skinny daughter of hers, such a sad little person,' said soft-hearted simple Mary.

Matt was looking at his watch. 'You'd be a sad little person if your father never noticed you, and your mother couldn't walk a straight line towards breakfast.'

'There are several of our regular clients with us next week,' said Isabella, wishing Matt wasn't such a good masseur (and anyway if she fired him Mary would probably go too). 'So pleasing, from Alba's point of view, to have old friends returning again and again.'

'Oh, dear, how muddling,' said Mary anxiously, 'I hope I don't get them mixed up. Only when people haven't got anything on, there's nothing to remember them by.'

'Never been a problem for me,' said Matt, picking up the guest list, 'oh, my Gawd, talking about problems, Desperate Diane and Sexy Sheila again. Hand me my

10

chastity belt, someone.'

'Matt, dear,' said Mary, 'I don't think that's quite . . . Oh,' she squeaked, 'oh, *Madame*, there's that old mother and daughter coming as well, and the old lady's so difficult, I know I'll get confused.'

'Even you couldn't confuse a flat-chested old spinster with an anorexic schoolgirl,' said Matt.

Isabella gave him the look of one in whose veins ran the blood of generations of Infantas, and said, 'We never confuse clients' names at Alba, Mary. It is merely a matter of concentration.'

Matt smiled blandly, looked at his watch again, and said, 'Is that the time? Oh, well, *Hasta la Vista*, as they say.' The Lawsons exited on an appalled silence.

Rosemary gathered her papers and said, 'If there's nothing else, Madame? I've left next week's diet sheets on your desk. Right, I'll run along, then.'

Sister Monica stayed behind. 'I didn't like the way Meadows was looking at us,' she said, 'she's no fool, that one. Think I'll have a word with her. Now, Madame, about my salary review . . . '

*   *   *

Matt and Mary Lawson drove out of the palatial gates of Alba on their way to Sue's to pick up the children. Matt was grumbling. 'Two miles out of our way, I'll never get fed at this rate. Why couldn't Sue have taken them straight home?'

'You know I don't like them to be alone in the house, dear. You never know what might happen. And it's very kind of Sue, what with her own three and everything . . . '

'I thought old madame gas-bags would never stop. How I hate these weekly meetings. Bloody boring waste of time.'

'Madame thinks it's essential for Heads of Department to discuss incoming guests and their individual problems. You know that, dear.'

11

'Discuss? Don't make me laugh. She discusses and we nod.'

'Naturally she's going to be autocratic, with her background. Matt, I don't think you were quite ... well, co-operative today.'

'I was there, wasn't I? How much more co-operative do you want me to be?'

'Well, if you could even pretend to read the lists. And when you said that about *Hasta la Vista*, I could have sunk through the floor.'

Matt scowled at the windscreen wipers and said, 'Oh, for God's sake.'

Mary knew she should have waited until after the roast, but she blundered on. 'You know it's an absolute rule, Matt, that we must never talk about anything Spanish. It upsets Madame so, to be reminded of her past.'

'Just you leave Isabella to me. I know how to deal with her. What's for dinner?'

Mary brightened. 'Your favourite, dear, roast pork.'

'A roast? Whatever made you choose a roast? We'll be eating at midnight.'

*   *   *

Sister Monica had, on the Alba estate, what would have been called a Grace and Favour cottage, if Isabella had been royalty. Of course, thought Monica, putting on the kettle, she practically is. And her family goes a lot further back than, say, the Greek Royal family. Fancy me speaking to a Cordoba de Zarate like that. I'm not one to mince my words, even if her ancestors did have battles with Drake and Raleigh.

The decor of Monica's sitting room reflected her complexion and her ankles. You could say that she imbibed her decorating ideas from the playing fields of Huddersfield Grammar School for Girls. The curtains were very nearly the same regency stripe as the wallpaper; a reproduction of

Monet's *Irises* (or was it Manet? Monica was blowed if she could remember) faced a blown-up poster of a baby eleph-ant standing between the rears of two grown-up elephants, which Monica found really rather sweet. In pride of place on the mantelpiece was a collection of china thimbles which Monica had bought, complete with display rack, through a Sunday colour supplement. She had just sent away for Vivid and Inspirational Ceramic Depictions of the Four Seasons (two-thirds the size illustrated). They would look very nice on either side of the thimbles. Cul-turally, Monica was a desert; but the instincts of the Mafia were ranged amongst the irises, the baby elephant and the cocktail glasses with transfers of hunting scenes on them. Monica couldn't have been more ruthless if Huddersfield Grammar School for Girls had been sited just outside Salerno.

Monica had asked Rosemary Meadows over for a drink. Ostensibly 'to discuss one or two of next week's more difficult clients'. But really because she wanted to find out if Rosemary had any idea about what was going on. Rose-mary had hesitated before she accepted. It would without doubt be sweet British sherry, and what she hankered for was a severe gin and tonic, well iced and with a strip of lemon peel, in her own immaculate sitting room. However, she had agreed, in the end, because she could swear there was something going on and she had every intention of getting to the bottom of it.

Now, sitting in Monica's perfectly frightful sitting room, drinking sticky warm brown stuff out of a glass called 'Gone Away', and trying to think of something civilised to say about twenty-seven thimbles with herbs on them, she wished she'd gone straight home.

'How lovely. What a *charming* idea. I've always been very interested in herbs. I thought Madame was looking rather tired this evening. How old is she, exactly?'

'That's for you to ask and me to tell,' said Monica, not telling, and taking a sip out of her own glass ('Hounds,

13

Gentlemen, Please'). 'Naturally she looks tired. Running a place like this is jolly hard work. A drop more sherry?'

'Thank you, no. Delicious, but I am driving.' Rosemary needn't have bothered; Monica was putting the bottle away even as she offered. 'No, it's more, I get the impression the old bird has something on her mind.'

'Between you and me, and I know it will not go beyond these four walls . . . ' Rosemary looked at the regency stripes and wished she hadn't, ' . . . Madame's health has been giving her a little cause for concern recently. Nothing very serious. But of course at her age she has to take care.'

'Oh, well,' Rosemary gratefully put down her glass and rose to go. 'Nothing to worry about, then? I really must be off.'

Monica thought, as she shut the front door on the renewed thanks of Rosemary (' . . . and such amusing glasses, Monica, where did you find them?') that Isabella had, and always would have, the constitution of a goat, but she had to think of something to put that nosy dietician off the track.

*   *   *

Rosemary's cottage did not belong to Alba. It belonged to the bank and, increasingly, to Rosemary. Her sitting room was almost totally cream, with a few touches of cinnamon here and there. Monica, who had been over once, for a glass of very dry Fino (Rosemary watched her puckered lips with deepest pleasure) considered it Rather Drab for My Taste.

Lighting a log fire and thankfully erasing the taste of British sweet sticky with a gin and tonic, Rosemary thought, Health giving cause for concern, my foot, the old bat's as tough as a boot. There *is* something going on.

*   *   *

It was half past eight. Matt was watching *A Question of Sport* and nagging Mary. 'Isn't supper ready, yet? . . . Must we have those old photographs of your father's all over the place? . . . Sam's boots need cleaning . . . I told you not to get a roast.'

Monica was savouring a Lean Cuisine Cheese Cannelloni with Sauce Napolitana fresh from the microwave; Rosemary was pouring herself a second G and T and thinking seriously about a baked potato with lots of butter and two poached eggs.

Isabella, though, was still at work. Accompanied by cross Flora, she was making her routine end-of-day patrol to ensure that all was well in the small kingdom of Alba.

You could have set your watch by her. First, the linen room, which would have done credit to a small hospital. Piles, stacks, mountains of snowy towels, sheets and pillowcases, all embroidered with a discreet blue 'A' in one corner. Racks of white bathrobes, Large, Medium and Small, with the 'A' on a breast pocket. A plateau of white cotton squares, for people to sit on in the Steam Cabinet, or modestly drape themselves in the Sauna. Isabella had long noticed that the people with the good bodies tended to be the more modest. It was the bodies that were best hidden from sight that lounged about with the luxurious abandon of a Rubens. The washing machines barely paused for breath at Alba. Clients moved from towel to towel during their carefully planned day. In other establishments, Isabella understood with a fastidious shudder, clients were given a clean towel each morning, and expected to hang on to it for the rest of the day; here, towels were lobbed about as if there were no tomorrow, as Matt put it.

Alba had suffered, during its early months, from a certain amount of pilferage. Isabella put a stop to that by displaying printed notices on bedside tables: 'Clients have occasionally evinced a desire to take home with them some items of Alba's distinctive linen. They are very welcome to

15

do so. Please enquire at Reception.'

The linen room approved, Isabella moved on to the Treatment Area, built on to the back of the original Victorian mansion. Flora, whose ancient hind legs were giving cause for concern, limped, grumbling in her throat, through the doors marked 'Massage – Gentlemen' and 'Massage – Ladies' and lay down while Isabella checked the curtained cubicles, pristine for tomorrow's pummelling. 'Come on, Flora, Sauna and Steam Cabinets, and just a quick look round the public rooms, then we'll go and get your supper.' Flora grunted and staggered to her feet.

Later, back in her private study, furnished with the cream of several centuries, Isabella opened her account books and allowed herself a dignified smile, a cigarette, and a sparse nightcap of brandy and soda. The fact that all over Alba people were paying well into three figures to enjoy nightcaps largely consisting of hot water made the brandy tingle on the back of her tongue in an even more delightful way. The figures were looking good, very good indeed, even allowing for vast outgoing expenses. She paid her excellent staff well above the going rate, the equipment was of the highest possible standard, the bedrooms sumptuously furnished in turn-of-the-century country house . . . and how it paid off. And we mustn't forget the Extras, thought Isabella demurely.

Not everything, of course, ran as smoothly as it appeared to Alba's cosseted clients. After the meeting, for instance, Monica was quite . . . peremptory was really the only word for it . . . about more money. Admittedly Extras had been her idea, but it was Isabella's flair for organisation, Isabella's contacts, and above all, Isabella's cool head in an emergency that had made Extras the moneymaker it was.

Who was it, Isabella thought irritably, who kept her wits about her when that silly young Viscount overdid things disastrously? All Sister Monica contributed on that occasion was shouting, 'Stop that at once,' in a bossy fashion.

Pathetic, not to mention ill-bred. Isabella came from tougher stock, and something that could have been a disaster was turned adroitly into a rather amusing incident. Luck, admittedly, was with her, as it always is on the side of strong battalions. There was only one other client in the swimming pool at the time; that vague writer, Ballard, with the thick glasses and the rather suspect vowels and the air of living in another dimension. He wouldn't have noticed an earthquake if he'd been in San Francisco in 1906, or whenever it was. Anyway, he was booked back for another visit next week, so young Lord Harry's lapse obviously hadn't impinged on him.

Isabella helped herself to another brandy, not quite so sparse this time, and lit another cigarette. She really ought to cut down. What was it she had said to that woman in mustard velour she'd caught smoking in the Drawing Room last night? 'There is no addiction that cannot be conquered.'

Well, she would conquer it tomorrow, or perhaps next week. Right now she had too much to think about, too much to organise, too many worries. She was, after all, rising seventy-five, and however good she looked, even she couldn't go on for ever. She needed someone to pick up the reins, someone to ease the burden from her shoulders. She needed an heir; and to her intense irritation, there was only one available. Her granddaughter Cordelia. That Woman's daughter.

She picked up a pen and took out a sheet of Alba's heavy creamy writing paper. 'My dear Cordelia,' she wrote. 'You will no doubt be surprised . . . ' Her eyes strayed, unwillingly, to a photograph of That Woman occupying a discreet shelf of the bookcase. Olivia Ledbury, with husband, child and dog, four portly, complacent creatures posed on the steps of a slightly run-down manor house. How Isabella could have given birth to such a lump she would never know. Olivia did not look like someone whose ancestors had ruled a considerable part of

17

Andalusia; she looked like somebody's cook, thought Isabella sourly. Somebody's cook who eats too much. Inconsiderate right from the start. A difficult birth, absolutely typical of Olivia, choosing to emerge in the middle of a London blitz. Nine pounds two ounces fighting its way through an aristocratic pelvis was bound to lead to discomfort. True to the tenets of her ancestry, Isabella didn't utter so much as a whimper through twenty-six hours of undignified pushing and pulling; the nurses thought her so brave, under the circumstances. In fact she had found the noise of gunfire and bombs and the smell of broken plaster a welcome distraction from what was going on inside her. During the All Clear she had plenty of time to wonder if she could ever have anything in common with a creature that insisted on idling its way through a simple journey of six inches. Once born, the baby wrenched at the breast in a manner which ensured it was bottle-fed within forty-eight hours.

'Don't worry, dear,' the nice little nurse had said as she carried hefty wailing Olivia off to the nursery, 'sometimes it takes days for mummy to feel at home with baby.'

More like decades, Isabella thought. She looked fondly at the old dog, asleep at her feet, and bent to rub her ears. 'Basket-time, Flora. Mummy carry you?' She was a much better mother to Flora than she had been to Olivia, her real daughter; but Flora, as a puppy, was sweet and slim and wriggly. Olivia was a podge who had grown up and given birth to another podge; a tiresome large girl obsessed with food.

Isabella felt no tug of affection for either of them; she only liked pretty things.

CHAPTER
ONE

Eight ounces plain chocolate, four egg yolks, half a pint of
cream . . . Cordelia Ledbury was seriously interested in
food. Every morning she lay in bed contemplating the day's
pleasures. Would it be croissant and honey for breakfast,
or toast, unsalted Normandy butter and a dollop of her
mother's ginger marmalade? How about that left-over bit
of bacon? A lunchtime quiche, perhaps, or spaghetti
carbonara? Sometimes she luxuriated for a further ten
minutes, compiling a shopping list of the ingredients she
might need for dinner.

Occasionally she was nudged by guilt. Shouldn't she be
thinking about the ozone layer or the Third World instead
of *boeuf en croûte* or spiced scrambled eggs? She had to
remind herself, sternly, that food was, after all, her business. Magazines paid her good money to tempt their
readers and advertisers with lavishly illustrated recipes.
Dipping a wooden spoon into the chocolate mixture,
Cordelia took a professional lick. Mmm . . . almost perfect. How lucky I am, she thought, actually to make money
out of my hobby. Another luscious spoonful. Nobody
could see her, so it wasn't fattening. Making a note on her
pad, 'Add dessert spoon strong black coffee to bring out
flavour,' she carried the mixture to the table, poured it
fondly into a charlotte mould and put it into the refrigerator.

Sally Rhodes, her flatmate, had left a large carton of
cottage cheese and a box of salad stuff in the front of the
fridge. Cordelia, who was now considering lunch, gazed

unseeingly over these wholesome items, seeking out a glass dish stashed at the back. It contained the remnants of a cassoulet, redolent of goose fat and garlic sausage, which she had prepared a couple of days before for a Food with a French Accent feature in *Homes and Gardens*. The cold congealed texture was curiously satisfying. Standing at her window, Cordelia surveyed the world below. Her idea of a view was one containing people and bustle and noise, and there was always plenty of that in Shepherd's Bush. The September sun, filtering through the spindly trees on the Green, was agreeably warming. She took a mouthful of cassoulet and waved her spoon merrily at the passengers on the top deck of a passing bus who gazed glumly back at her.

Cordelia had never been able to understand people who say: 'If only I'd realised it, I was so happy *then*.' She knew when she was happy; it swamped her in a warm glow and was usually accompanied by a need to sing and smile at strangers.

'Oh, what a beautiful morning . . . ' she sang into the fridge, searching eagerly for the remains of the apple crumble. She stopped singing as she remembered the meeting coming up that afternoon, with Janet Marmont, her agent. Janet, who had been handling Cordelia's cookery books and articles for the last five years, had suddenly turned critical.

'Nobody wants to eat all that heavy food any more,' she had said on the phone the day before.

'I do,' said Cordelia, and wished she hadn't when Janet, a skinny size eight, replied rather insensitively, 'Lucky you, not worrying about putting on weight. All the best-selling cookery books these days are diet conscious, Cordelia. Vegetables, pulses, yogurt; that's the current thinking. Come in tomorrow; we'll have a talk about it.'

Cordelia had heard enough about calories and cracked wheat. Only last week *New Woman* had sent back her Party Pâtés feature, and after she had spent all that time working out the exact number of juniper berries to add piquancy to the chicken livers, too.

'Stir-fry,' they said, 'that's the sort of thing we're after. Nutritious dishes our readers can whip up in a few minutes when they get home from the office.'

Cordelia came from Yorkshire where a good meal meant plenty on the plate. Her mother had worked as conscientiously at home-making as her father worked at stockbroking, and would have considered it wilfully feckless to push a few bean sprouts around a frying pan.

'My word, Olivia, you've got a bonny baby there,' the neighbours always said when Olivia pushed Cordelia out in her pram. Lovingly primed with hearty stews and nursery puddings, the chubby baby had turned into a pretty plump teenager who had grown into an even plumper adult. Whenever she went home to Yorkshire, Cordelia's mother's friends were still full of compliments. 'You've got a fine looking girl there, Olivia.'

Cordelia's own friends were less complimentary. 'You know what, Cordy?' Sally had said that morning, 'If you ate more of this . . . ' she waved her Low Fat Yogurt container, 'and less of that . . . ' she gestured at Cordelia's plate (she had come down in favour of croissants, honey *and* butter) 'you'd be bloody attractive.'

Scooping up the last of the cassoulet with a chunk of granary bread, Cordelia was forced to admit that the sort of food she enjoyed had gone out of fashion. And, what was worse, her income was beginning to reflect this unfortunate trend.

The aroma of chocolate was still drifting enticingly around the warm kitchen; Cordelia sniffed appreciatively and filed her last bank statement to the back of her mind. Stewart was coming back from New York today. She looked at her watch. He'd be touching down at Heathrow in less than half an hour. She thought about being in bed with Stewart again, the excitement of his familiar body. Maybe they'd have time for a pre-coital tandoori at that new Indian place in the Uxbridge Road. She passed there yesterday and really liked the look of the menu.

*   *   *

'I've had a "no" from Hodders and Century said they weren't interested, either.' Janet Marmont pushed a slim manuscript across her desk at Cordelia. 'I'm sorry, Cordelia, but I did warn you. People just aren't thinking Warm Winter Casseroles these days. Couldn't you come up with a book on healthy living? I was talking to Fran at Penguin, she's terrifically hot on the Food is Good for You idea; you know, The Larder is your Medicine Chest sort of thing. Couldn't you have a go at it? With your name I'd guarantee you a £10,000 advance.'

Seeing Cordelia's resentful expression, Janet wondered why she bothered. God knows, her files were bursting with letters from authors who'd be only too pleased to put aside their current *oeuvre* and make a mint with the definitive cookbook. And they'd be grateful for her advice.

'Well, maybe even £15,000.' Janet was fond of Cordelia; she had been a steady source of revenue to the agency, and her book on bedsitter cookery (Janet shuddered fastidiously at the memory of the myriad starchy meals Cordelia had managed to produce out of a Wee Baby Belling) was heading for a sixth reprint. 'Why don't you think about it? Rough out a few synopses?'

Cordelia subjected Janet to a long reproachful look, which Janet interpreted as petulance. 'No, thank you, Janet. Sage may very well be an excellent remedy for a sore throat, but so far as I'm concerned it's better lightly bound with egg, onions and breadcrumbs and stuffed into a joint of pork.'

Pleased with this witty précis of her viewpoint, Cordelia had planned to rise from her chair and deliver the final bit of it from the doorway. But the chair was so low, and it was such an effort to get up, that she was forced to throw away, 'I'm a cook, not a chemist,' from an undignified half-crouch in front of Janet's desk.

*   *   *

Before her meeting with Janet, Cordelia had rehearsed what she intended to wear that evening; last year's plaid skirt and the dark green cashmere sweater she had treated herself to a couple of weeks before with the *Bella* cheque. But, when she tried on the skirt, the zip had stuck half way up her hips. She tried pulling the sweater down over the gap, but it sprang up to her rib-cage every time she raised her arms. And anyway, Stewart was bound to spot the gap when she removed the sweater, which she fully intended to do at some point of the evening.

Leaving Janet's office she had made a quick dash into Big and Beautiful, a boutique at the back of South Molton Street which usually had some really nice things in her size. But all the skirts she tried on shared the plaid's problem. She looked around at the dresses, and the ones with size sixteen to eighteen labels inside seemed to have been designed for mature women to take Afternoon Tea in. Anything that tactfully skimmed the waistline came complete with a concealing granny bow at the neckline, and Cordelia had no desire to conceal her slim unwrinkled throat or her becomingly rounded cleavage.

And then she saw the perfect garment, in a far corner of the department. A rack of black cord dresses, flaring out from a low rounded neckline. Brilliant. And she fitted into the Medium.

Cordelia took a lot of trouble getting ready that evening. She squeezed half a tube of Perlier's Honey Cream into her bath, and hesitated only briefly afterwards, before smoothing Sally's Guerlain Body Moisturiser all over herself; Sally was, after all, three weeks behind on her share of the milk bill. She brushed her straight blonde hair until it shone. She smoothed Pretty Polly Nylons on to her long slim legs and

23

they gleamed a satisfactorily seductive Silver Grey. She added a gold brooch and bracelet to the black dress, and decided that she looked knockout.

Stewart seemed to think so, too. 'Cordy,' he scooped her into his arms, 'I came straight from the office, couldn't wait to see you.'

Cordelia felt the bottle of duty free champagne, enticingly chilly against the low back of her new dress, as he kissed her. Thank goodness Sally, an assistant floor manager at the BBC, was on location that day; with any luck she'd get caught up in a cast party after the day's shooting and wouldn't be home in time to raise an intrigued eyebrow when she and Stewart went into the bedroom together.

'Let me look at you. Darling, I've missed you. Do you realise it's been nearly a week?' Stewart disentangled himself, busied himself with the champagne. 'It's definitely celebration time. Come on, Cordy! Glasses! Quick!'

The cork popped festively and Cordelia caught the champagne in a Jet 'Free Tumbler'. (*What* had Sally done with the wine glasses?) They sat together on the sofa, while Stewart told Cordelia that NASA had approved his onboard software for their space programme in Houston, which meant he was in line for promotion, and Cordelia (deciding not to spoil the moment by mentioning the return of her manuscript) told Stewart how she'd created the truly perfect Chocolate Marquise. Without realising it, they had drained the bottle, and Stewart was gazing hopefully towards the kitchen.

'I thought we'd go out,' Cordelia said. 'There's this new tandoori place . . . '

'Much rather stay in,' Stewart said grumpily. He took her in his arms again then, and listed all the pleasurable things he'd been planning for them to do. 'Besides,' he added tactfully, 'I've missed your cooking almost as much as I've missed you.'

'I don't feel like cooking.' Why did everyone always

expect her to cook for them? Typists weren't expected to come home in the evening and type out bills of lading for their lovers. 'I'd been looking forward to the chicken tikka . . . '

Stewart stumbled very slightly as he rose, and spilt the last of his champagne over Cordelia's new dress. 'Sorry about that. Had a few nerve-steadying Scotches on the plane.' He took her hand. 'If you've been looking forward to a chicken tikka, my darling, then a chicken tikka you shall have.'

They had another bottle of wine with the tikka, and, back in the flat, a glass of brandy, with Billie Holliday singing 'My Man', which made Cordelia, now rather maudlin, wonder how she would feel if her man deserted her.

'You do love me, Stewart?'

'Of course I love you. What do I have to do to prove it?' said Stewart, taking advantage of Cordelia's plunging neckline.

Cordelia twisted away. 'Not like that. I don't mean that. I mean, *really* love me?'

'Oh, Christ!' Stewart dragged Cordelia up off the sofa and pushed her into the bedroom where they had an unsynchronised scuffle with Cordelia trying to remove her brooch and Stewart trying to remove her dress, ripping the Silver Grey Nylons in the process. 'I've been promising myself this all week.' He drew the dress over Cordelia's head and her arm got caught in the sleeve the way it always used to do when her mother was undressing her for bed. This made her feel even sadder, and she stood there in her underwear, with the tears splashing her cheeks.

Stewart threw Cordelia's dress on the chair. 'What's up with you, Cordelia? I bring you back a bottle of best Moët, I take you out to dinner, I make love to you and you start crying all over the place . . . '

'It's not love,' Cordelia mumbled. She'd so looked forward to this evening. Why was it all going so wrong?

'Oh, Christ!' Stewart flung himself down on the chair, on the dress, and because he felt guilty about Cordelia standing there semi nude and sobbing, and even guiltier that he was gazing at her critically (my God, she'd put on a bit round the waist) he looked at his feet instead. What he saw, down there on the floor, next to his brown leather brogues, focused his anger.

'Oh, that's just great,' he said, getting up, and waving the neckline of Cordelia's dress in front of her face. 'That's wonderful, that is . . . '

'What? . . . I don't know what you're . . . '

Stewart jabbed a finger at the designer's label. He was beginning to sober up and needed to justify his behaviour. 'Elegance Maternelle!' He spat out the words like an obscenity. 'Do you really think any man wants to go out with a girl who's so . . . ' he couldn't quite bring himself to say it, ' . . . that she has to dress in maternity clothes?'

Cordelia jumped into bed and pulled the covers over her head.

As he left, Stewart heard her sobbing under the duvet. 'Go away, go away, I never want to see you again.'

*   *   *

Cordelia was only half-listening to Sally, who had just come home with noisy news of her day in Studio B. She was curled up in the comfortable armchair (the one with a missing spring so you could really sink into it), trying to blot out yesterday; the meeting with Janet, the awful evening with Stewart.

'So then Peter shouts down the earphones, "Tell that bloody woman to stop waving her arms around when she's delivering that line,"' Sally threw down her shoulder bag and collapsed into the other armchair, 'and just as I'm suggesting to Miss Temperament that although Peter absolutely *adores* her interpretation, he does feel that the subtlety of the text would be enhanced if she stood very,

26

very still, he's crackling into the earphones again about the shine on Bob's bald head, and where are the bloody make-up girls? Still at their tea break as usual, he supposes. God, what a day. And there's an unofficial strike in the offing next Wednesday . . . '

'Ghastly,' Cordelia murmured. She knew that Sally thrived on studio dramas.

'Ghastly. Is that all you can say?' Sally gave Cordelia a sharp look. 'Cordy, are you all right? You look a bit down yourself.'

'Pretty low,' Cordelia admitted cautiously. She was prepared to tell Sally about yesterday's gloomy scene in her agent's office; but not about Stewart, she would never tell anyone about that.

'What's for supper?' It was an unwritten rule in Sally and Cordelia's flat-sharers' charter that Sally did all the practical chores like changing plugs, and Cordelia, with the Domestic Science degree, did the cooking.

'Nothing.'

'You mean there's nothing to eat?'

'There might be some shepherd's pie in the fridge.'

'Well, what are we waiting for?' Sally got up and then sat down again when Cordelia said she wasn't hungry. 'My God, Cordelia, you really are low.'

'I think I'll have a bath.' A warm bath was very nearly as consoling as a warm hug, and she could lock the door on Sally's concerned questions.

'Aha, making ourselves lovely for the Incredible Hulk. Is Stewart coming round again tonight?'

'There's a bottle of French *petits pois* and baby carrots in the cupboard over the sink,' said Cordelia, leaving the room.

*   *   *

Cordelia's appetite had returned by the following morning. She was actually quite hungry, and as she prepared

27

kedgeree, she brooded about the unfairness of life. Most people lost weight when they were miserable, wanly pushing away proffered plates – 'Oh, I couldn't,' – but even though life had lost every glint of lustre, and she had fretted through a sleepless night, Cordelia found herself reaching eagerly for the smoked haddock, eggs, butter and cream. She decided to blame her mother, who had always responded to disaster with a sweet treat. When Cordelia fell down in the school playground and got gravel in her knee, when Mr Bear's leg came tragically apart from his furry brown body, Olivia Ledbury would pop a slice of freshly baked fruit cake into her daughter's mouth. 'Cheer up, Cordy, it'll soon be better.'

'Bugger salmonella,' Cordelia murmured, recklessly stirring soft moist eggs into the brown crunchy rice, and sniffing appreciatively. She was hesitating over the wisdom of dotting in another ounce of butter and a further blob of cream, when Sally sprang into the kitchen, alert with health and bossiness.

'Letter for you.' Throwing the envelope over to Cordelia, she poured herself a cup of weak tea without milk, sat down at the kitchen table and started peeling a clementine.

'What's that weird smell?' Her eyes lit on Cordelia's cast-iron casserole. 'Oh, Cordelia, how could you? Risotto for breakfast. No wonder you're so . . . '

Cordelia was too busy gazing gloomily at the embossed envelope to pick up the slur. 'Oh, God, it's from my grandmother.' She opened it slowly and methodically with her favourite sharp kitchen knife, unfolded the letter and read it as enthusiastically as if it were a rejection slip. 'Oh, God, she wants to see me.'

'So?' Meticulously scooping up the fragments of her clementine skin and dropping them in the waste bin, Sally looked reproachfully at Cordelia's empty eggshells and fragments of haddock bone. If only Cordelia would stop fiddling around with food and go on a sensible diet she'd soon find someone more appealing than the Incredible Hulk. Cordelia hadn't said anything but Sally knew they'd split up. Stood to reason. When she had got back from the studio party the other night, there had been no sign of Stewart in the bedroom, and no washing up in the sink; all that selfish bastard ever seemed to want from Cordy was a good meal and a good screw. 'Cordy?'

'Yes?'

Sally looked at her watch. It was the Acton Rehearsal Rooms today and the traffic would be hell. She decided, on reflection, to postpone the Stewart saga until she and Cordelia had time to sit down and dissect the nuances of what he said, what she said, and exactly how he looked when he said it. 'Nothing. Got to rush.'

Cordelia was still absorbed in her letter. 'She wants to talk to me about something.'

'So, what's the problem?' Sally was half out of the door. 'Isn't she splendidly rich, your grandmother? Isn't she the one with the health farm?'

'Health *manor*, Sal. Farms are for the peasants, darling.' Cordelia rolled her Rs in a gutteral Spanish manner, which was rather unfair of her since Isabella Cordoba de Zarate spoke with scarcely a trace of accent. 'She wants to see me on Thursday.'

When Cordelia phoned her mother to tell her about the summons to Alba, Olivia said, 'She's written to you? I haven't heard from her for three years. Not since your father was in hospital having the cataract operation and she said he'd ruined his eyesight with whisky. Poor lamb. He does so enjoy his Scotch before dinner. What does she say?'

'She wants me to go down there next Thursday afternoon. She says she has something important she wants to discuss with me.'

'When mother says something is important, she means it is important to her,' said Olivia. 'Be careful, darling.'

CHAPTER
TWO

Although she had laughed at her mother's warning ('What on earth can she do to me, mum?') Cordelia had to shrug off a tremor of unease as she skirted a golf club, passed a farm and a lake and got a sighting of the turrets and chimneys of the Alba Health Manor. There was a touch of the gothic about them which she found appropriate. Cordelia had been brought up on horror stories about her grandmother, and even now found it hard to distinguish Isabella from the wicked witches of childhood fairy stories.

It was, of course, Isabella and not some villainess stepmother in the Brothers Grimm, who, when Olivia asked for a second helping of chocolate blancmange, made her finish the whole pudding until she was gagging and sobbing. 'It's for your own good, Olivia. I won't have greediness in this house.'

And it was Isabella who managed, every week, to find some small naughtiness calling for a spanking with one of the special bamboo canes she kept in the hall cupboard for that purpose. 'Spare the rod and spoil the child,' she would say, putting Olivia over her knee. Cordelia used to beg her mother to tell her this story again and again, because it ended satisfactorily, with Olivia snapping every one of the canes in two. 'That was the last time she beat me, Cordy,' Olivia would say, 'I was fifteen then. Old enough to stand up to her.'

Cordelia felt another shiver of apprehension as she pulled the bell rope. The door opened to reveal a wood-panelled hall, containing leather sofas and chairs, several tastefully arranged vases of flowers on highly polished mahogany tables, a reception desk like a hotel, and an unfriendly looking woman in a nurse's outfit barring the doorway.

'Yes?'

'I've come to see, er . . . ' Isabella Cordoba de Zarate. Why couldn't her grandmother be plain Mrs Somebody, like everyone else's grandmother?

'Er . . . my grandmother.'

'Your grandmother?' Sister Monica didn't budge. 'Is she one of our guests? I must advise you that we don't encourage visitors during treatment hours.'

'Actually, she owns . . . she's Isabella Cordoba . . . '

'Madame's granddaughter?' Sister Monica ushered Cordelia quickly into the hall, wondering why the old lizard had never mentioned a family, and goodness knows there was nothing foreign looking about this one. 'If you'd like to take a seat here, I'll see if I can find Madame.'

She marched off and Cordelia sank into a leather armchair by the fire. Sitting near her were two women, thumbing through the magazines on the coffee table. Cordelia smiled at them agreeably and wondered why they looked odd. Of course. They were lolling around the entrance hall in their dressing gowns and slippers. The old one was wrapped in expensive red plush velvet, the meek middle-aged one in faded blue candlewick.

'Good afternoon,' said the old one, picking up *Country Life* and putting it down again with a sigh of exasperation. 'My reading glasses, Rachel. You left them on the little cupboard next to the bed.'

'Won't be a minute, mother.' The meek one jumped up and disappeared up the oak staircase.

'Silly girl,' said the old one. 'She knows I can't read without my glasses. Is this your first time here?' She gave Cordelia a beady once-over, suggesting that Cordelia hadn't signed on a moment too soon.

'Yes it is, actually.'

31

'Oh, you'll enjoy Alba. My daughter and I have tried them all, of course, but we keep coming back here.' She leaned forward confidentially, 'Mind you, they charge enough. The seaweed treatment has gone up again and I swear they're recycling the lunchtime salads . . . '

She gave a whinny of pain as Sister Monica reappeared and slapped her roguishly on the shoulder. 'Time for your massage, Mrs Gillespie.' She placed a firm hand under the old lady's elbow. 'Upsadaisy!'

'Thank you, Sister, I can manage perfectly well by myself.'

If looks could kill Sister Monica would have been pole-axed on the oriental rug, but after more than twelve years at Alba, Monica was adept at deflecting a killing gaze with cheery badinage. 'That's the ticket!' Heaving Mrs Gillespie on her way, she smiled ruefully at Cordelia. 'Such a splendid character. Now, Madame is waiting for you in her office. If you'll come this way.'

Following Sister Monica along the carpeted corridor, Cordelia agonised about what to call a grandmother she hadn't seen for seventeen years. Isabella seemed too familiar, Madame a shade formal. Was she a Contessa or a Señora? She should have checked with her mother. Just cosy old Gran, perhaps?

Last time Cordelia had seen her grandmother it had been Christmas time at her parents' house in Yorkshire and the heavy silences of things left unsaid had been even more discomforting than the unfestive exchanges around the tree.

'What on earth is this supposed to be, Olivia?' Isabella had said, unwrapping a pale blue bedjacket, which even Cordelia, at twelve years old, could see was not her grandmother's style.

'It's a bedjacket, mother.'

'Olivia knitted it for you herself,' father said proudly.

Isabella tossed the gift casually on to the pile of wrapping papers. 'I'm not in my dotage yet, Olivia.'

Isabella's bed had been lumpy ('You know I always sleep in linen sheets, Olivia'); the house was like a refrigerator ('I can see why you've taken up knitting woollen jackets'); and Olivia's painstakingly prepared Christmas dinner was inedible ('Just make me an omelette, Olivia. That's all I can manage').

Cordelia's mother had cried and dropped the turkey, her father had locked himself in his study with the decanter, Cordelia had watched Bing Crosby and Rosemary Clooney having a lovely old-fashioned happy Christmas on television, and Isabella had packed her bags and left. 'That's the last time that woman sets foot in this house,' Olivia said, as the hired Mercedes turned out of their drive.

No, definitely not cosy old Gran. Cordelia stifled a giggle which caused Sister Monica to eye her suspiciously as she tapped diffidently at the door.

'Come in, come in.'

Isabella was sitting on a Victorian button-backed chair, framed by brown velvet and old mahogany. She was dressed in immaculate black, which contrasted elegantly with her upswept wings of pure white hair. The hand extended in welcome, criss-crossed with fine veins and tiny brittle bones, had a claw-like quality. She's like a bird, Cordelia thought uneasily, a small black predatory bird.

Sister Monica was still hovering in the doorway, alert with interest. Isabella gave her a brisk nod of dismissal and turned back to Cordelia. 'There you are, child.'

'Yes, here I am . . . grandmother.'

Isabella looked at Cordelia, draped in just the sort of floral smock Olivia would have considered appropriate for the occasion, and wished she hadn't put pen to paper. Ah well, it was done now. She gestured towards an unaccommodating *chaise longue*, tightly upholstered in silk. 'I have a proposition to put to you, Cordelia, but first . . . ' she stamped an imperious high heel on a bit of carpet which set a bell jingling in the distance, ' . . . first we'll have a cup of tea, and then I expect you'd like to see round.'

33

'Well, yes,' Cordelia looked at her watch. At this rate, she wouldn't be home in time for *The Victorian Kitchen* on BBC 2.

Tea arrived on a trolley, pushed by a competent looking young woman, wearing her overall casually open, to make sure nobody mistook her for a servant. The trolley was shrouded in a lace-edged white cloth. Isabella whipped it off, like a conjurer, to reveal cucumber sandwiches, golden scones, a sponge cake lightly dusted with sugar. She gave another of her dismissive nods. 'Thank you, Rosemary.' Folding the cloth neatly into four she placed it on the bottom level of the trolley. 'Most of our guests are on special diets. We try not to upset them unnecessarily.'

Cordelia took a scone which turned out to be crumbly. She had it delicately balanced between plate and mouth when it went to pieces all over the pale golden carpet. Not, thank God, the *chaise longue*. 'Oh, goodness, I'm sorry.' Cordelia bent to scoop up the crumbs and came eyeball to eyeball with a cross dog which had lumbered out from behind Isabella's chair. It hoovered up the remnants of scone and moved on purposefully towards Cordelia's ankles, growling in a deep-throated Scottish manner.

'She won't hurt you if you sit still.' Isabella patted a velvet cushion next to her chair and smiled at the dog in a way she had not smiled at Cordelia.

'Oh, you've got a picture of mum and dad and me and dear old Bessie.' Cordelia, looking around the room for some conversational ice-breaker, had noticed the family group all but concealed behind a begonia on the bureau. She added untruthfully, because it seemed polite, 'Mum sent you her love, by the way.'

Isabella glanced idly at the photograph then turned to stroke the dog who was eyeing Cordelia balefully from under a heavy black fringe. 'Flora is very much a one woman dog, I'm afraid. Now, if you've finished your tea I will show you around Alba.'

Cordelia had been planning on two or three cucumber

34

sandwiches, a slice of sponge cake and a top up of tea, but quickly relinquished the notion when her grandmother, who had done no more than nibble at a quartered sand-wich, dabbed at her mouth and put down her cup in a final sort of way.

What am I doing here? Cordelia asked herself as they passed the indoor swimming pool and made for the door marked Treatment – Ladies. Why am I being given this grand tour? Alba reminded her of boarding school; the same giggling groups in the corridors, which quickly dis-persed at the sight of the Head; the daily time-tables and rules on the notice-board ('Guests are Requested Not to Use the Swimming Pool Unaccompanied' . . . 'Please Note There is No Smoking in the Green Drawing Room'); even the warm pervasive smell of onions plus something unplea-sant, which Cordelia, with a professional sniff, identified as cauliflower.

The goings-on behind the closed doors were, however, nothing like school. More like a video nasty, Cordelia thought, as she entered a room and six heads nodded and smiled at her from the top of boxes, as though they had just been freshly garotted. 'Steam Cabinets,' her grandmother said, snapping her fingers at a woman anxiously plucking fresh white towels from a cupboard. 'Mrs Gerard is ready to come out, Mary.'

The next room contained a semi-naked woman being pummelled by a young man with strong hairy arms. 'Our chief masseur, Mr Lawson,' said Isabella. She shot him a look of distaste and briskly shut the door.

In the third room, people were attached to large pieces of machinery, one of which looked suspiciously like a rack. ('We have all the latest equipment, of course.') And next door to that, another group of people were lying around the floor, gazing hopefully at a lithe young woman, spring-ing up and down in an emerald green leotard ('Miss Watson is proficient in keep-fit and aerobics.').

Back in the sitting room Isabella sat down again on the

button-back chair, and Cordelia resumed her perch on the *chaise longue*. She was sorry to see that the tea trolley had been wheeled away.

'A few questions,' Isabella said, 'before we discuss my proposition.'

'Questions?' said Cordelia. 'What proposition?'

Disregarding the interruption, Isabella asked Cordelia if she enjoyed her work, how much money she made each year after tax, and was she contemplating marriage in the near future? Cordelia considered the questions rather nosy, but answered them equally briskly (yes, she loved being a cookery writer, she supposed she made about twenty-something thousand a year, no she wasn't getting married) in the hope that her grandmother would say whatever it was she had to say and she might still be able to catch the last half of *The Victorian Kitchen*. She was about to add, 'My boyfriend and I have just broken up, actually,' when her grandmother rose from her chair, strode over to the french windows and, with a sweep of the arm, made a theatrical gesture towards acres of green, taking in a size-able lake and an outdoor swimming pool.

'What would you say, Cordelia, if I was to tell you that one day all this could be yours?'

'Mine, grandmother?' Cordelia was so appalled at the idea of wasting her life away at a health farm that she only dimly heard something about salary, working hours and the pleasant suite of vacant rooms above the stable block. 'But I already have a job.'

'Exactly. You know something about diets and nu-trition. In theory at least,' Isabella added sourly. Did she really want to hand over her lifetime's work to That Woman's lumpen daughter? But at least Cordelia was family, and even the short tour of inspection had set up a series of niggling anxieties. Seeing that tricky masseur ma-nipulating silly little Mrs Steinberg made her wonder if he was manipulating her in some way, too. Was Rosemary cheating on the housekeeping? When she had queried the blemished apples at lunch, Rosemary had assured her they were organic. And then there was Monica, with her money-grabbing ways. 'I can't go on for ever, child. I need an heir.'

*　　　*　　　*

Driving back to London, Cordelia, usually a competent driver, wondered why she kept crashing her gears. And her hands were shaking. She slammed on the brake a second before hitting the car in front, which had quite properly stopped at a red light.

Pulling the Fiat into the side of the road, she slotted in her soothing Rigoletto tape and lit a cigarette.

Why was she even considering accepting her grand-mother's offer? All those people, all that machinery, all that boring countryside. And the old woman hadn't been exactly charming.

'You'll have to lose at least three stone, of course,' she had said, 'and get something done about those teeth. Who-ever does your hair, Cordelia? He should be shot.'

On the other hand, Cordelia thought, what am I doing with my life? Work is falling off, I've chucked Stewart, and I'll soon be thirty. Judging by the number of bedrooms, there must be at least a hundred guests at Alba at any one time, paying top hotel rates for a cuisine apparently based on boiled water.

Cordelia did some sums; the answer added up to some-thing a good deal more appealing than a £10,000 advance on a book she didn't want to write, anyway. And wouldn't it be rather nice, a small voice muttered at the back of her brain, not to buy clothes at places called Big and Beautiful?

CHAPTER
THREE

The day after her visit to Alba Cordelia drove up to York-shire to ask her parents' advice. The three of them were sitting slumped in front of the *Des O'Connor Show*, un-comfortably replete, after finishing every last buttery crumb of one of Olivia's steak and kidney pies.

'I'm not even sure I want to own a health farm,' Cordelia said.

'Of course you don't, darling,' said her mother, 'you can't possibly want to work for that mad woman.'

'She didn't seem mad to me, she seemed awfully ef-ficient.'

'You don't know Isabella,' said Olivia. She gazed around contentedly at her comfortable cretonne-covered sofas, the cheerful wood fire, the plump labrador dozing on the balding rug. 'You remember the last time she came here? As good as said we lived in a slum. An exceptionally cold slum, at that. Your grandmother, Cordelia, has a cruel tongue.'

'Funny thing about your mother, Olivia,' said Alec Ledbury, his eyes still on the television set, 'I never thought of her as particularly foreign, but when she came down here that Christmas, she looked as though she'd just dropped in from the Inquisition. Isn't that Val Doonican? Can't stand the chap.'

'It's Des O'Connor,' said Olivia. 'You can't stand him, either. I think it's because she always wears black, and has tortoiseshell combs in her hair.'

'One of the guests at Alba called her Contessa,' said

Cordelia, who quite liked the idea of aristocratic lineage. 'Are we . . . I mean, is she very grand?'

'We owned castles all over the place before the Spanish Civil War, mother was always talking about them,' said Olivia. 'Darling, do think about this carefully, before you make up your mind. Isabella can be very destructive . . . '

'Oh, come on, Livvy,' said Alec, 'at the worst Cordy can just get into the Fiat and drive away. At the best . . . I've been looking at those Alba brochures you brought with you, love, that place must be a goldmine. If she's really thinking of leaving it to you . . . '

'If I were you, I'd get it in writing,' said Olivia.

'Not good enough,' said Alec. 'Legally, you need signatures. I'd go for a proper Will.'

*   *   *

Cordelia left the flat in Shepherd's Bush with regret and as much furniture as she could prise away from Sally.

'What am I supposed to eat off?' Sally said, as Cordelia labelled the dining room table, the big brass bed, some linen and most of the cutlery.

'Well, they are mine,' Cordelia said, 'I'm going to need them at Alba.'

'I thought your grandmother was rolling in it,' said Sally. 'I thought you'd be dining off Chippendale and sinking your feet into Aubusson.'

'Not in the staff quarters,' said Cordelia, remembering the bleak rooms over the stable, barely furnished with basic chairs and tables her grandmother had described as the very best Utility. ('I bought them after the war from an old friend in Bayswater, Cordelia. They are practically antique.')

'You know why you're doing this, don't you?' Sally said, sifting through the cutlery and repossessing a fancy cork-screw Cordelia had never liked, anyway. 'You're on the rebound from the Incredible Hulk. You've been mooning about the place, looking lovelorn, ever since you had that row.'

'No, I'm not,' said Cordelia. 'I'm simply making a career move. When is the new girl arriving?'

'The day after you leave.' Sally shot another sharp look at Cordelia's pile of belongings. 'Only she did agree to share a *furnished* flat.'

'I am leaving you the sofa, and that carpet.' Cordelia gazed mournfully around the flat, looking, Sally thought, unusually vulnerable. 'It is all right about the little back boxroom, isn't it?' She had shifted her desk, her word processor and her files into a cupboard-sized room behind the kitchen which the estate agent had described as Third Bedroom cum Study. Cordelia had decided to give Alba a try, but was not prepared to relinquish her old life entirely. Besides, she needed somewhere she could moonlight the occasional cookery article when overwhelmed by too much healthy abstinence. 'You did say I could . . . I'll pay rent . . .'

'Of course you can have the boxroom, Cordy. Use it whenever you like, and you don't have to pay me anything,' Sally was still looking wistfully, at the We Move U pile.

'Oh, all right, Sal,' said Cordelia, 'I'll leave the bed.' The hard, narrow single bed at Alba would, she thought gloomily, be ideal for her new, spartan regime.

*   *   *

Isabella had insisted on supervising the We Move U team as they carried Cordelia's belongings up the narrow staircase into the rooms above the stable, and her eyes narrowed as Cordelia unpacked her white china and looked around for somewhere to hang her pans. 'What is all that cooking equipment?'

'My pans. My crockery.'

'You won't be needing those. It will be the Light Diet for

you, Cordelia. I want you to take advantage of everything Alba has to offer. Sensible eating, exercise, swimming, jogging, brisk walks, and be sure to make good use of all the equipment in the gym. Stay, Flora! Friend!' she added, as Flora moved resolutely towards a removal man's ankle.

The removal man dodged behind the gateleg table. 'He's not my friend, lady. Can't you chain it up, or something?'

'She won't bother you if you don't bother her.' Isabella laid a restraining hand on Flora's quivering rump, and gazed with distaste at Cordelia's provençal print smock, wishing again that it didn't remind her so vividly of Olivia. 'I have enrolled you in Carolyn's class, tomorrow morning.'

The removal man gave Cordelia a sympathetic smile. Nice little armful, what could she be thinking of, moving in with this old battle-axe? 'I'll be off now, then.'

*   *   *

Carolyn's class was at eight thirty, and since Sister Monica had asked Cordelia if she could help deliver the breakfast trays at seven, it seemed like lunchtime when Cordelia arrived at the gym. Especially as she had been allowed only one slice of Ryvita for breakfast.

'Do join us . . . one, two, three . . . the mat over there, dear . . . one, two, three . . . ' Carolyn was limbering up, lightly dancing from foot to foot, exuding vitality in her glossy emerald green lycra leotard.

'Left, right, left, right, gently, gently . . . ' Following the exercises, Cordelia experienced that fantasy she always had when she went to a really good film and came out transformed into witty, sophisticated Jamie Lee Curtis or pretty Meg Ryan with long blonde hair, long brown legs, and a smile that drove men mad. 'Now, roll shoulders forward, roll shoulders back, ear down to the right shoulder . . . ' Cordelia, moving to the music, felt as slim and trimly in control of her body as Carolyn Watson.

' . . . up to the centre, down to the left shoulder . . . straighten up . . . '

As she straightened up, Cordelia glimpsed reality in the mirror behind lissom Carolyn. A large, sweating woman in black leotard and an XL T-shirt at the front of the class. She was distressed to recognise herself.

* * *

Cordelia worked hard at Alba. She wanted a definite job, an independent role, but Isabella insisted she should gain experience in every department. 'You can help out, where you're needed.'

So, Cordelia helped out with all the most boring chores. She helped Sister Monica fill out the Appointments for Today cards, which were delivered on the breakfast trays, to make the Ryvita and the lemon tinted water look less lonely. She was sent to Steam Cabinets where she helped Mary Lawson process the towels and the clients, and where, one day, she was surprised to see two familiar faces; the old woman and her daughter, the couple who had been sitting in the hall on her first visit.

'Mrs Gillespie and her daughter Rachel,' Mary whispered. 'Regulars. They come here every few months. A lot of people do that, you know.'

'Really?' Cordelia had been constantly surprised by the shared intimacies at Alba. Perhaps it was because they were all old friends. She tried the theory out on Mary. ' . . . they say things I wouldn't even murmur to a friend. There was a woman in the Light Diet Room, yesterday, confiding to the whole room about her husband's lack of sex drive and the compensations she found elsewhere.'

'That would be Mrs Renfrew, I expect. Always talking like that. I suppose she thinks it makes her more interesting.' Mary shoved two more towels into the machine. 'I've often thought it's the dressing gowns; the clients tend to shed their inhibitions with their clothes.'

42

'Mary! Stop gossiping. I've been in here five minutes too long, already.' Sybil Gillespie's head swivelled crossly towards them, and Cordelia stepped forward to open the Cabinet. 'Mary will do it, thank you. She knows how I like to be put down for my rest.'

'I'm on my way, Mrs Gillespie.' Mary bustled over with a conciliatory smile, and Cordelia, releasing Mrs Gillespie's uncomplaining daughter, wondered how many times a day Mary Lawson had to remind herself of the Alba rule that clients should be humoured at all times.

Cordelia also put in a few hours each day in the Light Diet Room, doling out soup to serious dieters who crouched protectively over their mini bowls, fantasising about the delicacies being served in the main Dining Room. Word had got through, from those who were only at Alba to rest, that the table groaned with a splendid selection of salads, home-made bread and oatcakes, cheese, fruit and yogurt.

The only area where Cordelia was not allowed to help was in the kitchen. She had thought up a delicious way of beefing up the broth, and worked out a calorie-conscious recipe for extra light quenelles, but when she went into the kitchen, she found Rosemary Meadows guarding her pans defensively. 'I don't need any help or advice in the kitchen,' she said, 'it states quite clearly, in my contract, that I am in charge of the cuisine at Alba.'

'Cuisine!' Cordelia said derisively to Isabella, who was pinning up a notice about a theatre outing on the board. 'Honestly, grandmother, there aren't enough calories in those tiny bowls to keep a fly active. Why don't I work out a series of menus with nutritious, well-balanced dishes?'

'I think Madame would be more appropriate than grandmother in working hours.' Isabella turned from the notice-board and looked at Cordelia. 'Our clients come to Alba to get into shape, Cordelia. And you, I fear, are hardly an advertisement for our regime.'

Under her grandmother's critical gaze, Cordelia's thighs

seemed flabbier, her waist thicker, and her pretty bosom sagged apologetically. She was back at school, the butt of a sadistic teacher's sharp-tongued sarcasm. Only, this time, there was nothing and nobody to stop her absconding if she felt like it.

CHAPTER
FOUR

Cordelia might well have left Alba if it hadn't been for the boxroom in Shepherd's Bush. She had started a regular cookery column, monthly mental orgies (with the occasional necessary testing and tasting) of puddings lavished with cream, stews laden with dumplings. It was the perfect antidote to Alba and, on her days off, Cordelia drove happily up the A3 to put in six useful hours on the word processor.

'Out of London they still want all that heavy food you're so keen on,' said Janet. 'If you let me have twelve hundred words a month, I can shift it, no problem.'

'Not under my name?' If her grandmother ever found out that she was moonlighting in this disloyal manner . . . 'How about Jennifer Tremayne?' An appalling name, but less appalling than the prospect of Isabella's disapproval.

Cordelia hadn't had a chance to mention the Will. She only saw Isabella when she had something to impart, usually about Cordelia's appearance. 'Your hair is not quite right, yet' . . . 'Those teeth are an improvement' . . . 'Carolyn tells me you missed Aerobics yesterday.' Only last week she had sent for Cordelia to tell her that the state of her rooms left a great deal to be desired.

Cordelia assumed that her grandmother was not referring to the spartan conditions. She had thrown a rug over the bare board floors, covered the rigid sofa with a quilt, softened the contours of the hard chairs with down cushions, but the place still looked marginally more homely than a nun's cell in a rigorous Order. 'My rooms?' she said.

45

'What were you doing in my rooms?'

'Making sure, Cordelia, that you are genuinely dedicated to the Alba ethos. Speaking of which, Sister Monica tells me you used the word "fat" in Aromatherapy, yesterday. That is not a word we use at Alba.' Isabella was sitting in her high-backed authoritarian chair, with Flora on her knee bristling and growling. With one hand she placated Flora, with the other she lifted the lid of a latticed wood casket on the table next to her and withdrew two Yorkie bars. 'I found these in your chest of drawers, Cordelia.'

There had followed a ten-minute lecture about food dependency, the weakness of Cordelia's willpower, the untrustworthiness of her nature ('But what else can one expect, the way you were brought up'), and the fact that Cordelia's bed was still unmade at midday.

'But I was filling in the appointment cards and checking the diets and then I had a workout in the gym.'

'Excuses, excuses,' said Isabella. 'All beds must be made by 10 a.m., and it is absolutely forbidden to keep food in your room. If you can't abide by our rules, Cordelia, I shall have to reconsider our arrangement.'

'Talking about our arrangement, grandmother,' Cordelia had begun, but Isabella, consulting her fob watch, pointed out that Cordelia should be in the Light Diet Room making salads.

'*She'll* have to reconsider!' Sally had said, when Cordelia arrived at Shepherd's Bush and reported the conversation. 'What about you? Why do you stick it? You've been there six months, haven't you?'

'And three days,' said Cordelia. 'I nearly didn't, I nearly walked out, but look at me, Sally.'

'I have to agree you look wonderful.'

'I feel better, too. Horribly healthy. And some of the guests are so nice. There's an actress, Sylvia Someone, she was in that sit-com, and an author called Tod. Rather attractive. Tod Ballard.'

'Never heard of him,' said Sally. She looked keenly at

Cordelia. 'I begin to understand.'

'It's nothing like that. We have an occasional orange juice together in the pub, that's all.'

*   *   *

Sister Monica saw Tristram Bartholomew coming out of Massage – Gentlemen with a look in his eye which meant Complaint, and took evasive action by dodging into the Ladies' Steam Cabinet Room. This gave her an opportunity to harangue Mary Lawson in a hissed whisper about a pile of damp towels in the corner. 'You know Madame insists that the treatment rooms be kept tidy at all times, Mary.'

Tristram flip-flopped on, in his G for Gucci slippers, towards the Light Diet Room, bristling with indignation. He had always had Matt before, of course. Everyone who was anyone had Matt, the best masseur at Alba, the best on the health farm circuit; that's why all those silly women flocked here. The vulgar Renfrew creature speculatively eyeing Matt's jeans, old Mrs Gillespie, with the sharp nose and the sharper manner, even the gracious Miss Travers who called herself an actress but seemed to spend her time 'resting'; they all insisted on Matt.

And this morning, Tristram Bartholomew, whose tension knots were every bit as important as the ladies' libidos, had been relegated to Gary.

'What star sign are you, Mr B? No, no, don't tell me. I can guess. Aries. Warm, lovable and impulsive and just waiting for a lovely Leo to turn up. Am I right?' In Tristram's experience, when men with mournful moustaches started talking about Ariens and their compatibility with Leos, they were signalling their intent as clearly as if they had leapt out of a closet brandishing a Gay Pride badge. He had not welcomed the unnecessary intimacy of Gary's leg massage. People did get the wrong idea about him sometimes – just because he wasn't

47

married. He would have to have a word with somebody in authority and absolutely insist on Matt for the rest of his stay.

He found Cordelia behind the counter in the Light Diet Room. 'I'll have fruit and soup today,' he said, 'and a private word, if I may.'

Cordelia, referring to Tristram's notes, said firmly, 'I'm afraid you're only allowed the soup, Mr Bartholomew.' She handed him the bowl and followed him to a window seat.

Tristram slurped down the thin soup eagerly. He was starving, even though he had managed, that morning, to filch a dry Ryvita unaccountably left on the breakfast tray outside the room next to his.

'Too much onion, not enough chicken,' he said, scooping out the last mouthful and licking the spoon.

'That's right,' said Cordelia, who had said as much to Rosemary Meadows earlier and been told to mind her own business. 'And a smidgin of tarragon wouldn't have come amiss.'

Tristram looked at Cordelia in surprise. The first time he had ever studied any of the staff at Alba, they had always just been servants in uniform. But this girl . . . he vaguely remembered seeing her around last time he was at Alba. Dressed in one of those poncho things that look marginally better on a Mexican peasant. A nice face, still a bit plump perhaps, but pleasant, and oddly familiar. 'What do you make of the yogurt here?'

'It's home-made,' said Cordelia loyally, thinking how much better Loseley made it.

'A great many unpleasant things are made at home,' said Tristram. 'Personally, I find it . . . '

'Too runny?'

'Exactly.' They beamed at each other, and Tristram remembered where he had seen that rather appealing grin before. The *Sunday Express Magazine*, about nine months ago. Although he had a regular restaurant column in another Sunday paper, the *Express* had asked him to do a round-up of country house hotels for them. Bloody hard work, slogging up and down the country on British Rail to eat filthy food in outlandish places. And he'd ended up, his prose cut to ribbons, at the bottom of the page. At the top of the page was this girl, grinning away, as well she might, over a feature about pheasants. How to pluck them, stuff them, roast them, casserole them. 'I know you . . . you're . . . '

'Isabella Cordoba de Zarate's granddaughter,' said Cordelia.

'You're Cordelia Ledbury, the food writer.' Cordelia Ledbury, the dedicated foodie had defected to the yogurt and yoga business. It had to be a good story. Tristram grinned at Cordelia in a way he believed to be attractive. 'Now, I don't want to be difficult, but there is something I simply must insist on . . . '

*　　　　*　　　　*

'I've put Mr Bartholomew down for Matt,' Cordelia said to Sister Monica, as they filled in the Appointments for Today cards.

'No, Cordelia. He has Gary.'

'He complained about Gary yesterday. Something about Aries . . . said he always had Matt.'

'Matt's fully booked. It'll have to be Lucy.'

Cordelia filled in 'Massage – 8.15. Lucy'. She hadn't actually made a deal with Mr Bartholomew but perhaps, in the circumstances, it might be wise to have a word with him and ask him to be discreet about the cookery books.

Sister Monica wrote 9.15 next to Sauna, and 10.10 beside Massage on Antonia Fellowes' card. 'I do wish that Fellowes child would spend less time with the Gerard girl. When Carolyn arrived early for Movement to Music yesterday, she caught them both smoking in the gym.'

'Sarah Gerard smokes like a chimney,' said Cordelia.

'She probably put Antonia up to it. Seems odd, somehow, for mothers and daughters to come to a health farm together.'

'Middle-aged women and their adolescent daughters, both at a difficult age and in need of pampering,' said Sister Monica. 'Some establishments do special mother and daughter weekends, but Madame doesn't hold with it.'

'Why ever not?'

'I don't think she is particularly fond of young people.' Collecting the cards into a pile, Monica pushed them towards Cordelia. 'Pop these along to Rosemary in the kitchen, dear, and then you can give me a hand with the laundry.' And after that, she thought to herself, I'll have a word with Madame about Antonia Fellowes. She could be a candidate for Extras . . .

*   *   *

'Morning, Cordelia.' Tristram Bartholomew strolled into the gym, pleasurably aware that the scarlet towel draped casually around his neck was a perfect accessory for his grey Armani track suit.

'Hi!' Cordelia could hardly speak. She had already done half an hour on the exercise bike, after helping Sister Monica with the Appointment Cards, and all on a breakfast of segmented orange.

'You don't call that exercise, do you?' Tristram flicked a switch on Cordelia's bike and giggled maliciously as she pushed ineffectually on the pedals and ground slowly to a halt. 'And how's my fellow foodie?'

'I hate the word foodie,' said Cordelia, 'and I'm not one, anyway.' She dismounted and collapsed thankfully down next to Tristram on the hard bench at the back of the gym. 'I finished with all that, ages ago.'

Stretching out his short plump legs, Tristram gazed complacently at his Reeboks. 'I can see you wouldn't want it spread around.'

Surely Tristram Bartholomew didn't know about her cookery column? 'Wouldn't want what spread around?'

'That Isabella Cordoba de Zarate's granddaughter is the author of one of my favourite books. *The English Tea*, one could put on pounds just glancing at the illustrations.' Tristram eyed Cordelia slyly. 'Why the little sigh of relief, my pet? Don't tell me you've got something else to hide? I do adore spreading things around, especially at Alba. What else is there to do here but gossip?'

'I'd just rather you didn't mention it to anyone else, about me having been a cookery writer, that's all,' said Cordelia. 'It might be embarrassing for my grandmother.'

'Well, of course, it would be enormous fun to embarrass the Grand Isabella, but I really quite enjoy secrets, too. Shall we make it our secret?'

'That would be very kind.' Cordelia guessed gloomily that the whole of Alba would be discussing their secret by lunchtime. 'By the way, Tristram, I am sorry about Matt. Sister Monica says he's absolutely booked up and Lucy is awfully good.'

'Perfectly all right, dear.'

Tristram had, of course, been furious to find himself downgraded to Lucy, but he wasn't about to discuss it with this useless girl; he would speak to Sister Monica, or Madame, later. And he had managed to wheedle one or two interesting titbits out of Lucy. She'd all but admitted that The Invisible Man in the next room to his had a booze problem, and, under close questioning, had revealed that Cordelia's really rather fetching highlights had been done by Giovanni in Hairdressing. Tristram thought he might drop in on Giovanni during the next few days. A touch of ash blond at the temples would add *gravitas* and lend further credibility to the small hair extension Ivan had woven for him so expertly. He needed to look his best for the New York trip next month.

Tristram thrust out a hand, 'To our little secret.'

Cordelia reluctantly took Tristram's hand which was

51

unpleasantly moist, or was it her hand that was moist after all that uphill pedalling?

They hadn't noticed Tod Ballard enter the gym. He wandered over, and sat down, cross-legged, on the floor in front of them. 'A secret? Can I be let into it? No, let me guess. Erica Gerard has handed in her illicit vodka still? Lady Drummond has been sighted in the same housecoat two days running?' Cordelia grinned and Tod smiled at her. 'Rosemary Meadows has confided in you that she is planning to serve lasagne and chips in the Light Diet Room?'

'Really, Tod, how can you be so cruel?' Tristram wished he wasn't going quite so thin on top and that he was as tall as Tod Ballard. Mind you, he'd do something about that accent. Well north of Watford, and from the wrong side of the Odeon, by the sound of it. 'Fancy mentioning lasagne and chips to the starving. No secret. Just a bit of a joke between a couple of old hacks.'

'I didn't know you were a journalist, Cordelia,' said Tod.

'Oh, I used to do freelance work, you know, the odd article here and there. And Tristram . . . '

'We all know what Tristram does,' said Tod, 'he gives us a critical résumé every time he munches a lettuce leaf.' He looked up at Cordelia. 'What sort of things did you write about?'

'Just, you know, general features.' Cordelia wished she could be franker. She really liked Tod Ballard, he seemed so normal compared to the other Alba clients. 'You're a novelist, aren't you?'

'Well, not exactly. I do a bit of writing.'

'Now you're being modest. Every time I see you, you're scribbling busily in your notebook.' Tristram smiled wickedly at Cordelia. 'I expect he's really Jeffrey Archer or Frederick Forsyth. What name do you write under, Tod? We'll all go down to W. H. Smith in Guildford after our bowls of gruel and bombard them with demands for your books.'

'I use my own name,' said Tod, 'only I haven't actually got anything into print yet. I mean, I sent a couple of books to the publisher and they wrote back saying they would let me know in due course.'

Tristram was rather enjoying himself. 'My dear fellow, don't tell me you just pop your books into the post? Haven't you got an *agent*?'

Uncrossing his legs and jumping to his feet in a manner which would have pleased Carolyn, Tod said, 'Of course I have. Well, excuse me, I've got an early Sauna . . . '

'Hardly a runner-up for the Booker prize,' said Tristram, when Tod had left.

'Maybe not, but I think he's nice.'

'Nice? What a silly word; whenever has being nice had anything to do with talent?'

*   *   *

'Light Piano Music is Available in the Drawing Room after Dinner', it said on the notice-board.

Dinner! It had taken Tristram two minutes to finish an inadequate bowl of chopped fruit, wheatgerm, yogurt and honey. And now, the evening stretched before him, with nothing more amusing to fill the time than listening to a vapid young man tinkling away at Strauss. For this he had changed into a loose navy blue cashmere dressing gown, which, he noted with satisfaction, looked remarkably well with his Gucci slippers.

If he was in London he'd be dropping in at Groucho's about now, for a drink and a chat with an intelligent media contact about something more elevating than how many ounces they had both shed the previous day, or how wonderfully relaxed he felt after a Seaweed Wrap. A fatal thought, it reminded him of Alastair Little's inspired seaweed-wrapped sushi, which led on to musing about the same chef's outstanding griddled scallops served with a spicy cabbage salad. Tristram drooled nostalgically as he headed towards the strains of Strauss.

He'd promised to take Nicolette to Alastair's, that evening when they were eating at Sally Clarke's in Kensington. 'My partner reacted joyfully to the roasted red peppers with basil,' he had written in his review. Nicolette often played the 'my partner' role in his restaurant columns; some of his friends thought they were an item. No harm them thinking that, but Nicolette was just a good friend. She was also a Contributing Editor to *Vogue*, and he'd been trying to get into *Vogue* for years.

He popped his head around the door of the Drawing Room and withdrew it hurriedly. Nobody in there. Well, nobody he wanted to speak to, anyway. Just that awful old bat, Gillespie, with the put-upon middle-aged daughter, and the worthy Fellowes woman with her sulky bluestocking offspring. All nodding their heads seriously to show how much they were appreciating the music.

A bridge game was in progress in the Small Drawing Room. Tristram lounged in and circled the players, studying their hands. Adam Shepherd, partnering Erica Gerard, poor sod, waved his cards in a friendly greeting. 'Hullo there, care to join us?'

'Later, perhaps,' said Tristram. Adam Shepherd headed a public company and was nobody's fool. Tristram guessed he was keen to ditch that particular partner for someone who could tell a club from a spade. Judging by the way she was bidding, Erica Gerard must have introduced a tot of something stronger into her Highland Spring cocktail of honey and lemon.

'Two no trumps,' said Sheila Steinberg. She raised an eyebrow at Diane Renfrew across the table, but there were no need for signals between these two; Sheila and Diane had been playing together for so long that they could semaphore a complete hand with an arch of the eyebrow. 'Oh, Mr Bartholomew, what a handsome gown. What's the fashion item underneath?' Sheila winked at Diane.

'You're nearer to him than me.'

Diane leant over and flicked Tristram's dressing gown in an impertinent manner. 'Matching navy pyjamas, would you believe? With pale blue piping. Hand-stitched by the look of it.'

'Shall we continue with the game,' said Adam Shepherd.

'Sorry, I'm sure,' said Diane. 'Pour me out another glass of Highland Spring, would you, Mr B.? It's over there, on the sideboard. And a little bit of ice and a strip of lemon makes it more exciting, doesn't it?'

As Tristram poured, it occurred to him that this group might be ideal for his plan. On the day he arrived, he had spotted, a few hundred yards before the entrance to Alba, a most agreeable looking new pub called The Barley Mow. It was hung about with ivy and signs reading Free House, Comfortable Restaurant, Real Log Fires and – this was the message that haunted him – Fresh Lobsters and Game.

It had not taken Tristram long to justify a visit to The Barley Mow. He was a paying guest, after all, not a prisoner. He had been starving himself and exercising strenuously for five days. He had lost two pounds. He needed another restaurant for the Out of Town column he was planning for next month. He was hungry.

He was also something of a coward, and didn't fancy the idea of climbing the wall, as it were, by himself; anyway, it made a better restaurant review if there were several people in the party.

Tristram waited until they had finished the hand and were wrangling over their score cards, before broaching his plan. 'I've had an idea,' he said, 'and I'm wondering whether any of you would be interested?'

*   *   *

'How about a drink?' Tristram led the way into the bar.

'Well, perhaps I'll have a gin and tonic if everyone else is having something,' said Erica Gerard, making that quick gesture with thumb and middle finger which barmen the world over recognise as Make it a Double. 'How about you, Sheila? Diane?'

'I'll have a sweet sherry, dear,' said Sheila.

'Me, too,' said Diane. 'I'm sure there aren't many calories in a small sherry.'

Tristram wondered if the outing was a mistake; Erica Gerard, Sheila Steinberg and Diane Renfrew were not the dinner companions he would ideally choose. Adam Shepherd had opted out, making a pompous speech about the foolishness of coming to a health farm if you weren't going to stick to the rules, and had gone to talk to Sylvia Travers.

The three women slid away from the bar, giggling like truant schoolgirls as the barman passed Tristram the bill. Yes, the outing was a mistake. But the dining room was cosy, the tablecloths and napkins white and properly starched, the waiter suitably deferential. Tristram began to feel at home.

'I'll have the potted shrimps, please,' said Sheila, 'and then the roast pheasant.'

'That sounds nice,' said Diane. 'I'll have the same.'

'And me. And while you're at it, get me another gin, will you?' said Erica. 'Don't bother with the tonic. It's terribly fattening.'

'You can't,' said Tristram. Really, it was too much. He was prepared to buy these women dinner, on expenses of course, but they had to play by the rules. 'You can't all eat the same. The idea,' he leant forward, lowering his voice (a restaurant critic was, after all, meant to eat anonymously), 'is that we each sample a different dish, so that I can judge the strengths and weaknesses of the chef's cooking.'

The waiter's eyebrow flickered. He must warn them in the kitchen that there was an inspector out front. Last time the *Good Food Guide* man had been in he had found the roast duck in rosemary and red-currant coulis 'poorly sauced' and chef had been in a tantrum for weeks. Bending courteously towards the ladies in the party, he ran a pen

56

professionally down the starters. 'May I recommend the terrine of monkfish, sole and fresh herbs? Deliciously light. Or you might care to try the Stilton and Brie filo pastry parcels in a gooseberry sauce.' Sheila Steinberg shuddered with distaste . . . 'Perhaps madam would prefer the Mediterranean fish soup?'

It took the combined persuasive skills of Tristram and the waiter a full ten minutes to sort out a varied selection of dishes for the party. Typically, Tristram fumed to himself, I am stuck with the filo pastry parcels. They were not, however, half bad. Rather good, in fact. He was quite enjoying himself.

'You don't think they've missed us, do you?' Sheila giggled over her soup spoon. 'This is very tasty, Tristram. Do you want to try some?' She filled her spoon and pushed it archly under his nose.

Firmly ignoring the proferred spoon, Tristram picked up his pudding spoon and helped himself. 'Mmm . . . a little heavy on the saffron.'

'No, of course they won't,' said Diane. 'I told Cordelia we were going for a walk. "Lovely evening," I said, "just the night for a pleasant stroll."'

Tristram poured himself another glass of the excellent claret. The women, thank goodness, had opted for the House White. Well, two of the women. The Gerard creature was still on the G and Ts.

Cordelia. He was reminded of their conversation in the gym. The story was really too good to waste on present company, but he couldn't resist it. He gave an introductory chuckle to alert his audience. 'I've discovered something *rather* amusing about Isabella's granddaughter . . . '

'That hairstyle,' said Sheila. 'A great improvement, I grant you, but no body to it.'

'She should have gone to Sheila.' Diane patted her glossy blonde bob complacently. 'She's been doing my hair for years.'

Sheila nodded approvingly. 'That's right, seventy-six

57

wasn't it, you first came to me? The trouble with Giovanni is that he doesn't know how to layer properly.'

Tristram was just about to get the conversation back on course, when Erica Gerard said, 'She's done something to her teeth.'

'False?' said Diane.

'No, she's had a Shirley Bassey. Costs a bomb, I can tell you . . . ' Sheila's husband, Gerald, was a dentist who watched television with a keen professional eye. The other night Shirley Bassey had come on in a tight dress, opened her mouth to sing, 'I . . . I who have *nothing* . . . ' and Gerald had jumped up from his armchair and cried, 'Capped. That's what they are.'

'A Shirley Bassey?' Tristram wondered if he had drunk too much. Cordelia didn't look anything like Shirley Bassey to him.

'Talk of the devil.' Erica Gerard waved her glass welcomingly towards the door.

'Why, Mrs Gerard?' said Cordelia, walking over to their table. 'And Mrs Steinberg and Mrs Renfrew? Good evening, Mr Bartholomew.'

58

CHAPTER
FIVE

'Mrs Gerard! Your carrier bag's clinking. I thought you said you were going to look at antique shops?'

Isabella, looking slightly more amiable than a camp commandant, stood between Erica and the bolthole of her bedroom.

And Erica thought she'd been so clever, cancelling her Steam Cabinet session, because, 'I've got this little sniffle and you can't be too careful,' and mentioning casually that she'd heard there was an awfully good antique shop in Paxborough, and she thought she might . . .

Unfortunately Sarah had offered to come with her.

'If we put the L-plates on I could practise for my test. Oh, mum, do let's. I haven't got anything until Aerobics at three. Hey, why don't we have a secret wicked lunch at that Little Chef? Think of it, poached eggs and American hash browns and coffee with cream.'

But Erica had been thinking of tall bottles with brown smoky liquid in them. She could almost feel the reliable triangular shape of good old Grant's, hear the chummy little click as the bottle cap parted from its sealing ring, taste . . . 'Oh, darling, such a waste of your time,' she'd said, peering into her dressing table mirror and patting too much expensive make-up on the bags under her eyes. 'If you've got a couple of hours free, shouldn't you be studying for A-Levels, or something? *Now* what is it?' she'd added, as Sarah's tall frame slumped visibly. 'Do cheer up, darling. It's not much fun for me, you know, with you sulking all the time.'

'I've done my A-Levels. I did them in June. Alba was supposed to be a treat because I'd worked so hard.'

Erica had applied lipstick in a puckering manner which Sarah found irritating. 'Of course you've done them. I hadn't forgotten, darling, I was just teasing. Why don't you play ping-pong with that nice Fellowes girl?'

'Antonia? That vedge? That *quiche merchant* ... ?' Erica had contemplated asking Sarah what on earth she was talking about, but decided instantly that the last thing she wanted at that moment was an update on the young's boring slang ' . . . three As and a B and she's going to read History at Caius. And guess what she's doing for her gap, the sanctimonious prig?'

'I haven't the faintest idea,' said Erica, moving purposefully towards the door, 'see you later, darling. Have a lovely time.'

Sarah, left alone in her mother's bedroom, had turned sideways to the mirror and gazed distastefully at her gross thighs, her disgusting stomach and the vile way her boobs flopped under her outsize T-shirt. She had better go and weigh herself soon, and she knew what the scales would say. She bet she was very nearly up to seven stone again. What on earth had made her suggest lunch at the Little Chef? She could feel her bile rising at the mere thought of hash browns, greasy, dirty things smelling of burnt dead animal fat and old man's breath. Poached eggs, looking like yellow eyeballs in white, dead faces, and when you broke the yoke, the eyeball burst like something . . . Sarah searched for an unpleasant word and found suppurating. And perfectly good coffee ruined by stuff from some manury old udder that separated into sweaty droplets when you poured it in. How could she have even thought of Little Chef, let alone suggest it to her mother?

An averagely intelligent psychiatrist, or even somebody's grandmother, could have told her that if Erica had sat opposite her at a Little Chef table, or any other table come to that, coffee with cream in it might have seemed quite acceptable. And if Erica, while companionably spooning in sugar, had said things like, 'I still can't get over you getting a C in History when that ghastly Miss Slater said you'd be lucky with a U. Sucks to her. Why don't you try for Durham?' or, 'That new branch of the Gap's got some amazing things. You'd look knock-out in them.' Or even, 'You look a bit tired, darling. What time did you put your light out?' the hash browns would have had a working chance of smelling something very close to delicious.

Erica refused to admit that Sarah's painful thinness was anything but a passing teenage whim. We are just like sisters, Erica always said; Sarah told her everything. In actual fact, Sarah never got much of a chance to tell her anything at all.

Erica, now trying to outface Isabella (a testing task at any time, and hopeless when accompanied by a clinking carrier bag) was certainly not thinking about Sarah as she eyed her bedroom door wistfully. She was thinking resentfully that she *was* a paying guest; why should Madame, who looked as if she was about to shout, 'Raus!', delve into her carrier bag like some Hanoverian customs officer?

'Just as I thought,' said Isabella triumphantly, as she extracted half a bottle of Martell. 'How many times must we . . . '

'A little bit of an upset tummy. All that rich food you force on us,' said Erica, trying for a laugh and failing, 'I didn't want to bother you or Sister Monica, so I thought I'd just . . . '

'The bottle will be returned to you when you leave,' said Isabella, holding the Martell with distasteful fingertips. 'Really, Mrs Gerard, we have told you. We cannot help you if you don't co-operate. And after last night's disgraceful episode, too! I will speak to you in my study at three o'clock this afternoon.'

'I know, I *know*. Now, if you don't mind, I *would* like to get into my bedroom.'

Erica swept past Isabella and banged the door behind

her. Safe in her haven, she was not as downcast as she might have been. At the bottom of her capacious handbag was a half of vodka; tucked into an inside pocket of her coat was a half of whisky. With any luck and a bit of self-control, they would see her through until Thursday. Well, Wednesday, anyway.

She did not consider herself to be an alcoholic, merely someone who needed a bit of help to get through the day, and she had evolved her own method of shopping for drink. It was her habit to wander into Victoria Wine, or Unwin's, or Peter Dominic's, and peer vaguely about her, as though she had never been in a shop which sold bottles before. Drifting to the counter, she would say, 'So silly of me, I've forgotten what brand my aunt likes. Was it Teacher's or Bell's? Only old ladies are so fussy about their bedtime tots, aren't they?'

'Both brands are excellent, madam,' the assistant invariably replied, 'I'm sure that either would be acceptable.'

'I'd better take a half of both, to be on the safe side,' Erica would say firmly, leaving the shop in the complacent belief that she had behaved like a confirmed teetotaller. Since wine merchants are not fools in these matters, the glances that followed her out were either pitying or contemptuous.

Erica hid her little friends in the legs of a track suit in the long drawer at the bottom of her wardrobe. She was not going to have a drink right then. That would be silly.

How dare Isabella talk to her like that? I really ought to complain, thought Erica, I simply will not put up with paying four hundred a week to be spoken to as if I were a schoolgirl. Disgraceful episode, indeed! Simply four friends having a congenial meal in the heart of the English countryside. What could be more respectable than that?

Only, now that she came to think about it, what exactly had she been doing in a rather common pub with an overblown castrato droning on about samphire, or something, and two . . . hairdressers, or whatever those ghastly women did for a living?

Remembering how embarrassed she'd felt when Cordelia walked into The Barley Mow, Erica thought she would have a drink, just a small one.

CHAPTER
SIX

Isabella was suffering a day of really wearisome interviews. Her first was with Matt, unattractively eager to hand on the bad news, 'I couldn't believe my eyes, Madame, but I thought you'd want to know.'

And then, naturally, she waited for Cordelia to come to her, and Cordelia didn't come. Ungrateful, disloyal, treacherous, Isabella was quite pleased she hadn't yet made her Will. That letter she sent to Cordelia six months ago, confirming her terms of employment, would not, as Isabella very well knew, stand up in law. So if Cordelia thought she was going to inherit all this, she had better pull her socks up. If she could get them, Isabella thought venomously, over those calves.

At twelve o'clock Cordelia had still not appeared, and Isabella called Reception on the house phone. 'Miss Mayhew, would you find my granddaughter and tell her to come to my study immediately.'

'Now, that might be just a little difficult, Madame. Dear Cordelia is quite busy in the Light Diet Room. Shall I ask her to come as soon as she's finished? What a joy she is to have about, just like a ray of sunshine.'

'Immediately, Miss Mayhew.' I am surrounded by fools and incompetents, thought Isabella, slamming down the phone, and rather unfairly forgetting that fluffy, chatty Mayhew had not been chosen for her ability to place a decisive hand on the wheel in an emergency; her talent lay in making new clients feel instantly at home, and old clients feel that Alba was so enchanted to see them again that it could hardly contain itself.

Two minutes later, Cordelia poked her head warily around the door. After relaying Isabella's message, Miss Mayhew had added diffidently that dear Madame didn't seem quite herself this morning, which Cordelia readily interpreted as trouble.

'You wanted to see me, grandmother?'

'As I think you must know, Cordelia, I have been expecting to see you since early this morning. Oh, do stop hanging on the door and sit down, child. What on earth have you got on?'

Cordelia was wearing a very large, very expensive jersey over track suit bottoms. 'Don't you like it, grandmother?'

'It is a myth, Cordelia, that clothes four sizes too large make big women look small. They simply draw the on-looker's attention to how many yards of material are necessary to cover an overweight body. How much did you lose last week?'

'Two pounds,' said Cordelia sulkily, 'and Sister Monica said my upper arm measurements had gone down an inch.'

'I suppose that is a step in the right direction. I am waiting, Cordelia.'

'What for, grandmother?'

'You know perfectly well what for. You have something to tell me.'

Oh God, thought Cordelia, she's heard about the cookery column. 'Something to tell you?'

'The Barley Mow.'

Not the cookery column. Thank God for something. 'You mean last night? I wasn't going to bother you. I know how busy you always are, and I thought . . . '

'You thought that the fact that four of my clients had broken ranks and gorged themselves was so trivial that it was not necessary to bring it to my attention?'

'Well, not exactly, no. I was going to tell you, but . . . '

'But what? I am very disappointed in you, Cordelia.'

'I felt sorry for them. They looked as though they'd been

caught smoking in the dorm, or something.'

'And what, if I may ask, were you doing at The Barley Mow?'

'Nothing, we just had orange juice.'

'We?'

'Mr Ballard. We went out for a short walk after supper, just a stroll, he hadn't seen the knot garden, and I showed him our rhododendrons, and then we felt thirsty, so we went to The Barley Mow. He's so interested in Alba, grandmother, he asked me all sorts of things about how we run it, and where we get our supplies from, and so on. And you've always said client relations were important in this business. I thought you'd be pleased.'

'I hope you were careful, Cordelia. Other, less reputable, establishments are always trying to discover our secrets. Only last week a client who had been very highly recommended was caught taking notes in the Aromatherapy Room.'

'Tod Ballard, an industrial spy? Oh really! Actually I think he's a bit slow on the uptake. Was it him who told you we were at The Barley Mow?'

'Certainly not.' Cordelia felt a slight and surprising nibble of relief. 'Matt and Mary Lawson were having a drink in the saloon bar. Naturally he couldn't wait to get in here this morning and tell me. I found myself in a very undignified position when he gave me that common look of his and said, "But surely Cordelia's told you all about it?"'

*   *   *

It had been something of a relief to discover that Betty Drummond, Isabella's next visitor, had not dropped in for a consultation, a discussion about the less savoury parts of her digestive tract, or a complaint about Steam Cabinets. She was simply there for a good old homely chat.

Lady Drummond had first come to Alba three years before; wife of Sir William Drummond, a noted benefactor and member of charity committees, she was just the kind of client Alba welcomed.

Isabella reigned graciously behind her desk; Lady Drummond, dressed in a simple Italian track suit with a few simple diamonds strung about her, sat in a comfortable armchair.

'As this is your first visit to Alba, Lady Drummond, let me tell you a little about our aims. Our years of experience have taught us that where . . . '

'You haven't twigged, have you, love?'

'Twigged, Lady Drummond?' Looks all right, thought Isabella, but what an unfortunate voice.

'Come off it, Bella. You haven't forgotten Betty, have you? Your old friend on the shell casings bench?'

'Betty? *Betty!* I don't believe it. It must be forty years.'

'Nearer fifty, but who's counting? Do you remember that foreman with the Brylcreem and the hands? And *Workers' Playtime* in the canteen? And that time when you and I . . . '

*   *   *

Isabella was remembering her first day at the munitions factory; the blare of light and noise and people and the way the other girls stared at her because she was new. And remembering the bosomy blonde who bounced up to her and said, 'Hullo, love. Don't worry, it'll get worse. Here, there's a spare place on the bench next to me. Haven't you got lovely hands? Tell you what, I know where to get hold of some lanoline . . . '

Isabella had been a penniless refugee when she first met Betty, her young husband (scion of just such another Great House as hers) tragically killed on the beaches of Dunkirk.

She had worked hard during the war, at first in munitions. The other girls envied the continental way she tied her protective headscarf and the brave way she dealt with her widowhood. Isabella did not talk much about her antecedents; it didn't seem democratic, in those we're-all-in-it together days, but inevitably, details leaked out.

Tiring of broken finger-nails and community singing fairly quickly, Isabella manoeuvred herself out of the war effort and into more satisfying efforts on her own behalf. Pendleton's, the long-established family draper on a corner two minutes from her bed-sit, were delighted to employ such a personable, hard-working, and elegant young woman. Her landlady, who had also lost a husband at Dunkirk, was delighted to baby-sit the young Olivia. Though nobody said 'baby-sit' in those days; 'Of course I'll keep an eye on the little pet for you, dear,' said kind Mrs Thingummy (what was her name? Anderton, Andover, something like that) 'she'll be company for my little Tommy. Don't you worry about a thing.' Isabella had no intention of worrying about portly Olivia; particularly since, under Mrs . . . Wendover, that was it, Mrs Wendover's benign regime, she rapidly put on even more weight.

Everyone was delighted to help Isabella, the wistful, frail young widow who was so obviously incapable of looking after herself. And she'd kept one useful contact from the munitions factory.

'Street-wise' was another phrase not in use during the war, but it described Betty Drummond to a T.

Betty Drummond, who could lay her hands on hair-dye, mascara, wholesale boxes of Kit-Kats and 'a coupla extra eggs for the kiddy'; whose husband, Bill, escaped conscription by a subtle mix of 'his arches' (fallen), 'his eyes' ('I think the next line's got a G in it, but I couldn't swear to it'), and the fact that he was in the semi-reserved occupation of printing. Betty Drummond, who, when she heard Isabella was going to work in a draper's, had an interesting business proposition to put to her.

'Bill can print them by the hundreds, love, there's no problem with the printing. He does a lovely job, Winnie himself couldn't fault them, bless him.' Betty cast an affectionate glance at the photograph of Churchill, with cigar and V-sign, that stood on her mantelpiece. 'It's getting them to the public that's been a bit of a problem.'

Pendleton's regular clients learnt quickly that they could always depend on Isabella. Was a daughter getting married? 'I simply don't know how we'll manage. Of course the poor darling wants a traditional wedding dress. And a train, and a veil, and *everything*. And what am *I* going to wear? Thirty-six coupons between the pair of us, and that won't even *begin* to buy her underwear.'

Isabella thought she might be able to find some clothing coupons. Alas, it would, she was afraid, cost a little, but . . .

Was a husband due home on embarkation leave? 'Not a decent rag to put on my back, and, oh, Miss Isabella, he wants to take me to the Café de Paris, and I may never see him again.' Isabella was almost certain she knew of a little old lady who really didn't need all her coupons. Not very well off, though, so if a small contribution was possible . . . ? 'Oh, you are wonderful, of course I'll pay anything.' Anything usually turned out to be two pounds per coupon, but nobody grumbled.

Betty and Bill and Isabella did so well out of clothing coupons that they soon moved effortlessly into ration books. But when Bill said he reckoned he could do a very nice line in identity cards, Betty put her foot down.

'I'm not getting mixed up in anything dishonest, Bill Drummond; fair's fair is my motto, and always has been.'

To a foreigner, Betty's cockney standards of morality were confusing; she was a patriot who stood up, even if she was alone, when the National Anthem was played. A photograph of Their Majesties and the Little Princesses was ranged next to Winston Churchill on the mantelpiece. She wept for Our Boys Out There, and worked like a dog at the munitions factory. When a rumour swept London that dockers were stealing the iron rations from lifeboats, Betty indignantly wondered how they could look themselves in the face. On the other hand, anything that had fallen off the back of a lorry (a phrase almost certainly invented by Betty's father) was Finders Keepers. In her simple philosophy, clothing coups were all right, they just gave pleasure, didn't they? And if someone's son was home on leave, naturally they wanted to give him tinned salmon. But forged identity cards? She didn't think Winnie would like that. You never knew who might lay their hands on them.

Betty's sense of what was Right and what was Wrong was eccentric, but written in stone.

*   *   *

So it was rather a shock for Isabella, all those years later, to find Betty Drummond sitting across her desk.

'And you needn't look at me like that, Bella love. Mum's the word, and always will be. Clothing coupons? Never heard of them, dear. My Bill went into property and local government after the war. What a combination! Nothing dishonest, of course, you know me, dear. But when money's lying around asking to be picked up, it would be flying in the face of nature not to, wouldn't it? Now he's Sir William Drummond, with a photograph of him standing next to Princess Anne that time he handed over the cheque for the Save the Children Fund. And you've done all right, haven't you? The moment I read about this place in *Harpers*, I thought, Oi oi, Bella's gone up in the world. So I couldn't resist surprising you. Come on, tell us all.'

With a cautious eye on Betty's view of what was, and what was not, Quite the Ticket, Isabella had told her hardly anything at all.

*   *   *

70

True to her genes, Isabella had put every penny she could save from the clothing coupon deals into property. Her ancestors had always bought earth, in small packets and large. Wait until your neighbour is in trouble, and then offer to help him out, was the family motto, which sounded better in Latin.

It was early in 1943, when Isabella came home from Pendleton's to find Olivia and Mrs Wendover's Tommy fighting over a disreputable bar of chocolate in the hall. Mrs Wendover was crying at the kitchen table.

'Dear Mrs Wendover, what has happened?'

Mrs Wendover thrust a letter at her. 'I've never understood money. Ted did it all. They're going to take the house away from me.'

'Nonsense. They can't. May I read it?'

'Oh, please. Come and sit on Mummy's knee, Tommy, we're going to be thrown out into the cold to starve.' Tommy bellowed and dropped the chocolate. Even while reading, Isabella noticed distastefully that Olivia swooped on it like a seagull.

'Mrs Wendover, the letter says you haven't been making the mortgage repayments. The house cost £279-17s-6d in September, 1939 . . . '

'Ted said whatever happened I'd always have a home,' wailed Mrs Wendover.

' . . . a down payment of £87-15s-6d, leaving £192-2s to be paid off at the rate of 17s-6d per week. I don't understand. Even allowing for interest at, let me see, five per cent, you should nearly have paid it off, by now. There must be some mistake.'

'I didn't know I had anything to pay. Ted said the house was ours.'

'Well, it is, in a way, but didn't they send you reminders?'

Mrs Wendover waved a despairing hand at her filing system, an old Huntley and Palmer biscuit tin. Taking the contents out and turning them upside down, Isabella found a letter starting, 'We fear it may have escaped your notice that . . . ' Later letters came more briskly to the point. The letter that had arrived that day made no bones about it.

'But when you got these letters, why on earth didn't you . . . ? Couldn't you afford the payments?'

'Ted always said the house was ours,' said Mrs Wendover obstinately. 'Anyway,' she added, 'I never really took to reading.'

'You mean you can't . . . ? But how did you read this one? The one that came today?'

'Oh, I didn't. That secretary in the basement, that Miss Vavasour, she read it for me. It came registered, you see, and she said it must be important, and I said . . . well, anyway, she read it, and now I'm bally homeless,' said Mrs Wendover resentfully, leaving Isabella with the impression that as far as Mrs Wendover was concerned, it was all Miss Vavasour's fault because she could read.

'Mrs Wendover, you've been so kind to me. I have some savings. Would you allow me to help you out? I think I could manage to pay off the mortgage.'

'Whose house would it be then?' said Mrs Wendover, displaying, Isabella thought, a rather unappealing vein of shrewdness.

'Yours, of course. Yours and little Tommy's. And bit by bit, you can pay me back.'

Next day, Isabella came back from the bank. 'All your worries are over,' she said gaily, 'the bank was so helpful, once I'd explained the position. All you have to do is sign this little piece of paper to say that you agree to my taking over the mortgage. Oh, and we need a witness to your signature.'

'I see, dear. Why don't I pop down and ask Miss Vavasour?'

'Well, yes, I suppose she would be all right. Oh look, there's that nice Polish gentleman from the second floor, coming up the steps. Why don't we ask him. I always think,' said Isabella, who thought nothing of the kind, 'that a man's signature carries more weight, somehow.'

So Mr Volski, who was doing quite well at his English lessons considering he was seventy-two, witnessed Dora Wendover's signature.

*　　　*　　　*

Betty Drummond had listened, fascinated, to Isabella's version of her launch into the property business.

'I see, dear. So when your landlady decided to live with her sister in the country . . . '

'Better for little Tommy, she said.'

' . . . and she couldn't find a buyer for the house, you saved her bacon. And I bet you paid over the odds for it, now own up. You always had a heart of gold.'

*　　　*　　　*

Well, it was roughly true. Except that Mrs Wendover had decided to move to the country after Isabella bought the house from under her.

'But, Mrs Wendover, nothing's changed,' Isabella had said soothingly. 'Some silly legality, apparently the bank insists on the house being in my name because I paid off the mortgage. You and Tommy will still . . . '

'It's not what Ted wanted. I know you did it for the best, dear, but I think I'll up sticks. You must let me know how much I still owe you.'

'Nothing,' said Isabella, whose heart, while not being pure gold, wasn't totally black either, 'nothing at all.'

The episode was not a memory she cared to linger over; nor the way Miss Vavasour looked, not so much at, as through her, next time they met on the stairs. 'People like Dora Wendover shouldn't be allowed out by themselves,' said Miss Vavasour, 'I am herewith giving you a week's notice. I will be moving out on Saturday the fourteenth.' Mr Volski moved out quite soon, too, but that was because his radiator stopped working, and it was February.

*   *   *

'Hullo, love, and how's life treating you today? You all right? You're looking a bit under the weather.'

'Oh, Betty, I sometimes wonder whether it's all worth it. You've heard about The Barley Mow escapade, of course?'

'Mary Lawson told me all about it in Steam Cabinets this morning. Nice woman, but not a lot of gumption. And then I happened to be passing Sister Monica's office, and I heard her speaking to Renfrew and Steinberg about their disgraceful and irresponsible behaviour, and how you'd considered asking them to leave. Laying it on a bit thick, I thought.'

'Nonsense, Betty, rules are rules and have to be adhered to. I myself instructed Monica to speak to them severely. Mrs Gerard and Mr Bartholomew I shall deal with myself.'

'Poor swine.' Betty took out a packet of Silk Cut, lit one, waved it at Isabella, and said, 'May I?'

'You already have, Betty. As a matter of fact, I think I might join you.'

They puffed companionably for a few moments, and Betty said, 'What was it we used to smoke in the canteen? Players, was it?'

'Those ones in a green packet. I can't remember their name, but you could always lay your hands on a couple of cartons, Betty.'

'Woodbines. Takes you back, doesn't it? I say, Bella, I don't give a fig for horrid little Mr Bartholomew, he eats veal, so cruel. But Erica Gerard, don't be too hard on her. There's a nice woman there, behind the alcoholic haze. I'm thinking of getting her on to one or two of my committees. Apparently she's really interested in donkeys.'

'Pity she isn't more interested in her seriously anorexic daughter,' said Isabella, looking at her watch, 'she should be in the waiting room now. Ask her not to come in for five

74

minutes, would you, Betty? There's a phone call I've got to make.'

'Right.' Betty stubbed out her cigarette and rose. 'By the way, love, anything funny strike you about Mr Ballard?'

'What do you mean? Don't tell me he has been misbehaving too; he was recommended by a perfectly respectable politician.'

'Are there any?' said Betty.

'I am told Mr Ballard is a novelist.'

'It's just that he reminds me of someone, and I can't think who. Oh well. I'll be off. I'll tell Erica to crawl in humbly in five minutes.'

*   *   *

Erica was sitting in the anteroom outside Isabella's study, pretending to read *Harpers & Queen*. Her eyes flicked unseeingly over the *only* shape for autumn coats. She couldn't even concentrate on the social pages (always full of friends and acquaintances) because she knew that she would be Spoken To about the half of Martell Isabella had found in her carrier that morning, as well as last night's dinner at The Barley Mow. 'Clients who break our scientifically based rules are no longer welcome at Alba,' would be the least of it. Two rules broken, would she get away with it?

Erica's eyes, focused on a photograph of a woman she had never really liked curtsying to Princess Michael, glazed slightly. Half of her was thinking, 'Ghastly dress, where does Alice find them?' The other half was saying defiantly, 'So what? So Isabella does chuck me out, do I give half a hoot? Why do I come here for twice a year starvation and bullying and those boring exercises, anyway?' She was quite pleased with her new, courageous attitude, until she remembered why she kept on coming to Alba. Sister Monica's Extras, which for some silly reason she couldn't seem to do without, these days.

Isabella's door bounced open, and Lady Drummond bounced out. She was wearing the kind of earth-brown track suit that Erica never seemed to be able to find, and a lot of that particular gold jewellery that very wealthy women wear for shopping in the morning.

'Hullo, love!' said Betty Drummond. 'Cheer up, it may never happen. Bella's busy on the phone, she says will you go in in five minutes.' She sat next to Erica, and looked over her shoulder at *Harpers*. 'There's that dreary Pangbourne woman, sucking up to Princess Posh. If I had a hot dinner for every time I've told her she's too old for mini-skirts.'

'You know Alice Pangbourne?'

'She's on the Badger Committee with me. Mind you, only in it for the social side, and we only invited her because of all that money. If you ask me, she doesn't give a toss.'

'The Badger Committee?'

'What they're doing to those poor little bleeders you'd never believe, love. If you're interested, I've got some pamphlets in my room. These gangs go out baiting. God, if I caught them at it I know what I'd hang them up by. And of course the Min of Ag's about as much use as . . . you got any spare time for committee work, Erica? We're going to chuck Alice. She came to the Otter Conservation Meeting in a fur coat, would you believe it? I mean, who wears fur coats these days, I ask you?'

Erica thought of the mink (ranch mink, not wild, so that's surely not so bad?) hanging at home in her wardrobe (thank heavens she hadn't brought it) and rose to her feet.

'I think perhaps I'd better go in now.'

'You're in for a right royal ticking off, I can tell you. Who's been a naughty girl at The Barley Mow, then?'

Erica stiffened. 'I really don't think Isabella should discuss a client's private . . . '

'Bella didn't tell me. I heard all about it in Steam Cabinets at half past eight this morning. The place is

76

buzzing with it. That old trout Tristram looks like some-one sat on his hairpiece. And I rather gather that Sheila and Diane nearly got their marching orders. But you'll be all right. I said to Bella, (we go back to the Norman Conquest, so I can say anything to her) go easy on Erica, I said, she's the right sort, she's as good as promised to take over as fund-raiser for Mexican Donkeys.'

'Did I? I don't remember.'

'Yes you did, the other night. I was telling you how much those filthy bastards loaded them with, coming down from the mountains, and you said . . . '

'I said it was dreadful, and somebody ought to do some-thing about it.'

'Exactly. You're just the caring type of person we're looking for. Tell you what, I'll meet you after what Bella has the brass neck to call supper, and I'll bring the infor-mation with me. Ivory, that's something else we've got to keep an eye on. That Diane's got ivory earrings, I'm going to have a word with her.'

As Erica approached Madame Cordoba's door she was feeling marginally more confident. Betty Drummond, as boundlessly warmhearted as she was wealthy, had de-scribed her as a caring person. And what was David going to say when he heard that his wife had been invited on to a charity committee by the wife of Sir William Drummond? He was always getting at her for not being more help socially. Totally disregarding, of course, how often she had produced dinner for eight at three hours' notice on a Sun-day. Not bothering to remember the time that Frenchman from Lyons had kissed her hand and said, 'You are a better cook than my wife, *madame*.' Taking for granted the num-ber of times she had gazed at photographs of quite plain American children with metal all over their teeth and said, 'What a heart-breaker she's going to be, Al.' Erica didn't mind doing all that. She quite enjoyed it, actually. It would *just* be rather nice if *just* occasionally David said, 'You've done it again, darling. We've got the Chile contract. How

77

the hell did you know his English grandmother used to give him apple crumble?'

*   *   *

It was extremely unfortunate that J. Bevington & Daughter's telephone was engaged; Isabella only got through on her third try, and had barely started her conversation when Erica tapped on the door and entered. She thought, on the whole, that she covered herself pretty well, but it was all extremely difficult.

'Miss Bevington, I did explain to your father . . . hold on one moment . . . do sit down, Erica, I will not be long . . . and he quite understood . . . what? . . . no, no, half past nine at the very earliest . . . I should have thought that was obvious . . . if it is a question of overtime, then of course Alba will . . . ten o'clock, then? And of course, the tradesmen's entrance . . . thank you. Goodbye.'

Isabella put down the telephone and said, 'These local tradesmen, so set in their ways. Our last batch of yogurt has failed, so I have had to order some in from outside. Naturally, since Alba takes a pride in only serving homemade products, I trust you will be discreet.'

'Not a word from me,' said Erica staunchly, 'actually we were saying, at lunch yesterday, it was rather runny.'

'No doubt. Erica, what are we going to do with you? Lobster Thermidor at The Barley Mow, I am reliably informed, preceded by terrine of monkfish and followed by profiteroles. And accompanied throughout by gins and tonic. Four I believe. Doubles.'

'I honestly can't think what I was doing there. That dreadful Bartholomew man and those two frightful women.'

Isabella made an ineffable gesture, composed of eyebrow, shoulder and wrist, which Erica easily interpreted as, 'I cannot, of course, comment on my clients. But my mother would never have received them.'

Encouraged, Erica pressed on. 'So silly of me, I hope you're not going to be too cross. I am really beginning to feel the benefits of your regime. And Sarah is having such a happy time here.'

'We are, of course, here to help. And clients with special problems need special help. But we cannot help you unless you are willing to help yourself.'

'But, Isabella, you know I haven't got a special problem.' Erica caught sight of Isabella's eyebrow, and faltered, 'I admit I occasionally do like a little drink now and then, but who doesn't?'

'Many people like a little drink now and then, but they do not secrete bottles of brandy in the bottom of their carrier bags and . . . ' Isabella opened a drawer, and took out half a bottle of Bell's and half a bottle of Smirnoff ' . . . further supplies in their track suits in the bottom drawer of their wardrobe.'

Erica's first reaction was of shame. It was swiftly overcome by irritation; she felt as though she had been caught at the Customs with more than her allocation of duty-free liquor. Now she was going to have to go through the whole shopping charade again.

'Oh, really, Isabella, searching my room as though I were some common criminal.' Erica was so cross at the thought of having to repurchase her supplies that she spoke quite boldly, 'I don't seem to remember, in your brochure, that you say anything about clients' rooms being searched daily.'

'We wouldn't search if there was nothing to find. This is your last warning, Erica. Either you control your drinking, or our special infusions will no longer be available to you.'

Erica exited, shaking, but the interview had not been quite as bad as she had anticipated. Isabella had been surprisingly, well, tolerant wasn't perhaps quite the right word; tolerant was not a word you would use about the last daughter of the Cordobas. Understanding? No, that wasn't it, either. Abstracted, thought Erica, that's what she was.

Tristram Bartholomew was sitting outside Madame's office, listlessly studying *Horse and Hound*. 'How was it?' he said, looking up dolefully. 'Did she slaughter you?'

'It was all your fault. I can't think why you suggested that wretched Barley Mow in the first place. And I've had a gyppy tummy all morning.'

'You needn't have come if you didn't want to. I intend to be very firm. For one thing, I am not going to put up with lesser masseurs. I'm going to insist on going back to Matt. Lucy has fingers like a very old moth, and as for that impudent Gary . . . '

*   *   *

Tristram was not such a long-standing client as Erica, so he called Isabella Madame.

'I'm so glad you asked to see me, Madame, because there was something I wanted to mention. I really must insist on Matt. It's not that Lucy isn't an excellent masseuse in her way, but . . . '

'If you do not care for the manner in which I run Alba, Mr Bartholomew, you may, of course, leave this afternoon. The fees for the remainder of your fortnight will be re-funded to you. I must admit I am not particularly interested in retaining as a client someone who behaves as improperly as you did last night.'

'Ah.' The interview was going even worse than Tristram had envisaged. 'Improperly is hardly the way I would have put it. Evaluating restaurant meals is, as you know, my livelihood, Madame. I see now I should have asked your permission.'

'If you had, it would not have been granted. Not content with wilfully breaking your own carefully planned diet, you saw fit to lure three of my other clients into your nefarious scheme. I am not convinced, Mr Bartholomew, that there is any good reason for you remaining here for longer than it takes to pack your suitcase. Have you anything to say to make me change my mind?'

Tristram, usually so adept with the small witticisms and the sly threads of gossip, could, at the moment, think of nothing coherent to say at all. And, like Erica earlier, he asked himself why he was so keen to stay on anyway. He had just been spoken to like a housemaid caught stealing the silver, and last night's large meal at The Barley Mow had had the usual effect of making him even hungrier today. Ten minutes to pack his bags, a fast train to London; he could be eating at the Capital that night, or something quite restrained at the Savoy Grill. A vision sprang into his receptive mind of perfectly pink cutlets in cosy conjunction with a purée of potatoes, lambent with milk and butter. Lambent, a nice word, he must remember that.

Tristram swallowed to get rid of the saliva which had rushed excitedly into his mouth, and gazed pleadingly at Isabella. Because he knew why he didn't want to be chucked out ignominiously. He was a dedicated snob, and Alba was the Eton of health farms. It was the Royal Enclosure, the I Zingari tie, the table in the corner at the Ritz. Would-be new clients were wasting their time if they rang up and said, 'I read about you in *Vogue*. Could I come for a week in September?' New clients had to be introduced by old clients, and while Isabella was remarkably tolerant, considering her background, about class, she was positively National Front about behaviour. Tristram desperately wanted to be able to go on saying, 'Oh, I go to Alba, of course. Is there anywhere else?', so he must think quickly.

'Madame, what can I say? Except to apologise wholeheartedly, of course. A moment's aberration, so silly of me, but we all make mistakes sometimes, don't we?' Isabella raised her chin just enough to inform him that she, for one, never did. He blundered on. 'And anyway, it's not quite fair, is it? I gather that Diane . . . Mrs Renfrew and Mrs Steinberg are being allowed to stay on. Mrs Gerard certainly didn't say anything about being asked to leave. And what about that man in the room next door to me?'

Isabella looked down her nose in a manner that made Tristram feel he was sitting on the floor. 'What about him?'

'Well, he never appears for exercises, or anything. His breakfast tray is positively littered with cigarette stubs, I thought we weren't supposed to smoke in our rooms. And last night, after we got back from The Barley . . . after I went to my room, I couldn't get a wink of sleep. Moaning and groaning and the television on so loud, I mean, I made one small transgression, and he seems to be able to get away with . . . '

Isabella looked at her watch, a Fabergé fob, Tristram noted enviously, and rose decisively.

'Very well, Mr Bartholomew, but this is absolutely your last chance, is that clear? Now, I am sure we both have other things to do. I make no promises, but I will ask Matt to see if he can arrange his timetable to accommodate you.'

Tristram left the presence with alacrity. Of course he had always congratulated himself on his way with words; but not being expelled *and* getting Matt back? He couldn't remember exactly what he had said, but it must have been pretty telling stuff.

*　　　*　　　*

It was nearly bedtime at Alba. A few guests were playing desultory and irritable bridge. Most, exhausted, were in their bedrooms, watching television, reading, or wishing their tummy muscles didn't hurt quite so much. Betty, ensconced in the best bedroom in the place, was collating statistics on Live Horse Exportation; something was going to have to be done before 1992, when those inhumane foreign bastards' rules would come into operation. She was

82

also drafting a letter to every MP she knew (nearly all of them, for one reason or another) on the subject of dog farming, beagles, and Swedish experimental laboratories. Isabella had completed her nightly round, noticing coldly that two damp towels had been left by the shower stall in the Steam Cabinet room. Mary Lawson had been so busy gossiping about the Barley Mow incident, thought Isabella, that she had completely gone to pieces. She picked up the towels fastidiously and dropped them into the linen hamper, leaving a note that would have Mary whimpering in the morning, and exited, trailed by Flora, who wisely elected not to play the arthritic card that evening, as her mistress was plainly not in a mothering mood.

One more task, thought Isabella wearily, and she would have come to the end of a particularly disturbing day.

Sister Monica was in the kitchen, smoking a cigarette and drinking coffee. Clients, of course, were not allowed coffee, but members of staff, as long as they were discreet, might absorb as much caffeine as they fancied.

'Nothing yet?' said Isabella, looking down the passage to the back door.

'Not a sausage. Anyway, you told them ten o'clock, didn't you?'

'I told Miss Bevington ten o'clock, certainly. But I much prefer dealing with her father, always so discreet. The younger generation, Monica, are often haphazard in their ways.'

'Why don't you go to bed, Madame, and leave it all to me? You've had a hard day, and you know I can manage.'

'Do you know, Monica, I think I will. I'm not sure if I was wise in letting Mr Bartholomew stay on. Such a trouble-maker.'

'I think you had to. He's a dangerous gossip, that man. Now, off you go, Madame. I'll cope.'

*   *   *

Antonia Fellowes and Sarah Gerard were drinking Diet Coke and watching *MASH* in Sarah's room. They had not, on the face of it, very much in common, beyond the fact that they were both female, eighteen, and had finished A-Levels. Antonia thought Sarah was a witless Sloane, and Sarah thought Antonia was a work-mad prig. However, they spent a lot of time together, because nobody else at Alba understood a word they said. They were both heavily into Australian soap.

'What did you do this arvo?'

'Shot through to Paxborough. Lob me a tinny.'

'I reckon Tod Ballard's hunky, behind those speccies.'

'Hunky? He's a total dag, Tones. You show me a hunk at this place, and I'll show you,' Sarah paused to think of something really unlikely, 'Harold pashing Bronny.'

Antonia, convulsed with merriment at the thought of this unlikely occurrence, got up and wandered towards the window. Sarah's room was not quite on the luxury scale of her mother's. True, like most rooms at Alba, it had its own bathroom; but instead of looking out on to rolling pastures, venerable chestnuts and pedigree Herefords, there was a dull view of outhouses and the gates through which tradesmen were obliged to enter.

'You've got an even crappier view than me,' said Antonia, 'anything on after *MASH*?'

Sarah dropped the television page of the *Daily Mail* on the floor and joined Antonia. 'Nothing. Something about kitchen gardening. And snooker.'

'Gross. I say, what's that van doing?'

'It's probably delivering food, or something.'

'At this time of night? Hang on ... I can just see ... J. Bevington & Daughter, it says on the side. And underneath, Fun.'

'Fun? What does that mean?'

'Don't know, can't see the rest. Funny Hats, Ltd? Perhaps Isabella's going to give a party.'

'Fundamental Foods? More sacks of that ghastly muesli,

I bet.' Sarah lost interest, and picked up the telly page again. 'Hey, this might not be too bad, a real-life story about some woman whose husband beats up on her, and then she kills him. It says it's not for the fastidious.'

'Cool,' said Antonia vaguely. 'Go for it.' The van was moving off now, it was under the lights by the back gate, and she could see what J. Bevington & Daughter did for a living. 'Sarah . . . '

'What?'

'Oh, nothing.' What J. Bevington & Daughter did for a living was so riveting that Antonia thought that, for the moment, she would keep it to herself.

CHAPTER
SEVEN

'Mum, you're snoring again. Anyway, it's nearly time to get up.'

Antonia Fellowes was sharing a room with her mother. Partly because it was cheaper, and partly because Mrs Fellowes felt safer when Antonia was about.

It was seven o'clock, and Antonia had been awake for ages. She was reading Nabokov's *Invitation to a Beheading*; not strictly her field, but stimulating, and it provided plenty of material for the pretentious discussions about love, freedom and the State with which she and her friends filled their evenings.

Little chance, thought Antonia, of having a worthwhile discussion with that airbrain Sarah, unless you fancied a detailed comparison of plot lines of *Home and Away* and *Neighbours*. Antonia, like most of her contemporaries, was well into Aussie soap, but was not, like Sarah, your actual twice-a-day merchant.

She stretched and thrust a foot out from under the blankets; Alba, in her view, was unbearably over-heated. To be fair to Alba, a tent on the north face of the Eiger would have seemed musty to a child brought up in Partington Manor.

Antonia, the oldest of six children, looked across at her mother, still snuffling gently in sleep. She must, thought Antonia in amazement (and not for the first time) have done it with her father at least six times. Since they never seemed to speak to each other during the day, except when her father said, 'That light bulb's gone in the kitchen corridor again,' Antonia wondered how on earth they broached the subject of procreation.

*   *   *

Antonia was the product of a not unusual University family; father a professor of Modern Languages, mother a promising anthropologist who gave up measuring skulls and interpreting marriage rites to bear the first of his children. They'd had an unspoken agreement (well, unspoken by Henry Fellowes, anyway) that she would return to research as soon as Antonia was at kindergarten. By the time Antonia was five, Susannah had arrived and Harry was a positive pregnancy test.

Henry expected the large house to look immaculate, he expected to eat well, and he expected his wife to know exactly where he had left his notes on Comparative Consonancies of Northern Swedish Dialects. (In theatrical terms, five was an unusually good house for Professor Fellowes' lectures.) It was taken for granted that she would do it all on a remarkably small housekeeping allowance.

Antonia put her foot back under the duvet and wondered, not altogether charitably, why mum let dad get her so on the defensive.

'I mean,' she'd said to Sarah, on one of the rare occasions when they were not discussing Summer Bay, 'he's dead easy to deal with. All you have to say is "Shut up, dad, you're being mega-boring," and he folds up like a newspaper. Well, you know fathers.'

Sarah, who hardly knew her father at all, said, 'Right.'

'You won't believe this,' said Antonia, 'but she gets up and gives him a cooked breakfast.'

Sarah gaped in a suitable manner. 'Every day?'

'And irons his handkerchiefs. A first in Anthropology, and she behaves,' said Antonia scornfully, 'like someone from Easter Island.'

Sarah, who had no idea what people from Easter Island

87

behaved like, said, 'Is that why your mother's here, then? For a rest?'

'Not exactly,' said Antonia evasively. She had no intention of revealing all that embarrassing hoo-ha.

Four weeks ago Jane Fellowes, when collecting her youngest from school, had found herself unable to get out of her car. Nothing physical; as she tried to explain to a friend, also collecting, 'I know it sounds silly, but it's not safe out there.' Since tears were streaming down her face, the friend sensibly said, 'Move over, I'll drive', and took them all home.

The house looked, as it always did, perfect; children played, in the manner of a prestige BBC 2 serial, in the lower branches of a chestnut tree. Urns, planted with lesser periwinkles, were overshadowed by Albertine roses. A couple of labradors regarded them with elegant benevolence. Jane looked out of the car window at the evidence of her ordered and enviable life, and trembled.

'No need to rush,' said the sensible friend, 'just sit there and take your time.'

'I'm so sorry,' said Jane, 'and oh, Susan, what about your car? How will you collect it? I'll be better in a minute, I'll drive you back, and . . . '

'Jane,' said Susan, 'my car doesn't matter. Nothing matters. Stop fussing.' She got out of the car, and pushed her seat forward. 'Come on, kids, out you get. Go and talk to the dogs, or something.'

After ten minutes, Professor Fellowes and Antonia wandered out of the front door, looking puzzled. Jane did not usually have time to sit about in cars, chatting with friends.

Jane looked at them, and wept.

'Mum?' said Antonia. 'Mum? What's the matter?' She had nearly added *now*, but an unusual, for her, shaft of percipience had made her think that perhaps it would be better not to.

'Good afternoon,' said Henry Fellowes, 'it's, er, Mrs Jamieson, isn't it? Has my wife had an accident?'

'Susan Jamieson. She's had six accidents, if you ask me.'
Susan ran a highly popular Assertiveness Class, but even
she didn't feel she could add, 'Seven, if you count you.'
However, she did feel she could add, 'She is totally worn
out. Any fool can see that.'

The Regius Professor of Modern Languages did not care
to be called, even by implication, 'any fool'. On the other
hand, this bossy woman had plainly extricated Jane from
one of her silly mishaps, so it behoved him to be courteous.
Antonia was still crouched by the car, patting her mother's
knee.

'Do get out of the way, Antonia,' he said coldly, 'and let
your mother move. I am afraid we have kept you far too
long, Mrs Jamieson. Come along, Jane, pull yourself together. Antonia will make you some tea, or something.'

'She needs, for Christ's sake, far more than tea,' said
Susan, crossing her arms and leaning against the car;
which, if Henry Fellowes had attended her classes, he
would easily have interpreted as body language for,
'You're not getting rid of me that easily.'

'Well, a brandy, then, and early to bed. You can manage
supper, can't you, Antonia?'

'You're dining in college, aren't you, dad? And we could
have a Chinese take-away. Mum would like that too,
wouldn't you, mum?'

Henry and Antonia made firmly for the house, with Jane
between them muttering, 'Sorry, so sorry . . . '

'Excuse me.' Susan Jamieson's arms were still folded.
'Has it occurred to anyone to wonder how I'll get home?'

'Perhaps we could telephone for a taxi,' Henry Fellowes
said.

Antonia, who had caught the astounded look on Susan's
face, offered to ferry her back to her car.

'I gather you're on the bright side,' said Susan, as
Antonia changed gears in the careful way of someone who
passed her test last week.

With three As and a B, and a firm offer from Caius,

Antonia privately thought she was a good deal more than on the bright side, but she shrugged her shoulders in a modest way, and said, 'Oh, I don't know . . . '

'You certainly don't seem to be using your brains, as far as your mother's concerned.'

'Mum gets a bit tired sometimes.'

'Six of you, and the house, and the garden, and a husband who would probably have voted against women's suffrage, if he had had the chance.'

Naturally Antonia admired confident women who went out and did things, instead of having things done to them, all her contemporaries did. But not when they were talking about her family.

'It was very kind of you to bring mum home, Mrs Jamieson, but I really won't listen to dad being talked about like that.'

'I'm sorry, Antonia, I'm cross, that's the problem. I'm fond of your mother, and I'm very worried about her.'

*   *   *

Breakfast trays were delivered at seven thirty at Alba. Antonia made eagerly for the Ryvita and honey, and scanned the appointment cards.

'Mum! Come on, mum, breakfast. It's half past seven, and you've got underwater massage at eight fifteen.'

Jane Fellowes stirred sleepily, sat up, and gazed at her tray with deep pleasure. 'Oh, darling, isn't this lovely. What luxury.'

Antonia, already dressed in her track suit, picked up her mother's tray and put it on her lap. 'A slice of Ryvita and some honey? Luxury?'

'I didn't have to organise it. That's luxury. And I don't know what's for lunch, and I don't know what's for supper, and somebody else is going to make the beds. Such a brilliant idea of yours, darling, this fortnight. I feel quite different already, and we've only been here . . . how long is

90

it since Susan had to come to my rescue?'
    'Four weeks.'

                *   *   *

Four weeks since assertive Mrs Jamieson had sat in
Antonia's car, as good as told her she was a selfish incubus,
warned her that her mother was on the edge of clinical
depression and suggested, in a way which sounded more
like an order, that she needed a fortnight at Alba.
    'What's Alba?' said Antonia sulkily.
    'Health farm. The best. Two weeks of mindless inac-
tivity, punctuated by a little healthy exercise. It would do
Jane the world of good. It wouldn't do you any harm,
either. Why don't you go with her?'
    Henry Fellowes was in a benign and amiable frame of
mind when he got home that evening. It had been a guest
night at High Table, and the food had been quite admir-
able. As he forged cheerfully through a melting cheese
soufflé, rack of lamb and crême brulée, he thought distastefully of Chinese take-aways. The wine from the college
cellars would have cost sixty quid a bottle had it been
drunk in a London restaurant, but there was nothing very
unusual about that. Even more pleasing, he had been able
to put ghastly Susan Jamieson's husband right on a question of phonetics in Estonia.
    He was met by his beautiful and bright daughter, who
led him prettily in the direction of his study and the bottle
of fine old Armagnac (bought from the college buttery at
cost and still, Antonia thought disapprovingly, not all that
much of a snip).
    Next morning, Henry Fellowes, rather less mellow,
found himself wondering why, exactly, he had promised
Antonia ('Oh, you are an old duck, dad!') that she and her
mother could visit an extremely expensive establishment,
in order, as far as he could make out, to eat three pounds'
worth of lettuce leaves and drink a lot of water. He might

                          91

just as well throw eight hundred pounds into the wind, he thought crossly as he shaved; and went downstairs determined to put a stop to all that nonsense.

*   *   *

Just as well, Antonia thought, as she lay in the Sauna, the sweat pouring out of her in ticklish trickles, that she'd had the nous to ring Alba and book a room before Dad came downstairs with his liver. She had anticipated that a fortnight at a health farm would be tedious at best; but if it would do mum good, then fair enough, she'd give it a go.

It was turning out to be exceptionally interesting. And also dreadfully embarrassing, but she wouldn't think about that now. For a start, she quite liked all this healthy pampering stuff. Though the part of her that intended spending six months of her gap helping to build a schoolhouse in the mountains of Patagonia disapproved of the unguents, the warmth and the self-obsession, another part revelled in the combination of luxury and discipline. Anyway, she was feeling more relaxed than she had for years, what with Os and then As, and dad always taking it for granted that she'd get top grades.

Besides, there was something funny going on here, and Antonia intended to get to the bottom of it. J. Bevington & Daughter. The way Tod Ballard pretended to be rather dim. If that awful Matt and glossy, dreadful Diane weren't having it off, Antonia would personally pay the national debt. And what was in Sister Monica's delicious bedtime drinks? 'Honey and lemon and a few herbs,' she'd been told when she'd asked. If that was true, why were they so expensive?

CHAPTER
EIGHT

Antonia first became aware of Lady Drummond's obsession when she overheard her tackling Diane Renfrew about her earrings on the stairs.

'Now, love, you're not going to mind me asking, but those aren't ivory, are they?'

Antonia grinned, enjoying Diane's dilemma. If she said, 'These? Goodness, no, just plastic,' she would be openly admitting that she wore Cheap Copies. If, on the other hand, she said, 'Yes, they are actually, Derek bought them at Mombasa for me,' she would lay herself open to being made to look at several pictures of baby elephants nuzzling desolately at dead mother elephants with their tusks cut off.

Diane took the coward's way out (most people did, when dealing with Betty), declared that she wouldn't be seen dead in ivory, and these particular earrings came from a basket marked 'all at 75p' from a gift shop in Huntingdon. Actually Derek had bought them for her in Mombasa, when he was there tendering for a construction job he was quite glad not to get; and she must remember not to wear them again while she was at Alba.

Antonia was into ecology and conservation, and fully approved Betty's attitude, as far as it went; but while Betty seemed largely uninterested in her own species, Antonia thought people were more important than animals. She had quite liked Lady Drummond at first; pity, though, about the voice. True to her upbringing, Antonia found a cockney accent appealing and attractive when used by somebody who was saying, 'Yes, Miss' to her. It jarred, rather, when it came from an extremely wealthy woman who didn't seem to give a toss about Antonia's educated opinion.

That evening, a desultory party in the Television Room were watching, at Antonia's request, or insistence, a documentary about the plight of a South American tribe, their land wrenched from them by Commercial Interests.

Tristram was thinking queasily that they looked like exactly the kind of people who ate maggots.

Diane was thinking how disgusting breasts looked when they hung down like that, you'd think there was some way they could hitch them up.

Sarah was thinking that you had to admire Antonia for wanting to work with third-world people; but she bet there wasn't a telly within two hundred miles, and what did you do about having baths?

Erica was thinking, with some complacence, about the half of gin she had secreted in the first aid box in her car.

Tod was thinking that *The Bill* was on on the other channel, and what a pity Cordelia didn't spend more time with the guests. Though if this was the kind of programme they were forced to endure, he added gloomily to himself, he could hardly blame her.

The camera homed in on a decrepit shack made of large leaves which gave the appearance of being second-hand; Mrs Dispossessed-Tribe hunkered in a corner, chewing vaguely. Mr D-T waved a branch of leaves in an un-interested manner at a cloud of flies. A large number of children squabbled or sucked their thumbs, and several pigs rootled pessimistically amongst them.

'So much work needs to be done,' said Antonia earn-estly, 'and it's not just a matter of pumping in money. We've got to reeducate, give them a sense of their own worth, teach them.'

'Those poor pigs!' said Betty, looking up from a pam-phlet about kangaroo meat in dog-food. 'Fancy having to

94

live with all those frightful people.'

'Oh *really*,' said Antonia, 'you can't be serious.'

'Yes, I can,' said Betty, who had actually made the remark in a semi-humourous vein, but was not going to be told what she was serious about by some humourless teenager, 'it's not the pigs' fault they are there. I'd like to know why those improvident idiots produced what looks like about fifteen children when any fool can see they could hardly support one? And can't someone tell them about handkerchiefs?'

'How can they possibly know about birth-control? Nobody's ever taken the trouble . . . '

'There is a species of wild dog in Central Africa,' said Betty, 'that doesn't breed when its territory is fully populated. That is what I call civilised behaviour.'

'Anyway,' said Diane, catching Tod's eye and giggling, 'what else are they going to do on those long winter nights?'

'I don't know,' said Betty, gathering up her things and rising, 'basket work, or something. Renovating old Welsh dressers, how do I know? Oh good,' she sat down again, 'it's the *News*.'

'Is that the time already?' said Erica. 'How silly of me, I've left my cardigan in the car. I'll just . . . '

'I'll get it for you, shall I, mum?' Sarah rose obligingly.

'Nonsense, darling, I'm perfectly capable of going out to the car park.'

'You said you had a cold, mum, and it's getting chilly. I won't be a moment.'

'I will not be treated like a child, Sarah. Just for once, would you please do as you're told and sit down.' Erica swept out. Diane and Sheila exchanged 'fancy that!' glances, Sarah went pink and Tod took off his glasses.

Poll tax riots filled the television screen.

'Did you see that?' said Betty, 'bloody bastard.'

'Fascist pig,' said Antonia companionably, 'you wouldn't believe it if you hadn't seen it, would you?'

95

'Seen what?' said Tod.

'That mounted policeman thug beating up some poor bystander.'

'Bystander?' said Betty. 'He'd just kicked that police horse. Got what he deserved, if you ask me. Those wretched animals must be frightened out of their wits.'

'Oh, rubbish, they probably enjoy galloping about and treading on people. Anyway, how can you sit there preferring horses to children?'

'What people tend to forget,' said Tod mildly, 'is that policemen are human beings first and policemen second. I think you can safely assume that those coppers are just as scared as the horses.'

'Oh, pull the other one,' said Antonia, 'they're the ones who are armed, after all.'

'They're also the ones who are outnumbered, and the ones who have to try to stick to some pretty inflexible rules under very unpleasant circumstances.'

'Rules? You mean, like don't hit old ladies while you're on camera? If he's a nig-nog, he's fair game? Poofters ask for it? Those sort of rules?'

'I don't imagine that is the kind of briefing that is commonly handed out by Scotland Yard. In my experience, the less one knows about a subject, the more easy it is to make facile and rather silly judgements.'

'Oh, don't be so bloody patronising,' said Antonia.

'There's quite a good film on Four,' said Sarah.

'Tears before bedtime,' muttered Sheila to Diane.

Erica returned, in a frightfully good mood. 'Such a lovely night, I had a little stroll. Anything on the news?'

Antonia burst into tears, and left the room.

*   *   *

Antonia was sunbathing behind a yew hedge and moping. How could Tod have spoken to her like that last night, as though she was some ill-mannered child? Up to then he

96

had been looking at her, well, as though she was a woman. And she hadn't imagined it, he *had* sought her out. She knew it wasn't just coincidence, that nearly every time she sat about doing nothing, he seemed to be in the next chair. He was so funny, with his comments on life at a health farm, and so interested in her, and what she did all day. All the boys she knew only wanted to talk about themselves; Tod had made her feel grown-up and sophisticated.

She looked up, scowling, as Tod wandered up, sat down, lit a cigarette and companionably offered her the packet.

Yesterday she would have thought, He does fancy me, he must. Today she just hunched a shoulder at him. 'Go away, I'm trying to read.'

'There's something I think you should know.'

'How could you have taken that silly woman's side against me?'

'Well, I wasn't. I was simply trying to point out . . . '

'Poor little baa-lambs, and sick doggies, that's all she thinks about, silly cow.'

'I think she cares about animals because she's afraid of loving people too much.'

'You sound like some crappy psychiatrist. I would like to get on with my book, if you don't mind.'

'Until three years ago, Lady Drummond was a tireless worker for Save the Children.'

'So?'

'Three years ago, her twin sons, two days' short of their twenty-fifth birthday, set off to drive five miles to a friend's party. Perfect driving conditions, nobody drunk, nobody's fault . . . '

'Oh, shit.' Antonia sat up and reached for the cigarettes.

'One way of putting it. Oil on the road, jack-knifed lorry. One boy was killed instantly. The other survived two days. Until his birthday, by one of those hideous coincidences. Since then, I suppose animals seem safer.'

'Oh, Christ, what did I say to her?'

'Something about preferring animals to children,' said

97

Tod inexorably, 'but you shouldn't blame yourself too much. You didn't know, after all.'

'How did you know?'

'I read the papers, and I have a trained . . . I have a good memory. Oh,' Antonia noticed, irritably, that his voice had brightened, 'here's Cordelia.'

He took off his glasses; without them, Antonia thought, he looked bloody attractive, not to put too fine a point on it.

'Hullo,' said Cordelia, 'what are you two doing, lurking behind a yew hedge?'

'Just waiting to see who might come by,' said Tod.

'Trying to read, actually,' said Antonia, picking up *Invitation to a Beheading*, and holding it so they could both see the title.

'Is it a horror book?' said Cordelia, 'I love Stephen King, don't you?'

Antonia gave Tod a 'Can you believe the ignorance?' look, but he didn't notice, because he was looking at Cordelia and saying, '*Dead Zone*'s his best, don't you think?'

'I liked *The Stand* best,' said Cordelia. 'But I didn't think much of *Misery*, did you?'

'I say,' said Antonia, who had picked up Tod's glasses and put them on, 'what funny glasses. They don't make any difference at all.'

Tod jerked his attention away from Cordelia, and said coldly, 'Do you mind giving them back? I have a slight astigmatism, and I really don't like other people . . . '

'If you ask me, your optician's bent,' said Antonia, taking off the glasses and tossing them at Tod. 'Those aren't lenses, they're just plain bits of glass.'

'My father has an astigmatism,' said Cordelia.

'Has he?' said Tod, charmed by this delightful coincidence.

'Well,' said Antonia, 'I think I'll go for a swim.'

'Good idea,' said Tod.

'The pool's seventy-eight,' said Cordelia, 'I might join you later.'

Antonia picked up her travelling rug and tucked *Invitation to a Beheading* under her arm. Neither of them was listening to a word she said with the kind of attention she was accustomed to; Tod had been quite snappy about his silly glasses, and Cordelia, thought Antonia venomously, had horrid thick thighs considering how long she'd been at Alba. She felt like a child over whose head the grown-ups are talking, and had a sudden urge to shout 'Knickers!', so that they would at least look at her.

No, not 'Knickers!'; something much better.

'I say, Cordelia,' said Antonia, 'what was that undertaker's van doing parked outside the kitchen the other night?'

That caught their attention, all right; Tod's head had snapped round, and Cordelia was gazing at her in a moony, puzzled way.

'Undertaker's van?' said Tod.

'Oh, I don't think so,' said Cordelia, 'you must have made a mistake. Was it dark?'

'J. Bevington & Daughter,' said Antonia, 'Funeral Directors. I saw it in the light from the kitchen.'

'What else did you see?' said Tod.

'Nothing.' Antonia slouched off up the path through the rhododendrons. 'See you later, then,' she said. Nobody answered.

Emerging from the shrubbery, she looked up at the house. There were the windows of the telly room that led out on to the terrace. Next to them was the Dining Room, and beyond them the Drawing Room where smoking was not allowed; she'd only been in there once. And above them . . . wouldn't that be the window of Madame's private office? Isabella and Sister Monica were standing there, looking down at the yew hedge. Sister Monica was holding a pair of binoculars to her eyes. As Antonia stared up, the binoculars swung in her direction.

*　　　*　　　*

Antonia shivered in her shower, though the water was pleasantly warm. Those two old bats, hitherto rather a joke in her opinion, had looked distinctly sinister, peering down like eagles from their eyrie. And who were they so interested in? Cordelia? Tod? Or even Antonia herself? But why should they be interested in her?

Mary Lawson popped her head round the shower curtain. 'Ah, it's . . . Antonia, isn't it? . . . ' Mary was still having to work at it, telling those two girls apart. This was the arrogant one from Oxford with the depressed mother. Sarah was the thin one with the drunk mother. She must remember not to get them muddled, Madame made such a point of getting names right. 'Like a nice salt scrub, dear? It would do those spots on your back a world of good.'

'No, thank you,' said Antonia, but Mary had bustled off obligingly, to return with a plastic container full of damp salt.

'I've put in a few drops of baby oil, to combat those dry areas. Turn round, dear, I'll do your back.'

Mary painfully rubbed handfuls of salt over Antonia's shoulders, chatting cheerfully about poor circulation and the problems of adolescence.

Antonia, who did not consider herself to be an adolescent, and who certainly did not have spots on her back, well, perhaps one or two, decided to put Mary in her place. She was not a particularly nice girl, and to be fair she was not very happy herself at the moment. 'There are some pretty ghastly people here, aren't there?' she said. 'How on earth do you manage to be polite to all of them?'

'Oh, there's nowt so queer as folks. That's what they say in Yorkshire, where my husband and I come from. Everyone has their little ways, I always say, but there's good in everyone, if you look hard enough for it.'

'You'd have to look for it with a pneumatic drill in that

100

bad-tempered Mrs Gillespie, always snapping at that wimp
of a daughter.'

'A martyr to her arthritis, poor old lady.'

'And Diane! Isn't she frightful? I gather she's having it
off with one of the masseurs. How could he?'

'Here's the salt tub, dear,' said Mary, 'you can do your
arms and legs yourself, can't you? I must be off to my
ladies in the Steam Cabinets.'

*   *   *

It was the end of another long day at Alba, and Isabella
was pouring herself a brandy from a bottle whose level had
dropped noticeably during the last few days.

One way and another, it had not been a good week. In
all her years at Alba, Isabella could not remember a more
ill-assorted, tiresome (and, in one or two cases, actually
dangerous) collection of clients. That child Antonia, on the
face of it such an obvious candidate for Extras; her weak
mother, opting out of life by being depressed (Isabella was
very much of the 'Pull yourself together' school), and her
scholastically ambitious father who had plainly pushed her
into academic excellence. 'Vulnerable, that one,' Sister
Monica had said, and for once Sister Monica was wrong.
Antonia turned out to be the kind of child who stayed up
late, looked out of windows, and saw things she shouldn't
see.

'I say, grandmother,' Cordelia had reported, 'I'm quite
worried about Antonia Fellowes. She's seeing things.'

'What things, child?'

'Undertakers' vans. Outside our kitchen, can you believe. We wondered if she's on drugs, or something.'

'We?'

'Tod and I.'

And *there* was another guest she wasn't too happy
about. Mr Ballard seemed to be everywhere. He was
spending far too much time with Cordelia, who had all her

101

mother's naivety as well as her thighs; and when he wasn't looking at her granddaughter without his glasses on, he was following Antonia about. Diane and Sheila were really going right over the top, she wouldn't have them here again, and there was something about Adam Shepherd that worried her. As for Erica Gerard . . . Sister Monica had suggested replacing her infusions with plain camomile tea for the time being. Perhaps it would be safer while she was drinking so much.

Flora stirred and muttered in her basket, and Isabella got up and went to kneel beside her.

'I'm losing control, darling,' she said, 'and I thought it would be easier with Cordelia here.' Flora yawned and rolled on to her back so that Isabella could rub her stomach. 'Mary Lawson's work is leaving a lot to be desired; she's obviously heard about Matt's behaviour. Whoever could have been trouble-making enough to tell her? Damp towels everywhere, no lavender oil in Aromatherapy, and Sylvia Travers left fifteen minutes too long in her Steam Cabinet. Oh, Flora, what am I to do?'

Sister Monica entered, not bothering to pause after her discreet knock.

'Not more bad news, I trust, Monica?'

'Mrs Gerard's got some more drink hidden somewhere, and Matt has been keeping his clients waiting again. If you ask me, our Mr Lawson is getting right above himself. Sometimes you'd think he owned the place, the way he talks. I really think, Madame, that you will have to speak to him.'

'I certainly will, if his manners have not improved after his week-end off. Are he and Mary going away?'

'Somewhere called Leyburn, in Yorkshire. Apparently he was born there.'

Leyburn? Isabella's stomach muscles clenched in a way which Carolyn Watson would have approved. Leyburn. But he couldn't know, could he?

CHAPTER
NINE

Cordelia resented writing letters. If she put creative pen to paper she liked to get a proper professional fee for it. Damn, instead of typing ' ... so looking forward to welcoming you to the Alba Health Manor ... ' she'd inadvertently welcomed a prospective client to the Alba Health Farm. She was helping Naomi Mayhew in the front office, but her mind was elsewhere; sauntering down the corridor towards the gym with Tod Ballard, actually.

A few minutes ago, Cordelia had spotted Tod strolling past, in navy track suit bottoms and a beige Aertex shirt. He looked considerably more appealing than most of the male guests who colour coordinated their leisurewear as carefully as a model springing into a Calvin Klein ad.

'Cordelia!' He had seemed really pleased to see her.

'Tod!' She came out of the office and leaned against the counter. They beamed at each other.

'I'm just off to the gym for a workout. You coming?'

'Sorry,' said Cordelia, 'I've got six more letters and a pile of invoices ... '

'Later then?'

'Yes, later.'

Tod started to walk off and then turned back. 'Oh, by the way, did you mention the funeral van to your grandmother?'

'She said Antonia had imagined it.' What Isabella had said was, 'That child would say anything to get herself noticed.'

'She's got an unusually vivid imagination, then,' said

Tod. 'I went into Paxborough yesterday. J. Bevington & Daughter are hidden away in that little lane at the back of the church, next to the Oxfam shop.'

'I expect Antonia noticed it when she was in Paxborough.'

Tod shook his head in a way Cordelia considered rather patronising. 'Aren't you being a bit naive?'

Cordelia was getting tired of people telling her she was naive. 'Perhaps I am. It's better than prying into other people's business. I'm surprised you didn't cross-question J. Bevington's daughter.'

'I did. She was not at liberty to divulge her customer's private affairs.'

'Quite right, too,' Cordelia retreated back into the office. 'I've got to get these letters finished before lunch.'

Tod had given her a cool nod, and wandered off towards the gym, stopping to chat to Antonia Fellowes who just happened to be hanging about by the notice-board. Cordelia Tipp-Exed crossly. She was irritated by the way Antonia had looked up at Tod as though he was George Michael and she was the president of his fan club.

'Oh dear,' said Naomi Mayhew, 'there's that new client, she's just had her initial interview with Madame, and Sister Monica hasn't given me a diet card for her yet.'

A tall girl, wearing a white towelling bathrobe and carrying a hand towel, was crossing the hall; looking, Cordelia noticed, as nervous as she had felt on her first day at Alba.

'Oh dear,' said Naomi Mayhew, 'she's got her hand towel with her. Should I say, do you think?'

'I wouldn't worry,' said Cordelia, knowing that Naomi was incapable of not worrying. 'She looks rather nice, who is she?'

Naomi Mayhew flicked her card index. 'Deborah Wynne-Jones, thirty, from Swansea in South Wales. Recommended by Mrs Steinberg. Booked in for a week. Of course Madame much prefers clients to come for a fortnight to get the most from our regime, but in the circumstances, as Mr Pullen has ... er ... vacated ... '

A couple of mornings before, Cordelia had tried to deliver a breakfast tray to Room 21, only to have her way barred by Sister Monica's firm nurse's arm. 'Mr Pullen isn't feeling very well, Cordelia. I've sent for the doctor.' And then she had raised her arm, very slightly, so that Cordelia couldn't see into the room, and said, 'Run and help Mary in the Steam Cabinets, will you? I promised I'd give her a hand.' Cordelia had heard her grandmother's voice inside the room. What had she been doing there? 'Naomi,' she said, 'why did Mr Pullen vacate, anyway?'

'He was taken ill, went off to hospital ... oh dear, here's Rosemary ... '

Rosemary Meadows swooped in. 'Have you got those diet cards ready, Naomi?'

'I am sorry, Rosemary, there's one missing.'

'Dear God, the inefficiency. How am I expected to organise the meals ... ?'

'I'll get it.' Thankfully, Cordelia stopped typing and went off to find Sister Monica.

'By the way,' Rosemary went over to Naomi's desk and lowered her voice, 'I'll need another £500 for Fred; we owe him on last week's fruit and veg.'

'Oh dear, Madame won't like that.' Naomi's hand trembled uncertainly over the cheque book.

'She'll like it even less if she has to feed proper food to the starving masses.' Rosemary scooped up the diet cards. 'An apple a day keeps the profits soaring. Madame C. knows that. Come on Naomi.'

'Well, I don't know.' Naomi Mayhew picked up her pen reluctantly; Madame always got so upset when the budgeting went awry, she could sometimes be quite unpleasant.

'And make it out to cash,' said Rosemary. 'Fred has promised me a cash discount. That'll please Madame Scrooge.'

Sister Monica, ushering Debbie Wynne-Jones into the small waiting room next to Treatment, clicked her tongue in annoyance. Didn't any of them ever bother to read the House Rules on the notice-board? 'You've brought your hand towel, dear. Mary! Mary!'

'Yes, Sister Monica.' Mary Lawson came running along the corridor.

'Miss Wynne-Jones has brought her hand towel, Mary. Fetch a proper towel for her, will you?' Monica patted Debbie's shoulder reassuringly, managing, at the same time, to press her firmly on to a chair. 'Now just sit here, dear, and Lucy will come and collect you when she's ready.'

There were three other people in the room, with nothing very much to do except stare at each other. They all stared at Debbie.

'Hand towels are not to be removed from the bedrooms.' Tristram Bartholomew shook a playful finger at Debbie to show that he was being amusing. 'Rule number six on the notice-board.'

'Oh dear, I didn't read . . . ' Debbie looked down, noticed Gucci all over Tristram's feet, and tucked her nylon fur mules further under her chair.

It was like being the new girl in one of those old-fashioned school stories. And she had already had a grilling from the head mistress.

*　　　*　　　*

A little note on her breakfast tray had summoned her to the presence. 'I do like to welcome new guests to Alba personally. Could you spare me a few minutes in my office before your morning Massage?' It was signed Isabella Cordoba de Zarate.

The old lady had turned out to be as daunting as her

106

name; one of those charmingly elegant women who make you feel your finger nails are dirty. In the time it had taken Isabella to pour out coffee, Debbie had revealed that she had been born in a semi-detached house in Penarth, just outside Cardiff, had been educated at the local school and the poly, and was now, ten years later, responsible for over three hundred staff at Hancock (Business Supplies) Ltd in the Swansea Enterprise Park.

'Poly?' Isabella had queried, with an amused little wrinkle of her nose. She knew perfectly well what a poly was, of course, but didn't want this rather common young woman to think that Alba's clientele usually had truck with polys, semis and enterprise parks.

'The Polytechnic.' Debbie blushed and had to remind herself that she was the Personnel Director of a company with a fifteen-million-pound a year turnover.

'And what brings you to Alba, my dear?' Isabella gave Debbie's towelling robe a disparaging glance. 'You don't need to lose weight, I can see that.'

'I really felt like a rest, I needed a change, to get away for a while, and Sheila Steinberg told me about Alba.'

'Sheila Steinberg. Of course.' That, Isabella said to herself, would account for Miss Wynne-Jones not being quite the class of client she usually welcomed to Alba. She smiled encouragingly, nevertheless. 'You've come to the right place. We can offer you plenty of exercise, a healthy diet to get rid of the toxins in your system and a peaceful, relaxed atmosphere. I know you young people in your high-powered jobs have so much stress in your lives.'

Debbie admitted that her life was indeed stressful, which was not entirely true. She loved her job and was good at it; she had a comfortable flat in Brynmor Road with a view of Swansea Bay, a white Escort convertible, and lots of friends. She went windsurfing with Evan Hughes, a biologist at the university, and hang gliding with Patrick Hailey, a bright young estate agent who lived in the same block. She slept with them both, when she felt like it. On

Thursdays she went to her women's group. What more could she want?

The answer was Isaac Roberts, Sales Director at Hancock's, thirty-five years old, black curly hair, seductive blue eyes, and a wife and two children in Dunvant. Isaac was the stress in her life, but she certainly wasn't going to tell this beady-eyed woman about any of that. 'I'm sure a week here will put me right back on my feet,' she said.

'Take everything Alba has to offer,' Isabella had said, rising to bring the meeting to an end, 'and do try and stick to our rules. No illicit snacks, no smoking and certainly no drinking. We can't help you if you don't help yourself.'

*   *   *

And now, here she was, Debbie thought morosely, being given the once-over by another beady-eyed old woman.

'We haven't met,' the old woman said, helping herself to a pile of *Vogue*s and *Tatler*s, and leaving a 1984 *Lady* and a dog-eared copy of *Hair Styles* on the communal table.

'I've just arrived,' said Debbie picking up *Hair Styles*, hoping to hide herself behind it.

'You'll soon settle in,' said a younger woman, wearing a faded blue candlewick dressing gown, which made Debbie's C & A model look positively Designer Label. 'Mother and I love it here, don't we, mother?'

'You love it, Rachel,' said the hard looking old person, 'I just pay the bills. My name is Sybil Gillespie, by the way, and this is my daughter, Rachel. Mr Bartholomew, over there, writes for the papers, about food, as you can no doubt tell from his girth.'

'You're very sharp today, Sybil,' said Tristram. 'Be careful you don't cut yourself.'

'I'm Debbie Wynne-Jones,' said Debbie.

'Introduced by?' said Sybil.

'Sheila, that is, Mrs Steinberg.'

Sybil Gillespie's '*aha*' suggested that she might have

108

known it; who else but a hairdresser from Harpenden would have recommended a girl called Debbie, dressed in a cheap towelling bathrobe.

*   *   *

Debbie had met Sheila the previous June, when she was in Dunstable for the annual sales conference. Going to the conference had been Isaac's idea. They had been sharing a congratulatory bottle of Muscadet in the No Sign Bar, after she had cleverly poached Smythson's Computers and Office Equipment (West Wales) Ltd's top salesman. 'You're a marvel, Debbie,' he'd said. 'What would I do without you?' Half-way through the second bottle of Muscadet, he had smiled engagingly. 'I've been thinking, Debs. Why don't you come up to the Sales Conference next month? You could learn a lot.'

On the Thursday, Debbie had learned about targets and quotas. On the Friday, how Mr Bernard (West Midlands) would go about selling a Rank Xerox Copier to Mr Fletcher (Tyne & Tees) role-playing the part of a balky customer, and on the Saturday afternoon, she'd had enough of speeches and presentations and decided to opt out and get her hair done. The Receptionist at The Moat House Hotel had recommended Sheila at Cut 'N' Dried in Harpenden High Street. 'It'll only take you about ten minutes by car. I'll give her a ring, if you like.'

It always amazed Sheila Steinberg how many really nice looking women overlooked the hair factor. Just as a carefully chosen quality frame gave the cheap prints in Diane Renfrew's boutique an Old Bond Street aura, the right hairstyle, framing a face, did classy things for the cheekbones. It could even make a quite large nose look adorably retroussé.

It was clear to Sheila that Deborah Wynne-Jones had never even thought about such important matters. She used her hair as a camouflage, lurking behind a boring brown curtain and parting it, with a flick of her fingers, whenever she wished to communicate with the outside world.

'I think,' Debbie had said, as they both studied her reflection in the mirror, 'that I probably just need a trim.'

'Leave it to me.' Sheila had picked up her scissors and proceeded to ruin Debbie's life.

As Sheila snipped, she revealed a profile that many an actress would kill for. As she daubed and dyed and conditioned, boring brown became a gleaming, swinging chestnut red. 'You could do with something on those cheekbones,' she said, producing a Lancôme blusher in a curiously appropriate orange, 'and I've got a lipstick that would look a treat with the new hair colour.'

Whipping off the salon gown, Sheila had given Debbie a critical up and down appraisal. 'If you don't mind my saying so, dear, you'd look even better if you lost a pound or two. You know what you ought to do? Give yourself a treat at the Alba Health Manor. They're ever so good on diets and it's a great place to rest up, and . . . ' she winked significantly into the mirror as she brushed off the stray hairs on Debbie's collar, ' . . . and have a bit of fun. My friend Diane and I go there twice a year, regular as clockwork.'

Isaac Roberts had always thought of Debbie as one of the blokes, a capable colleague to have in your corner in a crisis. Not like Susie, his wife, who was blonde and bubbly and had a pert bosom which showed to advantage in pink angora. Susie even put on her high heels to go to Sainsbury; Susie was Isaac's idea of a *real* woman. So, when Debbie sat down opposite him at the conference dinner, flauntingly out of character in a scarlet woollen dress, clashing vibrantly with her chestnut red hair and orange lips, Isaac was first confused and, four glasses of Chablis and two brandies later, intrigued. 'What's your room number, Debs,' he had said huskily, as they followed Evan Hancock, their Chairman, into the bar for a final nightcap. On Saturday night Debbie had learned that Isaac Roberts

110

didn't wear pyjamas in bed and liked to make love with the lights on.

*   *   *

Debbie discarded the dog-eared copy of *Hair Styles* as a tall, dark young man lounged into the waiting room, dazzling the obediently waiting group with the glint from the heavy gold bangle on his wrist watch, the knuckleduster-sized gold signet ring on his little finger, and the gold and platinum neck chain dangling in the open neck of his body-skimming white cotton jacket. There was a further flash of nine carat as he raised an arm to beckon Tristram Bartholomew, who jumped up eagerly.

The tall, dark man, who, Debbie observed, wasn't quite so young on closer inspection, ignored Tristram and walked straight over to Sybil Gillespie who was bridling resentfully over her *Vogue*. 'Forgive me, Mrs Gillespie, Madame asked me to fit Mr Bartholomew in, a special favour.' He murmured something in her ear and the old lady, complacently pink, returned to *Vogue* which was advising her to Go Pale and Pre-Raphaelite.

Debbie, now deep into the Classifieds in the vintage *Lady*, stopped fantasising ('Companion wanted for Active Elderly Lady, Norfolk. Car Driver Essential.' Should she, Debbie had been wondering, just disappear and start a new life?) and reflected gratefully that she was to be spared Macho Man. Although Lucy, a deceptively slight young woman, also turned out to have a steely touch of the Rambo's about her.

'Why do people do this?' Debbie moaned, as Lucy's strong fingers probed her neck muscles.

'They find it relaxing.' Lucy giggled. 'There's a lot of tension in your back, Miss Wynne-Jones.'

Debbie's backbone clicked like the keyboard on a dead piano, and by the time Lucy led her into the Rest Room, she felt as though she had been through three punishing rounds with a sumo wrestler.

Deftly removing Debbie's dressing gown, Mary Lawson shrouded her in a warm towel and took her over to a vacant bed. Debbie fell onto it gratefully, closed her eyes and instantly opened them again to confirm her first impression. Six women lay silent and still on hard narrow beds, each covered by a white cotton sheet. Debbie shuddered. It was like a morgue. This morbid thought was reinforced by Mary Lawson gently drawing the sheet over her body and closing her eyes with a moistened mask. 'Just rest now, and call me if you need anything.'

'It's Debbie Wynne-Jones, isn't it?' Only minutes later, Debbie's eye mask was whisked away and she found herself looking into the critical eyes of her hairdresser, Sheila from Cut 'N' Dried. 'Just look at those ends. The moment you came in, I thought, my, she could do with a good trim.'

'Ssh, Mrs Steinberg.' Mary Lawson tiptoed over. 'Excuse me, but other people are trying to sleep.' She turned to Debbie. 'Shall I give you a fresh eye mask, dear?'

'No, thank you.' Debbie, no longer sleepy, swung her legs off the bed.

'Quite right,' said Sheila. 'Life's too short to spend it in bed by yourself. Aren't I right, Mary?'

'I wish you'd lower your voice, Mrs Steinberg. I'll have Sister Monica in here, before we know where we are.'

'Come on, Debbie,' said Sheila, 'they should still be serving drinks in the Light Diet Room if we get a move on.'

They found Cordelia behind the counter. 'Bovril for two and go easy on the water,' said Sheila. 'Cordelia, this is Debbie, a friend of mine. Why don't you join us? You know what they say about all work and no play?'

Chatting to Sheila Steinberg was not Cordelia's idea of play. She had been planning to escape to her room for an hour before lunch; she was on chapter four of *Dark Half*. But after one look at Debbie Wynne-Jones, emanating tension and misery, she thought maybe she'd leave Stephen King for later. I seem to be helping out with therapy, as

112

well as everything else, she thought gloomily.

Pouring out three mugs of Bovril, she said, 'Let's go and sit over there by the window. You're on the Light Diet, I'm afraid, Debbie. Boiled water and fruit. I just got your card from Sister Monica. I'm not sure if you should even be drinking this.'

Debbie didn't smile or respond, but sat down, looked glumly at them over the rim of her mug and recounted her morgue scenario. 'It was as though we were all dead, useless bodies, lying there.'

'Steady on, Debbie,' Sheila shivered, huddled into her mohair robe and cupped her hands comfortingly around her warm mug, 'there's nothing useless about my body, I can tell you. What's got into you, anyway?'

'It was all your fault, really.' Debbie turned tragic brown eyes towards Sheila Steinberg, who shifted nervously.

'My fault?'

'Making me look so different, so Isaac noticed me. I was thrilled at first, of course. That night at the Moat House Hotel, he was wonderful, tender, passionate . . . I didn't know it could be like that . . . '

'Hold on,' said Cordelia, 'who's Isaac?'

'The sales director at the firm where I work. I've been in love with him for years, and then, when Sheila kind of transformed me . . . '

'I get it,' said Sheila. 'You've been having an affair.'

Debbie nodded. 'Isaac used to come up to my flat at lunchtime, we went on business trips together . . . we were always very discreet.'

'So nobody at your office knew what was going on?'

'Everybody knew. I was worried sick his wife would find out. They've got two young children, you see.'

'How sad for you all,' said Cordelia, wondering if it was Alba or her friendly face that caused total strangers to buttonhole her and recount the most intimate details of their lives.

Debbie's story was all too familiar. The affair had

113

meandered along a traditional course. When Isaac attempted to end it, Debbie had become tearful and clinging. When Debbie turned from him, saying she couldn't stand it any longer, they would have to part, Isaac swore he loved her, couldn't live without her. 'He said he'd get a divorce, when the children were older. "How old?" I said. "Soon," he said, "I promise."'

Capable Debbie Wynne-Jones had gone to pieces; she lost contracts, mislaid files, drove her secretary crazy. 'She said she never knew where I was from one moment to the next. And then I kept catching colds and flu, and migraine ... I've never had migraine before.'

'No man's worth it,' said Sheila.

'That's when I remembered what you'd said about Alba,' said Debbie. 'Somewhere I could get away for a complete rest.'

'You know what you need.' Sheila lowered her voice. Even in a place dedicated to health it didn't always do to let people know you had an emotional problem. 'Professional help. Mr Patterson, on the notice-board, comes regularly. He's a hypnotherapist, very understanding.'

'A hypnotherapist?' Debbie was reminded of all those boring variety shows where people zombied around the television screen, programmed to do things they'd be too embarrassed to do if they were in full possession of their faculties. 'I'm not going to be hypnotised.'

'He doesn't hypnotise you, silly,' said Sheila. 'Not unless you want it, to stop smoking or something like that. He's a therapist, sort of brings out your problems, talks about them, makes you see everything in a new light. And he's a marvellous herbalist.'

'I can't stand all that natural rubbish,' said Debbie, sounding suddenly a lot more spunky; she'd always felt a spasm of irritation at the high cost of mother earth's bounty in her local wholefood shop.

'He's done a lot for my nerves with his happy herbals, I can tell you,' said Sheila.

114

'Nerves? You?' Debbie looked at Sheila in surprise. 'But you seem so confident.'

'You can't judge a book by the cover, dear.' Sheila managed to sound jaunty and sad. 'It's not all roses being married to a dentist . . . '

'Sheila's quite right,' Cordelia interrupted quickly, before she was swept off into another personal Odyssey. 'If you ask Mr Patterson, he might prescribe Extras for you. They're herbal infusions, my grandmother has them specially blended for Alba.'

'Your grandmother?' said Debbie. 'Madame Cordoba?'

'Yes, she owns this place.'

'In that case,' said Debbie, 'if you recommend them, maybe I'll go and see the hypnotherapist.'

*   *   *

Key in hand, Debbie paused outside Room 21, at the end of the corridor. The door was slightly open. Funny, she must have forgotten to lock it when she left for Massage. She listened. Someone was moving around inside. It would be the maid, cleaning her room, just when she wanted to change for lunch.

Tristram Bartholomew, hearing footsteps, deftly shut the desk drawer, and checked his watch. The Wynne-Jones woman should still be flat out in the Rest Room with a mask over her eyes. He had popped into her room on an impulse, to see if he could pick up a clue as to why Madame Cordoba had reacted so immediately when he had mentioned the curious habits of his previous next door neighbour. Also, he would be *quite* interested to see if Room 21 boasted an en suite. *He* had to trail down the corridor to the communal bathroom.

As Debbie walked through the door, Tristram swiftly sidled past her. 'So sorry,' he said, 'wrong room. Too silly of me. I'm next door.'

115

CHAPTER
TEN

The title of Carolyn Watson's after-dinner talk in the Drawing Room that evening was 'Exercise is *Fun*'.

'By working these major muscles,' Carolyn concluded, running her hands complacently along taut stomach and thighs, 'you can attain the beautiful, springy body you deserve.'

She circled the audience with her ravishing smile, eyes sparkling, pink-lipsticked mouth wide, warm and generous. In the front row Sybil and Rachel Gillespie, Cordelia and Debbie gazed back at her in glum disbelief.

'Maybe I don't deserve a beautiful, springy body,' Cordelia murmured to Debbie under cover of the clapping.

'Nonsense,' said Debbie, 'you've already got one.'

'Me?' said Cordelia. 'But I'm enormous. I've been at Alba for more than six months now, exercising and dieting and working harder than I've ever done in my life, and I've only lost sixteen pounds. The trouble is, I do so love food.'

They moved over to the sofa in the corner, amiably discussing their favourite delicacies.

'Muffins,' said Cordelia. 'Dripping with unsalted butter.'

'Welsh cakes quickly browned under the grill and absolutely *sodden* with butter.'

They were interrupted by Sybil Gillespie. 'Talking about food isn't very helpful for the other guests. I'm sure your grandmother wouldn't approve, Cordelia. Come along, Rachel. You need your beauty sleep.'

'Poor woman,' said Cordelia, as Rachel smiled

apologetically around the room, and followed Sybil. 'Forty-six and still tied to that frightful mother.'

'She is pretty ghastly isn't she? She was saying this morning that they come here every few months. I wonder why?'

'Who knows? To be pampered, to get away from each other, to escape every day routine and problems . . . ?'

'Problems.' Debbie sighed. She hadn't thought about Isaac for at least two hours. 'He's never going to leave her, Cordelia. And if he *did*, how would I feel? She's a perfectly nice woman, and then there's the two children. I don't know what to do. Maybe I ought to resign, but I don't want to leave my job and I do love my flat, but if I don't get away . . . '

'I know,' said Cordelia. It was the first time for months she'd had the opportunity to talk to someone of her own age (except for Sally who always seemed too brisk and competent for in-depth confidences), and she found herself telling Debbie all about Stewart Ferguson; without expurgating the humiliating Elegance Maternelle incident, either. 'I wouldn't have come here to work for my grandmother if it hadn't been for Stewart; I mean, he was right and I still need to lose weight.'

Debbie briefly stopped thinking about herself and looked at Cordelia; gleaming blonde hair, a golden complexion, clear hazel eyes, long slim legs, enviably tiny ankles and a nice, rounded figure. 'I think you look just great,' she said, 'don't tell me you've been brainwashed into exercising and starving yourself just because of some man . . . '

'It's not only Stewart. I'm at least two stone more than I should be for my height.'

'Who says?'

'Everyone. My grandmother. Magazines . . . everyone.'

'Magazines have a lot to answer for,' said Debbie, 'endlessly projecting an idealised image of the perfect woman. We can't all look like models.'

'You do,' said Cordelia. 'You don't know what it's like

not being able to do up your trousers, always having to wear huge concealing sweaters and flared skirts. And the way people's eyes slide past you . . . '

'Men's eyes, you mean? I suppose you'd rather be whistled at by some sexist workman with a beer belly and bottom cleavage.'

'Yes,' said Cordelia, 'I would.'

They looked at each other and started laughing. 'I don't know what my women's group would say if they could hear us,' Debbie said, 'me and Isaac; you and Stewart. You won't be seeing him again, I hope?'

'Certainly not,' said Cordelia.

*   *   *

The following afternoon Cordelia and Debbie were lying beside the swimming pool, enjoying the last of the day's sun. Debbie was wearing a white bikini and Cordelia had on a black one-piece swimsuit; you couldn't see it, because she was swathed in a towel. She avoided being seen in a swimsuit; the ones cut high looked rude, and the others sliced across her thighs unbecomingly.

'Come on!' Debbie jumped up, dived into the pool and expertly crawled a couple of lengths in the time it took Cordelia to look nervously round to see if anyone was staring at her.

There was nobody, except a distant figure coming down the terrace steps. Cordelia dropped her towel and jumped in. She was actually quite a good swimmer. 'Fat girls float naturally,' her school swimming instructor had once said, and at the next lesson Cordelia had locked herself in the changing room.

'Race you to the other end,' said Debbie, competitively shoving off and disappearing in a cloud of foam.

'Right!' Cordelia, keeping her head down, reached the bar a second after Debbie.

'I'd put the Welsh girl in front by half a length, but I may

118

have to ask for an action replay on this one.' Cordelia spluttered up to see Tod Ballard smiling down at her. 'I'm certainly not going to compete with you two. Positively Olympic.' He sat down on the edge and dipped a toe in the water. 'My God, it's freezing.'

'Lovely once you're in,' said Debbie, clinging to the rail.

'It's seventy-eight,' said Cordelia. Tod looked even more attractive without his spectacles. He could call her naive if he liked, just as long as he smiled at her like that when he said it. 'Come on, Tod.' She hummed happily and flipped over onto her back. *And* he won't be able to see me properly, she thought complacently.

'Cordy! *There* you are!'

Cordelia's reaction was to submerge herself up to the neck, or even further. Stewart Ferguson was standing at the side of the pool. The man she least wanted to meet when she was wearing a swimsuit, and with Tod only a few strokes away, too. 'What on earth are you doing here, Stewart?'

'Came to see you, of course, darling. Ran into Sal yesterday, she gave me your address.' Leaning down, Stewart grabbed one of Cordelia's hands and pulled her out of the water. As she clambered out, rucking her swimsuit unbecomingly, Cordelia wished that Tod Ballard was not watching them.

Debbie, guessing that this must be the sexist pig from the maternity smock débâcle, loyally handed Cordelia a towel.

'Thanks, Debbie.' Cordelia introduced them.

'How do you do.' Debbie took in the cavalry twill trousers, the checked sports jacket and the complacent expression. How could Cordelia have fancied this . . . yuppie?

'How do *you* do,' said Stewart to Debbie's cleavage. 'What is this place, Cordelia? Women in dressing gowns flaunting themselves in the hall, beautiful girls,' he threw Debbie a standard ogle, 'wearing practically nothing in the grounds. Can anyone join?'

119

'If you've got the money to pay for it,' said Cordelia. Had she really ever loved this man?

'Look, you're shivering, you'll catch your death out here.' Stewart gave Cordelia a proprietorial smack on her rump, just as Tod Ballard put on his spectacles. 'Get some clothes on and we'll go for a drink. There's a pub around the corner which looks fairly decent. Why don't you join us, Debbie?'

'No, thank you,' said Debbie, 'I've got an appointment.'

The visit to Mr Patterson, which she had been dreading all day, suddenly seemed quite appealing.

'Another time, then. Cordy, are you listening? I've come all this way to see you.' Cordelia was watching Tod Ballard slope off towards the house. 'That silly nonsense about the dress, I was only joking.'

'Oh, do go away, Stewart, you're so boring.'

*   *   *

Debbie was wondering, on the way back to her room, if she would ever have the courage to send Isaac away like that. Right now she knew that if she opened her door and Isaac was standing there, she would throw herself into his arms and lead him to the bed.

She opened her door. Tod Ballard shut the dressing table drawer and turned to face her.

'Tod.' Debbie reached quickly for her dressing gown. 'Tod?'

'Oh dear,' Tod adjusted his glasses, 'this isn't Room 20, then?'

'Of course it isn't,' said Debbie. 'It's Room 21. What are you looking for in that drawer?'

'Drawer?' said Tod, looking vaguely at the dressing table. 'Oh, that drawer. Well, my Calotherm cloth, actually. To clean my glasses.' He took them off and wiped them on a handkerchief. 'Blurred, you see. I am sorry, Debbie, I must have turned right instead of left. I'm on the other side of the corridor. Room 20.' And he darted out of Debbie's room as swiftly as Tristram Bartholomew had the previous day.

One man in her room with a pathetic excuse was odd enough, two was very strange indeed. Could this be what Sheila Steinberg had in mind when she winked knowingly and spoke of the fun to be had at Alba?

*   *   *

'Haven't we met somewhere before?' said Debbie. There was something familiar about the fading beauty sitting next to her, engrossed in a novel, outside Mr Patterson's door.

'I don't believe so ... ' Sylvia Travers put down her book and smiled at Debbie. She spoke softly, in a voice that carried down the corridor and into the Treatment Rooms.

Of course, thought Debbie, how embarrassing. She's an actress, the put-upon wife in that unfunny family sit-com which disappeared from the screen after two episodes. 'Silly of me,' she said, 'you're a well-known actress, aren't you? I've seen you on television.'

'Sylvia Travers,' Sylvia liked to get her name in before anyone asked; less humiliating, somehow. Twenty-five years in the legitimate theatre and she was only recognised as the actress who had a bit part in a failed sit-com. I know the face, people were always saying to her, but I can't quite put a name to it.

'I know the face ... '

'Quite,' said Sylvia and smiled to show she hadn't taken offence, 'but you can't quite put a name to it. It happens all the time.'

'How irritating for you.'

'Not a bit,' Sylvia lied, 'it's very flattering to be recognised at all.'

'I saw you at the Grand. *Macbeth*. You were awfully

good. I live in Swansea, just down the road from the Grand, actually.'

'How sweet of you to remember,' said Sylvia. Ghastly production, appalling sets, and why hadn't anyone ever wanted her to take her clothes off when she was still young and beautiful? 'Such a ravishing theatre.'

'It must be terribly hard work, acting,' said Debbie. 'I expect you have to get away every so often for a good rest.'

'Yes, indeed.' Sylvia had no intention of telling this pleasant girl that she had done more Resting than she would wish since the sit-com, and was spared the necessity of replying by the sight of Mr Patterson beckoning to Debbie from the doorway. 'I think you're wanted,' she said, 'I have enjoyed our talk.'

'Me, too,' said Debbie. Just wait until I tell Isaac, she thought, as she followed the hypnotherapist into his consulting room. Fancy meeting Sylvia Travers.

*   *   *

She told Mr Patterson about Isaac; she seemed to be telling everyone about Isaac, which made a nice change from never mentioning his name.

'I can't tell you what to do,' Mr Patterson said, leaning back in his chair and studying her closely. 'I can only help you to get things straight in your own mind so you can come to the right decisions.'

Debbie's mind was no straighter after going round and round her problem with Mr Patterson. She talked for three-quarters of an hour and then she burst into tears. 'I don't know what to do, and what's more I keep forgetting things.'

'Understandable when you have so much on your mind.'

'And I can't sleep. I wake up at four every morning and just lie there, waiting for the world to come to an end.'

'Of course, of course.' Mr Patterson passed her a box of Kleenex. 'Now, what I'm going to do, my dear, is give you something which will help you to relax, and get your beauty sleep.'

'Pills?' Debbie abruptly stopped crying. 'Oh, I don't want sleeping pills, I don't believe in taking pills.'

'Quite right,' said Mr Patterson. 'What I have in mind is a natural herbal remedy supplemented by restorative vitamins.' He reached into a box and handed Debbie a small packet. 'Think of it as a good old-fashioned tonic. To be taken in water, three times a day, after meals. That's easy enough to remember, isn't it?'

Debbie took the packets and looked at them dubiously. 'Extras?'

'I beg your pardon?' said Mr Patterson sharply.

'Cordelia told me to ask for them.'

'Ah yes, Cordelia.' He looked surreptitiously at his watch; five minutes over the hour and Miss Travers would be waiting. He stood up. 'Pop that one into a glass of water after supper, and I'll ask Sister Monica to organise your daily supply.' He shepherded Debbie towards the door. 'Make an appointment if ever you feel the need for another little talk.'

Debbie took the herbal infusion after supper and slept through until six. But that could, of course, just be exhaustion after all the unaccustomed physical exercise. She sipped another after breakfast and there were two more packets in the small box Sister Monica had given her.

There was a buoyant spring in her step as she made her way to the bicycle shed, after lunch. She and Cordelia were planning to ride around the Alba estate, and Debbie felt full of energy. She had really enjoyed the half hour in the Sauna this morning, Lucy had given her a lovely massage and she had actually gone to sleep in the Rest Room. Nothing in her life had changed for the better since yesterday. Why then, Debbie asked herself, do I suddenly feel all right? Something must be wrong.

CHAPTER
ELEVEN

Cordelia didn't like Sister Monica because Sister Monica so obviously didn't like her. 'I'm afraid Cordelia doesn't understand the way we like to do things at Alba, Madame.' Monica's starched skirts would crackle with self-importance and her plain scrubbed face would shine with venom as she pointed out barely legible Appointment for Today cards or a bed not properly hospital cornered. 'I'll see to it myself in future.'

Alba was Sister Monica's life. It had given her everything her parents had never had in Oakley Terrace, Huddersfield, that she had certainly never had in the days when she emptied bed pans at Huddersfield General. And she was a confidante of Madame Cordoba, a real lady even if she was a bit on the mean side. Monica had no intention of letting the hoity-toity granddaughter take it all away from her.

She was looking for Cordelia this morning, because Madame had asked to see them both in her study. 'I'd like a word with you, Monica.'

'Of course,' Monica had said eagerly, 'I'll pop along now.'

'And ask Cordelia if she could join us, will you?'

'Will that be necessary, Madame?' But Isabella had already put down the phone.

She found Cordelia gossiping on the telephone in the front office. She always seemed to be chatting on the phone or with the guests instead of getting on with her work. Monica thought she might mention that to Madame after the meeting.

Sally had phoned Cordelia to sound her out about Stewart's visit to Alba. 'Is it true you refused even to have a drink with him, after he came all that way?'

'Yes, it is.'

There was a slight sigh at the other end of the phone which could have been irritation or relief. 'Stewart was madly impressed by Alba and all the acres. Said it was full of naked men and women eyeing each other speculatively.'

'Wondering if the person sitting next to them had been given a larger portion of kiwi fruit than they had, I expect,' Cordelia said.

'Oh, come on,' said Sally, 'everyone knows those health farms are a positive hotbed of sexual activity. There was a piece in the colour supplement last week . . . '

'If there's any heavy breathing going on here, I certainly haven't heard it,' said Cordelia. 'Everyone's far too under-nourished and worn out to do anything more passionate than flop into bed with *The Bill*.' She noticed Sister Monica waving crossly from the other side of the counter. 'Got to go now, Sal . . . '

'It's over, then, you and Stewart?'

'Yes, of course it is, I told you,' said Cordelia, putting down the phone.

'Sit down, sit down,' Isabella said, as Cordelia and Monica entered the study. She waved a hand towards the hard *chaise longue*, and they perched uncomfortably while she paced. 'I'm worried about Mary Lawson . . . '

'I've spoken to her about the lavender oil in Aroma-therapy,' Monica said. 'She won't forget that again in a hurry.'

'I don't think that's fair,' Cordelia said. 'Mary Lawson works so hard and the clients love her.'

'I'm not talking about lavender oil and I am all too aware that Alba clients value Mary's services,' said Isabella, irritated by both of them. 'The trouble is she's going to pieces; it's that husband of hers, giving extra-curricular services again. I intend to put a stop to it.'

'It's time you spoke to Matt Lawson, anyway,' said Sister Monica, 'he's a law unto himself.'

'And the best masseur in the business,' said Isabella. 'We can't afford to alienate him and we certainly can't afford to lose Mary. We can, however, dispense with a promiscuous client.'

'How can I help?' said Monica. 'Shall I have a word with Matt?'

'Certainly not,' said Isabella. 'I'd like you both to keep your wits about you, and if you chance to overhear who is receiving his attentions, perhaps you would let me know.'

'Listen in to the gossip, you mean?' said Monica.

Isabella barely nodded her head.

'But, except for poor Mary, is it so awful?' said Cordelia. 'There was an article in the colour supplement . . . '

'A lot of rubbish,' said Isabella. 'We do not countenance that sort of behaviour at the Alba Health Manor.'

*   *   *

In the room above Isabella's study, Matt Lawson and Diane Renfrew were lying, thigh to thigh, in Diane's bed, her head on his shoulder. 'You've got lovely hands, Matt.' Diane turned Matt's hand and gently kissed the palm. 'Not like Derek's, all hard and knobbly from messing about with cement and plaster.'

'And I know what to do with them, don't I?' Matt knocked a Silk Cut out of the pack on the bedside table with his free hand and lit it with a monogrammed Dunhill lighter (present from a grateful client, he didn't remember which one). 'Right, Di?'

'Right.' Diane giggled because that was what Matt expected. Actually, she wished he was rather more romantic. It's true you couldn't fault him on the foreplay, but the sex bit was always, well, a bit of a let-down really. There was hardly time for a twitch and a moan before he was reaching for his cigarettes and blowing smoke all over her.

126

Funny, that; when Jeff Bridges had lit up after making love to Michelle Pfeiffer at the Luton Cannon the other week it had looked dead sexy. Diane coughed reproachfully and slipped out of bed, smoothing down her satin nightie, hand-made, with the lace bodice cleverly cut to support her breasts.

'Where are you off to, then?'

'To the bathroom, of course.' Diane turned and gave Matt one of her provocative looks, eyes half closed, the slightest suggestion of a smoulder; a waste of time since he was stroking the dark curly hair on his chest admiringly. 'Sheila will be back soon.'

'Not if she's having a Cellutron treatment,' Matt looked at his watch (another grateful client). 'She'll be at least another half an hour. Poor old Sheil, she could certainly do with some help in that area.'

'And how do you know, may I ask?'

'I used to be her masseur, remember? Hard to believe she's two years younger than you, Di.'

Diane slipped back into bed and snuggled close; it wasn't often Matt paid her a compliment like that. 'One year and eight months, actually,' she said. 'Another couple of years and she'll be forty. You wouldn't think it, the way she goes on.'

Matt didn't want to hear about how Sheila went on, but thought he'd better look interested; payment for favours received et cetera, not to mention favours to come. He raised an enquiring eyebrow, and Diane snuggled closer.

'We'd gone to the Taj Mahal for an Indian; Sheila, Derek, Gerald — that's her husband — and me. And she made a real play for Derek, couldn't keep her hands off him.' Diane's hand slipped slowly down Matt's body. 'Know what I mean?'

'I get the idea,' Matt said. He took her hand, placed it firmly on his chest and gave it a perfunctory pat; what did she think he was, bloody Rambo?

'Gerald kept ordering wine. "Allow me, my pleasure,"

he said, putting on airs just because he's a dentist. "I'm sure the ladies would enjoy a glass of white wine." Derek stuck with the lager, of course, pints of the stuff; and by the end of the meal it was, "Let's finish the party at our house. Come on, Sheil, and you, too, Gerry. We've got plenty more bottles waiting to be opened at home." And then, what do you think she did?'

'Tell me,' said Matt, knowing Diane was going to, anyway.

'Well, Derek put on the Ella tape, dead sexy; "Love for Sale", we always used to call it Our Song, and he was dancing to it with her. There she was, swaying around *my* lounge, wrapped around *my* husband, with her head on his shoulder, if you please.'

'You'd all knocked back a few, I expect,' said Matt philosophically. 'What about you and the dentist? Bit of suburban wife-swapping, was it?'

Diane shuddered. 'Certainly not. He's a right nerd, I can tell you. No wonder Sheil isn't trustworthy where men are concerned. We were dancing, not like them, all very proper, and I looked up at him and kind of smiled, and he bent down and murmured something in my ear. I thought he was going to say something nice about my perfume, Rive Gauche it was, St Laurent, really expensive. But what he murmured was, "Those central incisors of yours are in a bad state, Diane. Why don't you make an appointment and let me cap them for you?" The nerve!'

'Doesn't sound a ball of fun,' said Matt, looking at his watch again. 'I'll have to be off in a mo, Di.'

'Let me finish,' said Diane. 'You ain't heard nothing yet, as they say. I couldn't go on dancing with that Gerald, not after what he'd said about my teeth, so I said, "Let's go and make some coffee, it looks as though *some* people could do with it," and when we came back they were sitting on the sofa, *my* sofa, kissing each other like there was no tomorrow. They sprang apart when we came in with the Nescafé, all right, but I heard them whispering. "Next

128

Thursday, then," Derek was saying, and she was looking all soppy. And . . . ' Diane jabbed a sharply manicured nail into Matt's chest, which made him flinch, ' . . . and don't tell me that it was just a coincidence that Derek was held up late on the Harrow job the following Thursday. Traffic jam on the Wealdstone Bridge, he said it was. Made sense to hang on at the site until the rush-hour was over, he said.'

Matt stubbed out his cigarette, and got out of bed. 'You didn't have it out with her, then?'

'Couldn't, could I?' said Diane. 'Not with her business being just down the road from my gift shop. Not with us being friends for so long . . . '

Matt stepped nimbly into his scarlet briefs, 'And what were you two old friends up to in The Barley Mow the other night, then? I heard you nearly got your marching orders from Sister Monica.'

Diane sat up in bed and scowled, which, Matt noted unkindly, accentuated the carefully pancaked wrinkles around her mouth. 'I can't think why Madame Cordoba didn't deal with the matter herself. I know she had a word with Tristram and Erica Gerard. Leaving it to that *minion* to tick us off. You can't stay here if you can't be trusted, she said, as if it's any of her business, she's only a paid nurse, after all.'

'She can do no wrong in old Bella's eyes.' Matt pulled on his jeans. 'I wonder why?' He hadn't particularly relished shopping Sexy Sheila and Desperate Diane, but when you came right down to it, you had to look after numero uno, although Madame hadn't seemed particularly grateful for the info.

'The sun may be shining out of her you-know-what, but we've been coming here for years, and paying through the nose for the privilege. I bet it was that bitch Cordelia who told on us. And Sheila was ever so upset, she had to take two of her infusions.'

Matt fastened the buckle on his belt. Satisfying that he'd had it at least ten years without having to let out a single notch. He looked over at Diane, sitting up in bed. She'd stopped scowling and had come over all vulnerable again. He picked up his sweater, and went towards the door. 'Well, I've got to be off now, Di. My first client's due in five minutes.'

'And you're doing me again at eleven.' Diane giggled and jumping out of bed, came up behind him and wound her arms around his chest. 'You do love me, Matt, don't you?'

'Course.' It was lucky she couldn't see him throwing his eyes about. Women! Do you love me, Matt? That's what they all wanted to know.

*   *   *

'Have you been having a rest, then?' Sheila and Diane both looked at Diane's bed which had a hastily drawn up, rumpled look about it.

'That's right,' said Diane, swiftly smoothing and tucking. 'I felt a bit whacked after Movement to Music. Carolyn's such a slave driver.'

'And you've been smoking.' Sheila sniffed and grimaced. 'You know I can't stand smoking in the bedroom, Diane.'

'Sorry,' said Diane. '*Sorry.*' There were times when she wished she wasn't sharing a room with Sheila, but she couldn't afford to come to Alba twice a year by herself. The way things were between her and Derek, she needed Alba; needed Matt Lawson, if the truth be told. And there was always at least one gentleman guest looking for a bit of fun. As a matter of fact, she'd been eyeing Tod Ballard with more than a little interest, these last few days.

'By the way,' said Sheila, 'I was meaning to tell you. I saw Tod Ballard coming up from the swimming pool, yesterday . . . ' Diane jumped. Had Sheila suddenly turned into a mind-reader? ' . . . I was just glancing out of the corridor window on my way back from Aromatherapy, and there he was. He looked really miserable. You know what I think?'

'That he's a bit of all right?'

'Well, yes, as a matter of fact, but what I was actually thinking is that he fancies Madame C.'s granddaughter.'

'Never. He's much too attractive.'

'I was watching him, watching her. They were down at the swimming pool with Debbie, the girl with boyfriend trouble. Then this young man roared up the drive in a sports car, disappeared inside the house, came out again and made a beeline for Cordelia at the pool. He was very familiar with her. You should have seen the look on Tod Ballard's face.'

'You couldn't have seen much from that window,' said Diane sharply.

'It was the way he walked away from them, kind of defeated looking. And then he came in the door, right where I was standing. "Don't worry," I said, "it may never happen."'

'And what did he say?'

'Nothing. I don't think he even heard. Too taken up with Cordelia and the guy in the sports car, I expect.'

'And she was the one who split on us. She was with Tod Ballard that night at The Barley Mow.'

'That's right.' Sheila gave Diane a complicit nudge. 'We owe her one, Diane.'

*   *   *

Diane allowed herself an ironic smile as she came out of the Massage Room, glowing pleasurably from Matt's Special Services as he put it, straight into the arms of Matt's wife.

'I hope you enjoyed your massage, Mrs Renfrew?' Mary said, making a great fuss of wrapping Diane in warm towels. 'I know you're one of Matt's favourite clients.'

Diane gave Mary a sharp look, but Mary's anxious blue eyes appeared to be focused on her towel work.

'It was very nice, thank you,' Diane said and, as a penance for all the pleasure she had received from Mary's

131

husband that morning, forced herself to listen sympathetically to tales of the Lawson children. Young Sam, it seemed, was a real little athlete, but always in trouble at school, a bit of a handful. 'Like his father,' Mary said, with a sideways look. 'Little Nicola is ever so good, but being dyslexic she needs a lot of help with her homework, and what with me working all day at Alba, and having to get Matt his dinner every evening, I can't always find the time to do as much as I should for her.'

'Can't he get his own dinner?' said Diane. 'After all, you're both working.'

'Oh, no. I couldn't ask Matt to *cook*.'

Diane stopped feeling guilty. Really, some women did ask for it.

*   *   *

'Any room for little me?' Diane was pleased to see that the only spare seat left in the Dining Room was next to Tod Ballard, sharing a table with Debbie and Adam Shepherd, who had been so snooty about joining them at The Barley Mow. Sheila, with her cellulite problem, was confined to yogurt, wheatgerm and a sliver of kiwi fruit in the Light Diet room. Diane was pleased about that, too.

Tod Ballard shifted his chair. 'And what healthful activities have you been up to, this morning?'

'Oh, just a spot of massage, a spell in the Steam Cabinet, and a nice lie-down,' said Diane. She looked at her plate disapprovingly. 'I say, this lettuce is as limp as my old man's . . . ' she put a hand over her mouth and twinkled boldly at Tod and Adam, who did not twinkle back. 'Oh, pardon me. And just look at these tomatoes, covered in black spots.'

'After starving in the Light Diet Room, it's ambrosia,' said Debbie, who had insisted on coming into the Dining Room for lunch.

'I shall complain to Miss Meadows,' said Diane. 'I've

132

been coming here for years and the fruit and veg has always been in tiptop condition.' She turned to Tod. 'Did you enjoy your swim yesterday? The pool's lovely, isn't it?'

'Very pleasant.'

'What about Cordelia and her young man, then?'

'What about them?' said Tod.

'The boyfriend's a real good-looker,' Diane said. 'They've been going out for ages, crazy about each other, I hear.'

Debbie's fork paused half-way to her mouth. 'That's been over for ages.'

'Not according to Sheila.' Diane gave Tod a playful nudge. 'She said they'd really got the hots for each other.'

'I wouldn't put it as crudely as that,' said Tod, coldly.

'Don't mind me, love, I always believe in saying what I mean. Are you going to be at the pool this afternoon? I rather fancy a swim, myself.'

'I've got a bit of writing to do,' said Tod, deciding to do a bit of writing.

'How about a game of tennis later? Fresh air would do those clever brain cells of yours a world of good.'

'I never play tennis,' said Tod untruthfully.

'How about you, then?' Diane turned to where Adam Shepherd had been sitting, before he had prudently left the table.

'Oh, he's gone. How about you, Debbie?'

'I promised to go for a bike ride with Cordelia,' said Debbie.

*   *   *

'That's three laps up the drive and back.' Debbie's knees were pink and tingling uncomfortably with the effort and the sun. 'Why am I putting myself through all this misery?'

Cordelia slowed down to let Debbie catch her up. 'Because you want to feel better and live longer?'

'I'm feeling better already. Must be the healthy regime.

Or the Extras.'

Cordelia jumped off her bike and pushed it through the main gate. 'Let's go and have a drink at The Barley Mow.'

'A drink?' said Debbie. 'What would your grandmother say to that?'

'Not a real drink, Deb. If I wanted to go on a binge I wouldn't choose The Barley Mow, it's littered with Alba informants. An orange juice, a mineral water, anything, I'm parched.'

'Double gins, is it?' said the barman. 'That's what you truants usually order, or a stiff Scotch.'

'Double apple juice for me,' said Debbie.

'And an orange juice for me,' said Cordelia. 'We're not truants, Mick, just thirsty. Oh, my God, Debbie, don't look to your right.'

Debbie instantly looked to her right. 'Tristram Bartholomew eating a sandwich and Erica Gerard drinking something colourless.'

'Don't tell me about it,' said Cordelia. 'I haven't seen them, I don't want to know. Sometimes I really wish I wasn't working in a place where it's a sin to eat a sandwich. My grandmother found two Yorkie bars in my drawer the other day. The way she went on, you'd have thought I was stockpiling Semtex for the IRA.'

'That's odd, it happened to me, too.'

'What? Grandmother riffling through your bottom drawer?'

'No, not your grandmother. Tristram Bartholomew was lurking around my desk yesterday morning, and Tod Ballard was searching my chest of drawers in the evening.'

'What on earth were they doing?'

'They both had some idiotic excuse about mistaking their room numbers. Tristram is next door to me, and Tod is across the passage.'

'What would Isaac say?' Cordelia was making a joke, and a pretty lame one. She didn't like the idea of Tod in somebody else's bedroom. Of course, Debbie was in Room

134

21, the room Mr Pullen had so suddenly vacated. 'You know what I think, Debbie? There's something odd about that room.'

'As long as Tristram and Tod keep out of it. By the way, Cordelia, how do you feel about him?'

'Tristram? Crazy for him.'

'Tod.' Debbie was wondering whether it was wise to pass on Diane Renfrew's version of the swimming pool incident.

'Oh, he seems nice enough.' Cordelia didn't want to tell anyone how she felt about Tod. It was beginning to matter too much. 'Why?'

'Just wondered.' Diane's malicious gossip had done no harm, then.

They were putting their bikes back into the shed when Debbie said, 'Did you hear about Diane Renfrew and Matt?'

'No . . . '

'Mary Lawson was in tears this morning, in Steam Cabinets, after Diane had been in. Everyone was talking. Mrs Gillespie said, "That man should be shot," and Mrs Fellowes said, "Ssh, Mary will hear you," and Mrs Gillespie said, "Carrying on with that common woman," and Mrs Fellowes said, "Please, Mrs Gillespie, keep your voice down," and when Mary left the room, I said, "What man? What common woman?" And it seems that Macho Matt provides Mrs Renfrew with more than massage.'

'How could she? He's so awful.'

Debbie slotted her bike into the rack. 'Not as awful as Derek Renfrew, I gather. Diane was telling me about her marriage yesterday. It's terribly sad. They're absolutely rolling in money . . . '

'That doesn't sound too heartbreaking.'

'Derek made a mint in the property boom in the 'seventies, they've got this lovely house in Harpenden, an Executive Home Diane said it was, with three bedrooms and a nice little garden with a sandpit corner, and they

135

can't have children.'

'Did they want them?'

'Diane did, desperately. She'd even stuck up the Miss Piggy transfers in the spare room. And she had to go through all sorts of unpleasant tests. I must say, she told me rather more gynaecological details than I wished to hear, and in the end it turned out to be Derek who had the problem. She got him to the clinic eventually, and they told him to put a bowl of iced water beside the bed, and immerse what Diane called his wedding tackle before they did it. Apparently he'd been overheating.'

'Makes him sound like a used car. Did it work, the iced water?'

'Didn't do much for their sex life, I gather. Diane found the whole performance hilarious. So now he plays around and so does she. "What's sauce for the goose is sauce for the gander," she said. Isn't it amazing, Cordelia, the intimate things people tell you?'

CHAPTER
TWELVE

Sheila had gone off to see that hypnotherapist again, and Diane thought she might stroll down into the village and do a bit of shopping. She was right out of cleansing milk, and there was that new, blue mascara she'd read about in *Vogue* while she was waiting for her massage. Diane had withdrawal symptoms if she went for more than two days without entering a shop.

She decided to take the short cut across the back yard, through the tradesmen's entrance, past the walled garden and up to the village, but she had only completed the first lap when Cordelia spotted her from the kitchen window and waved.

Cordelia was far too busy to gossip with Diane Renfrew, but she had the idea that if she spoke frankly to her, and warned her off Matt, she wouldn't have to mention the matter to her grandmother. 'Lovely day, Mrs Renfrew.'

'So-so,' said Diane, looking up at a grey, cloudy sky. 'I was just going to the village to do some shopping.'

'I'll walk with you a little way, if I may?'

'Please yourself,' said Diane.

They walked in silence for a couple of minutes before Cordelia said, 'Mary Lawson isn't very happy, you know.'

'Oh,' Diane said unhelpfully.

'It's Matt, you see ... ' Cordelia felt a blush begin around her collarbone. God, she was mismanaging this. 'She thinks he's having an affair, with one of the clients.'

'Really?' Diane could see where this conversation was leading and she suddenly had a picture in her mind of

Sheila, traitorously whispering and giggling with Derek on her sofa. 'Well, don't look at me, dear.'

'I wasn't,' said Cordelia untruthfully.

'I'd have a word with my room-mate, if I was you,' Diane said. 'Now, if you'll excuse me.'

'Of course,' said Cordelia, 'I'm terribly sorry. Well, I'd better get back ... '

Diane went on her way, passing the walled kitchen garden, and noticed that the wooden door was wide open. An ideal opportunity to check the fruit at source, since Alba's brochure boasted, 'Much of the produce served in our Dining Room comes from our own well-stocked kitchen garden.' She slipped through the door and looked around.

Not many fruit trees, but plenty of vegetables and herbs. Diane wandered along the raised beds, nodding approvingly at the neat lines of lettuces, spinach, cabbages and waving fronds which she guessed were carrots. Next to the herb bed were greenhouses full of tomato plants. They all looked healthy enough, not speckled like the ones served up for lunch. Behind the greenhouses she saw two vast plastic bell-tent things, almost the size of aircraft hangars. Diane peered through the plastic, but there was so much condensation all she could see were rows and rows of Gro-bags.

In the village she spotted Rosemary Meadows, crossing the street, and hurried to catch up with her. 'There you are, Miss Meadows. I want a word with you.'

'A word with me?' Rosemary had just done a satisfactory deal with Fred Pearson, Wholesale Greengrocer, which involved Fred pocketing a sizeable cheque for First Quality fruit and veg, supplying Alba with Rejects ('It's all good stuff, Miss Meadows, just as nutritious as my First Quality and you'll be peeling most of it, anyway, I expect') and splitting the difference two ways. She looked at Diane Renfrew with distaste. 'I'm afraid I have to get back to Alba, now.'

Diane stepped swiftly between Rosemary and her

Renault. 'What I have to say won't take more than a minute. That fruit you served at lunch today was a disgrace, covered in bruises and blemishes.'

'Organic. You'll find no alar on my apples, not a trace of tecnazine on my potatoes. You must expect to sacrifice appearance for good, wholesome food untouched by pesticides. Now, if you'll excuse me.' She got firmly into her car.

Diane was left standing at the kerb, biting her lip in frustration. Crossly, she hitched up her shoulder bag, and went into the chemist.

It was an excellent shop and she savoured the stock with an admiring professional eye. She instantly located her favourite cleansing milk, found the new blue mascara, bought a bottle of something expensive that promised to erase wrinkles, and a pot of cream which assured her it would firm up sagging contours; which it had better do since it cost about as much as a Harley Street face-lift. She was almost restored to her normal good humour as she left the chemist, and crossed the road to Fred Pearson, Wholesale Greengrocer.

'Mr Pearson?'

'That's me.'

'I'll have a pound of apples, please. Organic.'

'Best Cox's. Over or under the pound?'

'Under, please. And they are organic? No alure, or anything like that on them?'

Fred replaced the apples on his display and scowled. 'Don't waste my time, lady. We don't go in for any of that organic muck here.'

*   *   *

'I'm not going to stand for it, I shall ask to see Madame Cordoba, I shall demand an explanation of the way I was treated this afternoon. I shall tell her about Rosemary Meadows.'

Diane and Sheila were sitting on Sheila's bed, discussing Diane's visit to the village. At least, Diane was discussing and Sheila was brooding about her session with Mr Patterson.

'He took me right through my marriage, today, Diane. I hadn't realised before. It's a sham, an empty shell.'

'On second thoughts, perhaps I'll keep my own counsel. You never know when a bit of knowledge might come in handy.'

'You never know what's going on in your own life, do you, until you really think about it?'

'I think I'll put on my pink velvet track suit for dinner. The one I got at Dickins & Jones.' Diane went towards the wardrobe. 'Come on, Sheil, or we'll be late.'

'I'm not coming, I don't want any dinner.'

'You don't want to *eat*? You're not crying, are you?'

'I've never talked to anyone about Gerald before.'

'Oh, you don't want to think about Gerald. Get on with living, that's my motto. Come on, now.'

Sheila slipped between the sheets. 'I'm not coming. Leave me alone.'

'Suit yourself.' Diane went into the bathroom, unpacked her purchases and carefully applied the cleansing milk, the wonder creams and the new mascara. She returned to the bedroom, put on the pink track suit and admired herself in the wardrobe mirror. 'How do I look?' Sheila went on looking moony. Diane picked up her quilted pochette and had a final self-appraisal in the mirror.

'Before you go, Diane,' Sheila looked wanly over the sheets, 'pass me my happy herbals, and I think I'll have a little drop of sherry.'

'You certainly look as though you could do with something to cheer you up. Go easy on the sherry, Sheil.'

Sheila reached for the glass. 'There's not enough here to inebriate a flea.'

Diane left the room, muttering to herself. Really, some people. She'd come in positively laden with gossip, and all

140

Sheila Steinberg could do was whinge on about life with a capital L. So, she and Gerald didn't have the perfect marriage. So, what's new?

By the time she reached the Dining Room, Diane had a merry social smile stitched in place. Laugh and the world laughs with you, was her motto. Looking around the room, she wondered which table to enliven with her presence this evening. 'Ah, Mr Shepherd. Any room for little me?'

*   *   *

Adam Shepherd sought sanctuary in the Drawing Room after dinner. The evening talk was billed on the notice-board as The Preparation, Planting and After Care of Shrubs, Trees and Conifers. He rightly suspected that Mrs Renfrew was not a keen gardener, and would not willingly follow him into any room where she was unable to talk.

'Rhododendrons are happiest in an acid soil, and welcome frequent top-dresses of peat, leaf-mould or bracken . . . ' Adam settled into the armchair and prepared for a pleasant doze. It was almost as soporific as a board meeting.

Diane, cheated of her prey, stalked the corridors in search of a chat. She had suggested a game of bridge to Adam Shepherd and her other table companions, but none of them had seemed keen. At the notice-board she came upon Tristram Bartholomew putting his name down for Scrabble.

'I wouldn't say no to a game of Scrabble, Tristram,' she said, 'though I don't suppose I'd stand a chance with a wordsmith like you.'

'Did I tick the Scrabble box?' said Tristram, crossing it out. 'I meant to put myself down for golf.'

'Now, there you've got me,' said Diane. 'I'm afraid I've never had time for golf in my line of business. I'm in Fancy Goods, you see. A little gift shop. So, if ever you want a very special present for your girl friend, you'll know where to come.'

'How very kind.' Tristram looked at his watch. A Cartier, Diane couldn't help noticing, only it was hard to tell these days, the copies being so good. She'd ordered half a dozen for The Gift Box, the copies, of course, but still pricey.

'Goodness,' said Tristram, 'is that the time? There's an awfully interesting talk on shrubs in the Drawing Room.'

Diane looked up the staircase. Lady Drummond was sauntering down, obviously in no hurry to go anywhere. Diane quickly fingered her ears. The diamanté earrings, thank goodness. No chance of Lady D. delivering a Greenpeace lecture about *them*. 'Oh, Lady Drummond,' she said, 'I was thinking of having a honey and lemon in the Small Drawing Room. Would you care to join me?'

'What a nice idea.' Betty Drummond thought that if there was one thing worse than a glass of honey and lemon, it was drinking it in the company of Mrs Renfrew. She drifted up to the notice-board and took a swift look at Coming Events. 'Alas, I am on my way to the Drawing Room. Shrubberies, so rewarding.'

'I think I'll tag along,' said Diane.

'Rhododendrons make a dense, compact root ball and can therefore be planted any time between September and June . . . '

Diane nodded off. It was nine thirty when she woke to the discreet sound of clapping, and decided she had better go and see how Sheila was getting on. Besides, Lady Drummond and Mrs Fellowes had begun an amiable argument about whether a philadelphus or a mahonia felt more at ease on a sunny bank, old Mrs Gillespie was telling everyone that they ought to have seen her dwarf Russian almonds this spring, they were a positive picture, and even Diane was aware that nobody would be interested in how she planted geraniums and lobelia in her patio pots.

Sheila was fast asleep when Diane got back to their

142

room. She tiptoed about, slipping out of her track suit, cleansing her skin and carefully patting in Replenishing Night Creme. Sheila was usually such a light sleeper, complaining if she put on the light, making a scene if she got up to go to the loo, and Diane had completed her nightly routine without a whimper from the other bed. She looked across and saw that Sheila was gobbling for air, like a goldfish about to turn up its toes.

'Sheil? . . . Sheila?' Diane got out of bed again, went over and tapped Sheila's shoulder. 'It's me. Diane.'

When Sheila failed to react to a firm shake, Diane darted over to the desk and fumbled for the Information for Alba Guests leaflet tucked into the blotter. 'A fully trained nurse is on duty twenty-four hours a day; guests should not hesitate to call on their help at any time, no matter how trivial the problem might appear to be.'

Diane picked up the telephone, and dialled Reception. It was the final straw in a perfectly bloody day, and she intended standing no nonsense. 'I want a fully trained nurse now. Room 43. Mrs Steinberg's passed out.'

She had barely replaced the telephone when Sister Monica swept in, closely followed by Madame Cordoba. Talk about service; one brief phone call and you got the head nurse and the owner of the place.

Sister Monica pushed Diane aside, made a beeline for Sheila's bed, and lifted her into a sitting position. 'Upsadaisy, Mrs Steinberg.'

Sheila yawned and smiled pleasantly at them all. 'Why, Sister Monica, Madame Cordoba, whatever's going on?'

Diane wanted to kill her. 'You passed out, Sheila, that's what's going on.'

Isabella walked swiftly to the bedside table, sniffed the glasses, and held up one of them. 'Alcohol.'

'Just one tiny sherry,' said Sheila.

'When you are on a reducing diet, that is one too many,' said Isabella, 'which is why we request our guests to abstain from alcohol during their stay here.'

143

Sister Monica looked around for a bottle to confiscate.

Much as it went against the grain after the afternoon's aggravation, Diane felt the need to apologise for making an unnecessary fuss. 'I am sorry to have bothered you, Madame, but I was so worried.'

'No bother at all. You behaved in a most responsible manner, Mrs Renfrew.'

Diane gazed thoughtfully at the door as it closed on Isabella and Monica. What exactly was the expression on Madame Cordoba's face as she made that surprisingly cordial exit speech? Gratitude? Not quite. Relief. That's what it was.

She got back into bed. 'You know what I think, Sheil? I think you had those two really worried.'

'Oh, do turn out the light, Diane,' said Sheila. 'You're keeping me awake.'

CHAPTER
THIRTEEN

Rachel Gillespie had a secret vice. Once a week, when she went into Hindhead to buy the vegetables, she dived down a narrow back street where a small, grubby Indian shop sold newspapers, sweets, cigarettes, reels of cotton, unrecognisable lumps of frozen meat in plastic bags, and, on the third shelf on the right, thin volumes with such titles as *The End of the Rainbow* and *Midnight Serenade*. Rachel was unable to resist the lure of seriously trashy paperbacks.

She kept her collection where Erica Gerard stored her vodka, in the darkest corner at the back of the wardrobe, and when mother was asleep she took them out and had a good read.

Rachel was a romantic, although she had never had a proper romantic attachment. Just after daddy passed away, she had been friendly with Mr Moffat, a sidesman at her local church, but mother hadn't approved. 'He's twice your age, dear, and he works in Cullen's.' Rachel supposed that her mother's judgement was probably right. In any case, Mr Moffat would have been hard put to it to live up to dashing young Dr Carruthers who wooed Melanie in *The End of the Rainbow*, or devil-may-care Simon Brown, the lean-jawed hero of *Midnight Serenade*, who drove his Porsche recklessly through the night to claim Susan from the arms of an industrialist.

Like all true collectors, Rachel was discriminating. A Mills & Boon was too glossy. The packaging of a Barbara Cartland had a professional air about it she didn't fancy. But the sight of a cheap flimsy paperback with dark smudgy print seeping into blotched porous paper had her reaching excitedly for her purse.

She had been thrilled by such a sighting only yesterday. Mother had run out of her Crabtree & Evelyn, and Rachel was just popping into the local chemist for further supplies, when she spotted a small bookshop on the other side of the street. It was more of a bric-a-brac shop, really. A few oddly shaped animals made out of shells, one or two badly knitted jumpers in unbecoming colours, piles of dusty magazines and, at the back of the window, a pink plastic latticed bin full of paperbacks.

Rachel was in the shop in a trice, rummaging in the bin as keenly as anyone seeking the Big Prize in a bran tub. Some of them were old favourites from her collection, but she was delighted to find a slightly dogeared copy of *Cupid's Messenger* by Dorothy Witney, one of her favourite authors. She was paying for it at the till when she chanced to see Mr Bartholomew riffling through a pile of magazines with an enthusiasm she sympathised with and understood. She wondered if he, too, had made a 'find' and was just about to go over and ask him, when she thought better of it. He would be bound to notice *Cupid's Messenger* and Rachel felt sure Dorothy Witney would not be Mr Bartholomew's cup of tea. She could just imagine him holding it up and making one of his unkind, witty remarks about her taste in fiction. She scuttled out of the shop while he was still too absorbed in his magazines to notice her.

Mother had gone to bed early, and Rachel waited until her snoring achieved the raucous rhythm which signalled she was out for the count, before tiptoeing along to the sitting room, *Cupid's Messenger* concealed in her dressing gown pocket.

The first floor sitting room was an annexe off the corridor, and Rachel had just settled into a deep armchair, and Maryanne, the sweet-natured heroine, had fallen, for the first electrifying time, under the dark brooding gaze of the aloofly handsome Adrian Dobson, when she heard footsteps and voices coming along the corridor.

She slipped *Cupid's Messenger* down the inside of the chair, kept as still as a mouse, and experienced the guilty thrill of an eavesdropper as she heard Sister Monica saying, 'I hope to God we get there in time.' And another voice, which Rachel recognised as Madame Cordoba's. 'I don't want a repeat of last Friday.' 'Oh, I wouldn't worry about that,' Sister had replied, 'Mrs Steinberg isn't a drinker.'

They had spent only a few minutes in Mrs Steinberg's room, and Rachel had peeped around the back of the armchair as they emerged, Sister carrying two dirty glasses. Madame had thanked Mrs Renfrew most graciously for calling her.

And, as the footsteps receded along the corridor, she heard Madame Cordoba say, 'Oh, by the way Monica, the inquest is on Friday.'

Rachel had closed her book, she would finish it tomorrow. She had a pretty shrewd idea that Maryanne and Phillip were going to discover that they were made for each other, but half the fun of reading was spinning out the suspense. She drifted silently back to the bedroom, and lay in bed for some time unable to sleep. Her wrist was aching, she must have sprained it at Yoga, and the heavy snoring from the next bed wasn't exactly soothing.

An inquest? How tragic, somebody in the village must have died. Rachel reached for a glass of water and a Disprin, quietly, so as not to disturb mother. And how typical of Madame to be so concerned for her guests and still find the time to take an interest in local affairs.

When she ran into Mrs Renfrew, on the way down to breakfast, and asked about her friend's health, Mrs Renfrew was not very sympathetic. 'Just a stomach upset,' she said, 'a lot of fuss about nothing.'

*　　　*　　　*

'How does my hair look, Rachel?' Sybil Gillespie sat at the

dressing table mirror, complacently tweaking a stray grey curl into place. 'I think it needs a touch more Silver Ash. Make an appointment with Giovanni for me, will you? I'll be able to fit it in this afternoon between Hydrotherapy and Lip Waxing.'

'Are you sure that won't be too much for you, mother?'

'I'm not in my grave yet.' Sybil sighted her daughter's reflection in the mirror. 'You could do with a touch of rouge, you're looking very peaky today.'

'My wrist,' said Rachel, 'it's a bit painful.' She looked admiringly at the youthfully erect figure at the dressing table. Nobody would guess that mother was in her seventies, she was always full of life, and so particular; not like some of her bridge circle who had odd patches of stray powder on their cheeks, slipped lipstick and, quite frankly, looked as though they could do with a good bath.

Mother always insisted on taking a bath every day; not too hot because it was bad for her veins and not too cold in case it set off her arthritis, and Rachel had to remember to sprinkle in one tablespoon of Crabtree & Evelyn's lavender bath salts. Naturally, with the arthritis, mother had to be helped in and out of the bath, and because of her wretched wrist, Rachel had been obliged to phone down and ask Sister Monica if she could come and help.

'I don't see why you can't manage, Rachel,' mother said. She hated the nurses seeing her with nothing on. Rachel could understand that, but she stuck to her guns. She'd never forgive herself if her arm conked out and mother fell in the bath.

While mother was doing her hair ('I'm not having *her* seeing me a wreck,') Rachel ran the water to just the right temperature and scattered the bath salts, but Sister Monica, usually so reliable, failed to arrive.

Sybil was not best pleased when there was a knock on the door and Cordelia came in. 'Sorry if I've kept you waiting. Sister Monica has been held up with Mr Patterson; she asked me to come instead. Ready for your bath, Mrs Gillespie?'

'I was expecting Sister Monica,' Sybil grumbled, but allowed Cordelia to help her off with her dressing gown and ease her into the bath. Without her clothes Mrs Gillespie seemed less alarming, but trying not to look at blue veins and flaccid skin, Cordelia was grateful that her grandmother ran a health farm rather than an old people's home.

Rachel was making one of the beds when Cordelia came out of the bathroom. 'You don't have to do that, you know. The maid will do it later.'

'I know,' Rachel said, 'I'll leave mine, but mother insists on her bed being made a special way.'

Cordelia longed to ask Rachel why she put up with it all, but instead she said, 'I'll give you a hand with the bed. You do rather spoil her, you know.'

'Daddy asked me to take care of her,' Rachel said. 'Those were his last words, in the hospital. It was a terrible place, an institution with bars on the windows; a brain tumour, they said it was. Mother wouldn't go there after the first visit. She found it too upsetting, she's very sensitive.'

'How awful for you,' Cordelia said, 'and you visited regularly, I suppose.'

'Oh, yes. I rather enjoyed it, in a way. We'd never had so much time to talk together before. Most of it didn't make sense, of course, because of the tumour; daddy seemed to think he was back in Colonial Africa with the RAF, and the nice male nurse, who came from Trinidad, was one of his servants.' Rachel giggled. '"Fetch me a glass of barley water, boy," he'd say.'

Cordelia imagined NUPE rampant. 'Did he mind?'

'Oh, no, held the glass to daddy's lips, and when daddy said the servants here were a pretty good bunch, he'd wink at me and say, "We do our best to please, sir." We were discussing cricket on the day daddy died. "I was watching Compton this morning," he said, nodding towards the open window and the car park. "A fine innings. Shouldn't be surprised if he doesn't make another century."'

There was a shrill cry from the bathroom. 'Rachel, where are you? Cordelia?'

'Just coming, mother,' said Rachel.

Cordelia put a hand on her arm. 'Don't worry, I'll go.'

She helped Mrs Gillespie out of the bath and shrouded her in a towel. 'There you are, Mrs Gillespie. You can manage?'

'Gossip, gossip, that's all that girl ever does,' said Sybil. 'Of course I can.' She whipped the last corner of towel out of Cordelia's hand. 'Off you go.'

'And then?' Cordelia said to Rachel, who was looking tearful as she smoothed down the sheet. 'Look, don't talk about it if it upsets you.'

'Oh, no, it doesn't,' Rachel said, 'it was all so long ago. Fifteen years. Well, then daddy sort of fell back on the pillow and said such a strange thing. "Sybil can't cope, you know," he said. "I've done everything for her since we married. Not her fault, mine. Should have stood up to her." It was as though he was gathering up every last ounce of strength as he took my hand and whispered, "Take care of mother."'

'You certainly do that,' Cordelia said.

'I do my best,' said Rachel. She looked curiously at Cordelia over the meticulously turned down sheet. 'You're Cordelia Ledbury, aren't you?'

'Yes,' said Cordelia.

'I knew it. I recognised you from *The English Tea*. Your picture on the back cover. Cordelia's Calorific Chocolate Cake is mother's favourite. I always make it for her bridge afternoons.'

'I wrote that book ages ago. It is not, as my grandmother might say, in the Alba ethos.'

'No, I suppose it isn't, all those chunks of crystallised ginger, that's what mother enjoys. I say, Miss Ledbury?'

'Do call me Cordelia.'

150

'Cordelia, can you, you know, patent recipes?'

'It's very difficult, there are so many familiar standards, but most writers have the decency to switch the ingredients about if they nick a recipe from somebody else's cookbook.'

'Well, Jennifer Tremayne in the *Surrey Advertiser* hasn't bothered to switch any of yours. I was reading it in the Rest Room yesterday, and there it was in the cookery column, as large as life, Calorific Chocolate Cake, and with the ginger chunks, too. You ought to do something about it.'

'Thank you, I will,' said Cordelia, resolving to get hold of the *Surrey Advertiser* before busybody Tristram Bartholomew thumbed through it, and put two and two together. Quite gratifying, though, to know that her column was now selling in skinny Surrey.

*   *   *

Giovanni was fully booked, but as it was dear Mrs Gillespie (a poor tipper, but spent like an Onassis on her hair colour and could usually be persuaded to have a vitamin treatment) he would, of course, shift his other clients around and make time for her.

Rachel knew that it would take at least two hours for Giovanni to achieve the exact shade of tasteful ash her mother desired ('Now, Giovanni, I don't want to look as though I've been dipped in a blue bag, and I can't take that dreadful hard mauve'), *and* she'd have another hour to herself after she'd delivered mother to the beautician.

What luxury, Rachel thought gratefully, as she stood at the dining room sideboard, languidly deciding between a plain biscuit and a slice of low-calorie madeira cake. She helped herself to the cake and a cup of weak tea with a slice of lemon and, carefully balancing plate and cup and saucer, diffidently approached the nearest table. 'I wonder if I might join you?'

Adam Shepherd rose and drew up a chair. 'Mother's

all right, I hope?'

'Having her hair done.'

'How nice,' said Sylvia Travers. She was enjoying Adam Shepherd's company, there weren't that many personable males around Alba, and was not particularly anxious to share it with this poor, drab creature.

'Mother's very fussy about her hair,' Rachel said. 'Carolyn was saying, only yesterday in exercise class, how marvellous mother always looks.'

'Yes, indeed,' said Adam. 'Another cup, Sylvia?'

'I don't think I should,' Sylvia bathed Adam in one of her loveliest smiles and held out her cup. 'Just half, then.'

'This is delicious,' said Rachel, nibbling the cake. 'We always get our Madeira from Sainsbury's, mother says you know where you are with Sainsbury. We do a big shop there, once a week, and I get the fruit and vegetables and salad stuff from our local greengrocer. It's a bit heavy, with the potatoes, but it works out much cheaper that way.'

'I expect it does,' said Sylvia, who always had everything delivered from Selfridges. Thank goodness Jane Fellowes was heading their way; at least she'd have something more interesting to talk about than household shopping.

Jane flopped down with a weary sigh.

'My dear,' said Sylvia, 'you look utterly exhausted.'

'Couldn't sleep,' said Jane Fellowes, 'there was the most awful racket in the next room last night.'

'That would have been Sheila Steinberg, I expect,' said Rachel. 'She had a bit of a tummy upset, diets do affect some people like that, don't they? And her friend, Mrs Renfrew, had to ring for help.'

'Oh, that's what it was all about,' said Jane, 'I am sorry. She's all right now, I hope?'

'Right as rain,' said Rachel, 'and, do you know, Sister Monica and Madame Cordoba, *herself*, went to her aid. And they both looked after poor Mr Pullen when he was taken ill, last week. You couldn't ask for better attention, could you? Really, we're so lucky to be at Alba.'

'Very true,' said Adam. 'Now, if you'll excuse me, ladies, I'm going to get into my togs for Movement to Music.'

'Fancy him doing that,' said Rachel, when Adam had left, 'most of the men are too embarrassed to join us in the Movement to Music. They usually only take the exercise class. He's such a gentleman, Mr Shepherd, isn't he?'

*   *   *

After delivering her mother to the beautician, Rachel was idly glancing at the notice-board, when Cordelia came along, pinned up the dinner menu and asked after Rachel's wrist. She was closely followed by Lady Drummond, who took one look at the menu and said, 'Really, Cordelia, this is too bad.'

'What's too bad, Lady Drummond?' Cordelia wearily prepared to parry another customer complaint.

'Beef. And at a health farm, too.'

'Manor,' Cordelia corrected, automatically. 'The tart is absolutely delicious, I promise you.' It was an economical Josceline Dimbleby recipe Cordelia had suggested to Rosemary herself, and she'd featured it in her last cookery column, with, of course, a slight switch of the ingredients.

'Hasn't anyone here heard about bovine spongiform encephalopathy?' Betty looked accusingly at Rachel and Cordelia. 'Just look at the appalling misery we've caused, and all in the name of progress and protein.'

Cordelia didn't want to hear about appalling misery. She was only too aware that her cheerful temperament was the result of not facing up to Third World starvation, Romanian AIDS, and mad cows.

What, Betty wanted to know, did farmers think they were doing, feeding minced up bits of sheep to herbivores? If the government knew what it was doing, which it obviously didn't, it would be slaughtering all the infected herds.

'But wouldn't that mean killing an awful lot of cows?' said Rachel.

153

'You obviously don't realise that every cow produces two hundred litres of methane a day,' said Betty. '*That's* the greenhouse effect for you.'

'Goodness me,' said Rachel, deciding to go for the Vegetable Bake that evening.

'How frightful,' said Cordelia, deciding to look out something more ecologically acceptable than minced beef for her column.

Betty left them, crossly jangling her bracelets. 'I'm going to have a word with Bella. She can't possibly allow beef to be served at Alba.'

*   *   *

The dinner gong had already sounded. Rachel was waiting patiently for her mother in the Small Drawing Room. She had put on her good navy blue wool; some people came down to dinner in their track suits, but mother didn't approve of leisurewear in the Dining Room, and Rachel was inclined to agree with her.

She'd so enjoyed the interesting chat with Lady Drummond, about spongi-whatever it was and methane gas (she must remember to warn mother off the mince) and now that nice Mrs Gerard was coming over to talk to her. You did meet such interesting people at Alba.

'I can't think where Sarah has got to,' Erica said, sitting down next to Rachel on the sofa. 'I suppose she's watching some Australian rubbish on television with Antonia.'

Rachel couldn't help noticing that Mrs Gerard, who often seemed pale and wan and somewhat abstracted, had a healthy spot of colour in her cheeks and had been smiling quite pleasantly when she was complaining about her daughter's absence. 'Why, Mrs Gerard,' she said, 'you do look merry this evening.'

'Merry?' Erica stopped smiling. She had only taken one small sip, a pre-dinner aperitif to make Alba's Vegetable Bake more palatable.

'I expect you've been enjoying one of your little drinks.' Rachel wondered why Mrs Gerard was looking at her in that funny way. And then it struck her. Mrs Gerard must have thought she meant an alcoholic drink, and everyone knew it wasn't allowed at Alba. 'Oh, I didn't mean, you know, a *drink*. I was thinking of Sister Monica's tonic.'

'Couldn't do without it,' said Erica swiftly. 'Last year, when Naomi Mayhew forgot to send me my three-monthly supply, I felt so ragged I'm afraid I phoned her up and gave her hell.'

'I didn't know you could have it sent.'

'You can't get it any other way. Madame Cordoba guards the secrets of her ingredients as closely as any Scottish whisky distiller. She only sends it out to her regulars. That's where her profits come from, if you ask me.'

'Surely not,' said Rachel. 'Alba is so popular. Everyone we meet longs to come here, but mother won't give a recommendation. She says that if she recommended one of her bridge circle, they'd all come.'

Erica changed the conversation, she had no desire to hear about Mrs Gillespie's bridge circle. And Rachel noted, not for the first time, how people invariably changed the conversation when she started talking.

She listened intently as Mrs Gerard told her what a wonderful relationship she had with her daughter. 'She's so much closer to me than to her father, but it's hardly surprising. My husband has always been more interested in his balance sheets than in Sarah.'

'How sad,' said Rachel, remembering the cosy chats she used to have with daddy. 'A father's so important to a young girl, isn't he?'

'Forgot her birthday,' said Erica, who had been so busy arranging a crucial dinner party that she might have forgotten, too, if Sarah hadn't come into the kitchen and, glancing at the soufflé ingredients in the mixing bowl, rushed over and hugged her, 'Oh, mum, fabulous, a birthday cake!' 'Luckily, she and I have always been such good friends.'

'Just like mother and me.'

'Not quite,' said Erica. 'Sarah and I are more the same generation, don't you think? We even buy our clothes together. At least I buy them and Sarah appropriates them. I found her wearing my new Ralph Lauren jeans the other day.'

'Did they fit?' Erica looked a regular size fourteen, while Sarah, a sweet child, was a mite slim for Rachel's taste.

'Miles too big for her, of course, but she pulled them in with a big belt. That's the way teenagers wear them these days. I simply can't keep her out of my wardrobe.'

The word 'wardrobe' triggered an automatic response, and Erica visualised the cool green gin bottle nestling in a shoe bag next to her trainers. She could do with another drop after all that chat about Mrs Gillespie's bridge club. She stood up, 'I think I'll go and find Sarah.'

'Rachel! Oh, there you are.' Sybil Gillespie walked in, closely followed by Adam Shepherd. 'Run and get my cardigan, you forgot to bring it down again. And we won't need you for bridge tonight, dear. This gentleman has kindly offered to make up the fourth.'

CHAPTER
FOURTEEN

'Well, that's it for this morning then, ladies. And gentle-man,' Carolyn Watson gave Adam an encouraging nod, jauntily draped her shocking pink cardigan over her shoulder, and was just making for the door when she was stopped by Debbie Wynne-Jones.

'Excuse me, Miss Watson.'

'Yes?'

'I'm really feeling so much better.'

'Good.' Carolyn looked at her watch.

'I'm sure it's your exercises. I've tried the Hip and Thigh, and the Callanetics, and they really didn't work for me. I was wondering . . . ?'

'Could we talk about it another time, dear?' Carolyn lowered her voice and looked over her shoulder, to make certain Sister Monica, super-spy, wasn't anywhere about. 'The thing is, one of my little ones has chickenpox . . . I need to get to the chemist . . . '

'Oh, sorry,' said Debbie, 'of course. It's just that I was wondering if you could work out a set of exercises for me, that I can do when I get home?'

Carolyn took off her cardigan. She relied on the extra money she made from the private clients she picked up at Alba. 'Couldn't be easier, my dear. You tell me the areas you want to work on, your stomach or your thighs, and I'll devise a programme specially for you. Half an hour, three days a week, should do it, and then we can see how you're getting on and take it from there.'

'Unfortunately,' said Debbie, 'I live in Swansea.'

157

'Well, that's no problem.' Goodbye to £15 a visit, then. 'You can write and report progress and I'll send you a follow-up programme. I'm afraid I have to charge £35 for each of my programmes.'

'Fine,' said Debbie. 'Actually, it's stomach and thighs *and* the upper bits of my arms.'

'Isn't it always?' said Carolyn, with that jolly laugh her classes always found so heartwarming. 'How long are you staying?'

'Until the end of the week.'

'Splendid.' Carolyn put on her cardigan again and moved swiftly to the door. 'I'll see you before you go, then, with programme in hand.'

'Isn't she wonderful?' Rachel Gillespie finished stacking exercise mats and passed Debbie her sweatshirt.

'Magic. And she's going to give me a set of exercises to do at home. She's got young children, you know. One of them has chickenpox.'

'Oh, the poor thing. And she's always so cheerful, never seems to have a care in the world. I wonder if she could work out some special exercises for mother, to help her arthritis. Nothing too strenuous, of course.'

'Why don't you ask her?'

'I will,' said Rachel, 'another time.' Experience had taught her the error of independent action. The trick she had perfected over the years was to plant an idea in mother's mind and wait for her to reproduce it as her own.

Looking at Debbie, Rachel hardly recognised her as the forlorn figure who had arrived at Alba only a few days before. 'What a wonderful place this is. It's done you so much good already.'

'I know. I feel so much better.'

'I expect you're benefiting from Sister's little drinks. Herbs are amazing things, aren't they? Nature's way of pepping you up.'

'You're probably right. I missed out on an infusion yesterday, and I felt perfectly bloody . . . awful, I mean.'

158

Rachel gave Debbie a reassuring pat on the arm to show that she was not shocked by the bold word. 'As a matter of fact, I've often thought of trying Sister's Extras myself.'

'Well, why don't you?' If I had to live with that mother, Debbie thought, I'd be wallowing in the stuff.

'I don't think mother would approve.' What mother had actually said, when Rachel had tentatively suggested it, some years ago, was, "Pay through the nose for a few herbs stirred into hot water, Rachel? You must think I'm made of money." 'Besides, it is rather expensive, isn't it?'

'Is it?' Debbie had stopped worrying about the cost of Alba's various treatments. She had spent more than £20 having her legs waxed that morning, and was planning a Facial, at least another £20 plus the tip to the beautician, before she left at the end of the week.

'Oh, yes, I think so, several pounds a packet, and a lot of people continue the regime at home. Miss Mayhew is kept quite busy sending out supplies. Have a word with Sister before you go home. She'll organise it for you. I know Mrs Gerard, for one, has a regular order.'

*   *   *

Constant exposure to Rosemary Meadows' low-calorie mini meals had begun to have their effect on Cordelia. Every time she nibbled a characterless salad or sampled a simple vegetable soup, she couldn't help thinking of some more amusing way to zip up the ingredients.

She had driven up to Shepherd's Bush that morning, determined to have a word with Janet Marmont about the beef and lentil tart. It wasn't only Lady Drummond going OTT about mad cow disease; Cordelia's own tastes were changing; she was finding the culinary possibilities of fruit and veg endlessly fascinating. Yesterday, she'd made a perfectly delicious spinach and cherry-tomato salad, bathed in a basil and walnut dressing. Maybe she'd swap that for the tart.

159

'It's too late to change anything now,' Janet said, when Cordelia phoned her. 'I sent the copy out days ago. Besides, beef and lentil tart is right in line with current thinking. Wholesome, hearty and not a hint of *cuisine minceur*. There seems to be something of a backlash against sorrel purée and raspberry coulis.'

'Damn. I've got a brilliant way of doing sorrel soup in the column I'm writing now.'

There was a pause at the other end of the telephone. 'I can't believe I'm hearing this, Cordelia. Just as the rest of the country is regressing back to nursery food you've decided to go *nouvelle*.'

'It has a chicken stock base,' Cordelia said, defensively.

'Well, let me see it. You're selling so well, in Australia, as well as here, we don't want to rock the boat.'

'I'll put in a steamed pudding, if you like.'

'Steamed puddings are still unacceptable, but how about a seafood casserole? Fish is very Now.'

Cordelia was still ruminating over shrimps and mussels and fillets of sole bound in an anchovy sauce, when Sally came in, looking less than pleased to see her.

'Cordelia? I didn't know you were coming today. Goodness, you look great.'

'I've lost another three pounds.'

'I can see you have.' Sally gazed admiringly at the concave area below Cordelia's wide belt. 'How long are you staying?'

'Not very welcoming, I must say. I've got to be back at Alba this evening.'

'What sort of time this evening?'

'What time would you like me to go? Don't you want me to meet the new tenant?'

'Of course I don't mind you meeting her, but she's on location this week in Lincolnshire. Actually, I'm going out to dinner, someone's collecting me in about half an hour.'

'It's the someone you're worried about,' said Cordelia, 'who is he, and why won't I approve?'

'As a matter of fact, it's Stewart Ferguson.'

'The Incredible Hulk?'

'Please don't call him that.'

Cordelia gazed at her in amazement. 'You're going out with the Incredible Hulk?'

'With Stewart. Yes.'

'But he's a pain, Sally, you know he is.'

'Then you don't mind?'

'I don't mind,' said Cordelia, thinking of Tod, 'not if you don't.'

*   *   *

Roadworks at the Guildford bypass again. Cordelia looked at her watch anxiously. She had promised to be back by six thirty to help Rosemary with dinner. She drove swiftly through the back entrance to Alba; the quickest route to the stable block and conveniently concealed from her grandmother's window. Skirting the kitchen garden, she noticed Tod Ballard wandering about amongst the poly-tunnels. She was just about to hoot and wave when she was overcome by an unaccustomed feeling of diffidence.

Until a few days ago she had taken Tod's friendship for granted, but ever since Stewart had turned up ... was she imagining a coolness? It took a surprising amount of cour-age for her to press the hooter and wave. Tod looked up, startled, and came towards her.

'You're not allowed in the kitchen garden,' Cordelia said through the car window. It was not at all what she had intended to say, and she wished she hadn't sounded so bossy when she said it.

'Really? Is that Management speaking?'

'I'm not Management.' Cordelia smiled uncertainly. 'I only meant you'd better not let grandmother see you here. She's paranoid about those polytunnels.'

'I wonder why?' said Tod, not smiling back. 'Have you been up to London?'

161

Cordelia would have liked to have told Tod about her moonlighting. 'Yes, I had to go up . . . to see a friend.'

'Of course.' Tod raised a hand briefly and turned away.

*   *   *

What a nice young couple, Rachel Gillespie thought, as she hurried across the courtyard towards the stable block on her way to visit Naomi Mayhew. She remembered Cordelia arriving at Alba six months before, bouncy and plump, a lovely girl. But look at her now. Really pretty. And young Mr Ballard was every bit as dark and handsome and enigmatic as Adrian in *Cupid's Messenger*. An ideal match.

She was still smiling approvingly as she rang Naomi's bell. Mother was having a Hydrotherapy session in the warm Indoor Pool, it did wonders for her arthritis, and Rachel had a spare hour to spend with her friend.

'Come in, dear, I've just put the kettle on.' Naomi led Rachel into her sparsely furnished bedsitter. Rachel could see steam rising from behind the rickety wooden screen which divided the wash-basin and gas-ring from the living quarters. There was no bathroom, Naomi had to cross the courtyard to the Manor and use the showers in the Treatment rooms when the guests had finished with them.

'Still no kitchen or bathroom?' Rachel perched on a worn armchair. 'It's not good enough, Naomi. You ought to make a fuss.' She always felt uncharacteristically confident and in charge when she was with Naomi.

'Oh, I don't mind,' Naomi poured out the tea. 'White with one lump, isn't it? Madame has promised to see to it one day.'

'You mustn't let her put upon you, Naomi,' said Rachel, biting into a Garibaldi.

'Dear Madame has far too much on her plate to worry about my facilities. Another Garibaldi, Rachel? She's been having trouble with that Matt Lawson again.'

Rachel skirted the subject delicately. 'Not another romance?'

Naomi giggled. 'There's nothing new about Mr Lawson and the lady guests, Rachel. No, it's Mr Bartholomew this time.'

'Mr Bartholomew? Oh, surely not?'

Naomi giggled again. 'What will you say next? Of course not, dear. Matt barged in on Madame yesterday. I was taking dictation, and he was absolutely outraged, said he would, on no account, take Mr Bartholomew for massage again.'

'Why ever not?' Rachel put down her cup. A chat with Naomi was sometimes as rewarding as a good read.

'It seems that Mr Bartholomew purchased some rude men's magazines and insisted on showing them to Matt during Massage. Matt said they were very explicit. He told Madame that he was as broadminded as the next man, but he hoped he knew where to draw the line. He said he had never been so disgusted in all his life.'

'My goodness.' So that was what had so engrossed Mr Bartholomew in the village shop. Rachel thanked her stars she hadn't spoken to him. 'Just fancy that.'

'And coming on top of the police, well, no wonder Madame hasn't had time to bother with my bathroom.'

'The police?' Rachel was quite content, on this occasion, to find herself in her listening mode.

'They phoned up yesterday to warn us that there is a con-man about; working the health farm circuit, they said, preying on rich elderly women.'

'How dreadful. But you wouldn't find a con-man at Alba.'

'Of course not. That's what I said. But poor Madame Cordoba! When I went into her room and told her that the police wanted to speak to her, she went white as a sheet.'

CHAPTER

FIFTEEN

'You certainly gave us a fright last night, Sheil.' Diane carefully applied a layer of make-up that was meant to look as though the wearer didn't wear make-up at all, but was simply glowingly healthy. It took ages. 'You should have seen Madame and Sister Monica.'

'I did see them. I honestly can't think what all the fuss was about. I simply had a glass of sherry and went to sleep because I was tired. No big deal.'

Diane slid into a pair of lime green Dayglo jogging pants, gazing affectionately at her taut thighs as she did so. Sheila noted, distastefully, that they were spattered with bruises which were not the result of exercises in the gym; and came to a decision that she had been fidgeting with for days. She was not coming to Alba again, or if she did, it would not be with Diane.

Sheila was tired of being thought of as part of the man-hunting double act Diane-and-Sheil. The give-it-a-go sisters, they of the provocatively raised eyebrow and the suggestive laugh. It wasn't really Sheila at all.

'You're not going to lie there all day moping, are you?' Diane said, picking up Sheila's appointment card. 'Look, you've got your All-Over Tanning session at ten, then there's Yoga at half eleven, and then . . . '

'I know what I've got,' said Sheila snappishly, 'oh, do go on, Diane, I'm quite capable of getting myself to an appointment on time.'

'Pardon me for breathing,' said Diane. She left the room, twitching her hips because she insisted on wearing high-heeled shoes, even with a track suit.

Sheila was feeling rotten. And it certainly wasn't half a glass of sherry that had knocked her out last night. She was beginning to wonder about those infusions; if they were all that good for you, why didn't they tell you what was in them?

She was also feeling rotten because she was ashamed of herself. Egging Diane on to mess up Cordelia's possible love life had been really mean. Tod Ballard, though good-looking enough, was a bit nothingy for her taste; but years of hairdressing and listening to other women's hopes and wishes hadn't been wasted. She knew when women were in love, and if Cordelia wasn't smitten she'd dye her hair Chartreuse with Magenta tips. What Tod felt was another thing altogether, he didn't give much away. Maybe she could give Cupid a bit of a shove, thought Sheila, as she threw back her blankets and plonked her feet on the floor, it's the least I can do. She walked into the bathroom, and started to clean her teeth with her soft Oral B toothbrush, automatically brushing the gums with gentle, circular movements. She looked for her dental floss and found there were only two packets left. Gerald was very strong on dental floss, she must remember to get some more.

I will go and find Cordelia, she thought. My life might be in a mess, but that's no reason to mess up somebody else's. After searching by the Indoor Swimming Pool, the Outdoor Swimming Pool, Aromatherapy and the Gym, Sheila found Cordelia in Steam Cabinets, chatting conscientiously to Sybil Gillespie and Sylvia Travers, who, encased up to their necks in gleaming technology, had rather red faces with sweat pouring down them.

Sybil had obviously just Spoken Out about something, because Cordelia was saying, 'Oh, I don't think so, Mrs Gillespie. Mary is always very careful about the towels.'

'Quite damp, and a smear of someone's make-up on the corner.'

'Good morning, Mrs Steinberg, and how are you?'

Cordelia smiled wearily at Sheila, and turned back to the arena. 'I'll look into it, of course, Mrs Gillespie, but I think you'll find . . .'

'I must say,' said Sylvia Travers, 'she did leave me in here yesterday for fifteen minutes too long. And when she did get me out, she completely forgot my special Attar of Rose shower gel. She was in such a dither.'

'There you are!' said Sybil triumphantly. 'This place is falling apart. And I had the wrong breakfast delivered this morning. I never touch crispbread, and never will. My friend whose husband is a doctor, so of course he'd know, goes to a lovely place just outside Edinburgh. She's always at me to go with her, but up to now I have remained loyal to Alba.'

She flicked a quick glance at Cordelia, and was rather put out to see that Madame's granddaughter, who really ought to take more interest, was totally unmoved by the implied threat, and, indeed, went so far as to say, 'Scotland? How lovely. Tell me the minute you feel you want to get out, Miss Travers, I've got your towel all ready for you, and here is your shower gel.'

'Excuse me, Cordelia,' said Sheila, 'I wondered if you have a few spare moments this morning? There's something I wanted . . .'

'Good morning, Mrs Steinberg,' said Sybil meaningfully. 'Just because I'm sitting here in a metal box doesn't mean I am invisible, I hope?'

'Oh, good morning, sorry, I didn't want to interrupt. Good morning, Miss Travers.'

Sylvia smiled the smile which made one of her lovers once describe her as Garboesque; and like Sybil, was quite put out because neither Cordelia nor Sheila appeared to be appreciating her amazing bone structure.

'Are you feeling all right, Miss Travers?' said Cordelia, 'you're looking a bit . . . ah, here comes Mary, she'll look after you.'

Mary bustled in. 'Now, which of my ladies is ready

166

for her shower?'

'I am,' said Sybil swiftly, 'and I trust that, this morning, I will be honoured with a clean towel.'

'Well, actually, if you don't mind,' said Sylvia, 'I think I ought to come out first. After yesterday . . .'

Cordelia caught Mary's eye, stepped forward and started undoing the buckles of Sylvia's steam cabinet. Mary did the same for Sybil. They both waved towels around like matadors' cloaks, tactfully hiding the sagging bits from any straying eyes. Sheila, turning her back, gazed in a fascinated manner at a list of regulations pinned on the back of the door.

*   *   *

'I honestly don't know how you put up with it, you're so patient,' said Sheila. She and Cordelia were drinking orange juice on the terrace, after escaping from the stressful power clash in Steam Cabinets. 'That Gillespie woman is a malevolent old buzzard, isn't she?'

'The one I feel sorry for is her daughter, she's got her for life. I really shouldn't be talking about the clients like this. Though I bet they talk about me.'

'I haven't heard anyone say anything about you that wasn't nice.'

Cordelia looked across at Sheila, and for the first time saw her as Sheila Steinberg on her own; not the other half of Diane-and-Sheil, the nudge and wiggle twosome. This new Sheila had kind eyes, and wasn't using them for provocative glances at passing males; she was looking at Cordelia with a kind of searching sympathy that made her want to confide all about Tod. Only, if she did, would Sheila tell Diane with gales of giggles, and would she, Cordelia, be the lovelorn joke of Alba by this time tomorrow? Perhaps wiser to keep her worries to herself.

'I suppose you think I'm just like Diane,' said Sheila, so eerily echoing Cordelia's thoughts that for a frightful second she wondered if she'd said them aloud.

'What?'

'She calls us The Terrible Twins of Harpenden, and I'm sick of it.'

'Then why don't you . . . '

'Drop her? How? Her gift shop's a few doors down from my salon, she's always in and out. And that's another thing,' added Sheila, who had forgotten all about nudging Cupid, 'I do her hair for nothing, and all I get in exchange is cordless bloody telephones shaped like hamburgers, and extremely rude corkscrews.'

Cordelia laughed.

'I suppose I sound a bit mean. Only, honestly, Cordelia, she's taken me over, and it's so awkward with my husband; the other day, Diane said to me, "Your Gerald couldn't take his eyes off me last night, I could see he was intrigued. Don't be green eyed, Sheil, tell me what he said." She thinks everyone fancies her.'

'And he doesn't?'

'Can't stand her. What he actually said about her was that halitosis is always an indication of trouble, that she needed gum surgery, and he personally would recommend Eludril mouthwash.'

'I hear her husband's pretty ghastly,' said Cordelia, wondering whether her grandmother would regard this conversation as legitimate mingling with the guests, or frivolous and unproductive gossip.

'Derek? Rumoured locally to be well into shifty deals, substandard concrete, and other men's wives. Tells the kind of stories that make you wish he'd keep his voice down.'

'How does he get on with Gerald?'

'Thinks he's a toffee-nosed snob because he's got a private practice . . . ' Sheila took a sip of orange juice and thought back to those nice friendly days when she and Gerald had discussed everything, including going private.

'I'm tired of patching up teeth that have hardly seen a

168

toothbrush from one visit to the next,' Gerald had said. 'Don't look at me like that, Sheila, I know I had ideals, I know what I said when I was a student. There was this woman today, she brought in her four-year-old and it had a dummy dipped in sugar-water stuck in its mouth and six cavities. It'll be in false teeth by the time it's twelve. I tried to explain to her, but what's the use? At least when Joe Bloggs writes me out a cheque for seventy quid, I know he's going to look after his teeth. People only value what they pay for.'

They had bought a long leasehold on an elegant Georgian house in the High Street, and Gerald had set up his surgery on the ground floor. Sheila redecorated the upstairs floors, trying not to accept too many of Diane's generously offered suggestions. 'You want to paint that ceiling dark blue, Sheil, it'll bring it down a bit, these rooms aren't very cosy, are they? . . . I should go for leather settees, if I were you, they've got lovely blue ones at World of Leather . . . Look, we've just had a delivery of these new cushions shaped like bums from California. Killing, aren't they? As it's you, love, they'll only set you back a few quid.'

Cordelia began to feel uncomfortable. This was no longer a riveting gossip. Sheila hadn't spoken for some minutes, she was off on some reverie, and it didn't seem to be a very happy one. She looked as though she was going to cry, and it seemed to Cordelia that the change in atmosphere had coincided with the mention of Derek Renfrew.

'Sheila . . . ' she said, at exactly the moment when Sheila said, 'Cordelia, can I talk to you?'

Effortlessly decoding this as 'Can I tell you something that mustn't be repeated?' Cordelia said, 'I won't tell a soul, I absolutely promise.'

So Sheila told Cordelia about the time the four of them had been out to have an Indian, which was embarrassing to start with, because Derek talked to the waiters as though it was 1857 in Cawnpore, and they were about to mutiny.

But at least they all liked Indian food; Derek opting for Chicken Vindaloo. 'Hot food for hot blood,' he said, as he always did; Diane giggled obligingly like she always did, and said, a mite too loudly, that she'd have the prawns, at least you knew *they* weren't made out of Whiskas. They all had too much to drink at the Taj Mahal, and then they went back to Diane's and had too much to drink there.

How she came to be sitting on the settee with Derek's arm round her, Sheila didn't have the faintest idea. But there she was, with Gerald taking not a blind bit of notice. He was too busy dancing with Diane and murmuring into her ear.

Sheila paused at this point, and Cordelia said encouragingly, 'Honestly, Sheila, that doesn't sound exactly criminal . . . '

' . . . only I'd knocked over a photograph frame when I was dusting that morning, one of those double ones, you know, and when I picked it up I looked at it properly for the first time in years . . . '

On one side, there was she and Gerald as a bridal couple, gazing at each other as though nobody had ever got married before. And on the other, there they were, gazing at each other over Edward's newborn head in the same way, only prouder. 'So I thought I'd get him sweetbreads for supper, his favourite, and we'd watch *The Golden Girls* together afterwards. I rang up on the intercom to the surgery and told him, and he sounded so pleased. And then, when I got to my salon, Diane came in and told me we were all going to the Taj Mahal.'

'Why didn't you say you couldn't?'

'Oh, you can't with Diane, she likes things her own way. And when I told Gerald it was going to be the Taj Mahal instead of sweetbreads he went on for ages about how *Golden Girls* was his favourite, and how I never thought about anyone except me. I suppose that's why,' Sheila said to Cordelia, who was beginning to wonder if she would ever get to the point, 'I let that awful Derek kiss me. All

170

Gerald ever looks at is teeth and television. I wanted him to look at me, for a change.'

Hmm, thought Cordelia, all very touching. But hadn't she heard something else about Sheila that wasn't so touching? Aloud, she said, trying not to sound censorious, 'So did it lead to anything? I mean did you, er, see Derek again?'

'Certainly not. What do you take me for?'

'I just thought, perhaps that's why Diane . . . '

'Who cares what Diane thinks? What I don't know is what Gerald thought, and really, that's all that matters, isn't it? I say, Cordelia, you do swear you won't repeat any of this? Only everyone gossips so much here, and I don't want . . . '

'Not a word, I promise.' Cordelia plucked a wisp of honeysuckle that was growing from a crack in the wall, and gazed at it intently. 'I suppose everyone was gossiping about that ghastly scene by the swimming pool?'

'When your ex-young man turned up and threw his weight about? No. There weren't all that many people around at the time.'

'No, I suppose there weren't. Just me and Debbie. And I think Mr Ballard might have been there.'

Just as well you don't have any plans to go on the stage, thought Sheila. 'I don't suppose he thought anything of it,' she said, 'and if I get the chance . . . what would you like me to say?'

'Good heavens,' said Cordelia, 'why should I care what he thinks? Actually, Stewart and I broke up ages ago, not that there was anything much to break up, actually. I suppose, if Tod did ask, you could say . . . you're laughing at me, Sheila.'

'I'm laughing with you, sunshine. You're nutty about him, aren't you?'

'Oh, Sheila, isn't he wonderful? Every time I go into a room, I hope he'll be there. He's so . . . yesterday when we were talking, he took off his glasses, and do you know what it reminded me of? Richard Gere unbuttoning his shirt.'

'I know what you mean,' said Sheila, getting up and moving away to lean on a balustrade.

'Are you all right?'

'No, it's just . . . my orange juice went down the wrong way,' said Sheila. Richard Gere? She had got it badly.

'Oh, be honest, Sheila, someone like that's never going to look at me, is he? I mean, look at me.'

Sheila turned round and looked at Cordelia, who stood up and gazed back at Sheila in the manner of a puppy expecting blame but hoping for praise. 'You're very attractive. You've lost masses of weight since last time I was here. What do you weigh now, about ten?'

Even as she said it, Sheila was thinking, what a frightful thing for one woman to say to another woman. Imagine saying that at a cocktail party, you'd get a glassful in your face. But it didn't seem to matter at Alba, where nobody talked about anything but their upper arm measurement and how their bowels were that morning.

Cordelia took no offence. 'About ten, yes, on a good day. And I tried on some things when I went up to London last week, and I easily got into a fourteen.'

'Why don't you wear fourteen, then?'

Cordelia looked down doubtfully at the vast jersey and the jogging pants that had become her uniform. 'I feel safer in these, somehow, I suppose it's habit. Grandmother did say it was a mistake.'

'She's right. I tell you what, are you doing anything this afternoon?'

'I'm supposed to be doing Aerobics at three, and then I said I'd give Rosemary a hand with the supper trays.'

'Give it a miss, and come on a shopping ramp. Rosemary is paid to do the catering, isn't she?'

'Oh, I know, but I'm supposed to give a helping hand. And Tod does Aerobics.'

'All the more reason to avoid them. Nobody's going to

172

fancy someone when they're tightening their bottom and rolling their pelvis up.'

Cordelia laughed. Sheila laughed too, and said, 'Well, not under those circumstances. Not with Carolyn Watson saying, "And one and two aaand three and slooowly down again, relax those shoulders, feeel your spine melting into the floor, Mrs Gillespie . . . "'

'Right,' said Cordelia, 'you're on. Where shall we go? I say, can I ask you something else? Only, grandmother says Giovanni is first-class, and I must admit my hair looks better than it used to, but, I don't know . . . '

Sheila was rather hoping for this; she personally thought Giovanni was fifth-rate expensive, the kind of hairdresser who covered a multitude of technical sins with an excessive amount of pseudo-Italianate gesture and flattery; he should have been drummed out of the profession for sending Sybil Gillespie out with a row of curls that accentuated her eagle nose and diminished her clear grey eyes. Not that she, personally, gave a hoot what Sybil looked like; but she did care about professional standards.

'Well, I think, with your lovely clean jaw-line and those fantastic cheek-bones . . . what you need is width here, and . . . I wish we had a looking-glass, then you'd see what I mean.'

'This'll do.' The curtains in the drawing room windows behind them were still drawn (somebody would be in trouble) and Cordelia could see herself plainly in their reflection. 'You mean, cut some of this off?'

'Mmm,' Sheila stood behind Cordelia and lifted some of her hair back, 'shorter here, you see, and length here, and a longish fringe.'

'Would that be all right? I've never had a fringe.'

'With those eyes, it's madness not to. Come up to my room when we get back from shopping, and I'll . . . '

The curtains were majestically swept back, and Cordelia and Sheila found themselves face to face with Isabella, looking displeased, and Lady Drummond. Cordelia smiled

173

in a way which even Sheila could see was irritating, and Sheila herself let Cordelia's hair drop as though she had been engaged in some unsavoury activity.

Isabella unlatched the french window and stepped out. 'Good morning, Mrs Steinberg,' she said coldly. 'Cordelia, it is twenty-five minutes to ten, and these curtains have not been opened. What are you doing there, posturing in that foolish way?'

'Oh, nothing, grandmother, we were just . . . '

Sheila, only pausing to wonder why an intelligent woman in her late twenties should take to writhing about like an inarticulate teenager, said, 'I was just giving Cordelia some advice about her hair, Madame.'

'No doubt you meant well, Mrs Steinberg, but we do have a quite excellent hairdresser on the premises. I believe you are due at your Tanning session shortly?'

Sheila, to her rage, found she was sidling apologetically out of the room, nearly tripping over that snappy little black dog that followed Madame like a shadow. She managed, as she passed Cordelia, frantically flinging back the rest of the curtains, to hiss, 'One o'clock in the car park?'

Waiting until Sheila had closed the door behind her, Betty said, 'Quite excellent, Bella? That's pushing it a bit. I wouldn't let him touch me with a bargepole. Giovanni, my foot. I never met a Giovanni with vowel sounds like that. Born not a hundred miles from Sauchiehall Street, if you want my opinion. Not that it's any of my business, love,' she added. 'Who cares, as long as the punters are taken in?'

'Oh, Betty, how could you?' The last of the Cordobas (as she always thought of herself) was appalled to find that she was close to tears. 'How could you be so disloyal? Giovanni came to me with quite superb references. Everything at Alba is of the best, that has always been my principle. The finest linen, antique furniture, a highly qualified dietician . . . masseurs, I poached Matt Lawson from Park Lodge, I had to have the best for Alba. Alba is all that matters. And now it's all going wrong, Betty, I don't know

174

why, but it's not working any more.' The dog wandered over and nuzzled Isabella's ankle. 'And nobody had bothered to open the curtains, Betty, do I have to do everything myself?'

Cordelia stopped opening more curtains; shouldn't someone do something? 'Shall I get Sister Monica?' she whispered to Betty.

'Nonsense, love, your gran's just a bit tired, that's all. Leave it to me. Off you trot, when you've finished the curtains.'

CHAPTER
SIXTEEN

Sheila rather enjoyed her All-Over Tanning session; though she saw what Cordelia meant. Thirty quid and it would have faded by the week-end. But it made her feel good, having that brown glow, and the comments of the young operative as she busily exfoliated and smoothed, gave her self-esteem a badly-needed boost. 'I only wish all the bodies we dealt with here were in as good shape as yours, Mrs Steinberg, but then I suppose if they were, we'd be out of business. Just come in for a rest, have you?'

'Sort of, I'm here with a friend, actually, Mrs Renfrew.'

'Oh, Mrs Renfrew, yes. She was in here on Tuesday.' The operative did not add the usual, 'such a nice lady,' or even 'quite a chatty person, isn't she?' and Sheila was left with the pleasing impression that Diane had not gone down well in the All-Over Tanning department.

She met fluttery Miss Mayhew on the way to her Yoga class.

'Good morning, Mrs Steinberg, don't you look well? Isn't it a blessing of a morning? And where are you off to now? Yoga? So popular with our guests, they all simply love it.'

That was not actually true, thought Sheila, as she paused outside the door of the Exercise Room. A small card was pinned to the door, headed YOGA 11.30; underneath was the class list, which contained only five names. Mrs Steinberg, Miss Travers, Mr Ballard, and oh, dear God, Mr Bartholomew and Mr Shepherd. Sheila actively disliked Tristram, and knew nothing of Adam Shepherd, except that he was a top business man, and pompous with it.

One by one, people had dropped out of Yoga; Diane because, 'If I want to lie about on the floor pretending to be a carnation, I can do it at home for nothing.' Rachel Gillespie, because Estelle, the visiting Yoga instructress, had told her that a particular exercise would do wonders for her sex life. Antonia and Sarah because they giggled throughout in a silly way, and were asked to leave.

When Sheila entered, she found Tristram, Sylvia, Adam and Tod lying on the floor in abandoned poses.

'You are one with the earth,' crooned Estelle, 'your bodies are heavy, heavy . . . ' Well, that's certainly true of two of them, thought Sheila, ' . . . languorous, relaxed. Ah, there you are, Mrs Steinberg. I think you'll find there's some room next to Mr Ballard.'

Sheila lay down next to Tod, who muttered at her, 'Do join me on the sea of tranquillity. What are we doing this for?'

'It beats back-packing over the Andes.'

'Only just.'

'Now, we are not going to talk,' said Estelle firmly, 'we are going to raise our left arm . . . so heavy, so relaxed, and gently let mother earth reclaim it again. Not quite like that, Mr Bartholomew.' Tristram had lifted his left arm and put it down again in the brisk manner of someone hailing a taxi in the rush hour. 'What we are seeking for is a languor that is almost sensual . . . now, I'm sure you know what I mean by sensual, Mr Bartholomew? Try and think of something that gives you pleasure, some beautiful picture, perhaps.'

Tristram went rather red and scrambled to his feet.

'No, no, not like that, Mr Bartholomew, you are asking your back to do things Mother Nature did not design it to do. Roll over to your side and let your hands . . . '

But Tristram had collected his Reeboks and gone, banging the door behind him unlanguorously.

'Well, really,' said Estelle, 'some people, so unreceptive

to the Greater Truth. You can let your arm float down again, Mr Shepherd.'

*   *   *

'What on earth was all that about?' said Tod. He and Sheila were drinking yet another glass of orange juice on yet another terrace. Alba was littered with orange juice and terraces and very up-market garden furniture.

'You mean Tristram? I suppose he just got bored. The bit I liked best was when Estelle said we should lie there and listen to nature's silence, and Adam Shepherd's tummy rumbled.'

'I was careful not to catch your eye. No, I got the impression Tristram was really upset about something. Does he . . . ' Tod looked round furtively and got out a packet of Marlboro Light, 'is he on those infusion drinks, do you think?'

'Tristram? Shouldn't think herbal drinks are his cup of tea. I'm not bothering with them any more, actually. I say, Tod, you remember when Cordelia had that embarrassing time at the pool with that thuggy ex-boyfriend?'

'She seemed very pleased to see him,' said Tod shortly. 'I've been to see Mr Patterson, and he didn't prescribe me anything.'

'I expect he thought you didn't need them. No, actually, she wasn't pleased to see him at all. Apparently she knew him slightly ages ago, and he keeps on trying . . . '

'Why did she put her arms round him then? What's wrong with those bedtime drinks? Why have you stopped taking them?'

'Well, she didn't. He put his arms round her. I happened to be watching. And also I happen to know that he doesn't mean a thing to her.'

'Really? That's not what I heard. I can't think why you're telling me all this.'

'And I don't know why you're asking me all those boring

178

questions about a simple cup of herbal tea.' Sheila thought of a good way to bring Tod and Cordelia together. 'Why don't you ask Cordelia? She's bound to know all about the infusions.'

*   *   *

Sheila and Cordelia, back from their shopping trip, were lolling about, exhausted, in Sheila's bedroom. Diane was not with them. She had made plans for the evening that did not involve talking to a couple of women, even if one of them was her best friend. Sheila had got out the hairdressing tools without which she never travelled, and Cordelia was holding a burgundy linen jacket up against her and gazing dubiously into the looking-glass.

'A hundred and ten quid! I must have been mad. You do think it suits me, Sheila?'

'I wouldn't have let you buy it if it didn't. It'll look smashing with those mushroom trousers. Come on, come and sit down. I'll just pin this towel round you.'

'You won't cut off too much?'

That was a question Sheila, like all hairdressers, could have answered, reassuringly, in her sleep.

An hour and a half later, Sheila was rolling the flex round her dryer, and Cordelia was moving her head about trying to catch what she looked like sideways. She had, at Sheila's insistence, put on the mushroom trousers and the linen jacket, and she couldn't quite believe what she saw.

'Sheila, it's amazing. I always thought my neck was short. I love this bit up here, where it sort of blurs sideways. You're a genius, that's all, thank you so much. I say, when you've gone, will Giovanni be able to do it like this?'

'Don't let Giovanni anywhere near it. Blow dry it yourself, it's dead easy, and every so often get in your car, and I'll give you a trim for old time's sake.'

'That reminds me, how much do I . . . I mean, you will let me pay, won't you?'

'No, love, I owe you one.'

'Do you? I don't see why. You're looking sad again, like you did this morning, only I was too busy thinking about me. Sheila, you're not crying, are you?'

'I want to go home. I hate it here. I let him down just because Diane said we couldn't afford the cancellation fees.'

'Let who down? When?'

'Gerald. The night before we came here. He didn't come up from the surgery till half-past seven. He'd done an extraction that took two and a half hours because the tooth broke, they do that sometimes, and the patient was crying. It's every dentist's nightmare, you know, hurting people.'

'Really?'

'Dentists have the second highest job-related stress factor next to policemen. And I was packing to come here, and he said couldn't I put it off, he really needed me, so I rang Diane.'

'Yes?'

'And she said, if I cancelled she couldn't go by herself because the room would be too expensive, and she said how could I let her down. So I let Gerald down instead.'

Cordelia listened to all this with a certain amount of cynicism. She liked Sheila, but wasn't she being a bit hypocritical?

'Cordelia, why are you looking at me like that?'

'I'm not. Well, it's only . . . anyway it's none of my business.'

'What isn't?'

'Oh, Sheila, you've been so kind to me, but honestly, how you could . . . '

'How I could what?'

'Well, I mean . . . ' Cordelia could have kicked herself. Other people's morals were nothing to do with her, and here she was, plonk in the middle of a really embarrassing situation. ' . . . well, I mean . . . Matt.'

180

'Matt! What are you talking about? I don't even have him for massage any more, I think he's ghastly.'

'Oh, well, that's all right, then.'

'It certainly is not. What did you mean, how I could?'

'Only Diane seemed to think that, um, you had something, well, going.'

Fascinating, thought Cordelia. One's read it often enough in books, but people really do go white when they're angry.

Sheila picked up the phone. 'Miss Mayhew? Oh, good, you're still on duty. Could you get me my home number, please?' She glared over the phone and said, 'I really enjoyed shopping with you today, and all the time you thought ... you idiot, it's Diane who's got something going with Matt.'

Diane walked in, extremely full of herself. 'Can't wait to tell you, Sheil, you'll never guess what Matt told me about old Bella, as he calls her ... Cordelia? What are you doing here? And what on earth have you done to yourself?'

'Gerald?' said Sheila into the phone. 'If I leave now I should be there by eleven. There won't be much traffic. Yes, I'm coming home.'

'Oh, don't be so silly, Sheil, of course you're not going home. Put that case down, and listen to me. Sheila. I'm talking to you. I suppose you put her up to this?' Diane turned on Cordelia.

'I certainly hope I helped.'

'And another thing, Sheila, if you insist on pushing off, how do you imagine I'm going to get home? We came in your car because ... '

'Because you said it would be cheaper on petrol. And so it was, for you. You'll just have to get a train, or something.' Sheila chucked some socks and a sweatshirt into her case, slammed it shut, and made for the door. 'Bye, Cordelia. Good luck. And next time, don't believe everything you're told.'

'What did she mean?' said Diane. 'Would you believe it?

No idea of loyalty, some people.' She looked waspishly at Cordelia. 'If you don't mind my saying so, dear, she's made a terrible mess of your hair.'

CHAPTER
SEVENTEEN

'I don't know why you're showing me these.' Isabella handed Cordelia a clutch of Daily Menus. Nobody at Alba, not even her own granddaughter, was capable of independent action; they all came running to her with every problem. 'It's Rosemary's job to plan the meals.'

'It's just that I'd like to change one or two things,' said Cordelia. 'Madeira cake and milky tea aren't exactly slimming, and we ought to have lighter dressings on the salads, fewer pulses and potatoes ... are you sure you're all right, grandmother?'

'I'd be all right if I wasn't constantly being bothered with every detail,' Isabella said.

Cordelia noted the familiar abrasive tone with pleasure. She'd been worried about her grandmother yesterday, all that hysteria about the curtains; the menus had just been an excuse to check up on her. 'I'll be on my way, then.'

'Just a minute, Cordelia.'

'Yes?'

'Monica tells me you're seeing far too much of that vulgar young writer. Do try and remember, Cordelia, that you are a Cordoba.'

So much for good intentions, Cordelia thought to herself. Next time her grandmother would have to flail the floor and froth at the mouth before she, Cordelia, made a solicitous enquiry. 'I'm a Ledbury, actually,' she said.

Isabella noted Cordelia's reply with approval; it suggested a modicum of backbone, a touch of Cordoba character. Perhaps Cordelia might become a trusted ally, after all. 'Mr Ballard isn't the only unsatisfactory guest in this current group. Those two girls are trouble-makers, Antonia's mother, Mrs Fellowes, is always lurking about, and why do I have the feeling that Mr Shepherd, who came to us with unimpeachable references, is up to something? As for that silly Steinberg woman walking out . . . '

'It was personal, grandmother, her husband . . . '

'*Nobody* has ever walked out of Alba before. I want you to mix with our guests as much as possible, Cordelia. Mix and mingle. It's helpful for me to know how they react to our regime.'

'You want to know what's going on, you mean?' said Cordelia.

'Quite.' Isabella watched Cordelia as she went out of the door. The child looked almost stylish in that linen jacket and, she had to admit, with that excellent haircut. Perhaps Betty had been right about Giovanni. If he didn't improve she'd soon have him out on the streets pushing an ice-cream cart. She took a Bonio out of her desk drawer, and waved it to and fro under her chair. 'Come along, Flora baby, walkies.' Isabella quite enjoyed a row. She straightened her shoulders and began to feel much better as she and Flora set off towards Hairdressing.

*   *   *

'Wasn't Michael Gambon just great?' said Sarah Gerard, going over to the television set. 'Nobody wants the News, do they?'

'I do,' said Betty Drummond, 'there was an EC ruling today on the transportation of livestock.'

'Boring,' said Antonia Fellowes.

Cordelia often wondered why Alba's guests didn't watch television in their rooms, since there was always someone who must see David Attenborough when everyone else wanted to keep up with the current soap. She sat in a corner of the Small Drawing Room, mixing and mingling, hoping that Tod Ballard might also be eager to hear about the EC ruling on the transportation of livestock.

Sarah Gerard resolved the confrontation by flicking the switch over to the ITV news and slightly turning down the sound. 'Do you know him, Miss Travers?'

'Who, darling?' Sylvia Travers looked up from her tapestry; a prop for when she didn't want to talk to anybody; she hadn't put more than three stitches in it for the last year.

'Michael Gambon.'

'Know him, darling?' Sylvia put down her tapestry. 'We did a season together at Scarborough, back in . . . oh, aeons ago, I can't remember exactly. Michael is one of the very few truly unselfish actors I know.' Everyone except Betty, determinedly drawing her chair closer to Sandy Gall, looked admiringly at Sylvia, who saw no reason to add that she'd had the tiniest walk-on and Michael Gambon wouldn't recognise her if she went up to him in the street, tapped him on the shoulder, and said, 'Ayckbourn, '78.' 'Not like *some* actors I could mention . . . '

'Who?' said Sarah. 'Go on, Miss Travers, mention them.'

'There is one man, and I am most certainly not going to tell you his name, Sarah, because you've certainly heard of him, who is notorious for upstaging the rest of the cast. There's no end to the business he gets up to with a cigarette to demolish another actor's big scene. I've told Theo, my agent, not to put me up for a part if he is involved, and I know I'm not the only one.'

Sylvia held her audience spellbound with backstage gossip for an hour, and then insisted that she really must go to bed, she was absolutely exhausted.

'Oh, no, Miss Travers, not yet,' said Sarah, who was turning out to be rather a good feed, 'do tell us the one about the murderer who is meant to reach for his gun, and then realises that he's left it in the dressing room.' She turned to Cordelia. 'It's terribly funny.'

185

'I'm sure it is,' said Cordelia. She could see why Sister Monica introduced celebrity guests with such relish ('*This* is Rob McWhirter, the pop singer/Paul Naismith, the novelist/Sylvia Travers, the actress ... '). It obviously pleased Sylvia to be admired, and it also pleased the other Alba guests to be able to go home and say, 'I met this famous actress who knows Michael Gambon.' 'I'd love to hear it, Sylvia, if you're not too tired.'

'Another time, darlings.' Sylvia picked up her tapestry, acknowledged her audience with a smile, and made a gracious exit.

'Miss Travers, please, wait for me, Miss Travers.'

Sylvia sighed. God knows it was hard enough performing on stage, without having to sustain the public role of Sylvia Travers the Famous Actress. And she'd just given that excellent performance in the television room for free. She managed a radiant smile for Debbie Wynne-Jones; a nice girl who seemed to have been dogging her footsteps ever since the Swansea Grand reminiscences. 'Debbie?' Tears were spilling down Debbie's cheeks, and on to her pink track suit. 'What is it, my dear? What's the matter?'

'It's Isaac,' Debbie sobbed, 'he's been unfaithful.'

'Who?' Sylvia took Debbie's arm and led her towards a sofa in the empty reception hall.

'His wife's having a baby.'

'How do you know?'

'Everyone knows, my secretary says. I phoned her at home, just now, to check that things were all right at the office. Well,' Debbie sank down onto the sofa, 'they bloody well aren't. And he swore that they'd stopped sleeping together.'

'My dear, don't they all?' The script was familiar, but Sylvia realised that she was not quoting from some half remembered play. It was a rerun of her love affair with Dennis. They were going away together, an Australian tour. And then, Dennis's wife had selfishly got pregnant.

Just one of the rotten men who had messed up her life

since darling Will, her beautiful young husband, stepped out of a stage door into the path of a delivery van. She could still hear the screech of brakes, and the silence that followed. 'Don't,' she took Debbie's hand, 'don't cry. Is he really worth it?'

'No. That's what makes it worse. How could I have been such a fool? And they've got two other young children. Miss Travers, how could I have been so *wicked*?'

'Not wicked, surely? Infatuated. That's what being madly in love means, isn't it?' Sylvia patted Debbie's hand and added a sympathetic sigh which might, to anyone less traumatised than Debbie, have sounded somewhat theatrical.

Sylvia was used to patting hands and sighing sympathetically. A lone woman, she discovered very soon after Will's death, was a target for other people's tears. When any of her friends were deserted by lovers, struck down by illness, or failed an audition for a part that was absolutely them, they rang Sylvia. 'Darling, can you come round?' And round Sylvia went, dispensing cups of tea and tranquillisers. She had learned not to take a strong view ('I always thought he was a shit, darling, you're better off without him') or hand out advice ('If I were you, I'd sue the bastard'), because, when the protagonists came together again, they had an unfair habit of uniting in mutual loathing of the frank confidante. Sylvia knew it was safer to let them do the talking. 'So, Debbie, what are you going to do?'

'They all know about Isaac and me at the office. I can't go back there.'

'And lose your job as well as your lover? I wouldn't make any instant decisions, if I were you.'

Debbie's eyes filled with tears again. 'But I can't go on like this.'

'Come along, now,' Sylvia looked hopefully up the stairs. 'The best thing you can do is sleep on it.'

'How utterly blissful.' Sylvia was making her morning telephone calls. 'I'd adore to come for the weekend. No, darling, of course I don't mind if it's just family, you know how I dote on your children . . . She's got her As? Clever Emily . . . Give her a big kiss from me. See you on the fifth, then . . . Ciao.'

Another truth about the single woman's life, Sylvia had discovered, was the necessity of assiduously cultivating friendships, unless you wished to spend your evenings with Terry Wogan and baked beans. In the old days, when she and Will were invited down to the country for weekends, it was dinner parties and point to points and, 'What would you like to do today, darlings?' Now, her married friends expected her to slot gratefully into their everyday lives.

She picked up the phone and redialled. 'Deirdre! I've been trying to get hold of you for ages. How did the tour go? . . . Never. He didn't. I don't believe it. Of course you were wonderful, everyone said so, the critics raved . . . perfect, darling, I'll see you next week.'

Taking out her diary, Sylvia entered the two dates, noticing that the pages were satisfactorily full; an empty diary struck her with an almost physical chill. She had written herself a reminder, under today's date, to phone Theo, her agent, about the new play at the Greenwich. Casting started this week and Theo had promised faithfully to have a word with Ronnie Palfrey, the director. 'There's a brilliant part for you in it, darling,' he'd said, 'a perfect cameo role.' Sylvia knew what that meant; seek a coffee creme in your box of Milk Tray and you'd miss her. But better a small part in the West End, and Greenwich was virtually the West End, than the lead in an obscure Fringe production in the back room of some dreary suburban pub.

Theo was out of the office, but his secretary assured Sylvia that he had quite definitely lunched with Ronnie the day before yesterday, and she was terribly sorry, he hadn't mentioned anything about Greenwich before he went out. 'We have your number at Alba, Miss Travers, and we'll let you know the moment we have any news.'

*　　　*　　　*

Cordelia, en route to Naomi Mayhew's office, passed Sylvia Travers dressed for the Centre Court in a brief one-piece tennis dress with a pale blue cotton sweater slung nonchalantly around her shoulders. She was glowering at the notice-board and swinging her tennis racquet irritably. 'Anything I can do?'

'Sheila Steinberg has gone home, the court is booked for eleven and it's too late to find a fourth,' said Sylvia; she turned and noticed that Cordelia was not shrouded in an outsize sweater. 'My dear child, what have you done to yourself?'

'The hair?' Cordelia, looking over Sylvia's shoulder, saw the name Diane Renfrew and decided she simply must clean out the bicycle sheds. The next name she saw was Tod Ballard. 'Don't worry, I'll make up the fourth.'

'Darling, how wonderful. No, it's not just your hair which is quite stunning,' Sylvia stared at Cordelia in a frank manner which would be considered rude anywhere but Alba. 'That linen jacket, and how clever to put beige with maroon. My dear, you've turned into a sylph.'

'Not quite, unfortunately. Look, Sylvia, it's not eleven yet, I've just got to drop these in on Naomi Mayhew and then I can be with you. Would you and the others mind knocking up until I arrive?'

'Of course not, I'll tell them. Here's Diane Renfrew, now.'

Diane bore down on them, in a frou-frou of frilly white out of sync with her firm step. 'There you are, Sylvia. I'm just on my way to the Light Diet room, to see if there's anyone willing to make up the fourth.'

'No need,' Sylvia smiled at Cordelia. 'Cordelia has

189

kindly offered.'

'Really?' said Diane, not smiling at Cordelia. 'I should have thought the staff were too busy to play games.'

'I can spare an hour,' said Cordelia, equably. 'See you on the court, Sylvia.' As she sped off towards the office, she thought she might really enjoy lobbing a tennis ball quite hard at Diane Renfrew.

*   *   *

'Yours, partner.' Sylvia's tennis technique was to stand on the back line, slam a hard serve over the net and then look victimised if somebody sent it back. She was prepared to hit the ball if she didn't have to run for it. Her partner, a competitive games player, was sweating heavily and her frou-frou was limp.

'Love, forty,' said Cordelia, as Diane dived towards the net and just missed the ball.

'I think that was a net service,' said Diane.

'Nonsense, darling,' said Sylvia.

'Too late, anyway,' said Cordelia.

'Game and set!' Tod scooped up Sylvia's next serve and lobbed it gently over the net.

'I wasn't ready,' said Diane, 'and isn't it about time we changed ends? We've had the sun in our eyes all morning.'

'Good shot.' Cordelia looked fondly at Tod, and wondered why she hadn't noticed before that his brown eyes had interesting green flecks in them. 'I say, you're not wearing your glasses.'

'Safer without them when tennis balls are flying about,' said Tod. 'Poor Diane. Ought I to offer to play with Sylvia for a bit, do you think?'

'I'd rather you stayed with me.' Cordelia had a strong forehand, Tod had a wicked backhand, they made an ideal team. Anyway, she liked the way Tod smiled at her when she won a point, and the way he smiled at her when she lost one.

190

'Then stay I shall.' He put his arm casually around her shoulders as they strolled towards the back line. 'I'm enjoying this, aren't you?'

'Yes.' Cordelia trembled, pleasurably aware of Tod's arm.

'You're cold? Surely not?'

'Not,' Cordelia whispered, she seemed to have lost her voice. 'Your serve or mine?'

*   *   *

'I expect you've got work to do?' Diane said to Cordelia, on the way back to the house. 'Don't let us keep you.'

'I have, actually.' Cordelia looked at her watch. 'I ought to be helping Rosemary with the lunch. Thanks for the game,' she smiled straight into Tod's eyes, 'see you all later.'

'After lunch?' Tod called after her. She didn't smile like that at Stewart Cavalry-Twill, he thought. Perhaps Sheila Steinberg had been right, and he doesn't mean a thing to Cordelia any more. 'On the terrace?'

'On the terrace,' Cordelia shouted back, 'but can you make it before supper?'

'Somehow,' Sylvia murmured to Diane, 'I don't think we're included in that invitation.'

'Don't you speak to me,' said Diane. 'Some *partner*.' She turned to Tod. 'Do you know what I'd really, really like, Tod? A great big glass of orange juice.'

'Good idea.' Tod led the way towards the terrace outside the Light Diet Room. 'How about you, Sylvia?'

'Just a mineral water for me, darling.' Sylvia flopped down on a wicker chair, and Diane sat opposite and scowled at her until Tod returned.

'Bless you.' Diane adjusted her frills and made a little moue as Tod handed her the orange juice. Sylvia reflected that if she was casting an ingenué she would not instantly call up Mrs Renfrew.

191

'Goodness, I'm hungry,' Sylvia said. 'That game has given me an appetite.'

Diane abruptly abandoned her girlish role, and said tartly that in view of her partner's apparent inability to put one foot in front of another, she was surprised Sylvia had worked up enough appetite to toy with a radish. The word 'radish' reminded her of something she found even more irritating. 'I don't know about you two,' she said, 'but I am sick and tired of the third rate fruit they serve here, and those appallingly unimaginative salads. Would you be prepared to back me up, if I put in a formal complaint to Madame?'

Sylvia, who was not prepared to ally herself with Diane against anyone, particularly the ogre of Alba, looked quizzically at Tod, who winked back at her.

'It's not as if they don't have a kitchen garden bursting with produce,' said Diane, 'and have you seen inside those plastic tunnel things?'

'What plastic tunnel things?' said Sylvia.

Tod sat down next to Diane on the sofa. 'Polytunnels, at least half a dozen of them in the kitchen garden. Have you seen in them, Diane?'

'Just a little peep,' Diane inched closer to Tod. 'Isn't this cosy?'

This time Tod ignored Sylvia's quizzical eyebrow. He appeared to be bewitched by Diane Renfrew and was making no effort to edge away from her. What a curious young man; gazing adoringly at Cordelia one moment, and all but embracing the Renfrew woman, the next. Sylvia felt left out and put out. 'I think I'll go and change, I'm due in Steam Cabinets in ten minutes.'

Tod smiled briefly and Diane, simpering, carried on with her story. ' . . . and, what's more, my dear, there was nothing in there worth pinching. Just a few mushrooms . . . '

*   *   *

192

'Fifteen minutes for you, today, Miss Travers?' Mary adjusted the timer on the watch around her neck. 'I've got your Attar of Roses ready for you, when you come out.'

'Just ten, I think.' Sylvia was feeling wan after the tennis and the phone call to Theo's office. Why was he always out of the office when she needed him?

'Not too hot for you, is it?'

Sylvia realised that she was looking crossly at Mary Lawson, and switched on her smile. 'No, really, it's quite perfect, thank you.'

'That's all right, then.' Mary scuttled across to the door to greet Debbie Wynne-Jones. 'It's all ready for you, Miss Wynne-Jones.'

'Debbie,' Cordelia put her head around the door, 'telephone.'

Debbie shrugged back into her bathrobe. 'I'll be back in a minute, Mrs Lawson.'

Sylvia was emerging pinkly from her Steam Cabinet as Debbie returned, looking flustered and rather pleased with herself.

'Isaac?' Sylvia temporarily abandoned the pleasure of her shower.

Debbie nodded.

'I'll just pop you in the Cabinet, Miss Wynne-Jones,' said Mary.

'And?' said Sylvia.

'He said he loved me. He said the baby didn't make any difference.'

Mary Lawson muttered, 'Men,' and hurried to the other side of the room to fold towels.

'He said he was coming to pick me up on Sunday, he's booked a double room at the Atlantic.'

'And what did you say?'

'I told him,' said Debbie, 'to take a running jump at himself. And then go back to his wife.'

Mary stopped folding towels and came across the room

to slot Debbie into the Steam Cabinet. 'Well done, Miss Wynne-Jones,' she said.

*   *   *

Sylvia was sitting by the swimming pool wearing a black cotton jersey swimsuit which sliced inches off her waist and hips.

'Mind if I join you?' Adam Shepherd was standing next to her in striped boxer shorts.

'Of course not.' Sylvia gave Adam the full 120 watt smile as he spread a towel and sat down next to her. Was she imagining it, or was Adam Shepherd deliberately seeking her out? He had been attentive all week, saving a table for her at lunch, pouring out lemon drinks for her in the evening, waylaying her in corridors.

'Sheila Steinberg has gone home,' he said. 'I just ran into Mrs Renfrew in the corridor, fuming about disloyalty. She said her friend's husband phoned up and ordered her home, complaining that he hasn't had a decent hot meal since she left. I was somewhat surprised, I must confess. Haven't masterful men rather gone out of fashion?'

'What a shame, I liked Sheila Steinberg.' Sylvia wished she had a masterful man at home, yearning for her *boeuf en croûte*. She also wished she had asked Sheila to give her a trim before she packed up the tools of her trade and disappeared. Cordelia's new haircut was stunning.

'Really? Personally, I don't care for either of those women. Tough and vulgar. Not like you, Sylvia.' He leaned forward and took her hand. 'You're the sort of woman a chap wants to look after and cherish.'

'How sweet of you.' Now that she only seemed to be offered parts playing some other actress's mother, Sylvia was susceptible to flattery. She placed her other hand on top of Adam's, hoping the gesture appeared warm and responsive, rather than reminding him of that hearty children's game. 'Do you know, Adam, I could do with . . .

194

cherishing.'

'But surely, a woman like you . . . ?' Adam said, apparently lost in admiration of her perfectly manicured nails.

'My husband died a long time ago, there isn't anyone . . .'

Adam smiled with relief. 'I suppose you wouldn't care to dine with me at The Barley Mow tomorrow night?'

'Goodness me, Adam,' Sylvia withdrew her hands, 'I don't think Madame Cordoba would approve of dining.'

'I'm not asking Madame Cordoba,' Adam said, 'I'm asking you. Nothing more sinful than fruit juice and a little grilled fish?'

'Why not?' Sylvia said impulsively. 'What a delightful idea.'

As she swam slowly up and down the pool, being careful not to get her hair wet, Sylvia wondered how much of a delight it would actually be. Adam Shepherd, fifty-something-year-old City tycoon with a prosperous paunch all too visible above the striped trunks. Tricky, in the informal attire of a health farm, to pinpoint his exact social stratum and style, but probably the sort of Englishman who had his suits built by a traditional tailor, got them cleaned once a year and slung a watch-chain across his waistcoat as a badge of office. Not really her type . . .

'There isn't anyone,' she had said. *And* there wasn't any work, *and* she was weary of battling with life and taxes and mortgages by herself. She waved at Adam from the other end of the pool. Perhaps the time had come to try out a new role; gracious Mrs Weybridge, safely secluded behind her rhododendron hedges, renowned in Surrey and the City for her amusing dinner parties.

CHAPTER

EIGHTEEN

'I've got these dreadful lines, right here.' Sylvia Travers placed a finger at the corner of each eye and, deftly tightening the skin, turned a sombre slant-eyed gaze on Mr Patterson. 'And just look at my eyelids.' She closed her eyes, and gently massaged smooth lids to demonstrate their appalling flaccidity. 'The time has arrived,' she said on the note of high tragedy that went down so well when she toured Lady Macbeth, 'for plastic surgery.'

'Not my field, as you know.' Mr Patterson studied Miss Travers' admirably arranged bone structure. Forty-eight and she'd easily pass for thirty-eight if she didn't make such a performance over every wrinkle. 'I could, of course, give you an introduction to a colleague of mine in Harley Street, but are you quite sure, my dear? Plastic surgery doesn't last more than a few years, the skin loses its elasticity, and all you'll have achieved for the pain and expense will be some rather unsightly scars in your hairline.'

He knew that Sylvia Travers wanted her youth back. That's what they all wanted, particularly the ageing beauties who had lived on their looks. And Mr Patterson also knew that there was nothing he could do to help, except give them advice they didn't want to hear concerning fresh air, exercise and a sensible diet. 'You're taking the infusions?'

'Of course.' Sylvia always kept the magic packets in her purse, in case she needed to mix and sip before she went on stage. She had kept drying, when they were making the sitcom, there had been endless retakes, and the rest of the cast had stopped saying, 'It's all right, Sylvia darling, don't worry,' with any semblance of sincerity. Even darling Dennis, who was directing her so sensitively, had eventually lost patience. She had been forced to return to the dressing-room to down a quick draught to get her through the last scene of Episode Two.

'What I'm going to do, Miss Travers, is alter your prescription.' Mr Patterson scribbled a code on his leather-bound pad and passed it to Sylvia. 'Ask Sister Monica to make this up, then come back and see me in a couple of days.'

'It won't really alter anything, will it?'

'It should help you accept the inevitability of the passing years; something we all have to do.'

'But I don't want to accept growing old and ugly.'

Mr Patterson sighed. Why were the beauties always convinced they were plain, while quite homely women behaved as though they were irresistible? Something to do with early parental attitudes, no doubt, and it was simpler to hand out an infusion than delve into any of *that*. He came out from behind his desk and led Sylvia to the mirror. 'Look at yourself, Miss Travers.'

'No,' Sylvia buried her head in Mr Patterson's clinical lapel. 'No.'

Slowly, he turned her face to the mirror. 'You see. You're beautiful.'

*   *   *

After lunch Sylvia climbed into bed, emptied one of her new herbal packages into a glass, added a little water and switched on the television. A play; Sylvia adored watching television plays. It was a repeat, she could see that by the seventies hairstyles. Under one of them she recognised Penelope Wilton. She also recognised the lines and realised, with a spasm of pain, that Penelope was playing the part — admittedly rather well — that should rightfully have been hers.

'Sorry, darling,' Theo had said, when the role went to Miss Wilton. 'They adored you, of course, but Penelope is a Name.'

Sylvia switched off the television and downed her infusion in a gulp. It was no good Mr Patterson telling her she was beautiful. She knew she looked an old hag. Yesterday, when she'd had difficulty holding her yoga posture, Estelle had come over and said, 'We're none of us as young as we used to be,' and had talked tactlessly of Tiny Lines that Come with Maturity.

Sylvia decided to give Yoga a miss for the rest of her stay. She picked up the telephone, dialled the Beauty Room, and booked a facial. If she was to audition for Mrs Weybridge over dinner, she had better make herself look presentable.

*　　　*　　　*

Yvonne, the beautician, had pink lips matching her pink overall and pink décor and appeared to have been trained in the same School of Frankness as the yoga teacher. She scrutinised Sylvia's expertly made-up face and, as she helped her into the pink salon robe, spoke long and earnestly about The Necessity of Getting Rid of Dead Skin.

'Cleanse, tone, moisturise, that's our beauty motto at Alba, Miss Travers,' she lisped in a small voice which went oddly with the large bosom disconcertingly resting on Sylvia's arm, as she leant over to cleanse away Sylvia's handiwork. 'And when we've toned, we'll smooth on some of this aromatic oil,' she waved a small bottle in front of Sylvia, 'to rehydrate the skin and detoxify the body.'

'I didn't come to be detoxified,' said Sylvia through a mouthful of cotton wool, 'I came for a facial.'

'Oh, we believe in treating the skin in conjunction with the mind and the body. Our clients find the scent of Alba's oil wonderfully calming and restorative.'

198

Chatting cheerfully about Regenerating Tired Old Cells, Yvonne's pink-tipped fingers splashed, dabbed, smoothed, patted and massaged. 'And now for the herbal mask.' She smothered Sylvia with something that smelt like a wet pine wood. 'We'll just let those facial muscles relax.'

Sylvia's facial muscles knotted with irritation as they heard Yvonne tip-tapping across the room in her high heels to hold an animated conversation with someone on the other end of the phone about why she couldn't meet them for dinner that evening. 'That's the way,' Yvonne said, putting down the phone. 'Relax, Miss Travers. We'll have five minutes of perfect quiet.'

Sylvia spent the next five minutes trying not to hear Yvonne assembling her cosmetics, sharpening her pencils, and filing her nails.

'You've no idea how many of my clients just drift off to sleep under the mask.' Yvonne peeled it off, revealing Sylvia's face, naked, moist and bad tempered.

As Yvonne helped her out of the robe, twenty minutes later, Sylvia glimpsed herself in the mirror, and decided that although her cells didn't look noticeably livelier, Yvonne had done a good job with the pencils, mascara, creams and blusher. Almost as good as if I'd done it myself, she thought, tucking the tip under the telephone.

'How kind,' Yvonne discreetly counted the pound coins, 'and now, may I give you a wee tip? Alba's All Day Face Firmer would work miracles on those little laughter lines.'

*   *   *

Laughter lines! Tiny Lines that Come with Age! Is it any wonder I'm jittery? Sylvia was sitting on the terrace, waiting for Adam. She had taken another infusion, just a small one, as she was changing, and the effect had been even less calming than having a pine forest thrown on her face.

Gazing across the gracious lawns towards the lake (water was always so splendidly soothing) Sylvia had an uneasy presentiment of doom, and wondered if it was the prospect of dinner with Adam, or had she overdone the herbal drinks again? She had been aware, for some years now, that her magic packets didn't help her remember her lines, but they did make her feel better about forgetting them; just one sip and she had the confidence to step on the stage and make a fool of herself. This new prescription seemed to be galvanising her metabolism instead of encouraging it to nonchalantly lie back and relax. I'll have a word with Mr Patterson tomorrow, she decided, as Tod Ballard, carrying a large notebook and a sheaf of papers, came between her and the view.

'You're looking very elegant, Sylvia.'

'And you're looking very businesslike. Why don't you draw up a chair and join me?'

'The outline for my new book.' Tod carefully placed the notebook under his chair. 'I've been working on it, down by the lake. It's so peaceful there.'

'Is it a novel? Do tell – what's it all about?'

'Non-fiction, actually. I'd really rather not discuss it too much at the moment.'

'Of course.' Sylvia had met a lot of writers in her time, and knew how secretive they always were about their current project. 'I was just sitting here, Tod, looking at the lake, thinking how peaceful I ought to be feeling, and I was wondering . . . by the way, do you go in for these infusions?'

'Mr Patterson said I didn't need them,' said Tod. 'Why?'

'I've just been given a new prescription and I was wondering if that is why I am feeling so jittery. It's extraordinary, I've never actually asked what's in them. Herbs, I suppose and . . . what?'

'I haven't an idea,' said Tod, smiling tenderly at a spot behind Sylvia's left shoulder. 'Here's Cordelia, she might know.'

'What might I know?' Cordelia flopped down on the grass by Tod's chair.

'What's in the Alba infusions? Sylvia's feeling a bit jittery and thinks they may have something to do with it.'

'That's funny,' said Cordelia, 'Debbie was saying the other day how they'd changed her mood. Couldn't understand why she was feeling so cheerful.'

'Hullo there.' Adam Shepherd laid a hand on Sylvia's shoulder. 'Ready, Sylvia? I say, you look fantastic.'

'How kind.' Sylvia suppressed a frisson of gloom at the sight of the watch-chain looped across Adam's pinstriped waistcoat. 'Shall we go, then?'

'A romance?' said Tod, as Sylvia and Adam went off arm in arm.

'Yes.' Cordelia reached up and gently touched Tod's cheek.

Taking her hand in both of his, Tod leant forward. 'Cordelia, will you tell me something?'

'Of course.'

'These infusions?'

Cordelia took her hand away quickly, feeling foolishly vulnerable. 'All you ever seem to do,' she said, 'is ask questions.'

*   *   *

Cordelia went straight to her grandmother's study and tapped on the door.

'Just a minute, if you please,' Isabella called out, 'I'm in a meeting.'

The meeting Cordelia overheard behind the closed door was rancorous.

'You're surely not suggesting I've embezzled your money?' Rosemary Meadows' voice.

'A pretentious word for petty theft, Rosemary.'

Cordelia sat down on the chair in the corridor and assured herself that she was not really eavesdropping. 'I know all about your arrangement with Fred Pearson. You've been lining your pockets very efficiently at my expense.'

'How dare you speak to me like that?'

'And how dare you serve third rate food at my table and tarnish Alba's reputation?'

'I'm not listening to any more of this. My solicitor . . . '

'Your *solicitor*? Consider yourself fortunate that I have not called in the police. You can pack your bags, Miss Meadows, and leave Alba immediately.'

'Now, wait a moment, Madame, there's the matter of my salary . . . '

'Go, do you hear me. Go.'

Rosemary Meadows erupted out of the study. Behind her, Isabella was outlined against the french windows, arm aloft, like some fearful Biblical character. Cordelia shifted uneasily on her chair. Maybe she'd come back some other time.

'Come in, Cordelia.' Isabella was shaking with anger. Discovering that one of her staff had been cheating her was bad enough, but to be informed of the fact by a guest, and by Mrs Renfrew in particular, was especially galling. And now she would have to find another dietician.

'Sit down, child.' Isabella sighed, 'I regret to say that I have had to get rid of Rosemary Meadows.'

'I know. I couldn't help hearing. You were talking rather loudly.'

Isabella looked at her granddaughter speculatively. 'An idea has occurred to me. You, Cordelia, have all the necessary qualifications to take over the catering at Alba.'

Cordelia was not immediately enchanted with the idea. She was already on duty from seven thirty in the morning until the last guest went to bed. And she had no intention of giving up her forays to Shepherd's Bush. 'But . . . '

'No "buts", Cordelia. You are trained for the task, and I will, of course, recognise your new responsibilities financially.'

It occurred to Cordelia that this might be a good moment to mention the Will. Her father had nagged her about

202

it on the phone, only yesterday. 'I really don't need more money, grandmother, but now we're on the subject, there is something I'd like to talk to you about ... ' It was proving as awkward as Cordelia suspected, but ever since she had seen her grandmother going to pieces, Cordelia had felt more confident in her presence.

'Say what you've got to say, Cordelia.' Isabella was looking uncharacteristically benign.

'It's just that when I came here, you said you wanted me to take over Alba. Eventually, of course.'

'So I did.'

'Only it isn't legal, you see, unless you've made a proper Will, a bequest.'

'Of course. I have instructed my solicitor to draw up the relevant papers.' Isabella relaxed. Thank goodness the child was prepared to cooperate. She would get on to her solicitor about the Will at some later date. Much later. 'That's agreed then? You are prepared to take over Rosemary's duties?'

'Yes,' said Cordelia. 'I'd like to try.' She smiled at her grandmother. It hadn't been too difficult, after all.

'And now, Cordelia. What did you come to see me about?'

Cordelia was thinking about cost and quality control on a minimum of one hundred mixed salads daily, and how to make foolproof yogurt. Why had it seemed so important to talk to her grandmother? And then she remembered Tod and his questions on the terrace. 'Those herbal drinks, grandmother, the ones that Mr Patterson prescribes and Sister Monica doles out to some of the guests ... '

'What about them?' Isabella had stopped looking benign.

'People keep asking me what's in them.'

'Which people?'

'Well, Miss Travers, the actress, and Debbie Wynne-Jones, and ... and ... Tod.'

'That young man again. I thought I had made it clear,

203

Cordelia, that I do not approve of my staff fraternising with the guests.'

'Hardly fraternising . . . ' Cordelia began and stopped abruptly. Her grandmother was looking apocalyptic again.

'Our infusions have been expertly blended, especially for us, by a leading herbalist and pharmacologist. The ingredients would mean nothing to you or to any of our guests. If I hear that you have been discussing Alba's secrets with anyone, I repeat anyone, I shall have to ask you to leave. Do you understand me?'

'Yes,' said Cordelia, untruthfully.

* * *

Adam had noticed the Jasper Conran straight away, when they met on the terrace. Didn't know it was Jasper Conran, of course, just that she was wearing something well-cut in expensive material. 'That's a beautiful dress, Sylvia,' he said, as they picked up the heavily embossed menus. 'Looks well with your eyes.'

'It's a Jasper Conran,' Sylvia said, 'I'm so glad you like it, Adam.'

When women described a garment as 'a something-or-other', as in 'a St Laurent', Adam recognised that they were talking serious money. 'Something of an investment, then?' he said.

Sylvia heard warning bells. Men liked their women to be well-dressed, but even very rich men, she had observed, did not enjoy paying for it. 'A gift from BBC Wardrobe,' she said. 'I wore it in a series.'

They both did a certain amount of investigative thrusting and parrying over the melon (her) and grapefruit (him); the waiter had made a big thing of the Chef's Pâté and the escargots dripping in garlic and butter, but they'd agreed that it was pointless to come to a health farm and then ruin it all on a blow-out.

'Tell me about Weybridge? St George's Hill, isn't that

choc a bloc with Rolling Stones?' Sylvia propped her chin on her hand (it made her neck look younger and longer) and gazed at Adam raptly.

As they ate their grilled sole (her), and rare steak (him), Adam told her about Merrymount. Edwardian mansion, eight bedrooms, en suite, naturally, billiard room, five acres, lawns, rhododendron hedges and so on. 'Truthfully, it's not exactly St George's Hill, but in a private road just off it.' A certain amount of frankness always went down well with the ladies. He didn't tell her that the house belonged to Costas Karayiannis, who let him have a room at Merrymount for old time's sake; they'd been partners in a construction company at the time of the '74/'75 crash. Costas had recovered and prospered, Adam was still working on it. 'Perfect in the spring, birdsong and buds,' he said, 'but an appalling commute. I'm thinking of getting a *pied-à-terre* in town. You live in Marlborough Mansions, I understand? Prestige block, porterage, ten minutes from the City, just what I'm after.'

'I believe there are one or two vacant flats, but it's awfully expensive. I'm lucky, you see,' Sylvia smiled guilelessly at him over her sole, 'I've been there years and years. I'm what is called a Sitting Tenant.'

The words struck a chill in Adam's soul. It was the sitting tenants who'd knocked twelve per cent off the value of the Richmond block when the bank withdrew their loan and forced him to sell; it was, in effect, the sitting tenants who had put Trasker Corbett into the hands of the Receiver. If it hadn't been for the sitting tenants he wouldn't, now, be starving himself in health farms, jiggling foolishly in gyms, and ogling women whose main charm lay in their cheque books. 'Lucky you,' he forced himself to say, 'you're on a controlled rent, then?'

'Thirty pounds a week, would you believe? Isn't it brilliant? Inclusive of rates. I have to pay for the electricity and the telephone, of course. But, you know, Adam,' Sylvia reached across the table and laid her hand on his, 'I'm getting so tired of London. The noise, the dirt, the litter. Sometimes I yearn for the countryside; the song of the birds, the buds hopefully opening to the spring, as you so beautifully put it, my dear, the delicious peace.'

'Quite so,' said Adam, pouring out the last of the Mersault '87. He'd persuaded Sylvia that even Madame Cordoba would consider a light white wine acceptable; he had been planning to oil the wheels of commerce, as it were. It seemed a pity to waste an intriguing vintage. He cast one final, hopeful line over the coffee. 'Your husband? Please don't talk about him if it is too painful, was he in business?'

'Will? Gracious, no. How sweet of you to worry about my feelings, Adam, but it was all so long, long ago.' Sylvia told Adam all about her handsome young husband, 'A tremendously talented set designer, darling, but you know how tough it is in *that* world. Luckily, I was earning good money at the time.'

She told him about the delivery van and how she had sat by Will's hospital bed, waiting for him to regain consciousness. 'He never did. They wanted to put him on a life machine, but I wouldn't have it. He looked so peaceful, you see.'

Adam found the story heart-rending. He had wasted three valuable days courting an out of work, penniless actress.

CHAPTER
NINETEEN

'Enjoying the sunshine, Mrs Er ... ? Another lovely day, aren't we lucky! Though it did say on the forecast last night that there might be showers in the south. Well, I must be off, no rest for the wicked.'

Mary Lawson flittered off, thinking she really must try and remember people's names better. Madame always insisted on the personal touch ('We at Alba must never forget that we are, above all, hosts'), but really, there was so much to think about. She must remember to ask Madame if she could have Thursday afternoon off for the children's sports day; one of them must be there, and Matt certainly wouldn't go. Thinking of Matt muddled her even more. That little cat, Antonia, with her insinuations ('Having it off with some masseur,' she'd said, while Mary was obligingly scrubbing salt into her spotty little adolescent back. And giving Mary one of those 'you poor cow' looks over her shoulder as she said it).

Of course they weren't just insinuations. Diane Renfrew. How could he. Naturally, Mary knew that men had different needs, she'd found that out quite early in her marriage. But Matt always came back to her, so she supposed she could count herself lucky.

And give him his due, he'd been really lovely during their week-end off. It had been so thoughtful of him to suggest they visited his old folks in Leyburn; she'd always got on with his mum and dad. 'Well, lass,' his dad had said, when Matt first brought her home to tea, 'our Matt has had his flings, I won't say he hasn't. But when it's time to settle,

I've always said to him, go for a local girl.' Mary had blushed, because Matt hadn't said anything yet to her about settling, and then Matt's mother had brought in the tea-tray and made her feel really welcome.

And they were still fond of her, all these years later, and told her what wonderful grandchildren she'd given them. It had been a perfect little break, that week-end, made even more perfect when, on Saturday morning, Matt said they'd go over and visit Mary's father, two villages away. 'It's time he saw his grandchildren, and you and I can have a stroll round the cemetery, Mary.' Mary giggled, even at her age, because the cemetery had been where they did their courting. It was nice of Matt to suggest they go over there, because he'd never got on with her dad. Mum had liked him, most women did, but mum was dead now, and dad lived with Mary's brother and sister-in-law in a very smart new house with everything indoors, which dad hated. He had retaliated for having to leave his good old cottage with everything right about it, by insisting on bringing his live-stock with him.

In the end they hadn't strolled round the cemetery, be-cause Matt had spent all morning talking to her dad; really putting himself out, he was, and she could see her brother didn't like it. She'd heard him saying to his wife, when he didn't know Mary was sitting on the bench outside the kitchen window, 'What's that smarmy little creep up to? Never bothers to come here, doesn't even let Mary visit, and suddenly he's all over dad. Thinking of the Will, I bet, that Matt never did anything for nothing.'

'Ssh, love, Mary's in the garden somewhere, supposing she heard,' Tom's nice wife whispered, 'and you've got to admit, those children are beautifully brought up.'

'That'll be Mary's doing,' said Tom. 'The last thing that cheating womaniser ever did for them was nine months before they were born.'

And Mary had slid off the bench and crept round the corner of the house to find her children and show them the

208

pigeons and the rabbits and the little brown hens that crooned and chuckled in nesting boxes.

*   *   *

Mrs Er, who was used to people forgetting her name, watched Mary bustle towards the treatment wing. A sad little woman, she thought, who would have been perfectly happy in a different civilisation, where it was taken for granted that women did the work and the child-bearing, while the men sowed their seed as and when they wished, and occasionally rowed out to kill some fish, making rather a performance about it.

Monogamy, though a good idea in many ways, reflected the woman who twenty years before had been widely tipped for future professorship, puts a terrible strain on those for whom it doesn't happen to work.

Jane Fellowes laughed to herself at the idea of a brown-skinned Mary Lawson strolling about some Pacific isle with a vague piece of cloth round her loins and nothing on top. Mary herself would be affronted at the thought, but anthropologically such a life would suit her down to the ground.

Jane was actually toying with the idea of writing a paper on the study of anthropology in a health farm; she would, of course, have to think up some frightfully pretentious title; several frivolous ones occurred to her. 'Aromatherapy and the Incest Taboo' had a certain ring to it, or possibly 'Colonic Irrigation: The Neolithic Imperative'? More accurately, thought Jane, the way people at Alba here jostled for advantage, 'The Contextual Definition of Masseur Status'.

Anyway, whatever she called it, it would make a good beginning to her return to work. And whatever Henry said, she was going to work again.

Ten days away from the people who loved her best had done her no end of good physically. Things would take a turn for the better, once she got home, and in the meantime, she had plenty to occupy her mind.

Jane Fellowes was by instinct and training an observer, and in Alba she had found a rich field for scientific appraisal. Or, putting it a shade more truthfully, as she admitted to herself, there was a lot going on, some of it quite riveting.

To begin with, the love interest. Cordelia and Tod Ballard plainly took a great deal of delight in each other. But all was not going as it should. For several days Tod had been giving every evidence of going out of his way to avoid Cordelia. And yesterday morning he had been actually rude to her.

Jane had been sunning herself after Steam Cabinets; she had (almost, but not quite, unconsciously) chosen a protected corner near french windows which led into the Diet Room and the Drawing Room, and with a good view of the path along which staff members made their way from their quarters.

She watched, with some interest, Cordelia emerging from the rather stark buildings in which Isabella housed her employees. What has she done to her hair? she thought. And doesn't it look good? Jane was not all that interested in personal appearance, but even she could see that the outfit Cordelia was dressed in had cost about as much as Henry Fellowes allowed his wife per year to clothe herself in the sensible skirts suitable to a don's wife.

Cordelia wandered up the path towards the house, tossing her new mane about and smiling to herself. And looking, thought Jane, delightfully foolish in the process. She arrived at the point where the path forked to go left to the Treatment Block and right to the house proper. Jane watched Cordelia pause, lean against a tree, and light a cigarette.

Tod came out of the Treatment Block. Cordelia dropped her cigarette and stood on it, apparently deciding that the left fork was the one she had intended to take all along.

'Oh. Good morning,' said Tod when they met (rather unfortunately from Jane's point of view, just where the path curved behind some rhododendrons, a plant she had never cared for). Still, they were near enough to overhear.

'Hullo, Tod, I haven't seen you for ages.'

'Haven't you? Well, I've been here. Nobody told me Sheila Steinberg had left.'

'I don't suppose anybody thought you'd be interested. Anyway, didn't you notice she wasn't around?'

'When did she go?'

'She decided to go home the other night, after she'd done my hair. She did it awfully well, didn't she?'

'What? Yes, it looks . . . it's a bit shorter, isn't it? You actually saw her go, did you?'

'Not exactly. I say, Tod, I was thinking of going to . . . '

'I mean, did she take a taxi? Only she hadn't been feeling very well, had she?'

'She took her own car. Diane was frightfully put out.'

They had emerged from behind the rhododendrons; Jane rather liked Cordelia, and wondered if she would take it amiss if she advised her that walking sideways two paces in front of the beloved was puppyish rather than seductive.

'But, was she fit to drive? Those infusions she took. Surely . . . '

'She looked all right to me. I can't think why you're so interested, it's actually quite boring, talking about Sheila Steinberg all the time. Anyway, Tod, I thought it would be fun to visit that Rural Arts Museum in . . . '

'There's something I want to ask you.' Tod took off his glasses; Jane thought she really ought to stop eavesdropping, it did seem to be getting a bit intimate. Cordelia obviously thought so too.

'Do you, Tod?' She smiled up into his face.

'Well, you never actually told me about the infusions, did you, Cordelia? Sister Monica is in charge of Extras, isn't she?'

Jane noted, regretfully, that Cordelia was disappointed,

and had decided to stand on her dignity.

'I am Madame's granddaughter, after all, she takes me into her confidence about everything. Sister Monica just does what we tell her.'

Jane sighed to herself; it was so easy to see how the game was going when you were merely an observer. Cordelia was obviously trying to make herself sound as important as possible; equally obviously, Tod didn't care for the way she was talking, and Jane didn't blame him.

'I see,' he said, putting on his glasses again. 'Well, I must be off.'

'But don't you want to come to the Museum?'

'No. I don't think I do.'

*   *   *

Now, Jane, back in her warm position of observational advantage, was reflecting how much better they managed courtship in the rain forests, when she saw Rachel Gillespie and Adam Shepherd, with the *Financial Times* under his arm, strolling across the lawn. They were virtually out of earshot; all Jane could hear was an occasional polite laugh. They paused at a rustic bench; Adam was plainly inviting Rachel to sit down, but she shook her head and wandered off towards the Treatment Block. Adam, left alone, providently put the *Financial Times* on the bench (it had rained the night before) and sat down on it.

Antonia, attended by Sarah Gerard, drifted up. 'Hullo, mum, how are you? All right?'

'Lovely, thank you, darling. It's so warm and comfortable here.'

'Oh, good. Sarah and I are off to play tenny. See you later, then.'

Antonia, frightfully clever, frightfully confident, and (thought her mother) almost totally humourless and not all that hot on the kindness stakes, turned to go. 'Come on, Sarah, otherwise those ghastly old geriatrics will have

212

bagged the court.'

'Geriatrics? Who on earth do you mean, darling?'

'Adam Shepherd and Tristram. Sarah! You're such a slug, do get on.'

But Sarah had sunk down next to Jane's chair. 'They're just serving elevenses, Mrs Fellowes. Would you like me to bring you a cup of tea?'

'How nice of you, Sarah. I must say, that does sound . . .'

'Mum never drinks tea, do you, mum?'

'Only because I hardly ever have time. Actually, I would love a cup.'

'It'll take ages. Oh, boring, I suppose I'd better go ahead and bag the court then,' said her daughter ungraciously. 'Try and get there before sunset, would you, Sarah?'

Antonia strode off, and Sarah, ducking her head and giving a nervous smile to Jane, trotted off in the direction of the Light Diet Room.

Jane picked up her Dick Francis, read a couple of paragraphs without taking anything in, and put it down again. Antonia, her first child and her least favourite. Possibly, admitted Jane, attempting an objective view, because her birth meant the end of research, the end of the fellowship she had been unofficially promised, the end of using her brain as it was meant to be used.

But more probably because Antonia really was quite tiresome. Just like her father, thought Jane, revelling in a disloyalty which she had never allowed herself before. She stretched a luxuriously brown leg whose contours had improved considerably after several days' exercise. There would be some changes made. She couldn't wait to see Henry's face when she told him that if he wanted clean shirts he'd better learn how to work the washing machine, and who gave a toss if there was a stain on the sitting room carpet.

'I say, I'm terribly sorry, Mrs Fellowes, but I slopped a bit into the saucer.' Sarah was back, bearing a teacup in

Alba's distinctive china. (Mint green, with a thin blue line on the rim, and having about it an ecological air. Isabella was always ahead of her time.) 'I don't know whether you take sugar, but I brought some anyway, brown lumps, is that all right? And did you want biscuits? There's a couple of Garibaldis and a Nice, is that all right?'

'Oh, Sarah, you are kind. Everything's all right. I'll just have a Garibaldi. Why don't you have the others?'

'Oh, I couldn't, Mrs Fellowes. They're not on my diet. They're full of sugar, and stuff. I'm so overweight, you see.'

Jane sipped her tea, looked at Sarah's thin body, and said, somewhat to her own surprise, 'Crap.'

'What?' In Sarah's experience, her friends' mothers seldom said 'crap', but now that Mrs Fellowes had said it, it sort of made her easier to talk to.

'You weigh about as much as twenty humming birds, Sarah. If you put on a couple of stone, you'd still be a small size ten. You're a nice child, why are you doing this to yourself?'

'My hips are so gross. I say, Mrs Fellowes . . . ' Sarah had not engineered a moment alone with Antonia's mother in order to have one of those boring grown-up conversations about how she was nothing but skin and bones, ' . . . I say, I was wondering if you think those infusions are doing Antonia any good? Only Mr Patterson suggested this morning that I went on them, and I don't know if it's a good idea.'

'Infusions?'

'Yes, you know, those night-time drinks she has. Only I think she's got a bit edgy, sort of, in the last few days, and I wondered if it was them.'

'I shouldn't have thought so; she's always been a rather impatient kind of person, you know. Anyway, they're just some herbal preparation. I asked Sister Monica. "Nature's remedies are the best," she said, "garnered from the hedgerows."'

Sarah thought that for a clever person, Mrs Fellowes was

214

being a bit naive; foxglove was a plant, wasn't it, and you made digitalis out of it, didn't you? Not that she thought that Sister Monica sat up at night putting foxgloves into people's drinks, but the principle was the same. And when you got down to it, there were parts of the world where cannabis was garnered from the hedgerows. (Sarah didn't suppose for a moment that Mrs Fellowes knew that Antonia smoked pot. Antonia had several times offered her a joint, and Sarah had been made to feel an unsophisticated baby because she said she'd rather not. 'Everybody smokes at Oxford,' said Antonia, 'but of course you're not going to Oxford, are you?')

'I suppose Antonia's so impatient with me because she's so much cleverer than I am.'

Jane got up, looked at her watch, and said 'Massage in two minutes, I must rush. Thank you for the tea, Sarah. Antonia is very bright academically; she hasn't the faintest idea of how to deal with people, which you seem to be rather good at. Don't do yourself down.'

'Oh, right. Christ, Antonia will kill me. See you.'

Sarah bounded off, and Jane gathered up her things and made for the Treatment Block.

*   *   *

'I can really see a difference in the muscle tone in your legs, Mrs Fellowes, you must be awfully pleased.'

Lucy, the competent masseuse despised by Tristram, was doing her usual excellent work. Jane's shoulders were so relaxed she could practically feel them yawning; the sense of healthy well-being ran right down to her fingertips. Matt, she knew, was the masseur the 'in' clients at Alba insisted on. She couldn't think why. From what she had seen of him he was pushy, aggressive, and with a hot glow in his blue eyes that made Jane glad that Antonia went to Lucy, too.

Lucy's voice was as mesmeric as her hands. Jane, her

215

face comfortably ensconced in the little hole at the head of the massage table, drifted comfortably in and out of attention.

' ... Sharon's always liked to have her own way, of course, but mum's really putting her foot down this time. No daughter of mine is getting married in a mini skirt, she said, and as for Pete's idea of turning up at the wedding on a motor bike ... ! And as if I didn't have enough of arguing at home, coming to work's been quite a strain lately, Mrs Fellowes ... just relax that ankle, lovely ... Matt came back from his weekend off in a very funny mood, even more bumptious than usual. I know he's supposed to be head masseur, and I'm not one to take offence, but I don't see why I should have to put up with that sort of behaviour. And you should have heard the way he spoke to Sister Monica, she was fit to be tied. And when she said 'Madame will hear of this!' he said, 'That's not all she's going to hear,' can you imagine? I'm quite looking forward to Saturday, Mum and I are going into Guildford to get our dresses for the wedding, we thought we'd make a day of it. Mary Lawson's even more nervy than usual, have you noticed?'

*   *   *

Jane had her shower after Massage, thinking that one was seldom out of water in Alba, and that was possibly why one was so relaxed; back to the amniotic fluid, the first place of safety. Stepping frankly out of the shower without bothering to wrap a towel discreetly round her, she nearly bumped into Sylvia Travers, who was being similarly casual. Hardly surprising, thought Jane without a trace of envy; your average eighteen-year-old would have been quite happy to have Sylvia's body.

'Isn't it funny?' said Jane. 'When I first came here I behaved like a Victorian matron on Brighton Beach. You know, clutching towels and bathrobes round me in case

216

someone caught a glimpse of tummy. But now, just a few days later . . . '

'Oh, my dear, I do know,' said Sylvia, 'nudity is something we, in the profession, have to come to terms with.' Jane had known quite a few actors in her time, from undergraduates in OUDS to thespians visiting Oxford for lectures and needing to be entertained. They all, without exception, were adept at leading any subject of conversation, from the greenhouse effect to holidays in Tuscany, into What It Is Like Treading the Boards.

'Have you ever, er . . . acted without . . . ?'

'Only once, in the Scottish play on tour. Our director, so young and so talented, he's working at Greenwich now, said . . . '

'*Macbeth*?' said Jane incredulously. Sylvia shuddered slightly at the mention of the unlucky name.

'Well, yes. I was playing Herself, and Ronnie Palfrey felt . . . '

'Lady Macbeth? You played her naked?'

'Only in the mad scene. It is at night, after all, and Ronnie said they didn't wear nightdresses in those days, so, in the cause of realism, I was prepared . . . and of course the lighting was integral to my interpretation.'

'Jolly painful if you'd got wax from that candle on you,' said Jane practically.

'There wasn't any candle. It was a modern version, set in Milton Keynes. I was playing a rising young sales manager's wife whose boss is coming to dinner after a selling tour of Japan. Of course, we had to rethink the banquet scene entirely.'

Jane, who had had quite enough of this nonsense, finished drying off and got into her track suit, whose waist, she noted complacently, was much more comfortable than it had been a week ago. 'Goodness,' she said, 'is it time for lunch already?'

Everyone looked forward to meals much more now that Rosemary Meadows had left and Cordelia was in charge.

That made three people leaving inside a week, thought Jane. First, Mr Pullen, whose disappearance, according to Antonia, coincided with her sighting of a funeral van parked outside Alba's tradesmen's entrance. Jane wondered whether this was actually true, or whether (a) Antonia had been watching too many late night movies, (b) Antonia was naughtily stirring things up, or (c) whether Antonia thought she saw it because she had been smoking pot. Jane was considerably less naive about her daughter's habits than Sarah had supposed.

Then there was Sheila Steinberg, whose departure seemed to be perfectly above board; only why had Tod Ballard asked Cordelia all those questions about her this morning? And, of course, Rosemary Meadows, about whose exit there was no mystery at all. Diane had button-holed just about every client in the place with a detailed description of how she, Diane, had personally caught out Rosemary in the great Organic Fruit and Vegetable Fraud, had triumphantly presented Madame with the evidence, and had the satisfaction of seeing her, for once, slightly at a loss.

Cordelia was behind the counter in the Light Diet Room, handing out meals individually tailored to clients' requirements. In the days of Miss Meadows, Jane had noticed cynically, each and every client seemed to have identical requirements. But now, it was apparent that a great deal of time and thought had gone into making roughly two hundred calories into appetising and interesting combinations. Also, as Diane never failed to point out, the apples were crisper, the oranges juicier, and the melons did not resemble yellow cotton wool.

Those who were not at Alba for weight loss, and ate in the Main Dining Room, reported excitedly of *cuisine minceur* delights. 'Mousseline of sole and pistachio in a watercress sauce,' Jane had overheard Debbie torturing Tristram, 'and afterwards, the most delicious mango water ice.'

'Shut up,' said Tristram, 'you're being beastly.'

'And the menu for tonight,' continued Debbie inexorably, 'is homemade mushroom soup, followed by pasta *con vongole*, and . . .'

'Go away,' said Tristram, '*now*, or I will strangle you. If there's any justice the clams will have gone off, and you'll spend the night writhing in pain.'

In Jane's opinion, Tristram, though an odious little squirt, was the only man in the place who was completely genuine. He knew a great deal about food, (and had, indeed, kindly given Jane a completely foolproof recipe for Hollandaise) and, anyway, Jane had often read his articles while waiting for one of her children at the dentist.

Tod, on the other hand, though pleasant, diffident, and attractive, didn't seem much like a writer to Jane. God knew she had known enough of them, and they fell, in her experience, into two camps. Either they reacted to the lightest query about their work as though they had been asked to produce some grossly damaging information about their private lives; or they talked about it all the time. Jane, at some recent college function, had been enchanted to find she was seated next to a world-famous novelist whose works were composed of fifty per cent violence, thirty per cent sex, and twenty per cent plots so convoluted that you had to keep on turning back to page fourteen to see who Lermontov was. She had looked forward to steamy revelations of the underworld of international crime. What she had got was an hour and three-quarters of Things That Have Gone Wrong With my Word-Processor.

So, finding herself alone with Tod one afternoon she had kindly encouraged him to talk about his work. 'I expect you use a word-processor, don't you? Nearly everybody seems to nowadays,' she said, in the gentle manner which worked so well with worried undergraduates.

'Not really, no,' said Tod. 'Are you doing Aerobics this afternoon?'

'I expect you've got a good old faithful portable, then?'

'Yes, I have. So much less to go wrong, and really, I'm such a fool with computers and things.'

'Which one? My husband won't be parted from his old Olivetti.'

'That's what I've got, an Olivetti. Very fond of it.' And before she could ask him anything else, he was gone. Jane suspected Tod was not a fool about anything; his eyes were alert behind those dreadfully thick glasses. She hadn't quite worked out yet why he should pretend to be stupid.

As for Adam Shepherd, he might have been a business-man once, but she would bet the Bank of England to a banana that he wasn't one now. True, he made a point of taking the *Financial Times* every day, and flourishing it about a lot, but Jane had looked at the copy he'd discarded on the bench, and as far as she could tell from its un-crumpled appearance, all he'd done to it was complete three clues in the crossword puzzle. And one of them was wrong; Jane spent the next twelve minutes finishing it.

Taking her tray from Cordelia, Jane looked round the room, hoping to find an empty table so she could eat and read. Unfortunately she caught Erica Gerard's eye in the process.

'Do join us, Mrs Fellowes, Sarah and I would love it, wouldn't we, darling?'

Sarah stood up obligingly, smiled warmly at Jane, and started moving things around on the table so that there was room for Jane's tray.

'Oh, thank you, how kind. Doesn't this look good? Things are looking up, aren't they?'

'Only they give you far too much,' said Sarah, moodily pushing sections of melon round her plate.

'These girls and their diets . . . ' said Erica in a manner which Jane could only describe as bibulous (no doubt she had had a couple of quick ones before lunch, and fruit salad, no matter how exotic, was doing nothing to muffle the alcohol) ' . . . always talking about calories. I expect your nice Antonia does it too, doesn't she? It's just a stage, of course. You'll have to eat more than that when you go to university, darling.'

'I haven't definitely decided whether I'm going, yet.'

'Of course you're going. Exeter, such a beautiful city, you'll have such fun. And I gather such nice people go there.'

'More fun to drop out, actually. Celia's working in this bar in Amsterdam, she's having an amazing time.'

'Oh, there's that nice Mr Shepherd, I must just have a word with him about bridge tonight.' Erica fluttered over to the other side of the room and confronted Adam, who smiled warily.

Jane resisted an impulse to touch Sarah; if she did the child would almost certainly cry. 'If you do go, what will you read?'

'Oh, Geography, you know, one of those vague subjects for dimmos.'

'Come off it, Sarah,' said Jane briskly, 'Exeter doesn't take dimmos. What sort of A levels did you get?'

'Two Bs and a C. And one of them was a retake.'

'Extremely respectable. And don't knock Geography; I'm an anthropologist, you know, and one of the brightest people in my year transferred from Geography.'

'Really?' said Sarah, picking up a piece of mango and eating it, 'an anthropologist? So how do you view the people in this place?'

'Well, let's see. Two of them are almost certainly not what they pretend to be. Two of them are in love and making a frightful mess of it. One of them is a demanding and selfish old woman. One of them makes me want to pull her high-lighted hair whenever she comes in reach. And one of them,' said Jane, hoping she wasn't going too far, 'is starving herself to attract attention from parents who probably don't deserve her.'

'I suppose you mean me.' Sarah looked at Jane with eyes that were too bright. 'It's not mum's fault . . . she just gets a bit vague sometimes.'

'I'm sorry. I really shouldn't have said that.'

'It's all right,' said Sarah, picking up a slice of peach and putting it down again, 'I say, Mrs Fellowes, could I talk to you sometime? I mean, somewhere quieter?'

'I've got Underwater Massage at three. After that, nothing. I usually take a book to that little terrace just outside those french windows.'

*   *   *

Sarah rather wished, as she peered through the french windows and saw Jane sitting with a book on the terrace, that she hadn't suggested this meeting at all. It had been on an impulse, saying, 'I say, Mrs Fellowes, could I talk to you?'; but now she was about to, she couldn't think of anything to say. So, okay, dad was never around and mum's eyes were glazed most of the time, but what could Mrs Fellowes do about that?

Sarah contemplated forgetting the whole thing and going and watching telly in her room (only an hour and a half until *Neighbours*), then thought that no, that would be rude, and Antonia's mother seemed a lot more polite than Antonia herself.

So she pushed open the french window, which fairly typically caught in the wind and banged open, causing Mrs Fellowes to jump. 'I say, I'm awfully sorry. Did I give you a fright?'

'No. It's just that I've got to a rather dramatic moment in my book.'

Mrs Fellowes had by her a pile of books which were the kind Sarah supposed Clever Women read. *Sense and Sensibility*, the Pepys diaries, and a very thick book called *Lower Palaeolithic something-or-other*. What she was actually reading was a book by Dick Francis called *Straight*. Sarah had read it herself and thought it amazing, but it wasn't the kind of book you boasted about reading, at least

222

not round Antonia. Antonia only read books by foreigners; and when you asked her what they were about, she told you and you didn't understand.

'Are you enjoying it, Mrs Fellowes?'

'Yes, very much. Do call me Jane. Some poor chauffeur's just been shot.'

'That's got nothing to do with the missing diamonds. It was actually . . . '

'Don't dare tell me. His plotting is quite excellent, isn't it?' Jane put a Waterstone book marker between the pages, and laid the book aside. 'Feeling better?'

'I'm afraid I was a bit silly at lunch.'

'No, you weren't. One of the unfair things about life is that grown-ups expect you to listen to every word they say as though it was the latest epistle from St Paul; but don't feel obliged to listen all that carefully to what their off-spring say. I've done it myself, I'm afraid.'

'I thought they'd be proud of me, making it to Exeter. But I don't think dad has even taken it on board, and mum seems to think it's going to be one long party with a lot of nice girls and suitable young men. Her words, not mine. I could kill for a digestive biscuit, couldn't you?'

'I keep on thinking about risotto. Be fair, it's meant to be fun, along with all the work. Sarah, I hope you don't mind me saying this, but . . . I'm awfully sorry, but has your mother ever considered, well, treatment?'

'I've heard her and dad shouting,' Sarah's face shrank at the memory, 'but she says she's not an alcoholic, she's just someone who likes a drink occasionally.'

'It's a hard fact that the first step towards a cure is to admit that you need treatment.'

'So you think I should persuade her?'

'I suspect someone should.'

'Mrs Fellowes, Jane I mean, you're so clever. I suppose you wouldn't?'

'I hardly know your mother. I think she'd find it offensive. Have you talked to your father about it?'

223

'Never there.'

'Oh, come on. I suppose he sometimes comes home to eat and sleep, doesn't he?'

'Yes, but he's got this study on the third floor, and . . .'

'So tap on the door one evening, and go in and talk to him. I don't know, tell him you're going to a dance, and does he think your dress is right. Tell him you're worried about your mother, and is there anything you can do. Ask his advice about Exeter. Have you ever actually talked to him, Sarah?'

'He wouldn't be interested.'

'How do you know, until you've tried? My bet is he's the one who feels rejected, by you. The old are terrified of the young, you know.'

Sarah giggled and then stopped giggling because it seemed rude. She thought that although Jane was very clever, that was pushing it a bit. The idea of dad being terrified of her!

CHAPTER
TWENTY

'I'm not a natural mover, I'm afraid.' Adam was aware of the sweat trickling down the inside of his T-shirt, as Carolyn Watson switched off the cassette player.

'You're doing splendidly.' Carolyn's salary depended on keeping up the numbers in her class, and the gentlemen did have an inconsiderate way of dropping out of Movement to Music if they were not primed with constant reassurance.

'You wouldn't, by any chance, be pulling my leg?'

'Certainly not.' Carolyn looked round for confirmation and was pleased to see an actress in the offing. 'Aren't I right, Miss Travers?'

'What's that?' Sylvia came over and dumped her mat on the pile next to Carolyn.

'I was just telling Mr Shepherd how splendidly he's doing.'

'*Splendidly*,' said Sylvia, on cue. 'Adam, my dear, I've been looking for you, to thank you; such a lovely evening.'

Carolyn looked at the two of them. Another Alba romance. She had never been sure whether it was healthy living, boredom, or proximity that set the clients' hormones racing about so excitedly. Picking up her cardigan and cassette, she called out, 'See you tomorrow, everyone.'

'Divine, darling.' Sylvia took Adam's arm, 'Now, what are we going to do today?'

'Lot of papers to catch up with,' Adam mumbled, disentangling his arm.

'You're meant to be relaxing, remember? How about a

swim? It's glorious down by the pool.'

'And I've promised to go jogging with Tristram,' Adam said.

*   *   *

'I'm singing in the rain ... I'm singing in the rain ... singing in the ra-ain, I'm singing in the rain ... '

Adam stood in the shower, lathering on the Palmolive and thinking what a good thing it was that his first wife was not listening and tensing with irritation as he sang the wrong words. It had driven his second wife mad, too. Funny thing, that. Funny things, women.

Why hadn't he said, 'See you around, Sylvia,' the ultimate don't-call-me-I'll-call-you brush-off? Something had stopped him. Surely he wasn't getting sensitive all of a sudden? The truth of the matter was that he had enjoyed the dinner and Sylvia was good company, a damned attractive woman. They were two of a kind; each of them spinning a professional line in the hope of hooking the other.

He had marked Sylvia down as a likely possibility from the beginning. The flat in affluent St John's Wood, weekly deliveries of Daz and stuff from Selfridges (only women with expendable cash dallied with that extravagance), clothes he instantly recognised as the Real Thing, rather than cheap copies. He should have realised, of course, that actresses never stop acting, and he had to hand it to Sylvia for throwing her all into the County Lady role; she'd certainly had him fooled. 'TRAVERS, Sylvia: fortyish actress, stunner in her time. Affluent. Rich man's widow?' he'd jotted in his notebook. How could he have got it so wrong?

He put on his bathrobe, picked up his notebook and ran his finger nimbly through a list of the Alba clientele. No to the Gerards, likewise the Fellowes and Ms Wynne-Jones. Diane Renfrew? Almost certainly running that little boutique on a bank overdraft. He put a question mark next to Lady Drummond. Sir William probably kept a keen eye on the bank statements; he had not made his pile in order to watch his wife hand it trustingly to a stranger. A lady on her own was always a better bet.

It had astonished him how even the sharpest women could be persuaded to open their cheque books if they were subtly primed with flattery and the promise of a higher annual percentage on their widows' mites. Look at Delia Sargent, seventy-four years old, widow of a rich South African industrialist; Adam's first and most satisfactory hit, so far. The staff at the Essex Hydro had trembled every time she pursed her lips, but it had taken only a modicum of gallantry ('If only today's young women had your exquisite taste, Delia') and a minimum investment (one week in Torquay and he'd been quite prepared to fork out for Barbados) before he'd got a look at her portfolio, and managed to persuade her to transplant a quarter of a million into the Quinta da Vasco Development Corporation's exciting new holiday complex.

She had got on to her bank manager after marvelling at the colourful brochure, an artist's impression, of course. 'Only fifty minutes from Faro, a once in a lifetime chance for capital appreciation *and* a high yield,' Adam had told her.

After Trasker Corbett had gone belly up, Adam and Gerry Brookman, the Finance Director, had managed to lay their hands on forty barren acres of Portugal for less than the cost of a terraced house in Brixton. Fifty minutes from Faro if you happened to be a crow; you had to cross two mountain ranges to get there. Gerry had suggested that they each take a nominal five per cent shareholding ('In case anyone gets a look at the Share Register, old boy'), the gullible Mrs Sargent had fifty per cent and Adam had been working his way around the health farm circuit ever since, on the lookout for further impressionable investors.

The Essex Hydro had been splendidly rewarding, but

only recently he'd spent hours on the exercise bikes with the formidable Lady Withington at an expensive place in Sussex, and all he'd got for his effort was a request to leave, a tip-off to the police, and aching hamstrings. He must go carefully. His pencil hovered over Rachel Gillespie. Ripe for the plucking, but the purse-strings were held firmly by mother. He put a tentative tick against Sybil Gillespie, and gazed gloomily out of the window, thinking of the distasteful task ahead and how hard he had to work to turn a dishonest penny.

He always booked a room at the back, it was cheaper, and the view from the back windows of Alba Manor was of the kitchen garden, with neatly laid out beds of vegetables, only slightly marred by some rather unsightly plastic tunnel things. As he looked down, he saw Cordelia emerging from one of the tunnels carrying a laden trug, and going off towards the kitchen. For a moment he was quite excited by the sighting. Why hadn't he thought of Cordelia before? Granddaughter of the owner of this goldmine, obviously being groomed to take over, a bloody heiress right under his nose, and he'd nearly overlooked her.

He could turn Alba into a Rest Home, there was money to be made out of geriatrics. Individual flatlets, bring your own familiar furniture, home from home, warden on the premises, out you go when the waterworks give up; that was the way to cut down on decor and staffing. He was just phrasing an application for planning permission to build an exclusive estate of executive homes beyond the swimming pool, when common sense intervened. He had to admit, with all modesty, that he was a fairly good looking chap, kept himself in shape, pretty good on the charm stakes, but he was nudging sixty and wooing a young, attractive woman was a very different proposition to winning the hearts of elderly widows clutching hopefully at their last chance of romance. Besides, there was youthful competition. The writer chappie, always nosing about and asking questions which, of course, was what writers did, or they'd have damn-all to write about. The heiress had her eye on Ballard, Adam was certain of that. He recognised the courting rituals; those easy blushes, those long looks under downcast lashes, the way she smoothed down her skirts and almost imperceptibly thrust out her bosom when Ballard hove into sight. Adam sighed wistfully at the thought of that firm young bosom, which changed into a low whistle of surprise as Tod Ballard strolled into view.

He watched Tod watching Cordelia, as she wandered slowly towards the kitchen. Instead of following her, or calling out, Ballard hung about until she had gone inside and shut the door, before stooping and picking up something from the path. Adam couldn't see what it was, something small, a piece of jewellery, most likely. Tod examined it carefully, and then, taking a furtive look around to see if he was being observed, slipped it into his pocket.

Well, there you go, Adam thought, wrong again. He'd had Tod Ballard down as a regular guy, as likely as Mother Theresa to scour the pathways for illicit loot. The vignette he had just witnessed told another story.

*   *   *

Cordelia put the trug down on the kitchen table and regarded it with pleasure. Mushrooms, ninety-two per cent water, were an ideal dish for dieters, and these were firmly fleshed. A bit on the small side, perhaps, and unappealingly shaped, but they would make an excellent soup.

Cordelia hummed happily as she gathered together her ingredients. Onions, paprika, skimmed milk, yogurt, a drop of wine vinegar. It was good to be cooking legally again, she was really enjoying her new job. One of the major bonuses was that she no longer had to help Sister Monica with the Appointments for Today Cards, and Monica rarely ventured into the kitchens, considering that any sort of domestic chore demeaned her status of SRN.

'Cordelia!' Monica came bustling in, as if summoned by thought transference. 'I've just been looking at the dinner menu on the notice-board. Mushroom soup?'

'Certainly, dietetically impeccable.'

'I don't recall seeing mushrooms on Mr Pearson's list.' Madame had asked Monica to keep an eye on the fruit and vegetable orders after the Meadows fiasco. 'You're the only one I can trust, Monica,' she'd said, and Monica had preened her starched apron at the compliment. 'Where,' her eye fell on the trug, '*where* did you find those?'

'In the kitchen garden, of course,' said Cordelia, picking up the trug.

'Give that to me, immediately.' Monica snatched the trug from Cordelia. 'These are Madame's special mushrooms.' The note of outrage in her voice suggested that Cordelia had been plucking bunches of rare orchids and idly tossing them on the compost heap.

'But there are acres of them out there, in those plastic tunnels,' said Cordelia.

'They are not for general consumption,' Monica swelled with self-importance. 'I can assure you, Madame would be most displeased if she found you with her mushrooms. You'll have to order some from Mr Pearson.'

'But that's ridiculous,' Cordelia protested. 'Anyway,' she looked at her watch, 'he closed five minutes ago.' She went to reclaim the trug.

'No you don't.' Monica whipped it under her arm and marched towards the door. 'You can take the car down to 8 'til Late, Cordelia.'

Cordelia knew her grandmother had asked Sister Monica to vet the fruit and veg supply; perhaps Monica thought she was deliberately side-stepping her authority by not entering '10 lbs mushrooms' in the order book. Why else would her eyes be popping so antagonistically?

'But they don't sell mushrooms at the Paxborough 8 'til Late.'

'They sell packet soups,' said Sister Monica, 'and I've tried the mushroom one myself, it's very tasty.'

*   *   *

'Look,' said Tristram, 'there's a seat. Couldn't we sit down for a minute?'

Years younger than me, Adam thought complacently, and he's panting like an out of condition pekinese. 'We've only been jogging for five minutes,' he said. To describe their slow lope around the perimeter of Alba as a jog was a serious distortion of the truth; Adam, setting off at an easy pace, had skirted the swimming pool while Tristram was still ambling along the terrace.

'Nobody can see us,' said Tristram, sitting down.

'True.' Adam joined Tristram on the bench. 'Can't think why you suggested jogging in the first place. A pointless pastime, if not positively dangerous.'

'Good excuse to get away from the Monstrous Regiment,' said Tristram. 'Dangerous? What do you mean?'

'Not the way you do it, old son,' said Adam, 'but the really keen buggers are always slipping their discs and jolting their spines. Smoke?' He took a packet of Castella Panatella's out of his track suit pocket and offered it to Tristram.

As they puffed companionably, Adam reflected gratefully how chance had thrown them together. Rather on his uppers after the unfortunate Lady Withington incident in Sussex, he had been dawdling round Berkeley Square, contemplating a crab sandwich and a half pint at The Coach and Horses, when he'd run into an old business acquaintance, who had invited him to lunch at his club.

It was one of those places where the members joined in general badinage around an oak refectory table and Adam had been placed next to Tristram Bartholomew, who had muttered disapprovingly in his ear throughout lunch about the poor quality of the provender. 'These potted shrimps

231

are frozen, of course . . . Have you tried the pastry on the steak and kidney pudding yet? Soggy as a leftover pancake . . . I wouldn't touch that trifle, if I were you.'

'The man on your left is Tristram Bartholomew,' the business acquaintance had murmured, and added, as Adam raised a querying eyebrow, 'famous food writer.'

Adam had said the obvious about how did Tristram manage to keep his weight down while taking all the free calories aboard, and Tristram had told him about his regular visits to the Alba Health Manor.

'The Alba Health Manor?' Adam said. It was a damn sight harder to get through the front door of Alba than into this smug club, he'd been angling for an introduction for months. 'How about a drop of port?'

'A spot of Dow 1980 might go down rather well,' said Tristram.

Adam had spent a useful half hour flatteringly asking Tristram's advice about all the restaurants whose names he could remember, and in between appropriate responses ('Cockroaches in the fridge? I'd never have believed it') had managed to convey the impression that he was a high-powered executive heading for a heart attack if he didn't slim down and rest up pretty damn quick. 'Trouble is,' he said, 'most of these health farms are full of such frightful people.'

'You ought to give Alba a try,' said Tristram, as Adam hoped he might, 'they're very choosy about their clientele.'

'Maybe I will,' said Adam, 'if you recommend it.'

Tristram had given Adam his card. 'Give me a bell if you're interested.'

' . . . and isn't it the most delightful irony that little Miss Calorie-Conscious 1990 is none other than Cordelia Ledbury, whose cookery books are a celebration of butter and cream and all the good things that are bad for you?'

Adam was only half listening as Tristram rabbited on. He wasn't interested in gossip unless it told him something useful. 'Lady Drummond seems a good sort,' he said.

232

'NQOCD,' said Tristram. 'Don't be fooled by the couture trappings and the jangle of gold jewellery.'

'But rolling in it, I imagine?'

'Sloshing about in the stuff, her old man is in printing and property. Shrewd as they come, made a mint after the war and got his K by hurling the hard-earned at charities.'

'Very estimable.'

'Animal charities?' Tristram wrinkled his nose disapprovingly, managing to look even more like a Pekinese. 'I can think of better ways of spending money. She's the kind of woman who'll leave it all to her cat.'

Adam was appalled. 'Not like Mrs Gillespie. Now there's someone who knows the value of money.'

'Tight as a wad,' Tristram agreed. 'Another woman who has been left comfortably off after burying the breadwinner. Have you noticed the beadiness in her eye when she's down 20p at the bridge table?'

'Yes,' said Adam. 'Yes, I have.'

'*There* you are.' Tristram jumped guiltily and Adam stubbed out his Panatella as Sylvia Travers emerged from behind a nearby eucalyptus tree. 'It's all right, I won't tell Carolyn what you get up to when you go jogging.'

'Felt a bit puffed,' said Tristram.

'Just a brief rest,' said Adam.

Sylvia was carrying a stylish beachbag with the distinctive Chanel initial on the front of it. Probably another free gift from Wardrobe, Adam thought sourly. 'I had to tell you, Adam. I've had a call from Theo.'

'Theo?'

'My agent. I told you. He was going to talk to Ronnie Palfrey about a marvellous part in his new play. I'm dashing up to London tomorrow to audition for it.'

'Splendid.' Adam surprised himself by feeling a genuine glow of pleasure at Sylvia's good news.

'The lead?' said Tristram.

'A cameo, darling. Terribly sensitive, the sort of role that positively cries out for the critics' plaudits. And now I'm going to have a lovely swim and then beg leave of absence from the Ogre.'

'Saw her once in that thing at the National,' said Tristram, as Sylvia went off towards the swimming pool, 'about as sensitive as Sister Monica.'

'Oh, I wouldn't say that,' said Adam who didn't know what thing at the National Tristram was talking about, 'I thought she was rather good.'

*   *   *

Sylvia was feeling extremely cheerful as she drove up to London. Cordelia, also on her way to London, was not cheerful at all. She had gone straight to her grandmother's study after the mushroom incident and, as she parked the Fiat in the NCP above the Shepherd's Bush Shopping Centre and crossed the walkway to the flat, she was still simmering with things said and things she wished she had said, if only she had thought of them at the time.

Isabella had been sitting in the carved chair looking tired and, the first time Cordelia had noticed it, somehow diminished by the heavy oak ornamentation.

Cordelia had not been in a mood to sympathise. 'What is all this nonsense about mushrooms?' she had demanded, fuelled by anger and the humiliation of serving packet soup; even if she'd upgraded it with yogurt, paprika and chopped chives.

'Perhaps you would like to go out and come in again in a civil manner,' her grandmother had said, stroking Flora slowly and rhythmically.

'No, I wouldn't. I would like an explanation.'

'Very well. Sit down, Cordelia, and lower your voice, please. Sister Monica was quite right to request you not to use my special mushrooms.'

'Hardly a request. She snatched them. She was extremely rude.'

234

'That, I am afraid, is Monica's way. But she knows that the produce in the polytunnels is experimental. She knows how much it means to me to produce the perfect mushroom, both in flavour and quality. I've been working on it, crossing varieties, for over a year.'

'The perfect mushroom? But they're tiny.'

'Exactly. The taste is exquisite but the size and shape are still not acceptable for Alba's table.'

'Well, you might have told me.' How unfair, Cordelia thought, I'm right about all this silly fuss, there are acres of mushrooms there, she wouldn't have missed a few pounds. And I've been put in the wrong again. She should have said all of that, but instead she said, 'And have you heard from your solicitor, yet?'

'I have been busy with other matters in the last few days, since I have to do everything around here myself.'

'Well, anyway,' Cordelia had said, flouncing out, 'I'm taking the day off tomorrow. You'll have to get someone else to mix the packet soups.'

Putting her key in the flat door, Cordelia stamped her foot irritably. What a fool she'd made of herself. Once again, her grandmother's attitude had made her behave like a petulant child.

'Who's there?'

Cordelia checked her watch. Ten o'clock in the morning, Sally was usually at the studio by now. 'It's me, Sal. Cordelia.'

Sally came into the hall in her dressing gown. The fluffy pale blue winter one. In the kitchen Cordelia could see Stewart sitting at the table eating cornflakes, wearing Sally's summer kimono.

'Very cosy.' Cordelia was still in a bad mood.

'Stewart missed the last bus.'

'What happened to the Lotus?'

'It's over in the car park,' said Sally, repressing a giggle.

They fell into each other's arms, laughing uncontrollably.

235

'What's so funny?' Stewart came out of the kitchen, all elbows and knees in the mini kimono. 'Cordelia?'

'Stewart.' Cordelia found herself embracing him warmly, without a hint of passion. 'Don't mind me, I've come to do some work.'

Sitting in front of her Amstrad, Cordelia tried to concentrate on the instructions for Mousseline of Sole and Pistachio with Watercress Sauce, which had been a great success in the Alba dining room. Watching the Alba inmates had convinced her that there was money to be made out of a cookery book filled with recipes for people who yearned to stay slim while eating extremely well. She was thinking of calling it *Gourmet Dishes for Dieters*.

She'd been stuck at the 'put the sole in a blender' bit for five minutes because her mind kept wandering elsewhere. Into the kitchen with Sally and Stewart; back into the garden at Alba with Tod Ballard. Only six months ago she would have been stabbed with jealousy if Stewart had nodded across the room at Sally and remarked how well she was looking. Today, she had felt nothing but goodwill as she watched them intimately spooning up cornflakes together, the morning after the night before. As far as Tod Ballard was concerned, she had obviously blown it. It had been so lovely on the tennis court when he had looked at her like that. But then he had asked all those questions. Why on earth had she gone on about being Madame's granddaughter and knowing it all? Because she didn't want him to guess that she was hoping for something more important than how Sheila Steinberg got home, or what Sister Monica put in her infusions. Something more on the lines of, 'Do you love me, Cordelia?' or even, 'Would you like to come for a walk in the knot garden?' How impossibly smug and bossy she must have sounded; no wonder he decided to give the Rural Arts Museum a miss. No wonder he'd been avoiding her.

'Mix lightly; the texture should be smooth but not runny,' she typed firmly. And when I've done three more pages, she promised herself, I'll phone Janet and sound her out on my idea.

*   *   *

'I like it,' Janet said, 'not sure about the title, though. *Gourmet Dishes for Dieters* sounds slightly pompous, don't you think?'

'Not really,' said Cordelia.

'*Eat Well, Stay Slim,* might be better. Hang on, it would be helpful if we could link it with Alba; everyone knows about Alba. Why not *The Alba Manor Cookery Book*?'

'Because my grandmother would have a seizure.'

'Don't see why if they are genuinely slimming recipes. Good publicity for Alba, good publicity for the book. Let me have a brief synopsis and a few sample recipes. Are you there, Cordelia?'

'Yes.'

'This is going to be the big one, you know. Serious money.'

Cordelia was feeling more cheerful as she put down the phone.

*   *   *

Adam was browsing through the *FT* in the drawing room and keeping Sybil and Rachel Gillespie under observation. They were playing Scrabble, and Sybil had just cheated by scoring high with Zion which, as Sybil, Rachel and Adam were all aware begins with a capital letter and should, therefore, be disallowed. None of them, for different reasons, drew attention to this fact.

'Hi, Adam. Have you seen Sylvia about?' Debbie Wynne-Jones had a flush of achievement about her.

'Gone to London for an audition.'

'I say, fantastic. Are you busy?'

'Not at all.' Adam closed the *Financial Times* with relief;

BJS leaps by forty-four per cent to 7.9m. pre-tax, figures surge for Olivan. It was painful reading about the successes of his ex competitors. 'Come and sit down.'

'I've decided I'm going back to Hancock's,' said Debbie, joining him on the sofa.

'That's where your friend works, isn't it?' Adam never failed to be amazed by the way women in these health farm places confided in you as though you were Anna Raeburn.

'I had a talk with Mr Patterson yesterday . . . you don't mind me banging on like this?'

'Of course not,' said Adam uneasily.

'He said that it would be more humiliating to run away than to face up to the office gossip. Returning to work and dealing with the problem would make me stronger as a person.'

'That's the sort of thing therapists do say, isn't it? Not so easy, surely, if you're madly in love with this chap?'

'Mad's the word,' said Debbie. 'I don't love Isaac, you see. Getting away from Swansea, coming here has put everything into perspective. It was just a physical thing.' Adam was keenly aware of Sybil Gillespie's gaze swivelling towards them from the Scrabble board. 'Mr Patterson made me realise that it wasn't love at all.'

'It wasn't?'

'It was just sex.'

'Don't knock it,' said Adam.

'Oh, I'm not,' said Debbie, 'Mr Patterson says you should never underestimate the power of sexual passion.'

Adam gazed fixedly at the front page of his *FT*. He couldn't believe he was having this conversation.

'You know what I think?'

'I haven't the faintest idea.' Whatever she thought was certain to be something embarrassing, and Adam sighed with relief as Tod Ballard came across the room towards them.

'I think Mr Patterson is a genius. I'm sure I couldn't have faced up to the truth about my relationship with Isaac without those Extras.' Debbie looked up, 'Oh, hullo, Tod. I've felt so much more in charge of my life since I've been taking them.'

'Hullo, you two,' said Tod.

'Good to see you,' said Adam.

'I've bored poor Adam long enough,' Debbie jumped up, 'and I'm due for a sauna in five minutes. See you both around.'

'What was all that about?' said Tod.

'Sexual passion, mainly,' said Adam.

'About Mr Patterson?'

'Oh, I don't know, something about his medicine cheering her up; you know the way women go on.'

*　　　　*　　　　*

'I'm singing in the rain, just singing . . . ' Adam shuddered as the cold water cascaded over his shoulders; flicking the hot switch, he paused in mid-song to ponder the possibility that Tod Ballard was a bit of a weirdo.

Tod had trailed him about like a conscientious bloodhound ever since they had met up in the drawing room. Followed him into the sauna, jumped into a track suit and insisted on bicycling with him around the perimeter of Alba, jogged back to the house with him, and all the time asking questions about that tricky conversation with the Wynne-Jones girl.

'Tell you what, old son,' he'd said, as they entered the hall, 'isn't it a bit prurient, all this interest in somebody else's sex life? If you're so fascinated, why don't you ask Debbie? She'll be only to pleased to talk about it, I can tell you.'

'Fancy an orange juice?' said Tod.

'I fancy a double whisky,' said Adam, 'but what I'm going to have is a cold shower. Alone,' he'd added, firmly.

CHAPTER
TWENTY-ONE

Jane made a habit of staying up late at Alba; it was not exactly frowned upon, but it was preferred that guests should be in their rooms by ten. Most of them staggered off, yawning, by nine, but Jane found it so enchanting to spend an evening without giving children baths, tucking them into bed, and helping someone with an essay, that she stretched it out as long as possible. That night, she had settled herself in the deserted Television Room and prepared, with great pleasure, to watch an old Paul Newman film.

She had just moved an armchair to centre front of the television set, and covered a low stool with cushions to make a footrest, when the door behind her opened, and someone walked in.

Jane turned, feeling quite guilty for moving the furniture about, and saw, with falling heart, that it was Lady Drummond. Not that she had anything against Lady Drummond, as such; she had not actually come into contact with her, beyond saying 'Good morning,' and 'A bit cooler today.' But she seemed to Jane to be the kind of woman she had absolutely nothing in common with. Slim, flawlessly elegant, obsessed with animals and fearfully rich, not her type at all. Anyway, thought Jane like a cross child, she wanted to be Left Alone.

'Oh, hullo,' she said ungraciously, 'I didn't expect anyone else to be up.'

'Won't disturb you for a minute, love, just looking for ... ' Lady Drummond gazed around vaguely, and swooped on an untidy folder of papers, ' . . . ah, there they are. My notes for next week's meeting on 1992 and Cosmetic Testing on Animals. I've never liked foreigners, not since the Blitz, and why they should use good English beagles for . . . '

'I only use Body Shop stuff,' said Jane defensively.

'Quite right. How are you enjoying yourself here?'

Jane thought irritably that the film would be beginning about now, toyed with the idea of saying, 'It would be all right if you ever got any privacy,' and told herself sharply to stop behaving like a spoilt teenager.

'Very much indeed, actually. You can't think how wonderful it is to be away from the children. Well, Antonia's here, of course, but she looks after herself. I know it sounds selfish, but to wake up in the morning and know that they're not going to be here is such a rest. I don't know if you've got children, but . . . ' something in the quality of her companion's silence made her hesitate and look across. 'Oh, God, what have I said?'

'Twin sons,' said Betty economically, 'until two years ago. Car crash. Twenty-five. No sympathy, please, I can't deal with it.'

'I wish someone had told me.'

'Hardly anybody knows, except Bella, of course. I don't want to talk about it, you see.'

'No, of course.' Jane floundered for something to say. 'I do admire the way you keep yourself so busy. All I can look back on at the end of the week is a lot of clean washing and about a thousand fish fingers.'

'I thought you had a degree?'

'In Anthropology. A First, actually. I was expected to do great things. Then I met Henry.'

'So you got married and had children. What sort of degree did he get?'

'A 2-1. Anyway, what's the use? It's too late now.'

'Oh, bother,' said Betty, 'I meant to watch that Paul Newman film, I suppose it's started.'

241

'So did I.' Jane switched on the set, and the announcer said 'We must apologise to viewers that because of extra time in the semi-final replay, tonight's film is starting twenty minutes late.'

'Oh good,' said Betty. And, during the course of the film she said a lot more.

A lot more along the lines of, 'Only forty-three? You're a young woman,' . . . 'It's time for you to be selfish, love,' . . . 'Surely a professor can afford someone else to deal with fish fingers?' It was a very good film, and Jane forgot a lot of what Betty said, but the message was clear. It's time you lived your own life.

*   *   *

The film had finished an hour before; it was half past twelve, and Jane was scurrying secretively down the treatment block corridor. She was not doing anything wrong, of course, merely retrieving the book she had left in the Massage waiting room, without which she could not possibly get to sleep. Jane did not usually leave things behind, but there had been a lot to think about. Her interview with poor little Sarah that afternoon. And the rather curious scene in the drawing room after dinner, yesterday.

Tod had been there, reading *Country Life*, and Tristram, talking wistfully of Quenelles de Brochet to anybody who could be bothered to listen to him. Adam, Diane, Erica Gerard and that wicked old woman Gillespie were playing bridge over in the corner. Cordelia was talking to Rachel Gillespie and looking across the room over Rachel's shoulder at the back of Tod's *Country Life*.

Debbie bounced in and Tristram instantly raised a protesting hand. 'No, thank you, Debbie, we of the Light Diet Room do not wish to hear any detail at all, not one, about the sumptuous banquet you have just been regaled with.'

'Sumptuous!' said Debbie. 'Banquet? What a con . . . ' Cordelia, her face extremely red, looked round. 'Oh, sorry,

Cordelia, I didn't see you. Only that famous home-made mushroom soup we were all looking forward to came straight out of a packet, didn't it?'

'A last-minute adjustment,' mumbled Cordelia. 'It was burnt, so I had to . . . '

'How on earth do you burn mushroom soup?' said Debbie.

'Why don't you mind your own bloody business,' said Cordelia, exiting to the accompaniment of astonished stares.

'I've said it before,' said old Mrs Gillespie, 'and I'll say it again. This place is going downhill.'

*　　　*　　　*

Rather an over-reaction from Cordelia, thought Jane as she tiptoed towards the Massage Rooms, perhaps she was doing too much. She was vaguely aware, as she tiptoed, of a rhythmic thudding noise coming from one of the cubicles.

Oh, Lord, here came Madame and that bad-tempered little dog. Wishing she had the nerve to say, 'Oh, good evening, Madame, I was just fetching my book,' Jane hid behind the towel locker in a manner not befitting a forty-three-year-old anthropologist.

Madame strode over to the Massage Room, flung open the door, and said, 'As I thought!'

Seconds later, Diane Renfrew flashed out of the door (almost literally, as she was pulling on her bathrobe) and scuttled away down the corridor.

Jane could hear perfectly well what was being said in the cubicle, and decency suggested that she should creep away. Fascination kept her behind the towel locker.

'How many times have you been warned, Matt? Your insolent manner, and now this flagrant misbehaviour with a client. How could you so let down the standards of Alba? I will give you and Mary a week's wages, exceptionally

243

generous under the circumstances, and you will leave tomorrow.'

'Oh, I don't think we want to leave, Bella, isn't that what your friends call you?'

'You have no choice in the matter, and how dare you speak to me in that impertinent way? May I remind you . . . '

'And may I remind *you* that I just spent a weekend in dear old Leyburn. I had a really interesting talk with Mary's father, Foster, her maiden name was. Marvellous memory, for his age. Oh, by the way, I bought you back a little memento.'

There was quite a long silence in the Massage Room. Then a sound of something being dropped, or even thrown. Isabella stormed through the door and down the corridor, Flora scuttling painfully after her.

Matt came out looking triumphant and venomous. Jane pressed back even further into the shadow behind the locker. Silly of a grown woman to be afraid of a masseur, but . . .

'Goodnight, Madame,' Matt called after Isabella, and grinning to himself in a repellent way, disappeared after her.

'Wow!' said Jane to herself, slipping into the waiting room and grabbing her book. 'What on earth was all that about?'

Although she was quite keen to get out of there and back to her room, she couldn't resist a quick look into the cubicle. Nothing out of the usual, except the towels on the massage table were crumpled . . . and a small blue casserole dish had rolled into one corner. The memento? Why on earth should that have stopped Madame in mid-flow?

Jane picked it up and turned it over. Perfectly ordinary, she herself had several like it at home. 'Denby stoneware' it said on the base.

CHAPTER
TWENTY-TWO

'You're not seriously going to Exeter, are you? It's full of Sloanes in green wellies, isn't it? Still, I suppose that would suit you, wouldn't it?'

Sarah was having a miserable time. To begin with, she and Antonia were at the shallow end of the swimming pool having just completed a four-length race which Antonia won, not so much effortlessly as insultingly. And to go on with, Antonia, though a little overweight perhaps, looked better curving out of a bikini than bony Sarah did in her old school one-piece.

And finally, Antonia was being seriously unpleasant.

Whatever Sarah may have said to her mother, she had no intention at all of opting out and going to work in some bar in Amsterdam. It sounded perfectly beastly to her, and quite dangerous; Celia bicycled back to her flat every night, which Sarah wouldn't fancy at all. Anyway, she was very proud of herself for achieving Exeter, which most of her teachers, even nice Miss Whipple, plainly thought was a lost cause as far as Sarah was concerned.

Sarah deeply resented Antonia's attitude to Exeter; it was apparently her considered opinion that the university world was divided into Oxbridge and the rest; the rest being inferior provincial universities that did a perfectly adequate job as long as you wanted to read Estate Management, and polys, which were for educating lower middle-class civil servants who Talk Like That. It was the way she had been brought up by her academic father, Sarah supposed, but did Antonia have to put her down all the time? Surely she had got nastier in the last week? Only a few days ago they had been chatting amiably about how *Neighbours* wasn't the same without Mrs Mangel, and wouldn't it be wicked if the hunk who plays Henry turned up to spend a week at Alba?

Now, every time Sarah opened her mouth, Antonia sat about despising her. Antonia's mother had implied that she was like that with everyone, but surely she had been friendlier when they all first arrived at Alba?

'You and my mother are getting very thick, aren't you?' Antonia was applying body lotion to her legs in a way that meant she had to stretch them out quite a lot; Tod was sunning himself on the other side of the swimming pool, next to Lady Drummond. 'What were you talking about on that little terrace yesterday?'

Sarah, for a wild moment, contemplated telling Antonia that they had been discussing recidivism in pre-war Bulgaria, or the later works of Monteverdi, but rejected the scheme as implausible.

'Oh, nothing, this and that, you know. She's awfully kind, your mother, isn't she?'

'Kind? Yes, I suppose so.' Antonia slid into the water, wasting a great deal of body lotion in the process, backstroked flashily across the pool, and flopped down next to Tod.

Since the pool, though as sumptuous as everything else at Alba, was not of Olympic size, Sarah could hear every word of the conversation on the other side. Antonia, despite oiling her limbs and showing off her swimming, was getting little change out of Tod Ballard.

'Hullo, Tod, what's that you're reading? A love-letter, I bet?'

'None of your business. Hey, look out, you're splashing me.'

'Yes, watch it, love.' Lady Drummond shook water off the piles of paper that accompanied her everywhere.

Antonia made a rude face at Lady Drummond, lithely

246

lifted herself out of the pool, splashing them some more, and laid herself down, with some ceremony, on the sun-bed next to Tod. 'Cordelia's up in London, isn't she?'

'I believe so,' said Tod, wishing she would go away. The letter he had been waiting for had only just been delivered; he only hoped nobody had noticed that it was delivered by hand.

'Meeting that hunky boyfriend of hers, no doubt.'

'I really wouldn't know.'

'You're not very friendly, are you?'

'I'm afraid I'm rather busy, at the moment.'

'It doesn't look very interesting, your letter. Interesting letters never come in brown envelopes.'

Tod said, 'Hmm,' and Antonia, with a fatal attempt at playfulness, snatched the envelope from where it was lying on Tod's stomach, and took a quick glance at it.

'Please don't do that, it's so childish.' He grabbed it back. 'Look, it's all damp.'

Antonia slid back into the pool, managing to displace a considerable amount of water.

'Oh, read your silly letter, if it's so important to you. Who'd want a girlfriend who works in a laboratory, any-way?'

*   *   *

Antonia swam back across to Sarah, this time doing quite an ordinary breaststroke.

'What a dag,' she said loudly as she flopped down on her towel.

'He's absolutely dripping, Antonia, no wonder he's cross. And Lady Drummond, and she's so nice. And if you ask me it's pretty babyish to snatch other people's letters.'

'Oh, I asked you, did I? That's what I said, was it? Sarah, do criticise my behaviour because you're so much cleverer than I am. Funny, I never heard myself say that, but if you say I did, then of course . . . '

247

Sarah found this tirade mildly alarming. She was used to being sneered at, of course; but not in a way that was very nearly hysterical. She noticed that Tod had put down his letter and was gazing across in his short-sighted way. Lady Drummond was lying back with her eyes closed, luckily she didn't seem to have noticed anything.

'I say, Antonia, give us a break. All I said was . . . '

'All you said was, as usual, a load of third-grade crap. God knows Exeter isn't much cop, but I do actually think someone should warn them that you're on your way.'

'May I remind you, Antonia, that guests are required to keep noise to a minimum round the swimming pool? There are other people to be considered, you know. And we do not care for language of that kind at Alba.'

For about the first time on record, Sarah was glad to see Sister Monica. Normally she considered her like about ten of the worst mistresses at school rolled into one. Now all she needed was a cask of brandy round her neck to look like the great rescue character of all time. On the other hand, Antonia was in a very funny mood indeed and would probably be frightfully rude to Sister Monica. Sarah thought that it was high time she went and had a shower, or something.

'Oh, I'm sorry, Sister Monica.' Antonia, to Sarah's astonishment, was just about cringing. 'Sarah and I were only . . . '

'Be that as it may, Antonia. Surely it is time for your appointment with Mr Patterson?'

'I don't think so. I don't think I've got one.'

'I think you have.' Sister Monica consulted her clipboard. 'As I thought. Three thirty. I'll take you up. We can only hope that Mr Patterson, an extremely busy man, will overlook your tardiness.' She raised her voice. 'There was a phone call for you, Mr Ballard. Your father, wanting to know how you're getting on.'

Tod put the brown envelope into his bathrobe pocket. Sister Monica and Antonia exited through the rhododendrons, looking, thought Sarah, like One Man and His Dog.

'Well, that young woman's certainly come to heel.' Lady Drummond, echoing Sarah's thoughts in a fairly eerie way, had walked round the pool and was standing between Sarah and the sun. 'Mind if I join you for a minute? It's nearly time for my Oil of Evening Primrose Face Massage. Personally, I don't think it makes a blind bit of difference, but I quite like it while it's going on. You and Antonia are close, are you?'

'Well, she's much cleverer than me, of course.'

'Clever? Poor little duck, that's not what I'd call her. Her mother's good news, though. I wonder . . . '

Sarah waited politely to see what Lady Drummond wondered, and after a few seconds realised that whatever it was, she was going to keep it to herself.

*   *   *

Antonia did not, as it happened, have an appointment with Mr Patterson; Sister Monica had suggested he fit her in as soon as possible, because, as she told him, there were certain contra-indications. ' . . . outside in the waiting room, edgy to the point of irritability, very nearly hysterical down at the pool just now. I would suggest, if you agree, of course, that some adaptation . . . '

So Antonia, looking subdued, was ushered in to Mr Patterson's office.

'I hear we're feeling a little irritable?'

'Everybody's so boring here, I can't wait to go home.' Now that Sister Monica had bustled off about her business, Antonia had regained some of her self-assertion.

'Boring? Oh, now why do we think that?'

'Because they are boring, that's why we think it. Boring little Sarah with a mind like a tortoise, boring Lady Drummond and her boring donkeys, boring Sylvia whatever her name is pretending to be Maggie Smith,

boring . . . ' Antonia was about to add, 'boring hypnother-
apists trying to look quizzical,' but thought better of
it. Mr Patterson, who found a quizzical expression quite
useful to hide behind, was thinking, 'Tiresome, spoilt,
humourless, but nobody's fool. I'd better go carefully.'

Aloud, he said, 'Well, we must see what we can do about
it, mustn't we? You must realise, Antonia, that as the body
frees itself, under Alba's beneficient regime, from toxins
that have accumulated over the years, there are bound to
be side effects. Some physical (I see you have an outbreak
on your chin, I will ask Sister Monica to give you some
Comfrey ointment) and some mental. In many cases this
reveals itself as a lassitude, a general lack of interest in
activity, but quite frequently . . . '

Mr Patterson's professionally soothing voice droned on,
making Antonia feel rather sleepy. Perhaps it's true, she
thought hazily, perhaps I have been a bit ratty lately.

' . . . and so, Antonia, we must look to the inner self.
You must tell me what is troubling you . . . '

So Antonia dreamily told Mr Patterson all about Tod,
and how he was being so beastly to her, and how, only just
now at the swimming pool . . . she was rather enjoying
herself, telling nice Mr Patterson everything.

'Well, now, we feel so much better for having got that
off our chest, don't we?' Mr Patterson raised his voice
slightly, and Antonia looked at him intently to show she
was paying attention. 'We mustn't forget, must we, that
Sister Monica is here to help us, and we must do what she
says at all times.'

Antonia yawned. 'At all times,' she repeated obediently.

'Splendid.' Mr Patterson slammed his hands down on his
desk, making Antonia jump, and got to his feet. 'I will have
a word with Sister Monica, and I think we will find we are
much more cheerful in the morning.'

*　　　　*　　　　*

While Antonia was being interviewed by Mr Patterson, Sarah was putting in half an hour on the exercise bike in the Gym. It was her intention to sweat at least four ounces off her bum.

However, she was bicycling rather slower than she intended, because she had company, and it was rather unexpected company. Well, neither of them would have surprised her separately, but together they made, in Sarah's opinion, a jolly weird couple.

Sybil Gillespie was attired in a mint green track suit with a matching sweatband. Which made Sarah giggle to herself anyway, because she doubted if Mrs Gillespie had ever done anything so unrefined as sweat in her life. She was lying on her back in front of the wall-bars, with her toes tucked under the lowest one, and was repeatedly raising her head about an inch from the floor, and putting it back again. If she were doing it properly, reflected Sarah, she would be taking the hell out of her stomach muscles; as it was, the only stomach muscles that were feeling pain were Sarah's own, which were killing themselves trying not to laugh.

Standing next to her, with his left side to the wall-bars, was that awful Mr Shepherd. His left foot was on the bottom rung, his left hand was holding on well above his head, and he was rhythmically raising his right arm and leg and letting them drop back again.

Sarah adjusted her eccy bike to resistance 5, which made her feel as though she was bicycling up the foothills of the Himalayas, and told herself severely that just because people are old, one shouldn't laugh at them. And what on earth were they talking about?

'Call me old-fashioned,' Mr Shepherd was saying, 'but I've always gone for freeholds. This time-sharing stuff, not for me, I'm afraid. Remind me to show you a snap of my little farmhouse in the Dordogne.'

'France!' said Mrs Gillespie, 'I've never fancied it. There! You've jogged my memory. I knew there was something

251

bothering me. Rachel has let me run out of Eau de Cologne again.'

'In a way, I know exactly what you mean. Our French friends, so civilised on the surface . . . perhaps you would allow me to drive you into the village? There is quite a respectable little chemist there, and they will certainly have Eau de Cologne.'

'They won't have the right brand. It's Crabtree & Evelyn, or nothing. Young people are so insensitive, Mr Shepherd.' For an awful moment, Sarah thought Mrs G. had caught her giggling; but it was her own Young Person she was talking about. 'With Rachel, I am afraid, it is self, self, self from morning till night.'

'Children,' said Adam vaguely, 'sharper than the serpent's tooth.'

Sarah thought that an extraordinary expression to use about poor old Rachel. The allusion had escaped her, because she did *Antony and Cleopatra* for A-Level. Sharp wasn't exactly the word. Were anyone to ask her opinion, she would reply frankly that Rachel was two petals short of a flower, that the lights were on but nobody was at home, and that if Rachel Gillespie were requested to fight her way out of a paper bag, she would start by investigating the possibilities of the closed end.

'Take my own son, Adrian, for instance. Twenty-eight and he thinks he knows it all. Only last week I took him to lunch (Claridges, so convenient for the office and considering the service, really excellent value), to advise him about his investments. And would he listen? I begged him to rethink his position on the yen, but need I tell you he knows better?'

'Never trust the Japs, my late husband used to say.'

'If you needed any advice on your holdings, Mrs Gillespie . . . or may it be Sybil?'

'My late husband never trusted shares,' said Mrs Gillespie, unhooking her toes, rolling on to her side and getting to her feet in an ungainly manner, 'he saw to it that

252

I was very well looked after, thank you, in other ways.'

'And some provision for dear Rachel, I suppose?'

He's got a nerve, thought Sarah, asking questions like that about other people's money. I wonder what dad would think of him? Not a lot.

'Now, how am I going to manage without my Eau de Cologne splash?' said Mrs Gillespie, who could not be bothered to talk about dear Rachel any more. 'I suppose I will have to make do with whatever the local chemist has in stock. I will be ready to leave in five minutes, Mr Shepherd, if you will be so kind.'

Rather unsatisfactory from Mr Shepherd's point of view, thought Sarah, who could see perfectly well what he was up to; how could he smarm up to that mean-faced old bat, just for money? Sarah, like most young people brought up in utmost comfort, had highly moral views about finance.

So Adam, hoping that it was going to be worth it, but fearing in his heart that it would not, got out his car, which he explained away as, 'My son's old Renault, my own is being serviced,' and drove Mrs Gillespie to the chemist.

Once there, she found that they did stock Crabtree & Evelyn; that they had a brand of Vitamin E moisturiser she had been looking for; that she had just remembered that she was running short of hair-spray; and that she had left her purse at Alba.

'Think nothing of it,' said Adam, gallantly fishing out his wallet.

He thought of little else all the way back to Alba.

CHAPTER
TWENTY-THREE

Sarah had asked her mother to go for a walk with her, and they were strolling down the drive towards Alba's portentous lodge gates. Erica, for several very irritating reasons, had not had a drink since the previous night; someone had stolen her private supply again, this time from inside the water tank above the loo in her bathroom, which Erica had thought was a cunning place. Not cunning enough for Alba's searchers, however, who from long experience were of a very high calibre.

Then, when she had tried to drive into the village to stock up, she couldn't find her car keys. 'Too tiresome, darling,' she'd said to Sarah, 'I can't find my keys anywhere. You haven't borrowed them, have you?'

'I haven't seen them,' said Sarah, who had put them in the bottom of her make-up bag, 'I expect you left them somewhere.'

'Oh, well, I suppose I'll find them eventually. I wonder whether that nice Mr Shepherd would drive me in?'

Nice Mr Shepherd, when asked casually if he could do Erica an enormous favour and drive her into the village had reacted, for some extraordinary reason, as though she had flown up to him, buzzing, and stung him.

So here she was, trapped without a drink; and as a result a good deal more clear-eyed than usual. When Sarah had, rather surprisingly, asked her to come for a walk, she had instantly conjured up several very good reasons why she couldn't; and then thought, 'She's looking a bit peaky. I wonder if there's something on her mind?' and said instead, 'What fun, darling. I'll just get my other shoes.'

Now that Sarah had got her mother alone, she was finding it frightfully difficult to come to the point. How does one say to one's mother, 'I think you ought to join Alcoholics Anonymous'? The thing was, thought Sarah, to lead up to it gradually.

'How are you feeling, mum?'

'Me? Top of the world, as usual, darling. Sarah, you don't think you're overdoing this dieting thing a bit, do you?' Out in the fresh air, the child's skin seemed almost dangerously translucent, and when Sarah had chummily thrust her arm through Erica's, just like they used to, her elbow had jabbed into Erica's side like a dagger. Her jeans, which Erica knew for a fact were size eight, were gathered about her waist in a way which might well be fashionable, but couldn't, thought Erica in rising alarm, be healthy. 'How much do you actually weigh, darling?'

'Masses,' said Sarah briefly, 'only I'm a bit worried about you, mum.'

'Needn't worry about me, darling. Now, if only I could find the car keys, we could sneak off to that Little Chef you suggested the other day, and have a good old gossip.'

'Hey, wicked. I bet I can find them, you know you're hopeless at looking for things.'

Mother and daughter, both intent on doing each other good, turned and walked back up the drive. A car turned in at the lodge gates and came up behind them but, deep in thought, they didn't notice it until it screeched to a halt beside them.

*   *   *

Sylvia couldn't believe it. She actually couldn't. She was in work! She had driven all the way back to Alba from London without consciously changing gear. Her mind was seething with plans and possibilities, and she recalled with deep pleasure her conversation with Ronnie.

'Now, do remember, Sylvia darling, that Ronnie Palfrey has rather a name for being a difficult director to work with,' dear Theo had warned her before the audition.

'Difficult? Ronnie's a baby lamb, Theo. You must remember I toured with him in the Scottish play, and he's just so inspirational to work with.'

'Really? That's not what I've heard ('Smug little bastard, and capricious with it' was what Theo had heard, but no point in repeating *that*) but if you know him, darling. Is that what you're going to wear?'

'No, of course not, Theo, don't be so absurd.' Sylvia had driven up from Alba in jeans and an old T-shirt. 'I've brought my divine Cerruti that I wore in *Comfort's Darling*. I can change here, can't I?'

'Of course.' Theo's suite of offices contained a bathroom cum changing room, in case any of his clients needed tarting up on the way to auditions.

When they got to the theatre, it turned out that they weren't going to an audition after all. It was more of a reunion.

'Sylvia darling!' Ronnie Palfrey had rather flatteringly detached himself with haste from the group he had been conferring with, and darted across, 'How long has it been since Milton Keynes?'

Sylvia, who didn't want to think about how long it had been, (and wasn't all that besotted by the Milton Keynes reference) contented herself with a brilliant smile, a fetching shrug of the shoulders, and a, 'Ronnie! When I heard it was you . . . so inspirational.'

'We try to please, darling. Now, I want you to meet the writer.' Ronnie lowered his voice, 'A first play, but you'd never think it.' He raised his voice again, 'Edgar. Come and meet your Cora Martell. Sylvia will be quite perfect, won't she?'

Edgar, who had about him the apologetic look common to most new writers, said, 'How do you do? Only . . .'

'Only what, Edgar?' said Ronnie briskly. When he had

said to Edgar, as he said to all his new writers, 'Remember you are part of the team. They are your sacred words, after all. I shall want your views on everything,' he had meant, 'You can come to rehearsals, if you must. Don't speak.'

'Only Cora isn't meant to be glamorous.'

Sylvia smiled graciously, and said, 'I won't look like this in your play, Edgar.'

'No, of course not,' said Ronnie. 'Cerruti, isn't it? Ravishing. Let's not waste time. Take the script away with you, darling, you're going to love it. Not a vast part, the Mother's Friend, but her brooding presence is felt throughout the piece. If any of your lines don't feel right, let me know, and we'll give them a bit of a tweak, won't we, Edgar? 'Bye, darling, Susie will call you with rehearsal dates.'

*   *   *

Theo had been delighted. And why not, thought Sylvia, since he'd be getting commission for a part she had virtually got for herself. Driving back to his office, he said, 'Nice one, Sylvia. Not massive money, of course, but quite a bit of prestige. And on the big money side . . . ' he paused and looked at Sylvia in an assessing way.

'Yes, Theo?'

'There's the possibility of a Soap. Sort of upper class *Eastenders* type of thing. I suggested you and they made quite interested noises. But, I don't know quite how to say this, darling. Oh, well, in for a penny. Sylvia, the drinking really has got to stop.'

'Drinking? I don't drink, Theo. Who was scheming enough to put that rumour around? People are such bitches.'

'That last thing you were in on telly. The word was that you had to be endlessly prompted, were vague as a boot, and kept on sipping out of a little bottle.'

'A little bottle? For heaven's sake, Theo, that's my herbal

257

drink, the one I get from Alba. Nothing alcoholic about it. Just nature's pick-me-up. Honestly.'

'Oh, come on!'

'I've got it here.' Sylvia fumbled in her handbag, and handed Theo a small bottle. 'Go on, sniff it.'

'Sorry, darling. I'll get back to the Beeb, then, and tell them no probs. And for God's sake leave nature's pick-me-ups to nature, in future. They're obviously bad for you.'

*　　　*　　　*

Sylvia, turning into Alba's gates with abandon, was delighted to see Erica and Sarah. She couldn't wait to tell someone her good news, and the Gerards would do very well. She banged on her brakes and said, 'Anyone for a lift? I say, guess what? I got the part!'

'Oh, Sylvia, how wonderful. Can you tell us what it is, or is it a secret?' Sarah opened the front door for her mother, and got in the back.

'Quite small, but rather important. And almost better . . . I may get a part in a big new prestige Soap.'

'I say, can I have your autograph now, before you get too grand?'

Sylvia laughed. 'Not much chance of that. And you'll never guess why I haven't been getting parts lately. The word went round that I was an *alcoholic*, can you believe?'

Not noticing that her audience was a shade subdued, Sylvia told them the whole story. ' . . . so I'm going to tell Isabella what she can do with her infusions,' she said gaily, pulling up at the front door.

*　　　*　　　*

Mr Patterson gazed across his desk at Sarah with smoothly disguised disfavour. Another of these rich young girls with nothing to worry about except their appearance. He didn't need to look at her case notes to know that she was severely anorexic, some pathetic bid to attract attention, no doubt; not a case that was likely to interest him very much.

However, Sister Monica, who in his view was getting above herself, had virtually ordered him to give Sarah a consultation and put her on Extras. 'Every time I turn round,' said Sister Monica, 'that child is sitting there looking at people. She notices things. Madame and I think she should be sedated a little. When she is more . . . tranquil, no doubt we will be able to get to grips with the anorexia.'

'Now then, Sarah,' said Mr Patterson, 'six stone ten. Are we really happy with that?'

'Actually, I weigh far more than that.'

'Nonsense. Sister Monica herself weighed you when you arrived here. Now listen to me, Sarah . . . '

Oh, boring, thought Sarah, another fireside chat about the body is a temple and we must treat it with reverence.

Sulky little bitch, thought Mr Patterson. Aloud, he said, 'Well, we must see what we can do about your little problem, mustn't we? You must realise, Sarah, that as the body frees itself, under Alba's beneficient regime, from toxins that have accumulated over the years, there are bound to be side effects. Some physical (I see your hair is a bit lacklustre, I will ask Sister Monica to give you some Sage and Geranium shampoo) and some mental. In many cases this reveals itself as a lassitude, a general disinterest in activity, but quite frequently . . . '

Sarah looked across at him, thinking irrelevantly that somebody must once have told him that he had got a voice like John Gielgud; and she wished he'd stop waving his pen back and forth. She was actually feeling quite tired, and would like to go and lie down somewhere.

'Now we must remember, mustn't we, Sarah . . . ' He was gazing at her intently. I know what he's up to, thought Sarah suddenly, the bloody old weevil's trying to hypnotise me. Well, he can save his breath to cool his porridge (a really cool expression she had picked up from Mary

Lawson); there had been a hypnotist at one of those debby parties her mother was so keen on, and he'd made people cluck and pretend to lay eggs, and everybody thought it was hysterical until he'd tried it on Sarah. After forty-five seconds of him staring at her and telling her she was a dog, and she was going to go over to that table and lift a leg, Sarah had said, 'Why don't you do it first and show me how?' Far from admiring her strength of character, her friends had considered her to be a wet little party-pooper.

This time, she thought it might be rather interesting to go along with it, so she let her head slide artistically towards her shoulder and made her eyelids look heavy.

' . . . that Sister Monica is here to help us, and it is absolutely vital to do as she tells us. I am going to ask her to give you some strengthening drinks that you will take at bedtime, and you will not tell anybody else about them. Now, have we got that clear, Sarah?'

Sarah wondered what the form was; should she leave it at a dreamy nod or actually say something? Since Mr Patterson's eyebrows remained raised, she mumbled, 'Quite clear,' and yawned.

'Very well, then,' Mr Patterson slapped his desk with his hands, which Sarah took to be a 'wake up and act normal' sign, so she lifted her head and said, 'I say, I'm awfully sorry. I think I dropped off.'

'A little hypnotherapy to help you deal with your problem. It is so much more efficacious to send instructions straight to the subconscious. I think we will find,' Mr Patterson smiled benignly, 'that we will be very hungry at supper tonight.'

*   *   *

Sarah was slumped in front of the television set, watching *Home and Away*. She had no idea what was going on down there in good old clean-limbed, sun-tanned Summer Bay. She had got to talk to somebody, that was obvious,

260

but who? Hang about, was she imagining the whole thing? She didn't think so. The way Antonia had been behaving lately (One Man and his Dog, she'd thought, when Antonia followed Sister Monica through the rhododendrons; you didn't have to be Hercule Poirot to work out that Patterson with the potent eyes had been at work on her, too); and hadn't there been a mini-panic about Mrs Steinberg one night? Sarah remembered overhearing vague-wits Rachel Gillespie telling someone how Sister Monica and Madame Cordoba had personally rushed to Mrs Steinberg's bedside. Now that she thought of it, wasn't that a bit . . . creepy? What were they both expecting to find in the middle of the night? Don't think about it. And that session she'd just had, she could make quite a funny story about it if she was back in London with her friends. But if she was rapping with her friends, she wouldn't feel so isolated. How about Tod Ballard, could she talk to him? He'd probably think she was coming on to him, like Antonia. Lady Drummond was awfully nice and sensible, but she'd known Isabella for yonks, maybe she was in on it too. In on what, Sarah? Pull yourself together. She could try Mrs Fellowes, Sarah supposed doubtfully; except that she'd have to tell her about Antonia, and it would all be a bit awkward.

Sarah remembered how she had conned Mr Patterson, and tried to make herself laugh. The pit of her stomach felt cold and empty, and her legs were shaking. She knew she was being silly, but she was dead scared. She wanted her mother.

*   *   *

'Ah, there you are, Mrs Gerard.' Sister Monica bore down on Erica like a battleship of the line. 'You're due with Estelle for Yoga.'

Sod Estelle and sod Yoga, thought Erica. Lack of vodka was making her rather short-tempered, but she was

261

thinking better than she'd thought for four years. Sylvia's exciting news had diverted her and Sarah from their Little Chef trip, and now she couldn't find Sarah anywhere.

'I think I'll give Yoga a miss today, Sister.'

'Oh, I don't think you should . . .'

'Yes, I will. Have you seen my daughter?'

'Sarah? She and Antonia went bicycling.' Sister Monica forged off to urge Mrs Gillespie towards her pedicure.

'I think you'll find Sarah's in the Television Room.' Mr Ballard, with several books under his arm, had paused beside Erica.

'No, I looked there, of course, at five thirty when it was time for *Neighbours*.'

'At five thirty I saw her going into Mr Patterson's room.' Tod gave her what Erica thought was a rather funny look. 'Did you know she was seeing him?'

'I certainly did not.' Erica rose, 'I suppose she's watching *Home and Away*?'

'Australian accents and surfboards?'

But Erica was already on her way out.

* * *

'Sarah, darling, are you in here?'

'Mummy!' Sarah scrambled out of a deep armchair and flung herself at Erica. 'I'm frightened.'

'Darling, darling . . . come on, we'll sit on this sofa. Why didn't you tell me you were going to see Patterson?'

'There wasn't time. Sister Monica said he had a cancellation, and I couldn't find you. Mummy, can we go home, *now*?'

How many years ago, reflected Erica, did Sarah drop the babyish 'mummy' in favour of the universal 'mum'? Cradling her child, she thought, 'Christ, there's nothing of her. What have I done?'

'Darling, tell me exactly what's happened.'

Sybil, Rachel and Adam walked in, Sybil telling everyone

where she had to sit.

' . . . if I don't have the high-backed chair by the window, my back . . . oh.'

'Would you mind?' said Erica, 'we won't be long . . . ' Even Sybil hadn't got the face to watch the *News Round-up* over the body of a distraught child, so the three of them exited awkwardly. 'Now, darling, what's it all about?'

'I think Antonia's on drugs . . . those infusions she has, I really think . . . and Mr Patterson tried to hypnotise me.' Sarah's story was muddled and nearly incoherent, but it was enough to turn a not very bright woman with a drinking problem into a cold-eyed tigress.

'Right. I'm going to deal with this. You stay here, Sarah, I'll be back very soon.'

'Please don't leave me alone, mummy.' Sarah clutched at Erica's track suit, and reminded her, almost unbearably, of a three-year-old Sarah at her first day at play school.

'Betty Drummond's in the drawing room. I'll go and get her.'

'Lady Drummond! But she's an old friend of Madame's. She may not be . . . all right.'

'Straight as a die, darling, I promise you. Don't move, back in two secs.'

She was back in ten secs, accompanied by Betty, who sat on the sofa next to Sarah, patted her knee, and said, 'I'll stay with you till your mother comes back, love. Had a bit of an upset? You'll be safe with me.'

'Lady Drummond, do you think Antonia's . . . taking something?'

'No, of course she isn't,' said Betty comfortingly. And wondered uneasily to herself whether Bella knew what was going on.

*   *   *

It was nearly time for supper, but Isabella and Monica were not in the mood for food.

'How I have managed to live through this day, I simply do not know,' said Isabella. 'That wretched actress telling me she didn't want any more Extras, so silly of her when they were doing her so much good.'

'At least you didn't have to deal with Mrs Gerard, Madame. I'm still shaking, and it takes a lot to get me flustered. Going on like a madwoman, telling me her daughter was not to have any of our filthy infusions, and what's more, she wasn't going to go on with them, either. There was no arguing with her, Madame, she was like a woman possessed.'

'Oh, really, what's happening to everybody? You try and do a little good, you try and help people . . . '

'And try and make a bit on the side,' interjected Sister Monica practically, but Isabella was having none of it.

'That has never been my main purpose, Monica, as you know.'

Monica knew nothing of the kind, but could see that there was little point in arguing. She opened her mouth to say something tactful, but was interrupted by a knock on the door.

'Oh, now what is it?' said Isabella, 'Come! Oh, it's you, Mr Patterson.'

'Something I think you should know, Madame. It may be nothing, but while I had Antonia Fellowes under today, she revealed that she had seen part of a letter addressed to Tod Ballard.'

'Well?'

'She remembered the word Psilocybe, because of the funny way it was spelt.'

*   *   *

The Gerards had firmly chosen a table for two in the dining room. Erica could have done with a gin and tonic (how many hours was it since her last?) but she was too busy comforting Sarah to actually do anything about it.

264

'Of course you're not going to go on Extras, darling. There's nothing wrong with you that two square meals a day won't cure. I wish you'd heard me giving Sister Monica the time of day. I didn't repeat myself in ten minutes.'

'Wasn't she cross?'

'No, darling, I was the one who was cross. Oh, lovely, Quenelles of Sole with Spinach and Almonds. I must say Cordelia has made a difference. Oh, darling, I do love you. Please try and eat something.'

Sarah picked up her fork. 'Would you do something for me?'

'Anything, darling, you know that.'

'I looked up the address of the Kensington branch of AA.'

'Oh, Sarah, you know I don't drink. Not really.'

Sarah put down her fork again. 'Bargain, mum. I eat and you don't drink.'

'Darling, do you really think . . . what a bully you are. I promise I'll try.'

Sarah grinned and said, 'This fish isn't half bad. I say, mum, do look at Antonia.'

Erica twisted in her chair and saw Antonia, on the other side of the room, standing on her chair and jabbing at the ceiling. Cordelia, who had been circulating the room and modestly accepting compliments about the Quenelles, darted across and said, 'Antonia, are you all right? What on earth are you doing?'

Antonia smiled brilliantly. 'I am counting all the pretty butterflies,' she said.

CHAPTER
TWENTY-FOUR

'I think I'll wear the navy blue housecoat this evening, Rachel. No, not that one, dear,' Sybil raised her eyes, may the Good Lord give her patience, 'that's the wool. Mr Shepherd admired the velvet.'

'He's nice, Mr Shepherd, isn't he?' said Rachel.

'Shrewd.' It was Sybil's highest accolade. 'He remarked on my hair yesterday, when he kindly drove me to the chemist. "Very becoming," he said.'

'Giovanni does do it beautifully.' Rachel fiddled diffidently with her own hair, which was neither long nor short and curled wilfully in the wrong places. 'I was thinking, mother, perhaps . . . ?'

'What, Rachel? Don't mumble.'

'Perhaps I could go to him before we leave Alba? Just for a trim?'

Looking at her daughter, Sybil barely concealed a quiver of irritation. Forty-six years old and never turned a man's head, except for that pathetic creature from Cullen's, and he'd gone back behind his counter fast enough when he'd seen their Maple suite and the kind of home Rachel came from. She averted her gaze from the furry slippers inappropriately teamed with a flower-sprigged nylon housecoat. It would take more than a trim to put Rachel to rights. 'Wait until we get home, dear. Phyllis always does your hair very nicely. Now, where's my hairbrush? You can give me twenty strokes before we go down to dinner.'

Sybil always made a point of descending the staircase into the main hall just before the dinner gong; she liked to make an entrance, and then decide which of the Alba regulars, thronging hungrily outside the dining room doors, she would invite to join her table.

That evening, her gracious descent was sabotaged by Isabella, coming up the stairs with her dog, which immediately made a play for Rachel's slippers. Rachel screamed foolishly, causing Sybil to trip and clutch dramatically at the banister rail. 'Really, Isabella, you should keep that dog under control.' 'It's all right, mother, I'm all right.' Rachel bent to pat Flora, and withdrew her hand quickly as the dog bared its teeth.

'Here, Flora.' Isabella clicked her fingers and Flora sidled over, wagging her tail. 'I do apologise, Sybil. Are you sure you're all right, Rachel?'

'Rachel may be all right, but I'm certainly not,' said Sybil. 'The fright it gave me. We didn't come here to be attacked by a mad dog. You should put a muzzle on that animal, Isabella.'

The hush that fell on the group at the bottom of the stairs throbbed with as much expectancy as if they were lobbing about the Forum, waiting for a lion to set upon a Christian.

There was a concerted sigh of disappointment as Isabella said, 'Thank you for your advice, Sybil. I'll bear it in mind.'

'What did you make of that?' Diane said to Tristram, over the gazpacho and garlic croûtons. 'I was expecting Madame to blow her top.'

'Not in front of the other guests, that's not her style. But if I were you I wouldn't count on running into Mrs Gillespie on my next visit to Alba.' Tristram was savouring the croûtons, life had certainly taken a turn for the better since he'd been upgraded to the dining room. He noticed that after taking a tentative taste Diane had firmly put down her spoon. 'If you're not going to finish that, Diane . . . ?'

At the table by the window, Adam was charming Sybil Gillespie. 'How well that blue robe sets off your hair, Sybil.'

Sybil patted her rigid row of curls complacently, 'I'm so fortunate to have thick hair. Giovanni always says it's remarkable for a woman of my age, like a young girl's. But that's quite enough about me. Now, Adam, I've been thinking of going into one of those home-owner equity release schemes. No more worries about leaking roofs *and* a nice little income to see me out. What do you think? It's so comforting to have a man's view.'

As Adam bored through the pros and cons ('One does, after all, have to consider one's dependents . . . ' he glanced significantly at Rachel, who smiled artlessly back at him) Sybil was agreeably aware that she was the subject of buzzing speculation at the other tables. Little do they know, she thought, that Isabella will never get rid of me.

She put down her soup spoon and only half listened to dear Adam describing the scenic delights of Portugal, as she reflected on the good fortune – no, she mustn't underestimate herself – the shrewd bargaining, which guaranteed herself and Rachel Special Terms at Alba.

It was five years ago, after that rude manageress at Park Lodge had all but asked her to leave when she'd complained quite legitimately about the state of the toilets, that Sybil had sent for several other health farm brochures. The moment she'd clapped eyes on the photograph on the inside cover of the Alba brochure, she had reached eagerly for her reading glasses. 'Madame Cordoba de Zarate, our directrice, is always on hand to welcome guests and discuss their individual requirements . . . ' Cordoba? Sybil knew that name, and even after fifty years there was something familiar about the arrogant foreign way the woman was staring out of the photograph. She popped the brochure into her handbag. Later, after she had perused it thoroughly, she said, 'We're going to Alba, Rachel.'

It was on the second afternoon of their first visit that Sybil's suspicions had been so agreeably confirmed. Rachel, selfish as usual, had gone off on her own devices;

on this occasion to have tea with a Miss Mayhew who worked in Reception.

'Very well, Rachel,' she had said, 'don't mind about me, I'll be all right by myself. But be sure to bring me up a cup of tea and a slice of Madeira at four.'

At four ten there was still no sign of Rachel and by the time Sybil had got up from her rest, put on her dressing gown and made herself respectable, the Madeira had all been eaten.

Thwarted of her treat, she had determined to find Rachel and give her a piece of her mind. She had located her, eventually, gossiping thoughtlessly with Miss Mayhew in her room above the stable. Sybil had opened her mouth to say all the things she'd been planning to say concerning selfishness, ingratitude and reprisals ('Just you wait, my girl . . . ') but her mouth had remained agape and silent as she gazed around the room.

'Oh, mother,' Rachel jumped up, 'I am sorry. Naomi and I got talking . . . '

'Be quiet, Rachel.' Sybil looked at Miss Mayhew's narrow bed with the mean slatted headboard, at the wooden table stained with the rings of countless solitary mugs of coffee, and she looked particularly keenly at the threadbare grey three-piece suite. Going over to the sofa, she picked up one of the hard seat cushions. Just as she had suspected. The fabric on the back of the cushion was a mess of pulled threads, and in the centre there was a murky stain.

Sybil gave a croak of triumph. That was the cushion Tibs, her little tabby, used to knead ecstatically when she'd managed to wheedle a few scraps for him, off points, from the butcher in Bathurst Street; the stain was where Tibs had had an accident that time the buzz bombs came over and she'd had to dive down the shelter at Marble Arch, and hadn't got home in time to let him out. 'Come along, Rachel,' she said, 'I've got some business to do.'

She'd asked Rachel for the loan of her handbag. 'The good crocodile one I gave you, with the initials on it.'

Rachel watched Sybil gaze fondly at the handbag as she buffed it with her handkerchief. She didn't know what her mother was up to, but admiring old handbags was certainly preferable to the lecture about dereliction of duty she had been expecting.

'I'm afraid Madame Cordoba has someone with her at the moment,' Sister Monica had said, when Sybil arrived outside Isabella's study.

'Never mind,' Sybil sat down, 'I'll wait.'

There had been none of the grandee Madame Cordoba rubbish back in those Bayswater days; she'd been plain Mrs Cordoba, and, so far as Sybil could remember, she'd worked in a munitions factory like everyone else. Gave herself airs, of course; typical foreigner. Tied her headscarf in a fancy way and always managed to lay her hands on nylons when Sybil and her friends had to make do with streaky leg make-up. Sybil couldn't actually prove it, but she knew, as sure as dried eggs tasted nothing like the ones chickens laid, that Mrs Cordoba had done poor, ignorant Dora over those mortgage repayments.

Sybil hadn't wanted to stay in Inverness Terrace after that. Anyway, she'd just met James. Bumped into him in the blackout. Squadron Leader Gillespie, very dashing in his uniform. Not so dashing after the war, though, when he put on a suit and turned into a small-town solicitor.

How like James to make such a production of his Will and then make a mess of it, Sybil was grumbling to herself, as Miss Meadows, the dietician, came out of Madame's room, 'Madame will see you now, Mrs Gillespie.'

Isabella had been sitting in a high-backed chair behind an imposing desk. She hadn't bothered to get up when Sybil entered the room. Still giving herself airs, Sybil thought, taking in the tortoiseshell combs in Isabella's hair and the ostentatious jet jewellery. I'll show her.

She drew up a chair and sat facing Isabella, the handbag four-square on her knees.

'What can I do for you, Mrs Gillespie?' Isabella had said,

'I hope you are enjoying your stay at Alba?'

'Very pleasant, thank you.'

Isabella had looked at Sybil enquiringly. Another difficult client preparing to voice some trifling complaint. The ones recommended by their doctors were always the most troublesome. 'May I get you a cup of tea?'

'That won't be necessary.'

'Well, then . . . ?'

'Inverness Terrace, 1944,' said Sybil, holding up the handbag.

Isabella studied the woman on the other side of her desk, and saw a determined chin, a mean narrow mouth, an ill-concealed gleam of triumph in the foxy grey eyes; and then she looked at the initials on the handbag, S.V.

'That's right, Mrs Cordoba,' Sybil said, 'Sybil Vavasour.'

They had come to an agreement after that. Sybil and Rachel could visit Alba as often as they pleased, (it usually pleased Sybil to come every six months), and were to be given the front room with lake and garden view, the services of Matt Lawson whenever Sybil fancied a massage, and a discount on the bill, to include all extra treatments and hairdressing. Isabella had offered a twenty-five per cent discount, Sybil went for seventy-five per cent and they negotiated to a mutually acceptable fifty per cent. Acceptable to Sybil, anyway. Isabella had to grit her teeth and stifle a scream of frustration every time she signed the Gillespie bill.

Sybil smiled. What a satisfactory meeting that had been. She gave a start as Cordelia tapped her on the shoulder. 'Would you like the spinach tart or the calves liver and sorrel purée, Mrs Gillespie?'

'I'll have the calves liver with spinach,' Sybil said, 'I can't abide sorrel.'

*   *   *

'May I fetch you a drink, Sybil?'

'Thank you, Adam. An apple juice, if I may.'

Adam returned with the drinks, accompanied by Tod Ballard, and Sybil remarked, not for the first time, how often the most eligible men seemed to prefer her company to that of younger women. Look at Isabella's granddaughter, for instance, gossiping away at the other end of the terrace with the girl from Wales. Both of them lounging about untidily, sloppily dressed in baggy trousers and even baggier tops. Goodness knows how often she had told Rachel that men liked to see a woman elegantly dressed in clothes that flattered the figure.

Sybil had never wasted her time on other women, except for her bridge group, who fluttered and squeaked like old hens when Dr Corbett joined them for an occasional game. Sybil despised their silliness, but always made sure that Dr Corbett was served the slice of cake with the cherry on top. She had come to rely on him for financial as well as medical advice.

She had missed James grievously when he died. He had been a good husband, in his way. Always on hand to fetch and carry and deal, uncomplainingly, with uncreative chores like filling in income tax forms, tussling over the rates with the Town Hall and emptying the dishwasher. And it had been so useful, when dealing with tiresome people who wanted her to do what she had no intention of doing, to be able to say, 'I am sorry, but I'm afraid my husband simply wouldn't hear of it.'

Adam Shepherd lit a cigar. 'You don't object, Sybil?'

'Certainly not, my dear.' Sybil liked to see a man smoking a cigar. Yes, Adam would do very nicely; the chairman of a large public company was a fitting consort for Sybil Gillespie. He'd told her the name of his firm, Trasker Corbett; easy to remember because her sister was married to Phil Trasker, a notorious layabout, and Corbett was the name of her dear doctor. Adam was, perhaps, a trifle young, but some men preferred mature women. And, of course, at her age he wouldn't expect her to go in for any of that nonsense. She'd put a stop to *that* after Rachel was born. It was single beds, thank you very much, the day she came back from the Nursing Home.

Listening to Adam talking business with Mr Ballard, Sybil was impressed by his obvious grasp of financial matters. Perhaps she would have a word with him about the annuity problem.

'Johnson Parvitt haven't a hope in hell, forgive me, Sybil, of sliding past the Monopolies and Mergers Commission with that one . . . ' Adam was saying, as Sybil leant forward and interrupted.

'Now that I've got you two knowledgeable men captive, I'm going to ask your advice. My late husband left me very comfortably off, as I believe I mentioned, Adam, but he was always a cautious man and he tied up all the money in an annuity . . . '

'An annuity?' said Adam.

'That's why I was thinking of raising money on the house, it would be so comforting to get my hands on a little capital.'

'I can understand that,' said Adam, who had been hoping to get his hands on it, too, 'but I'm afraid there is no way you get capital out of an annuity.' He turned back to Tod in a way Sybil considered really rather uncouth. 'We came up against the M & MC in my company, a few years ago, when we made a bid for Cartwrights.'

'Trasker Corbett, wasn't it?' Sybil was keen to get back into the conversation.

'I beg your pardon?' said Adam.

'The name of your firm, Adam dear. Trasker Corbett.'

'I think you've got it wrong there, Mrs Gillespie,' said Tod. 'Trasker Corbett went into liquidation about a year ago, I seem to remember the Serious Fraud Office had one or two pertinent questions to put to their Board.'

Liquidation? Serious fraud? Sybil decided she was already late for her Aromatherapy.

'Good Lord no, not Trasker Corbett,' she heard Adam say as she went through the french windows into the Light Diet Room. 'Poor old soul, I expect her memory is playing her tricks.'

Sybil twitched angrily. Old soul, indeed! And Mr Ballard wouldn't believe her, even if she went back and told him about her sister and Dr Corbett.

Climbing the stairs, Sybil decided to have another private session with Carolyn Watson; those exercises were really loosening her up. By the time she had reached her bedroom, she had rewritten recent events into a more flattering version. Some women might have been taken in by that shyster, but not Sybil Gillespie. She had always thought there was something fishy about Mr Adam Shepherd. What was it James always used to say? Never trust a man with close-set eyes.

*   *   *

'Did I tell you?' said Debbie, 'I'm going back to Hancock's.'

'Hancock's?' said Cordelia. She was trying very hard not to watch Tod Ballard talking to Adam Shepherd at the other end of the terrace.

'You know, where I work, in Swansea. Where Isaac works.'

'Isaac?' Adam had left, and Tod was scribbling something in a notebook. He pushed a stray lock of hair off his forehead; Cordelia wished she could do it for him. 'Sorry, Debbie?'

Debbie also looked across the terrace. Nice enough, but bookish, not her type. Then she looked at Cordelia; for someone who had professed a lack of interest in Tod Ballard, Cordelia seemed curiously absorbed.

'Isaac was my lover,' she said slowly and deliberately, 'we both work for the same firm. His wife is having a baby, and I do not love him any more. My office is a hotbed of gossip and conjecture on the subject. Nevertheless, I am returning there next week, because I don't give a damn what Isaac or the sales staff or the managing director or anybody says.'

Cordelia guiltily switched her attention to Debbie and was glad to see that she was laughing. 'I really am sorry, Debbie. Of course I remember, and I think you're very brave.'

'That's me sorted,' said Debbie, 'so what are you going to do about Tod?'

'There's nothing I can do. He won't speak to me, he actually dodges into doorways when he sees me coming.'

'He's not dodging now, he's coming over.'

'Hi, there,' said Tod, not looking at Cordelia, 'can I get anyone an orange juice?'

Cordelia would have liked to say something warm and welcoming. She shook her head and said nothing at all.

'Not for me, thanks,' said Debbie, 'I've had my quota of liquids for today.'

'Adam has told me about your decision,' said Tod, sitting down next to Debbie, 'I'm sure you're doing the right thing. It won't be easy, will it?'

'Mr Patterson has been so helpful . . . given me courage . . . '

'The herbal infusions?'

'And the therapy. He really talked me through it.'

'I don't like him much. What do you think, Cordelia?'

Cordelia, aware only of Tod sitting just a touch away from her, had not taken anything in except that Tod was talking about infusions again. 'About what, Tod?'

'Mr Patterson. Quite a few people seem to have had problems with his infusions, and he certainly messed up Antonia Fellowes, poor child. How reliable is he, I won der? Has he been here long?'

The happiness, which had come over Cordelia when 7 spoke to her, evaporated. Questions again, she thour resentfully, all he ever does is ask me question

275

Patterson is a professional hypnotherapist and herbalist,' she said, 'he has been at Alba since it started, and we think very highly of him.'

'I think he's marvellous,' said Debbie.

'And what's more,' said Cordelia sharply, 'Antonia Fellowes is a spoilt child who enjoys being the centre of attention.'

CHAPTER
TWENTY-FIVE

Adam was packing his bags. There didn't seem much point in hanging about Alba any more. In fact, there was a damn good reason for getting out fast. Who'd have thought there would be anyone lurking about a health farm with the Trasker Corbett facts at his finger-tips? He had skilfully helped the Serious Fraud Office with their enquiries, and they had gone away, apparently satisfied. He wasn't sure that he had been quite so clever with Tod Ballard who wasn't such a woolly-minded intellectual as he liked to make out. And old Mrs Gillespie was nobody's fool.

He was neatly folding the Harvie & Hudson checked shirt, the Old Wykehamist and Old Harrovian ties, the navy Gieves & Hawkes blazer, when the phone went. Adam glanced at his Appointments for Today card. No doubt it was Carolyn summoning him to Movement to Music.

He picked up the phone. 'Shepherd here.'

'Mr Shepherd?' The voice was quavery, oddly familiar.

'Yes, yes.'

'It's Delia . . . '

'Delia?' Oh, my God, Adam sank down onto the bed, his hand tensing on the receiver. Delia Sargent from the Essex Hydro, major shareholder in Quinta da Vasco. 'Delia, what a surprise, how did you know I was here?'

'You told me about Merrymount, your house in Weybridge, remember? A friend of mine found the number . . . ' (Oh, God, she's been on to her solicitor) ' . . . and I spoke to one of your servants, Costas, he told me where

277

you were.'

'Costas?'

'He sounded rather snooty. I just had to talk to you . . . '

'Now, Delia, you must realise that all investment is something of a gamble.'

'I know, Mr Shepherd. That's why I wanted to thank you . . . '

'A high yield inevitably carries risk. Thank me?'

'I had such a nice phone call yesterday, a Portuguese gentleman wanting to buy my shares. And he's offering ten times more than I paid for them.'

'Ten?' Adam clutched the bedhead for support. 'Ten times? But that's . . . that would be . . . '

'Exactly, Mr Shepherd. Two and a half million pounds.'

As Delia Sargent chatted on ('My dear, my stockbroker simply refused to believe it . . . ') Adam did a quick sum. If fifty per cent netted £2.5 million, five per cent would bring in . . . no, it wasn't possible.

'Great, Delia, great news; much appreciate your calling.' Adam put down the phone and dialled a London number with trembling fingers. Why didn't Gerry answer? 'Gerry?'

'Adam. You've heard, then. I was just about to get on the blower.'

'How? Who? I can't believe it.'

Gerry chuckled. 'Amazing, isn't it? They're going to build an airport on our land, open up the interior. That's £250,000 for you, old chap, and £250,000 for me.'

Adam slowly unpacked his suitcase. No need to rush away, he was a respectable businessman with cash in the bank. He looked forward to telling Sybil Gillespie how she had missed out on a once in a lifetime investment. Rather pleasing to drop a word to that know-it-all writer chap, too.

Besides, he hadn't yet had a chance to congratulate Sylvia on her success at the audition. A celebratory bottle of Lanson might well be in order.

*   *   *

'There's a funny atmosphere in this place, Rachel,' said Sybil. 'Where are my hair-pins, dear? I left them in the top drawer.'

'On the dressing table, mother.' Rachel didn't waste time telling her mother she had put them there herself two minutes ago. 'How do you mean, funny?'

'One child in hysterics, Mrs Gerard had the nerve to practically throw me out of one of the public rooms because her daughter was in there sobbing, and the other child babbling away in the dining room about butterflies.'

'Oh, mother, Antonia's only a child, really, I expect she was playing a game with us.'

Sybil looked at Rachel pityingly. The girl's simple-minded insistence on seeing the best in everybody and everything exasperated her beyond endurance. 'Antonia Fellowes was not playing a game with us, Rachel, she was hallucinating. It's something to do with that herbal quack, mark my words. I knew I was right not to let you near him.'

'He's been very helpful to Debbie.'

'Time will show. Her eyes are too bright for my liking, and it's not natural to be so cheerful when you've just lost your boyfriend.'

'*Really*, mother.' Rachel smiled affectionately at Sybil, how she did go on. 'Next thing you'll be telling me that nice Mr Shepherd is a mass murderer.'

'There's something fishy about Mr Shepherd, I said so all along.'

'You said he was shrewd,' said Rachel, bravely.

'How right I was. And on the make, if you ask me.' Sybil sat down heavily on the bed. 'Help me on with these stockings, Rachel. I think I'll need them this evening, I'm feeling a bit shivery.'

'You'll not be playing bridge with Mr Shepherd after dinner, then?' Rachel lifted up Sybil's foot and slipped it into a sheer stocking. How typical of mother to wear nylon rather than the lumpy lisle favoured by most old ladies.

'Not this evening or any other evening. Be careful you don't snag the nylon, Rachel, you should have put on those cotton gloves I gave you. Oh, never mind about them now.' Sybil was left with a dangling leg as Rachel dutifully scurried off to fetch the gloves. 'I wouldn't be surprised if Mr Shepherd turns out to be a con-man.'

'Never?' Rachel's eyes widened as she recalled Naomi telling her about the con-man roaming the health farms, preying on rich, elderly women. She had imagined a small man, sharp and rodent-like, gnawing away at his victims; not someone nice and jolly, like Mr Shepherd.

'He says he's the Chairman of a large public company, but I happen to know that company went into liquidation some time ago.'

'How do you know that?

'I have my sources, Rachel. I don't suppose the man has two pennies to rub together.'

'Oh, he has,' said Rachel, 'I heard him telling Sylvia in Movement to Music. "You're not going to believe this," he said, "I can hardly believe it myself, but I've just done a property deal worth a quarter of a million. And," he said, "we're going to crack a bottle of champagne to celebrate your success and my good fortune." And then he laughed.'

'Sylvia Travers would do well to look to her savings, if she has any. Come along now, Rachel, I'm ready to go down for dinner.'

*   *   *

'Celeriac and Walnut Patties again,' said Tristram fretfully, 'we had them only the other day.'

'They were Jennifer Tremayne's cookery column in the *Surrey Advertiser*,' said Rachel. 'I was reading it in Treatment Reception, waiting for Lucy. And they featured the Marrow Stuffed with Crab we had yesterday.'

'Bit of a coincidence,' said Tristram.

'I expect Cordelia read the column. I was telling her about it the other day, when she came in to help mother. And do you know, Mr Bartholomew, Miss Tremayne had the nerve to steal Cordelia's recipe for Calorific Chocolate Cake?'

'*The English Tea*,' said Tristram, 'quite a good little book in its way.'

'I find it a real boon for mother's bridge afternoons; Mrs Fortescue has such a sweet tooth, and Miss Phillips likes her sandwiches spread with just the tiniest trace of mayonnaise, she says nobody makes sandwiches like Rachel Gillespie . . . '

As Rachel prattled, a suspicion was looming large in Tristram's small mind. Three familiar recipes were more than a coincidence, and food writers were renowned for recycling their favourites. If he was not mistaken, Cordelia Ledbury, the ultimate foodie, was still busily scribbling away at a syndicated cookery column; a professional like Cordelia wouldn't waste her time on the pittance she'd receive from selling a cookery column to one local newspaper.

Madame Cordoba had asked him to drop into her study after dinner, 'to discuss a serious matter'. Some busybody had, no doubt, informed her of his lunchtime visits to The Barley Mow; he had, over the last few days, become seriously addicted to their Yorkshire Pheasant served with Forcemeat Balls and Redcurrant Jelly. Tristram smirked in anticipation of the meeting.

'May I share the joke, Mr Bartholomew?' said Rachel.

'Just thinking,' said Tristram. What he was thinking was that the tantalising tit-bit about Cordelia moonlighting would certainly stop Madame C. in mid venom.

*   *   *

Sybil looked at her bedside clock. Seven thirty a.m. and all was not well. She had a headache, a sharp pain around her left eye, and her tummy was playing her up. 'Rachel!' There was no reply from the other bed. 'Rachel!' Nothing for it, she'd have to struggle out of bed by herself.

Muttering resentfully, Sybil just managed to get to the bathroom in time. It must have been those queer nut patties, she thought, steadying herself against the washbasin. She inspected her eye in the mirror, and was appalled to see that it was circled by a cluster of red spots. They hurt when she touched them.

'Rachel!' Sybil staggered back into the bedroom and poked a sharp finger at her daughter's sleeping figure. Useless girl. Out like a light when needed.

'What's happened? What's the matter?' Rachel rose abruptly from a deep sleep; *Cupid's Messenger* having reached a satisfactory conclusion, she had been up half the night reading *Prisoner of Love*; she was still immersed in a misty aura of romance, dispelled by the sight of Sybil. 'You've got spots, mother.'

'I know I've got spots.' Sybil raised her eyes in exasperation, and gave a yelp of pain. 'Now look what you've made me do. And I've got a headache and my tummy's not right.'

'I'm sorry, mother. Shall I get the doctor?'

'I won't have that Patterson man near me. Help me back to bed, and then you can call Sister Monica.'

'Do you think I should?' Rachel found Sister Monica even more alarming than her mother.

'She's a nurse, isn't she?'

Sister Monica told Rachel to keep mother in bed, make sure she was warm and comfortable ('How could I possibly be comfortable when I'm in agony?') and she'd be along in a jiff.

When Sister Monica arrived, ten minutes later, she made a big production of temperature and pulse taking. 'Only just above normal.' She shook the thermometer briskly, studied Sybil's eye, then whisked up her nightdress and gave her a professional once-over. 'Just as I thought, it generally manifests in one or two neuroderm areas on one side of the body. Lucky for you it's only your eye.'

'Lucky?' said Sybil. 'What is it?'

'Shingles. Have you been near anyone with chickenpox?'

'Certainly not.'

'Well then,' said Sister Monica cheerily, 'you've been near someone who's incubating it. It's most infectious thirty-six hours before the spots appear. Painful, is it?'

'Of course it's painful.'

Sister Monica turned to Rachel. 'Keep mother in bed, I'll send her up a warm drink. And, later, I'll get a doctor to her.'

'I won't have that Patterson,' Sybil rose up weakly.

'No, no, the local GP.' Sister Monica pushed Sybil down and pinioned her with a zestful tuck-in of the sheets. 'I'll ask him to come in after Surgery, we'll need a doctor to refer you to hospital.'

'Hospital?' squawked Sybil.

'Certainly,' said Sister Monica, 'you can't stay here with shingles. This is a health farm.'

*   *   *

'I'm singing in the rain, just singing in the rain, I'm singing in the rai-ain, I'm singing in the rain . . . ' Down the corridor, Adam Shepherd was singing in the shower.

He could see her through the watery glass, walking slowly towards him; naked, slim as a girl, but infinitely more beautiful.

Sylvia stepped into the shower and put her arms around him. 'Wrong words, darling,' she said, as the water cascaded over them, 'my own darling, you're singing the wrong words.'

*   *   *

Rachel had gone for her morning Massage. 'You might as well, we're paying for it,' Sybil had said, and had been quite put out when Rachel readily agreed.

Sybil couldn't remember when she had felt more irritable. She was in pain, she was uncomfortable and the radio was too far out of her reach for her to turn off Brian Redhead, who was shouting down the telephone to somebody in the Sudan who couldn't hear him.

She struggled out of bed (Sister Monica might just as well have put her in a straitjacket), turned off the radio with a sigh of relief and went unsteadily towards the wardrobe.

She'd need to change into a new nightie and a pretty bed jacket for the doctor, and they were packed in her suitcase. It was hard work dragging the suitcase out from the bottom of the wardrobe, but Sybil finally managed to pull it free. As she did so, she noticed, tucked away at the back, a pile of paper books with lurid covers. She shuddered with distaste. They looked to her, at first glance, the sort of unpleasant material unpleasant people had sent to them under plain wrapper.

Cupid's Messenger? Sybil threw it aside and picked up the next. *Prisoner of Love, Winter's Bud, The End of the Rainbow*; a lot of cheap trash. She dropped them into the waste paper basket where they belonged.

She put on her best nightie, the satin one with ecru lace on the bosom, and the lacey bed jacket Rachel had crocheted for her birthday, and climbed back into bed, confident in the becomingness of her attire.

*   *   *

'Doctor's here, Mrs Gillespie.' Sister Monica bustled in, followed by the local doctor and Rachel. 'My, you do look smart. All ready, are we?'

'We've been ready for some hours,' Sybil said sourly.

'I'll get your sponge bag and bed jacket, mother,' said

284

Rachel, going to the wardrobe.

'It's all right, Rachel, I managed to get them myself.'

But Rachel was already ferreting about in the wardrobe. She was white-faced as she turned towards Sybil. 'Where are my books?'

'Your books?' Sybil had guessed straight away, of course, that the books were Rachel's; they were too cunningly hidden to have been casually left behind. 'That rubbish? I threw them in the waste paper basket, dear. Well now, doctor, Sister Monica tells me it's shingles.'

The doctor put down his case and, coming forward to give Sybil's eye a solicitous inspection, was stopped in his tracks by Rachel, pushing in front of him. 'How *dare* you touch my books?'

Sybil gave Rachel one of her Looks. Had the girl gone clean out of her mind? And in front of the doctor, too. 'Pull yourself together, Rachel.'

For the first time in her life, Rachel ignored the Look. She rushed over to the empty waste paper basket, and turned it upside down. 'Where are they? What have you done with them?'

'The maid took them while you were off having your Massage,' said Sybil, 'an hour ago.'

'The dustbin men came early today,' said Sister Monica. 'Least said soonest mended,' she added hopefully, as Rachel collapsed onto the chair by the dressing table, looking at Sybil in a way she had never looked at her before.

'How could you be so cruel, mother?'

'Oh, be quiet about your wretched books,' said Sybil. 'What do they matter?'

'Well, then,' said the doctor, stepping forward again. 'Yes, definitely shingles, I'm afraid.' He looked from the old lady to her daughter, who was sitting across the room waxen faced, as though somebody had snapped off her oxygen supply. A routine five-minute call, and the atmosphere in this room was as highly charged as if they were acting out something by Ibsen. At this rate he wouldn't get in all his visits before lunch. He was relieved when Sister Monica announced the arrival of the ambulance, and left her post at the window to push Sybil into her dressing gown. 'Well, then, have we got everything we need?'

He looked anxiously at Rachel, who was still sitting at the dressing table, staring bleakly at her mother. 'You mustn't upset yourself, my dear,' he said, 'mother will be right as rain in a few days.'

'My spectacles, Rachel,' said Sybil, from the doorway. 'I'll need my spectacles. On the shelf in the bathroom.'

Rachel made no attempt to move.

'I'll get them, Mrs Gillespie,' said Sister Monica.

'Right we are,' said the doctor. He looked at Rachel. 'I expect you'd like to come in the ambulance, with mother?'

Rachel was gazing at Sybil in disbelief. All the years we've been together, she thought, and I never realised how much she hated me. 'No, thank you,' she said, 'I wouldn't.'

CHAPTER
TWENTY-SIX

'When are you coming home, doll? I'm missing you something rotten.'

Betty was enjoying her nightly phone call with her husband. An eavesdropper might have raised an eyebrow at the absurdity of a seventy-year-old man addressing his not much younger wife in a manner reminiscent of mini skirts and bouffant hairstyles; but an eavesdropper wouldn't have known that Sir William and Lady Drummond met at school when he was ten, married when she was seventeen, and were still, some fifty years later, fresh as daisies.

'They looking after you all right, darling?' asked Betty fondly.

'They' consisted of a live-in staff of cook, butler and housemaid. (You had to laugh; little Betty Appleyard who used to go to school in her brother's cast-off shoes, saying, 'We'll be ten for dinner tonight, Mrs Cargill.') A gardener came in five mornings a week, and then there was Mrs Stainton, who did the rough.

'Of course they're looking after me. If one more person reminds me to turn off my electric blanket . . .'

'What are you having for supper?'

'Steak and kidney pudding. Now I know what you're going to say, Betty . . .'

'I told Mrs Cargill you'd got to watch your carbo-hydrates.'

'I won't eat the suet, then.'

'Yes you will, you wicked old devil. I told her. Salads, I said, and a little poached fish. You know what the doctor said. Oh Bill, do look after yourself.'

'Why don't you come home and look after me?'

'I'll be home tomorrow, about lunchtime. Bill, I'm worried about Bella.'

'Try worrying about something with a really soft centre, like the Rock of Gibraltar.'

'No, listen, Bill, seriously, you remember I told you yesterday about that girl Antonia . . . '

'The one who's starving herself?'

'No, that's Sarah, I knew you weren't concentrating. Antonia's the one who stood on a chair counting butterflies that weren't there.'

'The spaced-out one?'

'Well, what do you think? And where did she get it from, that's what's worrying me. I put it all down to Sister Monica, Bill, Bella's right under her thumb.'

'Betty, think about it, love. Bella hasn't been under anyone's thumb since about ten minutes after she was born.'

But then, thought Betty after they'd said goodnight, Bill never really took to Isabella, even when they were making all that money with the coupons, back in the war.

Kind Betty, only eighteen then, and already with an eye out for a lame dog, had hesitated when Bill suggested that the shop where Bella worked was a perfect outlet for his artistic forgeries. 'She's all alone, Bill, in a foreign country, with that little baby. We don't want to get her into trouble, do we?'

'She knows how to look after number one. Makes Goebbels look a sweetie, if you ask me. And there's another thing, Betty. If she's the daughter of dead Spanish aristocrats, why does she speak such flipping good English?'

'Doesn't she speak lovely? Actually, I did ask her that. Apparently she had an English governess. She looked quite surprised when I asked her. Well, I wasn't to know, but apparently all those people with titles on the Continent have English governesses. Hers was called Miss Merridew.

288

"Dear old Merry," she said, "so fussy about vowel sounds, I still hear from her occasionally." And sometimes she does have a little bit of an accent, Bill.'

'Anything you say, love.'

Bill thought she had a little bit of an accent, too, which he found difficult to place; born well before Englishmen of his class used the coast of Spain as a sunny back garden, he wasn't all that sure what a Spanish accent was meant to sound like. However, he wasn't about to upset his darling little Betty, so he shut up.

Isabella had drifted out of their lives towards the end of the war, but not before her considerable business acumen had had Bill whistling through his teeth with reluctant admiration.

Bombed properties that were little more than three walls and a staircase were going for peanuts; Bill himself had made several nice little purchases, but he was a fumbling beginner compared to Isabella. When he congratulated her on her perspicacity ('No flies on you, Bella'), she gave him an icy look and said, 'My family have always bought land. It is in my blood.'

'You'll be going back to Spain, will you, when the war's over?'

'I will never go back.'

'Won't your husband's family want to see little Olivia?'

'They too are dead. There is nothing for me in Spain, nothing.'

After she had gone, Betty said reproachfully, 'You know she doesn't like to talk about Spain, Bill, you know what happened to her during the Civil War. How could you be so tactless?'

'I know what she says happened to her,' said Bill heartlessly. 'Personally I'd rather ravish a V2 rocket. Talking about little Olivia, love, isn't it about time we got you in the family way?'

*   *   *

289

Betty hated remembering that; everything was ahead of her and Bill then. They were young and handsome and secure because Bill's mum adored Betty ('Don't you let him put one over on you, dear. If he gives you any trouble, you know where to come') and Betty's father went fishing every Saturday with Bill; putting him, in the process, on to quite a few nice little money-earners. Not strictly legit, perhaps, but who was counting?

It had taken her seventeen years to get in the family way; it really got to Betty, the first time she saw her babies, because Bill's mum had died in the meantime, and it seemed to Betty then that the worst thing that could happen to a woman was not to see her son's sons. She knew better now.

'Shut up, you silly old cow,' said Betty to herself. 'The dead can look after themselves. It's the living you've got to worry about.'

And she'd been really worried at Alba this time; it was all so different from her previous visits. Isabella had always had the place running like clockwork. Now it all seemed to be falling to pieces; and weren't some of the guests a bit peculiar? Adam Shepherd, it hadn't taken her long to suss him out, and Diane Renfrew was a nasty piece of work. Why hadn't Isabella thrown her out? She certainly had good reason.

One thing, Sarah was going to be all right. A sensible head on her shoulders, and her mother seemed to have come to her senses. What Erica Gerard needed, besides stopping drinking, was a purpose in life, and Betty thought she was going to be very useful in the Registration of Dogs campaign.

Antonia was probably a lost cause, though, and it didn't half make you think there was no justice in parenthood. Erica Gerard had got better than she deserved. Jane Fellowes deserved the best and hadn't got it. And Betty Drummond, who had never wished anyone any harm (unless you counted that air-raid warden on VE night) got

an inadequate young WPC knocking at her door one afternoon and saying something about road conditions and
nobody's fault.

It was after supper on Saturday, and after supper at Alba
there was not much to do, unless you played bridge, which
Betty certainly did not. She loved cards; she and Bill often
took a hand of whist after dinner, but she refused to put up
with the malice that seemed to affect even the mildest of
people once they'd said One No Trump. Of course, she
could have watched television in her own room, there was
rather a nice programme about zebras, but she fancied a bit
of company.

She would go downstairs and watch the programme
about zebras in the telly room; though now that she came
to think of it, there probably wouldn't be many people
about. Sunday was the day, at Alba, when guests were
firmly requested to vacate their rooms by twelve noon.
Unless they were staying on for another week, in which
case they were still considered important. Most people
would be packing.

Betty met Diane Renfrew, no doubt fresh from some
vulgar rendezvous, on the stairs. 'Off to do your packing,
Mrs Renfrew?'

'I've ordered a taxi for ten in the morning. We came in
Sheila's car, but of course she had to rush off home in her
hysterical way to look after dear Gerald.'

'Anyway, I'm sure you feel the better for your time here.'

'Not particularly. Alba doesn't feel the same, somehow.
I was toying with the idea of trying somewhere else, next
time.'

Betty murmured something, uninterested, and moved on
down the stairs. Isabella, in one of her lighter moments
(and there hadn't been many of those, recently) had told
her about walking in on Diane and Matt in flagrante
delicto.

' . . . in one of the massage cubicles, Betty, so unprofessional, and he hadn't even bothered to tidy up the

towels from the afternoon sessions.'

Betty had grinned to herself. Even during the war, when soap was short, Bella had kept everything compulsively clean; the impression that was coming across was that if the towels had been tidy, Isabella might have overlooked the adultery.

'You and your clean towels, Bella,' she had said, 'but seriously, love, I know he's a good masseur and all that, but you can't keep him on, can you? Messing about with the clientele is a bit off, isn't it?'

Isabella had, rather uncharacteristically, been noncommittal in her reply.

Betty found the telly room empty except for Sarah. A very different Sarah from the one she comforted while her mother tore Sister Monica off a strip.

'Oh, hullo, Lady Drummond. There's a programme about zebras in a minute on BBC 2.'

'Just what I came down for. You're looking a good deal more chipper than the last time we were in here.'

'I expect you thought I was being silly. Only I was worried about Antonia.'

'With reason. Where is she? I haven't seen her today.'

'Her mother took her home this morning. I don't know whether to like Mrs Fellowes, or not. I mean, she was very kind to me, but . . . '

'She should have noticed what was happening to Antonia?'

'Well, she should, shouldn't she?'

'I think that might be partly my fault. I told her she wasn't being selfish enough.'

'Oh,' said Sarah, who, being a polite child, didn't like to add, 'what a funny thing to say,' which was what she was thinking.

'I can see you don't approve. Jane Fellowes came here for a rest, because she was on the edge of a nervous breakdown. Antonia has five brothers and sisters, you know, and there's a vast house and no help. Jane got a first at Oxford, and her husband got a second. So guess who got to follow their career?'

Sarah's brow cleared. Now that they had got on to Women's Lib, she knew exactly how to think. 'I see what you mean. Bloody unfair.'

'Isn't it time for the zebras?' Much as she liked Sarah, Betty had had enough of the young. Seeing everything in black and white made them more exhausting to talk to than a Min of Ag inspector. Sarah manipulated the remote control and produced a restful scene of the African veldt. Zebras strolled about and flicked their tails and a couple of lionesses yawned and stretched and contemplated lunch.

'So cruel, nature, isn't it?' said Sarah.

'Not half as cruel as veal,' said Betty shortly.

'Actually, I was thinking of becoming a vegetarian.'

'Good.'

Sarah realised she was politely being told to shut up, which was a pity because she would have liked to ask Lady Drummond if she knew what happened at poor Mr Pullen's inquest.

Oh dear, here were that pillock Mr Shepherd and Sylvia Travers. They would want to talk, and Lady Drummond would get cross.

'Good evening,' said Adam jovially, 'anything decent on?'

'Just this programme about zebras which I am enjoying very much,' said Lady Drummond. Adam and Sylvia exchanged a look and tiptoed out, rather theatrically.

'They're very thick, aren't they? Oh, sorry, Lady Drummond, I forgot about the zebras. Only he's awful, Mr Shepherd, he goes after women for their money. You should have heard him trying to get off with Mrs Gillespie in the Gym.'

'I'm glad I didn't.'

'Yes, it was gross. Only I like Miss Travers. Do you think I should sort of warn her?'

'I really don't think she'd appreciate it, Sarah. She's quite capable of looking after herself. Anyway, they looked to me like friends, nothing more complicated than that, I think you'll find.'

'I didn't think they looked like just friends, Lady Drummond, I thought they looked sort of . . . laughing secretly. Oh, hullo, Miss Gillespie, any news about your poor mother?'

'The hospital says she's quite comfortable.' Rachel Gillespie had entered the room with rather more assurance than usual, and seated herself four-squarely in the arm-chair usually appropriated by her mother. 'I shan't go and visit her, though, no point. I don't want to catch shingles.'

Betty cast a regretful look at a zebra foal that had strayed rather far from its mother, got up, and left the room. She would go and have a brandy with Isabella; she hadn't seen her all day, and she felt the need for some intelligent conversation.

After the door had closed behind her, Rachel said, 'Was it something I said?'

'No, only she was trying to watch this programme about zebras.'

'Oh dear,' said Rachel vaguely. 'She threw all my books away, you know, and I was so much looking forward to reading *Winter's Bud* again. I'll never forgive her, never.'

'Lady Drummond? Surely not?'

'And what's more I am going to stay on for another few days, and whatever she says, I've made an appointment for Giovanni to cut my hair.'

'Goodness,' said Sarah, since Rachel seemed to think a hairdressing appointment was worthy of some remark.

'I don't see why I can't get a job, other people do. She'll just have to look after herself during the day, that's all.'

'Right,' said Sarah, who was finding her end of the conversation quite difficult to keep up. '*Winter's Bud*? I don't think I've read it.'

'It's Perdita Blane's latest. It's about a girl who takes a

job running a chalet, but she doesn't know that her cousin . . . '

Sarah smiled politely and let her eyes drift back to the telly. Oh dear, that poor little baby zebra.

*   *   *

Isabella was sitting bolt upright in her armchair; Flora was lying, whimpering occasionally in her sleep, in front of the log fire.

'I am afraid I am rather busy at the moment, so if you wouldn't mind . . . oh, it's you, Betty. I thought it was yet another grumbling client.'

'It's not like you to be defeatist, love. You surely don't get many grumbles at Alba, everything's so beautifully run.'

'There's always someone making difficulties. Shingles at Alba, it's really too much. And on half-rates too,' added Isabella darkly.

'Rachel just flounced into the television room, looking rather full of herself, I thought.'

'I dare say she'll be throwing her weight about before we know where we are. And then look at Mr Pullen.'

'Very inconsiderate of him, I'm sure. Why couldn't he wait to die until he got home?'

'It's not funny, Betty. The inquest was this morning, and Monica and I felt we both ought to go.'

'Showing the flag, sort of thing?'

'Well, she had to be there to give evidence, and I went so nobody could think we had anything to be ashamed of.'

'What was the verdict?'

'Heart attack brought on by drink and drugs. How were we to know that he was taking stuff like that? Monica did extremely well in the witness box, and the coroner said no blame could be attached to the highly reputable establishment the deceased had happened to be staying at, at the time of his decease.'

295

'All very satisfactory.'

'Up to a point. Only why was Tod Ballard there?'

'Was he? Writers are always looking for background stuff, aren't they?'

'You remember you said once he reminded you of someone?'

'Only vaguely, love; I nearly got it when he was asking Antonia questions the other day, but then it went.'

'Don't speak to me about Antonia. On some hallucinogenic, I gather. It's really too bad of people to bring that kind of thing to a place with Alba's reputation.'

'Bella, one or two people think . . . she might have got it here. Those extras that Patterson prescribes and Sister Monica hands out, people are beginning to ask questions about them.'

'Ridiculous! They wouldn't dare do something so reprehensible behind my back.'

'Yes, but Mr Pullen had them too, didn't he? And didn't Sylvia Travers say the Alba infusions made people think she was an alcoholic? And wasn't there some fuss with Sheila Steinberg one night? She was on Extras, wasn't she?'

'No. No. It's all nonsense. Stop it, Betty, I won't listen . . . '

'Dear me, dear me, and what's all this? The Princess getting hysterical, is she?' Matt Lawson walked in, with a bottle in one hand, and a glass in the other. The bottle was by no means full. 'Thought I'd join the party, if that's all right with you ladies.'

Betty, thinking, 'Well, she'll have to get rid of him now,' waited for Isabella to freeze Matt right out of the room. He sat down in an armchair by the fire and stretched his legs out. Flora growled in her throat.

'Get that bloody little dog away from me, unless she wants a kick.'

'Flora,' said Isabella, 'here, darling.'

'Oh really,' thought Betty, 'this is beyond belief.' Aloud, she said, 'Madame is not feeling very well, Mr Lawson, I

296

think it would be better if . . . '

'Now, now, Betty, you're not going to spoil the party, are you? I can call you Betty?'

'No, you may not. Please go. At once. Isabella, surely you're not . . . '

'I'll go after I've told you a story. You'll like it, it's interesting. And . . . ' he took a snapshot from his pocket and waved it at them, ' . . . it's a story with a picture.'

Betty instinctively looked towards the fireplace; surely the fire must be out, the room had got so chilly. But the flames were still flickering.

'Once upon a time, a very silly woman who I have the misfortune to be married to, got a letter from her father oop north, as we Yorkshire people say, don't we, Princess? Well, more of a package, actually. Full of family photographs the old fool wanted her to have. She never got round to looking at them, that idle cow never gets round to anything much, but I got round to looking at them. My word, I did.'

Betty looked at Isabella's frozen face, and rose. 'I've heard quite enough,' she said, 'I am not remotely interested in your wife's family, and in my opinion you have had far too much to drink.'

'Betty, please stay.' Isabella's voice was barely a whisper. Flora flattened her ears and pushed her nose into Isabella's hand.

'Yes, do stay, your ladyship. It gets better, I do promise you.' Matt poured himself a drink, and swallowed half of it. 'Now, where was I? Oh yes, the pretty picture. Harry Foster's lost love. Take a look at it, Isabella, for old times? No? Well, perhaps Lady Drummond might be interested.'

Betty, fascinated, and repelled by her fascination, took the photograph and looked at it.

The girl in the 'thirties clothes stared out at her with the hopeful, untested set of the eyes that everyone has before life gets to them. Standing in front of a fairground tent, she was holding a coconut like a proud trophy. Betty supposed she had known, since the moment Matt took the snapshot from his pocket, that it would be a photograph of Isabella.

'Do read what it says on the back. It's very touching.' Matt swallowed the rest of his drink.

Betty turned it over; in the disciplined copperplate that Harry Foster had learnt in the village school, it said, 'My beloved Bella.' And underneath, 'O where are you?'

'Brings tears to the eyes, doesn't it? So I went up to see my father-in-law the other day. Maundering old fool, he's forgotten most things. But he still remembers Bella Denby, the girl who ran away because she was carrying his child. He wanted to do right by her, more fool him. But she didn't want to do right by him, you see. She was meant for better things.' Matt looked round Isabella's study. 'Old furniture and velvet and ordering other people about. That was what she was meant for, not a farmhouse kitchen and a decent man who loved her.'

Betty was disconcerted to find that it had, indeed, brought tears to her eyes. She didn't want to cry in front of this odious man.

'This must have been taken . . . what, a year before I met you in the munitions factory, Bella?'

Isabella nodded. Matt got unsteadily to his feet, yawned, and moved towards the door. 'Not exactly a bundle of laughs, you two, are you? Oh, by the way, you might like this,' he dropped a folded piece of paper on to Isabella's lap as he passed. 'Harry Foster said it would be buried with him, but I managed to nick it while he was looking for some daft medal he wanted to show me.'

Written in copperplate learnt at the same school as Harry's, and dated May, 1940, it said, 'The child is a girl. Don't try and find us, there's no point. I wish you well. Bella.'

Matt opened the door, and paused. 'He waited quite a long time before he married someone else. You know what really makes me laugh? Little Mary Lawson, who does what everyone tells her, is practically your step-daughter,

Princess. Make a cat laugh, wouldn't it?'

* * *

Betty made Isabella a strong cup of tea and poured her out some cognac.

'I hope you're not going to let this upset you too much,' she said bracingly, 'lots of women take on foreign names for professional reasons. Look at Margot Fonteyn, she was born . . . ' Betty couldn't remember what she was born, and in any case her comforting wasn't cutting much ice with Isabella. She gave Betty a look which made her feel, absurdly, that the last twenty minutes had been some silly joke. Surely those eyes were handed down from ancestors who spoke sternly to Popes?

'Don't be ridiculous, Betty. My whole life has fallen apart, and you sit there talking about a ballet dancer. More to the point if you helped me work out how to keep Matt Lawson quiet.'

Give him one of Sister Monica's infusions, leaped into Betty's mind. A thought that started out by being funny, but was more, now she thought about it, unfortunate. Thank God she didn't say it aloud. Instead she said, 'Why don't I go and get Cordelia? After all, she is family, Bella. And when you get down to it, I suppose she has a right to know . . . '

'The right to know she is descended from yeoman farmers rather than one of the oldest noble families of Spain?'

She was still talking about the Cordobas as though they actually existed, thought Betty. 'To be fair to Cordelia, I don't expect she'll give a row of beans. I won't be a minute, I'll go and get her, then I'll leave you both alone.'

When Cordelia burst into the room a few minutes later, she was accompanied by Betty, who, against her better nature, couldn't resist seeing what happened.

'Gran! Lady Drummond's told me. Oh, poor Gran. I am

so sorry.' Cordelia knelt beside her grandmother's chair and wrapped her arms round her. 'That vile Matt, I never liked him, at least it gives us a good reason to get rid of him.'

Betty was about to cry again. The generous loyalty shining from Cordelia's face, the strength of the young arms encircling the old lady, the utter absence of any suggestion of blame; Bella's got a second chance, she'll end her days with love. Not the same love she stamped on fifty years ago, but the love of a beloved grandchild. Betty felt a dragging stab, and identified it as envy.

'Us, Cordelia?' The old lady's back was even more rigid.

'We're not going to let it bother us, are we? I was thinking, we could sort of make a joke out of it, you know, sort of brazen it out. Who cares who people's ancestors are these days? I don't, and I bet mum . . . '

'There will be no question of "us", Cordelia. I thought I told you to throw that dressing gown away?'

'I know it's a bit ancient . . . of course it's going to be us, gran, actually I've got quite a few plans.'

Isabella shrugged Cordelia's arms away. 'I'm sure you have.'

Dear God, thought Betty, she's stamping on it again; why could she never see the love and strength, only the outward appearance? A farmhouse kitchen then, an old dressing gown now.

Cordelia sank back on her heels. 'I don't understand?'

'The disloyalty, the treachery. How could you, after all I've done for you?'

'Come on, Bella, don't be a fool.' Betty raised an eyebrow at Cordelia, who made an I Haven't the Faintest Idea face. 'The child works like a dog, I think you ought to be very grateful.'

'For going behind my back and writing this kind of rubbish?' Isabella opened a drawer of her desk and took out a newspaper cutting which, by the way she handled it, could well have been the lowest form of pornography. 'The

Surrey Advertiser,' she said, in tones which some would have used for Naughty Nights of Silk and Leather. 'And, from what Tristram Bartholomew tells me, other, similar publications all over the country.'

Betty took the cutting, which was headed 'Jennifer Tremayne's Cookery Column'.

'"This week is indulgence week,"' Betty read aloud. '"My special Calorific Chocolate Cake is designed to put a couple of pounds right back on the hips, but who's counting? There's more to life than dieting."' Betty stopped reading. 'You didn't write this, did you, Cordelia? It's by someone called Jennifer Tremayne, Isabella. I must say, it does sound rich; preserved ginger, butter, a whole pound of grated chocolate . . . '

Isabella rose and pointed an accusing finger at Cordelia. 'That is Jennifer Tremayne. My granddaughter promulgating self-indulgence, going against everything Alba stands for. And not even having the courage to do it under her own name. I never want to see you again, you ungrateful slut!'

*   *   *

Two hours later Isabella busied herself in the small private kitchen leading off her study. Her own bedtime drink was ready, and she had put three chicken livers into a saucepan, covered them with cold water, and added the merest pinch of salt, since too much salt wasn't good for little dogs. She would bring them to the boil and simmer them for exactly four and a half minutes, so that they were still pink inside. A coffee-cupful of rice was boiling on the next ring. Chicken livers with rice was Flora's favourite supper.

'Won't be long, my darling,' Isabella said, returning to her study. Flora yawned and stretched cheerfully; she had smelt the chicken livers. Isabella stood in front of the elegant Chippendale looking-glass hung over the mantel-shelf. How many times had she said, casually, 'Given to my great-grandmother by the English ambassador, I believe there was quite a scandal at the time.' She had got it down the Caledonian Road just after the war for twenty-five bob.

Isabella Cordoba de Zarate had come to the end of her days. Life as Bella Denby seemed a poor thing in comparison. She could have dealt with the infusion business, just like she had dealt with everything all her life. It was Monica and Patterson who handed out Extras, after all, nothing to do with her. Naturally the police would have believed her. But Cordelia, her own kin who she had taken in and nurtured, groomed, trained to follow her as mistress of Alba ... cooking disgusting rich chocolate cakes in some murky corner and selling the recipes for money. No Cordoba blood in her.

The timer pinged in the kitchen and Isabella drained the livers and the rice, and mixed them in Flora's dish. She crushed several Mogadons, and stirred in the crumbs.

'Here we are, my best girl, eat up, and then we'll go to bed.'

Flora, her old tail moving with love and trust, ambled over to her dish.

CHAPTER
TWENTY-SEVEN

'One thing about pot,' said Tod's father, casting a professional eye on his son's paperwork, 'it may not be legal, but at least it's easy to spell.'

Tod grinned. 'You've got to the Psilocin, have you?'

Tod looked much better without an air of diffident apology and glasses. He was having dinner with his father, who had retired from the Yard the year before, but still liked to keep his hand in.

'If that's how you pronounce it, yes.' Ex-Chief Detective Inspector Donald Ballard looked across at his son; there was no greater form of flattery than having a child who chose to follow you into your career. However, he hadn't achieved the top of his trade by gazing fondly at people, so he put the report down and said, 'The word is out that the DPP think it's a Crown Court case.'

'Nobody's told me,' said Tod. 'Typical! The one who does all the ground work, the one at the sharp end . . . '

'Sharp end? Lying about on sunbeds and being massaged by young women? I never got that sort of obbo at your age.'

'Don't start, dad, do you mind? I've just about had enough of the funny jokes.'

Six months since Tod had done the Alba job, and his colleagues were still shouting across the canteen, 'Penelope, could you have a look at my thigh? It's feeling tense again.' And when he pointed out, huffily, that his masseur had happened to be a man, the humour got even more basic; a forest of limp wrists was the least of it.

'What I can't understand,' said his father, 'is how it took you so long. Two weeks, and Patterson and Monica Bains were under your nose the whole time.'

'The trouble was, it was all a bit of a muddle.'

'That's not how you put it in your report, I hope. I know things have changed since I first came into the force, but . . .'

'"Circumstances at the inception of the investigation were confused by the differing motivations of the various personalities gathered at Alba during the relevant period." That was how I put it in my report.'

'More like it. I suppose it actually means something?'

'So many people were trying to hide something which actually had nothing to do with drug abuse. Erica Gerard, for instance. Flitting about looking furtive, and all she was hiding was a drop of the hard stuff. Adam Shepherd. He smelt wrong right from the start.'

'I always said you had my nose.'

'He turned out to be a con-man who got lucky. I rather liked Adam. He's living with Sylvia Travers, now.'

'That woman in what's it called? BBC 2 on Thursdays? He certainly landed on his feet, she's very classy.'

'The biggest muddle was about the infusions themselves. I mean, at health farms you're drinking things all the time. Everyone had bedtime drinks, and mostly they were perfectly innocent herbal tea or hot water and lemon.' Tod shuddered reminiscently and took a long swig of beer. 'Out of the group I concentrated on, only five were on Class A drugs supplied by the establishment.'

Donald Ballard picked up the report and riffled through it. 'Mrs Gerard, the Wynne-Jones girl, Antonia Fellowes, Sheila Steinberg, Sylvia Travers. And, of course, Pullen.'

'Pullen was a complication. He was already on crack, and an alcoholic. Alba's infusions simply finished him off. They smuggled his body out after dark through the tradesmen's entrance.'

'And you didn't find that suspicious?'

304

'Not at a health farm, dad. Dead bodies at health farms are more embarrassing than sinister. People have been known to pop off as a result of unaccustomed exercise and near starvation. "Death from natural causes due to over-exertion," sort of thing. But however innocent the cause, the last thing a health farm wants is a hearse drawing up at the front door just before lunch.'

'Put the punters right off their lettuce leaf.'

'Right. Unfortunately, from their point of view, Antonia Fellowes happened to be looking out of the wrong window at the wrong time, and saw the funeral van. Shortly after she started telling people what she'd seen, they changed her infusion.'

'Bit nasty.'

'They jacked up the hallucinogenic part of it. Someone who sees butterflies in the dining room is quite capable of seeing hearses outside the back door, was probably their line of thought.'

'Pity Bella Denby is out of our reach; there's no doubt she was in on it?'

'None at all. Nothing went on in that place without her having a hand in it. I don't honestly see much point in stressing her role, though.'

'Why? Because you fancied her granddaughter?'

How did he know that, the jammy old bastard? 'I liked Cordelia Ledbury very much, yes. But . . . '

'For Christ's sake, Tod, you're not still seeing her, are you? Emotional involvement in a case of this kind is absolutely disastrous.'

'I haven't seen her since the day her grandmother was found dead.' (But she had phoned, twice; and he had told her, in the kind of language his father would have approved, that he was a policeman going about his duty, and might shortly be requesting an interview on matters pertaining to the case.)

'Good. So you've got your witnesses all nice and tidy?'

'Well, some of them. Not everyone is all that keen on

standing up in court and admitting that they are, or have been, dependent on drugs. Particularly as they were conned into their dependency by an elderly Yorkshire woman pretending to be a Spanish grandee, a hypnotherapist of murky background, and a bossy nursing sister.'

*　　　*　　　*

Debbie Wynne-Jones had been very firm.

'I'm certainly not going to testify against Patterson, look what he's done for me.' She had gestured round the vast new office in which Hancock's had installed her.

'We could subpoena you, you know.'

'And if you did, I'd say I'd had a few relaxing herbal drinks, and as a result, worked out what to do with my life. I say, Tod, fancy you as a policeman! You look much better without those awful glasses.'

'No doubt. Surely, Miss Wynne-Jones, as a responsible citizen, you would wish . . . '

'I went to Alba feeling just about useless. Silly little Debbie from Swansea, in love with a married man who was making a fool of her. Alba gave me the strength to come back here and face up to all the sneers and innuendos. And do you know what I found?'

'Are you still on drugs?'

'Would I tell you if I was? Anyway, I'm not, who needs them? No listen, Tod, I walked in here that first day back, thinking, Okay, do your worst, have a good laugh, I can deal with it. And guess what?'

Debbie had always enjoyed talking about herself, Tod thought wearily. 'What?'

'They were all on my side, even Mr Hancock. The first thing was, my secretary said, "Lovely to have you back, Debbie, it's been chaos." Then, when I went to the loo, Isaac's secretary was in there, and she said, "You should see the mess that dickhead's been making of everything. Tell you what, Debs, he's just about to lose the Conway

306

contract. Say no more, if you know what I mean." So I rang Conway's, I've always got on well with their buyer, and I said . . . '

'So where is Isaac now?'

Debbie sat on her desk and crossed her legs in a manner she had almost certainly acquired from *LA Law*. 'Whose office do you think this was? He's been seconded to Porthcawl, and I don't have to tell you what that means.'

Thank God there's something she doesn't have to tell me, thought Tod. 'Well,' he said, rising, 'if you really insist on not co-operating in this matter, Miss Wynne-Jones . . . but you might bear in mind that the police can do nothing without the help of the public.'

'It used to be Debbie, at Alba. I say, Tod, why don't I take you out to lunch on expenses?'

Because, Tod thought, I would have to listen to you talking. 'I'm afraid I've got to catch the twelve eighteen.'

'Another time, then.' She picked up a phone and pressed one of a bank of buttons. 'I say, Sally? Haven't those plot-sheets come through yet?'

*   *   *

Tod drove home after dinner with his father, feeling quite irritable. Fair enough, the old man had seen it all, and Tod realised it must be gratifying to hand on the fruits of experience to the next generation. He would probably do it himself, if he ever got married and had children. Which, the way things were looking, didn't seem a strong possibility.

Several times during the evening, he had felt very much as he had when he got his first bike for Christmas. In exactly the same tones as his father had used to the six-year-old Tod, 'It's all a matter of confidence, old chap,' so had he said to the thirty-two-year-old Tod, 'If the guests who were on Extras won't talk, why don't you try the one's who weren't? Take my tip, Tod (it was at this point that Tod had felt like killing him), I think you'll find they will have noticed some very useful stuff.'

'I already have,' said Tod grumpily. He could almost feel the bike wobbling beneath him. 'It's all in the report, if you bothered to read it. Page seventy-two.'

'Where? Oh, I see. "On the morning of June 17th, I proceeded to Woodlands, Maryatt Drive, Hindhead, to interview Mrs Sybil Gillespie and Miss Rachel Gillespie, both guests at Alba during the relevant weeks. I was not, on that day, able to speak to Rachel Gillespie . . . "' He must have been feeling unusually ratty that evening, because his father sounded as though he was reading, 'Tod has made no real progress in History this term.' Anyway, as dad would find, if he went on studying the report with his eyebrows raised in that infuriating way, the interview had left a great deal to be desired.

Tod had pressed the doorbell of Woodlands and waited for what seemed like ten minutes. The woman weeding her front garden next door watched him suspiciously. Eventually he heard wavering footsteps coming towards the door, which opened to reveal an old lady who bore no resemblance to the Grim Reaper, which was how Tod had tended to think of Mrs Gillespie.

'Who is it?' she said, keeping the door on the chain, 'I haven't got my glasses.'

'You may remember me, Mrs Gillespie. Tod Ballard. I was at Alba when . . . '

'Nonsense. He was a weedy young man with glasses. There's nothing wrong with my memory. Go away at once, or I will call Neighbourhood Watch. Mr Harrington mans the phone twenty-four hours a day.'

'Here is my warrant card; DC Ballard, Drug Squad. I did phone yesterday to make an appointment. Perhaps if I could see your daughter . . . ' The woman next door turned her attention to a bed slightly nearer the party wall.

'Rachel? Rachel is far too busy to have chats with acquaintances.'

'I am not an acquaintance, Mrs Gillespie, I . . . '

The garden gate behind Tod clicked open and shut. Mrs Gillespie brightened, and took the door chain off. 'Dr Corbett! Just when I needed a man. Please tell this person that I don't want any dusters, and if I did, I would ask Rachel to get them for me at Sainsbury's.'

Tod groaned mentally. 'But isn't it awfully dangerous, working in the drugs squad?' bright-eyed young women would ask him at parties. Tod could not remember ever having been in physical danger. He remembered an awful lot of interviews like this one, though.

'Dr Corbett,' he said, 'I would be grateful if you could explain that I am a policeman, here is my warrant card, making routine enquiries about a health farm Mrs Gillespie and her daughter were in the habit of visiting regularly . . . ' the woman next door had now given up all pretence of weeding. ' . . . perhaps if we could all go inside?'

Ten minutes later, Tod and Dr Corbett were seated in Mrs Gillespie's front room. Mrs Gillespie had twice gone out, at the Doctor's suggestion, to make them all a nice cup of tea. Twice she had come back, once with a photograph of Rachel, and once to ask if they would like a cup of tea. Doctor Corbett had said, with a patience for which Tod had the utmost admiration, how very nice, and should he put the kettle on? Mrs Gillespie had replied tartly that she wasn't helpless, thank you very much, and had left the room again.

'I'm afraid she's got a little vague,' said Dr Corbett.

'Is that the result of shingles? The last time I saw her, she was being rushed off to hospital with quite a bad attack, I think.'

'You were at Alba too, were you? For your health? Or . . . professionally?'

'I'm afraid I can't discuss . . . yes, of course I was there professionally. And now I would like to get some facts from Mrs Gillespie.'

'Good luck to you. I don't think it's the shingles that's done her memory in, though at her age you never know. I think it's her daughter.'

'Rachel? My estimation of her was that she wouldn't hurt a fly.'

'You haven't seen her lately, then? That worm has turned with a vengeance. I am not, of course, speaking professionally about my patients, you understand, Mr Ballard. That would be quite . . . unprofessional.'

Tod made the soothing noises that meant, I won't repeat a word, and the gesture that meant, look, I'm not writing anything down, and said, 'Anything you can tell me off the record that would be helpful?'

Mrs Gillespie returned, carrying, somewhat to Tod's surprise, a tray loaded with tea-pot and cups and a plate of Garibaldis. Even more to his surprise, she remembered who he was.

'Here we are, Mr Ballard, not like tea at Alba, is it?'

'Ah, you remember Alba, do you, Mrs Gillespie?' A ghastly mistake, he realised, even as he said it.

'There's nothing wrong with my memory, I could put you young people to shame. What do you want me to remember?'

Tod left forty minutes later. In the interim he had learned that *Winter's Bud* was not a book Mrs Gillespie would ever consider reading, and that Sarah what-was-her-name had thoughtlessly stopped her from watching *News Round-up* by crying in the Television Room. Sister Monica had pinched her when she tucked her in, and, mark her words, Adam Shepherd was on the make.

'Quite,' Tod had said, 'I believe you knew Bella Denby back in the old days?'

'Who?'

'Madame Cordoba.'

'Oh, her. I knew at once when I saw poor Tibs' cushion. I picked him up in the blackout, you know, somebody had thrown him out, grudged the milk, I suppose. I picked

310

James up in the blackout, too. He was a Squadron Leader then, but it turned out he was only a solicitor when the war was over.'

Dr Corbett left with Tod. 'I don't suppose any of that was much use to you. Go and see Rachel, I've got her address, and her telephone number.'

*   *   *

Rachel's address turned out to be Pelham Place, SW1. When Tod telephoned to ask if he could see her, she had said, sounding a good deal more self-assured than the Alba Rachel, 'Let me see. Three o'clock is a good time, how about Tuesday?'

This can't possibly be Gillespie country, thought Tod, arriving at the Pelham Place address. The cars on the res-park were Jaguars, Rolls Royces and Renault Monacos. Every house looked as though it had been painted last week, and ancient wistarias rambled over elegant balconies.

But it was Rachel Gillespie who answered the door. 'Do come in, Constable Ballard,' she said. 'Let's sit in the conservatory, it's such a lovely day. I've asked them to bring us some coffee.'

They sat in a glassed room built on to the back of the house, and a foreign manservant brought them coffee in fine bone china.

'What a lovely house,' said Tod, groping for words in a way which would have left his father in despair.

'Isn't it? I shall be so sad to leave.'

'You're not here permanently, then?'

'No, I never take a job for longer than a month. Though of course they're always asking me to stay on.'

'Quite. What exactly is it you do?'

'Didn't you know? What I've done all my life. I look after old people. Only now I do it for money, you wouldn't believe what I get paid.' She told him what she got paid,

311

and Tod believed her, but only just. 'And now people don't say, "Rachel, you've let me forget my glasses again," they say, "Rachel, dear, I know I'm being such a nuisance, but could you possibly pass me my cardigan?"'

'Why do you only stay for a month?'

'Because my speciality is post-op care. God knows mother always insisted on being treated as an invalid, I know it all backwards. You've no idea how grateful rich people are to someone who takes responsibility off their shoulders. They usually give me a present, when I leave.' Tod had already noticed the Cartier on Rachel's wrist. 'When mother threw away my books, she was doing me a kindness. About the only one she'd ever done in my entire life.'

'You mean, all this because you couldn't read . . . er . . . *Winter's Bud* again?'

'Of course not. I sat in my room the night mother was taken into hospital and thought, Rachel Gillespie, you're acting like a hysterical teenager because someone threw away your books, that's what you've come down to. A second-hand life of trashy potboilers. What would daddy have said? Pick yourself up, go and get your hair cut and start again.'

'Giovanni at Alba?'

'Sheila Steinberg at Harpenden. My old gentleman will be waking from his nap soon. How can I help you?'

The most helpful thing Rachel remembered was the way Sister Monica and Isabella had rushed to Sheila's room in the middle of the night. 'I thought then, like the silly twit I was, how conscientious. Now, I think they were afraid Sheila might be serious, like Mr Pullen, and they wanted to get to her before it was too late. Look, why don't I write down everything I remember, Mr Ballard, and send it to you? Because now I'm afraid I really must get back to work.'

*   *   *

312

At about the time that Tod was dining with his father and watching him fiddle through his report in such a way as to make the most loyal son see red, Tristram Bartholomew was entertaining Nicolette at a new restaurant in Islington. He was still hopeful of getting a column in *Vogue* (perhaps an occasional one, as she was being just a little evasive about a regular contribution) and reckoned that a few more exceptional meals might do the trick. Anyway, he was dying to gossip about the events at Alba to someone really knowledgeable.

'Of course I knew something was going on, darling, I recognised Tod Ballard at once.'

'You knew he was a policeman? Right from the start?'

'Not exactly, no. But I remembered he'd been at Alba before, because I was there too, when there was a fuss about young Harry Hopecroft; you know who he'll be when his father dies, of course. Anyway, Harry had to leave rather quickly, some commotion in the swimming pool, and next thing we knew, there he was at that drug addiction place for the children of the upper crust. Ballard left the same day, and if you ask me, that was what put him on to Alba in the first place.'

'Yes, but why was Ballard there, anyway? Losing weight? I thought you said he was rather weedy? I'm not sure about these snails, Tristram. A bit salty.'

'Right. "My companion found the escargots a shade over-seasoned." Well, obviously, darling, the drug squad were on to Hopecroft, and were checking up on his contacts. Try a spoonful of my jellied gaspacho. A shade diffident, but light to the tongue, wouldn't you say?'

Nicolette seriously wondered whether she could go on eating with someone who described gaspacho as diffident; they certainly didn't want stuff like that in *Vogue*. 'Didn't the policeman remember seeing you before?'

'He didn't recognise me. Of course, I'd lost a lot of weight in the meantime.'

'So, go on. Were you there when the shady hypnotherapist and his accomplice were arrested? How riveting, Tristram, do tell.'

'As it happens,' said Tristram fretfully, 'I was having lunch at The Barley Mow.'

*   *   *

Tod had approached Edwardes Square with some gloom; he was not going to enjoy interviewing the Gerard ménage. He had considered Erica to be silly and selfish; the father sounded, from the way Sarah spoke of him, like a self-absorbed businessman who thought of nothing but money. And Sarah herself was a pathetic little victim of parental neglect. He only hoped she'd managed to put on a bit of weight.

Erica Gerard opened the door, and said, 'Tod! How nice. Only we're supposed to call you Detective Constable Ballard, aren't we? Do come in, we're in a bit of a mess.'

The hall was full of suitcases, carryalls, and plastic bags. A pleasant-looking middle-aged man was sitting on one of the cases and saying, 'You'll have to take something out, darling.'

'There's nothing in there that isn't absolutely vital, dad,' said Sarah, who had indeed put on weight. 'Try bouncing. Hi, Tod, you sneaky bastard. To think I sat there drinking orange juice with the fuzz.'

'Sarah!' said the pleasant looking man. 'I do apologise for my daughter, Mr Ballard. She's a bit excited at the moment, off to Exeter tomorrow.'

'I knew there was something funny about you, didn't I say so, mum?'

'I don't think so darling, no,' said Erica, whose skin shone. She's joined AA, thought Tod, but it's more than that. The three of them, surrounded by placky bags with toasters falling out of them, a vast ghetto-blaster, a pile of rugs and a cuddly dinosaur with half its stuffing missing, looked like a very solid unit.

314

'I hope you're going to ask me to be a witness when you prosecute those two devils,' said Erica, 'because I can't wait.'

'I am delighted to hear it. I must admit that not everybody is as public-spirited.'

'Who have you seen so far?' said Sarah.

'Darling, I really don't think you can expect Mr Ballard . . .'

'Oh, shut up, dad, Tod doesn't mind, do you Tod? Hey, what about Sheila? Mum and I go out there quite often to get our hair cut, if she moved to the West End she'd be coining it. Imagine getting pregnant at her age.'

'Darling, she's only thirty-nine, that's not old,' protested Erica.

'Well, tottering,' said Sarah. 'Last time I was there I tried to get her to talk about Dreadful Diane, but she clammed up on me.'

'I don't believe they see a great deal of each other, these days,' said Tod. He had, in fact, interviewed them both, and got very little change out of either of them. Sheila was in a glow of happiness and hopelessly vague about her bedtime drinks. As a prosecution witness she would be a gift to the defence. Diane had declared total ignorance about Extras and had talked a lot about 'Some people's ingratitude', and 'A baby at her age, so sordid, don't you think?' and had pottered restlessly round her nasty little shop. Tod had particularly disliked the joke corkscrews.

'Mrs Gerard,' he said now, 'how long had you been taking Alba's Extras?'

'Three or four years. They were meant to make me stop drinking, Mr Patterson said. I suppose I was pretty naive to go on taking them, because they obviously didn't work. What I'd like to know is what exactly was in them?'

'The mushroom Psilocybe Semilanceata grows naturally in the wild or can, under certain conditions, be cultivated. Anyone who picks it will not be prosecuted. However . . .'

'Hey,' said Sarah, 'wasn't that the word Antonia saw in

315

your letter when she was being embarrassing at the swimming pool?'

'Unfortunately, yes. I had requested a rush report on a mushroom I had found in the kitchen garden, inadvertently dropped by Miss Ledbury.'

'Cordelia? You don't seriously think she had anything to do with it?'

'Sarah, that is more than enough. Do go on, Mr Ballard.'

'If, however, the mushroom is dried and processed, it becomes Psilocin, a Class A hallucinogenic drug. A supplier of this drug to another person can be prosecuted under the Misuse of Drugs Act.'

'Gosh! What will Sister Monica and slimy Patterson get?'

'If I have to tell you once more, Sarah.'

'All *right*, dad. If a hypothetical X and Y were supplying Psilothing, what would they get?'

'If they came up before a Magistrates' Court, probably six months or a fine of £2,000, or both.'

'Is that all?' said Erica. 'I don't call that much.'

'A serious case, a big supplier or a key dealer, could be referred to the Crown Court. In which case, the maximum sentence involving Class A drugs is life imprisonment.'

Sarah looked subdued. 'Life? It's not a joke, is it? When Patterson tried to hypnotise me, half of me was laughing and half was dead scared. He was telling me I needed infusions and must do what Sister Monica told me.'

'You'd be prepared to state that in court?' Sarah's face took on a faraway expression. 'You really needn't worry, Miss Gerard, there is nothing very frightening about giving evidence.'

'She's probably planning what she's going to wear in the witness box,' said her father. 'So that's all Extras was, then, this dried mushroom?'

'A clinical analysis has revealed that Extras was a combination of Psilocin, Guaranine, a natural and perfectly legal life-enhancer, and Librium, a standard Benzodiaza-

316

pam, a blotter-out of reality. They varied the ingredients to suit each client. And in some cases, overdid it disastrously.'

'Poor Antonia,' said Sarah sadly, 'when I first met her I thought she was so strong. Much cleverer than me, and so sure of herself.'

'I rang Jane Fellowes the other day,' said Erica. 'Antonia's at that clinic in Weston-super-Mare.'

'I haven't yet interviewed Mrs Fellowes. Someone told me she was planning to put her foot down, hire a housekeeper, and go back to research,' said Tod, thinking, not for the first time, that the line between gossip and legitimate interrogation is a fine one.

'What she actually said to me,' said Erica, 'was that she was definitely picking up her career. Possibly next year, after the twins start play school. She didn't say anything about a housekeeper.'

*   *   *

'I was the one who found her,' Betty Drummond had told Tod, when he called on her at her imposing Georgian house tucked away in Twickenham. 'Her and poor little Flora.'

'I understand she was an old friend?'

'Met her at a munitions factory during the war; she was so beautiful.'

'You knew her well . . . what made you think she was Spanish?'

'You should have been there during the war,' said Betty. 'London was full of foreigners then. Free French, Free Poles, Free Belges; what was one Spaniard amongst that lot?'

'Understandable,' said Tod, 'and she'd certainly done her homework. I heard from an informed source . . . ' dad, of course, ferreting around his old contacts . . . 'that Bella Denby came south when she was two months' pregnant and was registered as a domestic at the Spanish Institute.'

'So that's where she picked up the Grandee business. Mr Ballard, I know I've met you somewhere before.'

'The Hopecroft boy,' said Tod. 'You and your husband were weekend guests at their house in Gloucestershire when I interviewed his father. That knowing look of yours gave me a nervous moment or two at Alba.'

'It was those spectacles that put me off the track. It was terrible, you know, finding Isabella like that. And the Will took my breath away. She made me an Executor, she'd left a note for me on her desk. It said I was her only friend.'

'I'm afraid this is upsetting you . . . '

'It's all such a waste, you see. If only she had been able to accept Cordelia's love and support . . . ' Betty looked up at Tod through her tears. 'She's a lovely girl, that. Don't let her slip through your fingers.'

*   *   *

Cordelia. He doubted if she'd ever forgive him. Of course it was clear, after interviewing Bains and Patterson, that she knew nothing.

'Silly little girl,' Monica Bains had said, 'coming in here, thinking she was going to take over. Madame never took her into her confidence. I was the only one she trusted.'

He'd been fool enough to apologise to Cordelia for suspecting she had been involved. She hadn't taken the apology too well. 'All those endless questions about infusions. How could you have thought I'd be involved with anything like drugs?'

'You kept on saying you knew about everything at Alba.'

'I wanted to impress you. I can't think why I bothered.'

And there was nothing he could do about Cordelia, until this bloody case was wrapped up.

318

CHAPTER
TWENTY-EIGHT

Cordelia's syndicated column had gone from strength to strength, she had received a very pleasing advance for the new cookery book, and she could now afford the flat at Shepherd's Bush on her own.

Otherwise, it had been a bloody year, starting with her grandmother's suicide, and ending with the trial of Sister Monica and Mr Patterson. She hadn't particularly liked either of them, but it was disconcerting to hear people you had worked with called The Accused.

They had been sentenced yesterday. 'You grossly abused your position of trust,' the judge had said. 'Under the guise of medical treatment, you battened on your victims. The public must be protected from wickedness of this sort.' Bains and Patterson had asked for two hundred other offences to be taken into consideration, and got ten years for their pains.

She had only seen Tod twice; once, months ago, when he interviewed her on Matters Pertaining to the Case, and once in the witness box. On duty, Tod was self-confident and professional; the jury had listened to him with flattering attention. His assurance had contrasted sharply with Cordelia's own manner in the witness box; twice Prosecuting Counsel had asked her to speak up.

She didn't want to think about that, nor the way she kept on stammering and forgetting things, so she picked up the proofs of the *Alba Manor Cookery Book*. Janet had said the trial would give the book no end of publicity, and the new owners of Alba had been delighted with the idea.

Grandmother's Will had been something of a shock; not a word in it about Her Beloved Granddaughter, in spite of all her promises. 'Being of sound mind, I wish my estate to be shared equally between my daughter, Olivia Ledbury, who, with all her many faults, has never been treacherous, and her half sister, Mary Lawson, in the hope that she will rid herself of her worthless husband. I do this in memory of their father, Harry Foster.'

One of the few light moments of the year had been visiting Alba and seeing how well her mother and Mary Lawson were working together. Mary had lost no time in following the advice in the Will; she had filed for divorce, naming Diane Renfrew and a cast of thousands; Matt was now the second masseur at an obscure Hydro in Norfolk. Without Isabella criticising her every move, Mary's basic competence had come into its own.

Olivia had put Yorkshire pudding behind her and embraced the kiwi fruit. And her father hardly ever watched television now, he was so busy organising everything. Clients still flocked to Alba; the scandal had done no harm at all. 'Never underestimate the avid factor,' said Alec Ledbury.

Everyone is happy except me, thought Cordelia, putting down the proofs to answer the telephone. She was getting tired of old friends ringing to get the lowdown on what *really* went on at Alba, and what it was *really* like to give evidence in court.

It wasn't an inquisitive friend. It was Tod asking questions again, and not one of them about infusions.